NOTABLE BRITISH TRIALS

Trial of
JACK SHEPPARD

Edited by
HORACE BLEACKLEY
and
S. M. ELLIS

JACK SHEPPARD is the most famous criminal in the records of English crime : not by reason of his actual offences, which were merely petty thefts, but because he accomplished three very remarkable escapes from the prisons of Clerkenwell and Newgate. In the most celebrated of these escapes he effected his release unaided and alone, in darkness, and with merely a nail and an iron bar (wrenched from a chimney) for "tools." His pluck, gaiety, strength, and endurance, and the bravery with which he met his cruel death at the gallows at the age of twenty-two, have tinted his otherwise sordid story with pitiful romance. Through the course of two centuries his brief career has formed the subject of numerous romances, dramas in the theatre, and literary allusions by famous writers.

This volume provides a full account of Jack Sheppard's life and achievements, and of his Trial in 1724; an Epilogue relating his posthumous fame in Literature and Drama; an extensive Bibliography; three contemporary accounts of his career—two of them attributed to the pen of Defoe; a Note on Jonathan Wild, and a rare contemporary memoir of that arch-criminal, who was the associate of Jack Sheppard and the main factor in the early termination of his life.

NOTABLE BRITISH TRIALS SERIES.
General Editor—HARRY HODGE.

Dr. Pritchard. Edited by William Roughead.
The Stauntons. Edited by J. B. Atlay.
Franz Muller. Edited by H. B. Irving.
The Annesley Case. Edited by Andrew Lang.
Lord Lovat. Edited by David N. Mackay.
Captain Porteous. Edited by W. Roughead.
William Palmer. Edited by Geo. H. Knott.
Mrs. Maybrick. Edited by H. B. Irving.
Dr. Lamson. Edited by H. L. Adam.
Mary Blandy. Edited by William Roughead.
City of Glasgow Bank. Edited by W. Wallace.
Deacon Brodie. Edited by William Roughead.
James Stewart. Edited by David N. Mackay.
A. J. Monson. Edited by J. W. More.
Oscar Slater. Edited by William Roughead.
E. M. Chantrelle. Edited by A. D. Smith.
Douglas Cause. Edited by A. Francis Steuart.
Mrs. M'Lachlan. Edited by William Roughead.
Eugene Aram. Edited by Eric R. Watson.
J. A. Dickman. Ed. by S. O. Rowan-Hamilton.
The Seddons. Edited by Filson Young.
Sir Roger Casement. Edited by G. H. Knott.
The Wainwrights. Edited by H. B. Irving.
H. H. Crippen. Edited by Filson Young.
Thurtell and Hunt. Ed. by Eric R. Watson.
Burke and Hare. Edited by W. Roughead.
Steinie Morrison. Ed. by H. Fletcher Moulton.
G. J. Smith. Edited by Eric R. Watson.
Mary Queen of Scots. Edited by A. F. Steuart.
Neill Cream. Edited by W. Teignmouth Shore.
Bywaters and Thompson. Ed. by Filson Young.
Adolf Beck. Edited by Eric R. Watson.
Henry Fauntleroy. Ed. by Horace Bleackley.
Kate Webster. Edited by Elliott O'Donnell.
Ronald True. Edited by Donald Carswell.
Abraham Thornton. Ed. by Sir J. Hall, Bt.
Katharine Nairn. Edited by W. Roughead.
Charles Peace. Ed. by W. Teignmouth Shore.
H. R. Armstrong. Edited by Filson Young.
Madeleine Smith. Ed. by F. Tennyson Jesse.
Adelaide Bartlett. Ed. by Sir John Hall, Bt.
Duchess of Kingston. Ed. by L. Melville.
S. H. Dougal. Edited by F. Tennyson Jesse.
Charles I. Edited by J. G. Muddiman.
J. B. Rush. Ed. by W. Teignmouth Shore.
J. D. Merrett. Ed. by William Roughead.
Vaquier. Ed. by R. H. Blundell & R. E. Seaton.
The Bloody Assizes. Ed. by J. G. Muddiman.
Browne and Kennedy. Ed. by W. T. Shore.
G. Chapman. Ed. by H. L. Adam.
Captain Kidd. Ed. by Graham Brooks.
Harold Greenwood. Ed. by Winifred Duke.
Dr. Smethurst. Ed. by Leonard A. Parry.
A. A. Rouse. Ed. by Helena Normanton.
"Bounty" Mutineers. Ed. by Owen Rutter.
The Baccarat Case. Ed. by W. T. Shore.
J. W. Laurie. Edited by William Roughead.
The Royal Mail Case. Ed. by Collin Brooks.
Jack Sheppard. Ed. by Bleackley and Ellis.

IN PREPARATION.

Gardiner (Peasenhall).
Field and Gray.
Queen Caroline.
Sidney H. Fox.
Dr. Knowles.
Robert Wood (Camden Town).

Wm. Hodge & Co., Ltd., Edinburgh and London.

Notable British Trials

Jack Sheppard

NOTABLE BRITISH TRIALS SERIES
General Editor—HARRY HODGE

Trial	Date of Trial	Editor
Mary Queen of Scots	(1586)	A. Francis Steuart
King Charles I.	(1649)	J. G. Muddiman
The Bloody Assizes	(1678)	J. G. Muddiman
Captain Kidd	(1701)	Graham Brooks
Jack Sheppard	(1724)	Horace Bleackley / S. M. Ellis
Captain Porteous	(1736)	William Roughead
The Annesley Case	(1743)	Andrew Lang
Lord Lovat	(1747)	David N. Mackay
Mary Blandy	(1752)	William Roughead
James Stewart	(1752)	David N. Mackay
Eugene Aram	(1759)	Eric R. Watson
Katharine Nairn	(1765)	William Roughead
The Douglas Cause	(1761-1769)	A. Francis Steuart
Duchess of Kingston	(1776)	Lewis Melville
Deacon Brodie	(1788)	William Roughead
"Bounty" Mutineers	(1792)	Owen Rutter
Abraham Thornton	(1817)	Sir John Hall, Bt.
Henry Fauntleroy	(1824)	Horace Bleackley
Thurtell and Hunt	(1824)	Eric R. Watson
Burke and Hare	(1828)	William Roughead
J. B. Rush	(1849)	W. Teignmouth Shore
William Palmer	(1856)	Eric R. Watson
Madeleine Smith	(1858)	F. Tennyson Jesse
Dr. Smethurst	(1859)	L. A. Parry
Mrs. M'Lachlan	(1862)	William Roughead
Franz Muller	(1864)	H. B. Irving
Dr. Pritchard	(1865)	William Roughead
The Wainwrights	(1875)	H. B. Irving
The Stauntons	(1877)	J. B. Atlay
E. M. Chantrelle	(1878)	A. Duncan Smith
Kate Webster	(1879)	Elliott O'Donnell
City of Glasgow Bank	(1879)	William Wallace
Charles Peace	(1879)	W. Teignmouth Shore
Dr. Lamson	(1882)	H. L. Adam
Adelaide Bartlett	(1886)	Sir John Hall, Bt.
Mrs. Maybrick	(1889)	H. B. Irving
J. W. Laurie	(1889)	William Roughead
The Baccarat Case	(1891)	W. Teignmouth Shore
T. N. Cream	(1892)	W. Teignmouth Shore
A. J. Monson	(1893)	J. W. More
G. Chapman	(1903)	H. L. Adam
S. H. Dougal	(1903)	F. Tennyson Jesse
Adolf Beck	(1904)	Eric R. Watson
Oscar Slater	(1909-1928)	William Roughead
H. H. Crippen	(1910)	Filson Young
J. A. Dickman	(1910)	S. O. Rowan-Hamilton
Steinie Morrison	(1911)	H. Fletcher Moulton
The Seddons	(1912)	Filson Young
George Joseph Smith	(1915)	Eric R. Watson
Sir Roger Casement	(1916)	George H. Knott
Harold Greenwood	(1920)	Winifred Duke
Bywaters and Thompson	(1922)	Filson Young
Ronald True	(1922)	Donald Carswell
H. R. Armstrong	(1922)	Filson Young
J. P. Vaquier	(1924)	R. H. Blundell / R. E. Seaton
J. D. Merrett	(1927)	William Roughead
Browne and Kennedy	(1928)	W. Teignmouth Shore
A. A. Rouse	(1931)	Helena Normanton
The Royal Mail Case	(1931)	Collin Brooks

IN PREPARATION.

Gardiner (Peasenhall)
Field and Gray
Queen Caroline
Sidney H. Fox

Dr. Knowles
Robert Wood (Camden Town)

Jack Sheppard
Drawn from ye Life

The Hole he made in ye Chimney when he got loose from ye Castle in Newgate

JACK SHEPPARD

BY

Horace Bleackley, M.A., F.S.A.

Author of "Life of John Wilkes," "The Hangmen of England," &c.

WITH AN EPILOGUE ON JACK SHEPPARD IN LITERATURE
AND DRAMA, A BIBLIOGRAPHY, A NOTE ON JONATHAN
WILD, AND A MEMOIR OF HORACE BLEACKLEY

BY

S. M. Ellis

Author of "William Harrison Ainsworth and His Friends," "The Solitary Horseman," &c.

EDINBURGH AND LONDON
WILLIAM HODGE & COMPANY, LIMITED

PREFATORY NOTE

IT may be well to give a brief explanation why the names of two authors are attached to this volume, for I believe it is only the second time that such a conjunction has occurred in the history of the series of Notable British Trials. This book is not a work of collaboration in the usual sense: I did not see Horace Bleackley's manuscript until after his death. He had completed his account of Jack Sheppard's Life, Trial, and Execution, and selected three contemporary narratives of the young criminal's career for republication in the form of appendices. Other additions were considered necessary in order to give a complete conception of Jack Sheppard's remarkable posthumous fame, and at Mr. Hodge's request I have supplied these in the form of an Epilogue recounting Jack's perennial reappearances in pamphlet, romance, and drama, and in a full Bibliography. I have also contributed a Note on Jonathan Wild to precede the republication of a rare and little-known contemporary account of his career, and, finally, a short memoir of Horace Bleackley, for his share of this volume was the last literary work he accomplished before his sudden death.

The subject of my Epilogue, Jack Sheppard in Literature and Drama, is one of the most curious examples of a mouse giving birth to a mountain—to reverse the Horatian metaphor. It will be seen that Jack, a small thief but a great prison-breaker, has engaged the minds and pens of many eminent authors for over two centuries, and plays about his meteoric career have been produced from 1724 until the present day. His lasting fame is mainly due to his resuscitation in Harrison Ainsworth's romance of "Jack Sheppard" (1839). In view of the great interest now taken in all that appertains to Charles Dickens and the origins of his books, it is of biographical value to know that "Oliver Twist" and "Barnaby Rudge"—in their criminal and melodramatic phases—were written in emulation of the successes Bulwer and Ainsworth had achieved in presenting the Romance of Crime. Dickens at this period was one of The Newgate Novelists, and his "Oliver Twist" reacted in turn again on Ainsworth in the composition of "Jack Sheppard." That point is established by the contemporary (1841) mock-heroic lines of Bon

Gaultier, which he entitled "On Reading Ainsworth's 'Jack Sheppard' by Charles Chickens"—

> Much have I travelled 'mong the prigs of old,
>   And many goodly Sikes and Fagins seen,
>   With many Artful Dodgers have I been,
> Whom beaks in fetters for Sir Peter hold,
> Oft, of the Red-Room, too, had I been told,
>   That deep file, Sheppard, ruled as his demesne,
>   Yet never did I know his might serene
> Till I heard Ainsworth speak out loud and bold:
> Then I felt like some faker of men's clyes
>   When a new doxy rolls into his ken . . .

Truly, the influence of Jack Sheppard could furnish another chapter for "The Curiosities of Literature." What occurred during the course of his short life of twenty-two years, and what has resulted from it during the course of over two hundred subsequent years can be read in the following pages.

                                                           S. M. ELLIS.

3 KENT ROAD,
    KEW GARDENS,
        March, 1933.

In Gratitude.

I wish to express my thanks to the following persons for the help that they have given me:—

The Rector of St. Dunstan's,	Stepney.
Mrs. Charles Whibley,	- North House, Jesus College, Cambridge.
Mr. W. L. M'Carty, -	- Town-clerk, Stepney.
Mr. Sidney Phipson, -	- Inner Temple.
Mr. A. H. Thomas, F.S.A.,	- Guildhall Record Office.
Mr. J. G. Muddiman, -	- London.
Mr. Sidney Perks, F.S.A.,	- City Surveyor, Guildhall.
Mr. S. M. Ellis, - -	- Kew Gardens, Surrey.
Mr. N. Maskelyne,	- Maskelyne's Theatre of Mystery, London.
Mr. Seymour Hicks, -	- London.
Mr. J. E. Sharpe, -	- His Majesty's Theatre, London.

And I am grateful to the Corporation of the City of London for the permission to reproduce the plan of Newgate.

Horace Bleackley.

The Lord Chamberlain,	- St. James's Palace.
The First Commissioner of H.M. Office of Works,	- Storey's Gate.
Keeper of the National Gallery, - - -	- Trafalgar Square.
Mr. Leslie Bridgewater.	- Sudbury, Middlesex.
Mrs. Gabrielle Enthoven, O.B.E., - - -	- Victoria and Albert Museum.
Mr. H. Granville-Barker,	- Colyton, Devon.
Sir Arthur Keith, -	- Royal College of Surgeons.
Mr. James Lightwood,	- Lytham.
Mr. J. G. Muddiman, -	- London.
Miss Joan Sharp, -	- Cecil Sharp House, London.
Mr. Walter T. Spencer,	- New Oxford Street, London.
The Reverend Montague Summers, - - -	- Oxford.
Mr. Geoffrey Whitworth,	- The British Drama League, London.

S. M. Ellis.

CONTENTS

JACK SHEPPARD—   PAGE
- I.—Birth and Childhood,   1
- II.—Apprenticeship,   2
- III.—The Housebreaker,   5
- IV.—The Prison-breaker,   7
- V.—A Short Career of Crime,   9
- VI.—Newgate Prison,   12
- VII.—The Trial,   15
- VIII.—First Escape from Newgate,   18
- IX.—A Short Spell of Freedom,   21
- X.—Newgate Once More,   23
- XI.—The Great Escape from Newgate,   26
- XII.—Another Short Spell of Freedom,   33
- XIII.—Newgate Again,   38
- XIV.—Second Appearance before the Judges,   40
- XV.—In the Condemned Hold Once More,   43
- XVI.—The March to Tyburn,   46
- XVII.—The Triple Tree,   51
- XVIII.—The Criminal,   55
- XIX.—His Posthumous Fame,   57
- XX.—The Exploits of Jack Sheppard,   61

EPILOGUE—
- Jack Sheppard in Literature and Drama,   64

BIBLIOGRAPHY—
- I.—Contemporary Newspapers,   127
- II.—Tracts and Biographies,   127
- III.—Plates,   130
- IV.—Manuscripts,   130
- V.—Later Publications,   131
- VI.—Miscellaneous,   135

THE HISTORY OF THE REMARKABLE LIFE OF JOHN SHEPPARD,   137

A NARRATIVE OF ALL THE ROBBERIES, ESCAPES, &c., OF JOHN SHEPPARD,   159

AUTHENTIC MEMOIRS OF THE LIFE OF JOHN SHEPPARD,   170

A DIALOGUE BETWEEN JULIUS CÆSAR AND JACK SHEPPARD,   196

JONATHAN WILD—
- Introductory Note,   199

AN ACCOUNT OF JONATHAN WILD,   209

IN MEMORIAM: HORACE BLEACKLEY,   243

INDEX,   257

LIST OF ILLUSTRATIONS

1. Jack Sheppard drawn from ye Life in Newgate Prison, — *Frontispiece*
2. Jack Sheppard escaping from St. Giles's Round-House, — facing page 6
3. Jack Sheppard escaping from Clerkenwell Prison, — ,, 8
4. Plan of Newgate Prison, — ,, 12
5. Newgate Prison in the Eighteenth Century, — ,, 14
6. Jack Sheppard escaping from the Condemned Hold in Newgate, — ,, 20
7. Jack Sheppard's Escape from the Castle in Newgate, — ,, 28
8. Jack Sheppard escaping from the tiles of Newgate Prison, — ,, 32
9. Jack Sheppard, from the portrait by Sir James Thornhill, — ,, 44
10. The Execution of Jack Sheppard at Tyburn, — ,, 52
11. Jack as Harlequin Sheppard, Drury Lane Theatre, 1724, — ,, 72
12. Lord John Russell as Jack Sheppard, from *Punch*, 1841, — ,, 85
13. William Harrison Ainsworth as The Biographer of Jack Sheppard, — ,, 88
14. Mrs. Keeley as Jack Sheppard at the Adelphi Theatre, 1839, — ,, 97
15. Singing "Nix my dolly, pals," at the Adelphi Theatre, 1839, — ,, 99
16. Paul Bedford as Blueskin at the Adelphi Theatre, 1839, — ,, 100
17. Nellie Farren as Jack Sheppard at the Gaiety Theatre, 1885, — ,, 116
18. Peter Spagnoletti as Jack Sheppard at the Elephant and Castle Theatre, 1928, — ,, 124
19. Wych Street, Strand, — ,, 126
20. Jack Sheppard in Newgate from a contemporary print, — ,, 176
21. Jonathan Wild, — ,, 208
22. Jonathan Wild's House in the Old Bailey, — ,, 224
23. Horace Bleackley, — ,, 243

Chronology of the Story of Jack Sheppard.

1702,	March 4.	Jack Sheppard born at White's Row, Spitalfields.
	5.	Baptised at St. Dunstan's Church, Stepney.
Circa 1710.		Educated at the Bishopsgate Street Workhouse.
1717,	April 2.	Bound apprentice for seven years to Owen Wood, carpenter of Wych Street, before Sir William Fazakerley, Chamberlain of the City of London.
1723,	Spring.	Commits his first theft at the "Rummer" Tavern, Charing Cross. Rescues Edgworth Bess from St. Giles's Round-House.
	August 1.	Robbery at Mr. Bain's house in White Horse Yard.
	2.	Jack leaves Owen Wood and breaks his apprenticeship.
	October 23.	Robbery at Mr. Charles's house in Mayfair, Piccadilly.
1724,	February.	Commits various thefts.
	April.	Escapes from St. Giles's Round-House, Soho.
	May 19.	Arrested.
	20.	Committed to the New Prison, Clerkenwell, along with Edgworth Bess by Justice Walters.
	25.	Escapes from the New Prison along with Edgworth Bess.
	July 12.	Jack Sheppard and Blueskin commit a burglary at the house of William Kneebone in the Strand.
	20.	Highway robbery at Hampstead on John Pargiter.
	23.	Jack Sheppard arrested at the house of Blueskin's mother and taken to the New Prison.
	24.	Committed to Newgate by Justice Blackerby.
	August 13.	Tried and convicted at the Old Bailey of the robbery at Kneebone's.
	14.	Sentenced to death by Sir William Thompson, the Recorder.
	31.	Escaped from the Condemned Hold, Newgate, with the assistance of Edgworth Bess and another woman.
	September 1.	Jack is helped by his "trusty comrade," Will Page, the butcher-boy.
	10.	Captured at Finchley, near Highgate, by the turnkeys from Newgate.
	16.	Removed from the Condemned Hold to the Castle.
	28.	Rev. Thomas Purney, the Ordinary, is obliged to go into the country owing to ill-health.
	October 10.	Thomas Sheppard, Jack's elder brother, is transported.
	14.	Blueskin cuts Jonathan Wild's throat at the Old Bailey.
	15.	Jack Sheppard's great escape from the Castle at Newgate.
	16-18.	Hides in a shed in Tottenham Fields.
	18.	Gets rid of his irons.
	29.	Robs Rawlins's Pawnshop in Drury Lane.
	31.	Captured in Drury Lane and brought back to Newgate.
	November 6.	Duke of Newcastle, Secretary of State, writes to Sir Philip Yorke Attorney-General, ordering him to bring Jack Sheppard before the Court of King's Bench for sentence.

Chronology—continued.

	November 7.	The Attorney-General makes motion at the King's Bench Bar that Jack Sheppard should be brought before the Court to have execution of sentence of death awarded against him.
	10.	Jack Sheppard brought before Court of King's Bench, Westminster, where sentence of death is pronounced against him by Justice Powys.
	11.	Taken from Middle Stone-room and put into Condemned Hold.
	13.	Sir James Thornhill "takes a draught" of Jack Sheppard in the Condemned Hold.
	16.	Execution of Sheppard at Tyburn.
	16.	Buried at St. Martin's-in-the-Fields "before midnight."
	28.	"Harlequin Sheppard" produced at Drury Lane.
1839, 1840,	January to February.	The romance—"Jack Sheppard"—by William Harrison Ainsworth is issued periodically in "Bentley's Miscellany."
1839, October.		"Jack Sheppard" published in three volumes by Bentley.
	28.	Drama of "Jack Sheppard," by J. B. Buckstone, produced at the Adelphi Theatre with Mrs. Keeley and Paul Bedford as Jack Sheppard and Blueskin. Nine other theatres also produced versions before the end of the year.
1840,		"Jack Sheppard" issued in fifteen monthly parts.
1873,	February 5.	"Old London" by "F. Boyle" (John Oxenford), produced at the Queen's Theatre, Long Acre, with Henrietta Hodson (Mrs. Labouchere) as Jack Sheppard—here called "Dick Wastrell."
1885,	December 26.	"Little Jack Sheppard," a burlesque by Yardley and Stephens, produced at the Gaiety Theatre with Nellie Farren and Fred Leslie as Jack Sheppard and Jonathan Wild.
1928,	April 30.	"Jack Sheppard," adapted from Buckstone's version by Matt Wilkinson, with Peter Spagnoletti as Jack Sheppard, produced at the Elephant and Castle Theatre.

JACK SHEPPARD.

I.—Birth and Childhood.

On 28th February, 1697, a young carpenter, named Thomas Sheppard, and his wife Mary, brought their first-born child to the font of the church of St. Dunstan in Stepney to be baptised. The baby, a boy twenty-two days old, was christened Thomas after his father. Both parents were reputed to be honest folk, who resided in White's Row, Spitalfields—a road leading off Commercial Street about three-quarters of a mile to the north of the Tower of London—and so the journey to their parish church was a distant one, since until the year 1729 Spitalfields formed part of Stepney.

A year and a half later, on 19th October, 1698, another son was born to Thomas Sheppard and his wife, but this time the baby was a frail one and had to be taken to its baptism at St. Dunstan's on the day following its birth. This second baby, who was called John, died three years later and was buried in the graveyard of the parish church on 14th October, 1701. At that time Mary Sheppard was expecting an addition to her family, an event that happened on 4th March, 1702, when there was a repetition almost of the former misfortune. For there was little hope that the ailing, puny child would survive, and, once more, Thomas Sheppard had to go to a christening at St. Dunstan's without his wife on the day after the child was born. In defiance of bad luck the name of John was chosen again. This time the baby did not die, but lived to become one of the most notorious men of his generation.

The carpenter and his wife had only one more offspring, a girl, named Mary, who had a short life, dying on 23rd December, 1708. A worse calamity had fallen upon the little household in White's Row a year or two previously when Thomas Sheppard died after a short illness, leaving his wife with three young children.[1]

Mary Sheppard, however, was a woman of grit and initiative. When the death of her daughter made it unnecessary to keep up a home, she went into domestic service and found places for her sons. Thomas, the elder, became footboy in a lady's family, while Jack, now seven or eight years old, was sent to the Workhouse school in

---
[1] Registers of St. Dunstan's, Stepney; local information.

Jack Sheppard.

Half-Moon Alley, Bishopsgate Street Within. There he learned to read and write and figure, and was taught a trade, remaining a pupil, well-conducted and diligent, for several years. All the boys on the foundation wore the same costume, one of russet cloth with a badge upon the breast, representing a poor boy and a sheep. " Some of them are tailors," wrote a historian of London some years later, " some are shoemakers, some knit stockings. They brew their own drink . . . they kill their own mutton . . . in cases of sickness they have medicine and surgery gratis."[2]

Upon leaving the Workhouse, not being old enough to be put out as an apprentice, he was engaged as shopboy by the man who employed his mother as servant, one William Kneebone, a woollen draper, under the sign of the Angel, near the New Church in the Strand. This Kneebone is said to have been very kind to the boy, improving him in his writing and accounts, and himself setting him copies with his own hand. In this way some years were passed until Jack Sheppard had reached apprentice age when the charitable woollen draper persuaded Owen Wood, a house joiner and carpenter in Drury Lane, with whom he had influence, to take the lad into his business. So, on 2nd April, 1717, Jack was bound to Wood for seven years before Sir William Fazakerley, Chamberlain of London.[3]

II.—Apprenticeship.

Young Jack Sheppard served his time with Owen Wood for six years, becoming a clever carpenter and a locksmith of amazing skill. He acquired an uncanny knack in picking padlocks and unfastening bolts, being infinitely more adroit than any other apprentice whom his master had known. There was nothing to complain of in his conduct during this period, and Mr. Wood, who was a mild, indulgent person, regarded him as a promising young man.[4]

Jack had outgrown completely the weakness of his childhood. Although a tiny person—only 5 feet, 4 inches in height and very slender—he was all sinew and muscle, and his muscles were as tough

---

[2] Wilkinson's " Londina Illustrata " (1825), II, p. 146.

[3] " Authentic Memoirs of the Life of John Sheppard " (Joseph Marshall, 1724), p. 3; " Narrative of all the Robberies and Escapes of John Sheppard " (John Applebee, 1724), pp. 1, 2; " The History of the Remarkable Life of John Sheppard " (John Applebee, 1724).

[4] *The London News*, 16th November, 1724, says that Jack Sheppard was apprenticed at first to a cane-chair maker, in Houndsditch, who died.

Apprenticeship.

as whipcords, and his joints as strong as steel. For a man of his small frame he was of remarkable physical strength—a complete pocket Hercules. As agile as a cat and as daring a climber as a steeplejack, he was never daunted by the height of any roof that he was called upon to scale. His features were intelligent, but bore no little resemblance to those of a pug-dog, and he was very pale. By nature a merry soul he was usually in a good humour, although his passion would flame forth when provoked; and he had a keen and fluent Cockney wit, the piquancy of which was enhanced by a slight stutter in his speech.[5]

In the spring of 1723, when twenty-one years old, there came his first lapse in honesty. Later, when repentance overwhelmed him for a moment, he attributed his fall, as so many sinners do, to evil associates. His master was now living in a court off Wych Street, and in the evening, when his work was done, Jack began to frequent the " Black Lion " Alehouse in Newton Street, Drury Lane, a low tavern that was the resort of footpads and women of the town, the landlord being Joseph Hind. Before long he became enamoured of one of these sirens, Elizabeth Lyon by name, nicknamed Edgworth Bess, the doxy of a foot-soldier. This woman, a violent-tempered Amazon, who had accepted him as her lover soon after they met, Jack regarded subsequently as the cause of all his misfortunes. For his mistress was an expectant harpy, always ready to sit up and beg, and Jack was driven at last to picking and stealing to satisfy her voracity. While doing a job for his master at the " Rummer " Tavern (seen in Hogarth's picture of " Night ") at Charing Cross, he filched a couple of silver spoons, and, finding thieving such an easy way of gaining pocket-money, he was always on the lookout for opportunities of a similar kind.

At the same time his relations with Owen Wood underwent a change. The bumptious young apprentice began to bully the good-natured carpenter; on one occasion at the " Sun " Alehouse in Islington, when hours of hard work and a parsimonious midday meal had fretted his irascible temper, going so far as to " beat and bruise the old man in a most barbarous and shameful manner." Not long afterwards, when Edgworth Bess had the effrontery to visit him at Wych Street, Mrs. Wood, the carpenter's wife, begged him on her knees to have nothing more to do with the harlot. It is said that Jack's reply was to throw a stick at the old lady, damn her blood, and beat her to the ground. But he always denied this, declaring that Elizabeth and her soldier were quarrelling in Mr. Wood's yard, and that he bade them

---

[5] *Evening Post*, 15th-17th October, 1724.

Jack Sheppard.

begone and flung a piece of timber at them, which unfortunately struck his mistress instead, but caused her no harm. Still, the long-suffering Woods, who seem to have been much attached to this wild young apprentice, made no attempt to get rid of him.

Other measures, however, were taken to show their displeasure. Jack was now in the habit of staying out till past midnight, so his master began to try to read him a lesson by locking him out several times. Such attempts, however, were the merest farce. Jack's bedroom was on the third floor, but he managed to climb up thither with the greatest ease and opened the window in a few moments. He was always to be found fast asleep in bed when his master knocked at his door in the morning.

During the summer of 1723 Edgworth Bess fell into trouble. She had stolen a ring from a gentleman whom she took home with her, with the result that he charged her with the theft and she was committed to St. Giles's Round-house in Soho. As soon as he heard the news, Jack went off to St. Giles's, had a tempestuous interview with the custodian—Brown, the beadle—and commanded him to hand over his keys. The poor beadle was no match for the vigorous young thief, who soon had wrenched his keys away from him, in spite of the assistance of his wife who rushed to the help of her husband with screams of rage and terror. Jack then proceeded to unlock the doors and released his mistress.

Both Bess and Jack were now sorely in need of funds, so in the middle of July, while the apprentice was doing some repairs at the shop of Mr. Bains, a piece-broker in White Horse Yard, he stole a roll of fustian about 24 yards in length, but, being unable to find any one to buy it, he had to hide it in his trunk in his room in Wych Street. This led to trouble, profiting neither Bess nor her lover, for the cloth was traced to Jack's possession, and he was declared to be the thief. Although his mother swore that she had given it to him, while he went boldly to Mr. Bains and protested that his reputation was being sullied unjustly, the woollen broker threatened to prosecute unless his property was restored. Eventually Jack gave back the greater part of it.

Soon afterwards he had his revenge upon Mr. Bains. On 1st August, 1723, he once more broke into his house through an underground kitchen window. In the till of the shop he found £7 in cash, and, taking goods to the value of £14 besides, he came out at the front door, which he locked after him. All this loot he carried away to the lodgings of a girl friend, named Poll Maggot, one of the

Apprenticeship.

numerous rivals of Edgworth Bess. The next day he quitted his master's house in Wych Street for ever, eight months before his time had expired. Jack Sheppard's apprenticeship was ended.

III.—The Housebreaker.

At this period Thomas Sheppard, the elder brother, now twenty-six years old, had become as arrant a rogue as Jack himself. He too was a house joiner and carpenter, having grown tired of domestic service after a little while, and, according to some accounts, he had been apprenticed to Owen Wood along with Jack. Be that as it may, he was now combining the occupation of thief with that of his own trade. During August of this year it was discovered that he was stealing the tools of his fellow-workmen, and, being convicted at the Old Bailey, he was sentenced to be burned in the hand. After his discharge he persuaded Jack to make him a partner in his robberies.

Previous to this Jack had made a fine haul of silver plate. Since leaving the Wych Street carpenter, he had been lodging in the house of a Mr. Charles, in Mayfair, Piccadilly, who had had occasion to employ a joiner to do some repairs, and Jack was taken on as journeyman. The opportunity of having a free run of the establishment was too good to be lost and Jack was soon busy among the spoons. On 23rd October, 1723, he decamped with a large bundle containing his loot, which enabled Bess and himself to live in affluence for some time.

The partnership between his brother and himself began to bear fruit in February of the following year. During this month they accomplished two considerable robberies. On the 5th of the month they broke into the shop of Mary Cook, a linen draper of Clare Street, Clare Market, where they stole goods to the value of £55; and on the 14th they entered the house of William Phillips, in Drury Lane, where they found little of value. These burglaries had one important result. While trying to sell some of the stolen goods, Thomas Sheppard was apprehended and committed to Newgate, where the mean fellow, in the hope of being admitted King's evidence, impeached his brother and Edgworth Bess. But although the thief-takers of Newgate sought for them all over the town, no trace could be found of them.

In addition to his harlots, Lyon and Maggot, there were other even more disreputable creatures in Jack's entourage. Joseph Blake, nicknamed Blueskin, and James Sykes, known as Hell-and-Fury, were bosom companions of his, and both were well-known thieves. It was through the treachery of the latter that he was arrested.

Jack Sheppard.

The pursuit of Bess and Jack had now grown so hot that they thought it advisable not to expose themselves in public places. The man Sykes, however, persuaded Jack to go with him to Redgate's, a boosing-ken near the Seven Dials, to play at skittles, a game in which Sheppard excelled. Scarcely had play started than a constable appeared. Sykes had informed him previously of the choice quarry that would be awaiting him, and he proceeded to charge Jack with the two burglaries at Mary Cook's and Phillips's. So the young thief was haled before Justice Parry, the nearest police magistrate, who committed him for the night to the St. Giles's Round-house, the lock-up from which he had rescued Bess.

He was confined on the top floor, two storeys from the ground, with no serviceable tool but an old razor, but in less than three hours he was a free man. Spreading a feather-bed on the floor to deaden the falling of rubbish, he broke a hole in the roof of his prison. It was about nine o'clock at night and the street was full of people, one of whom, happening to be struck by a falling tile, raised the cry that the prisoners were escaping. Realising that there was no time to be lost, Jack struggled through the hole that he had made, scattering a shower of bricks and tiles upon the crowd below. Then, tying together a sheet and a blanket, he slid down at the back of the Round-house into St. Giles's churchyard. A moment later he had scrambled over the wall and mingled with the excited spectators, who were staring at the roof of the prison, crying to one another, " There's his head . . . there he goes, behind the chimney," and Jack pointed up, too, declaring that he could see Sheppard on the tiles.

His freedom did not last for very long. On 19th May, 1724, while passing through Leicester Fields with a fellow-thief, he came upon a gentleman in altercation with a woman of the town and snatched a gold watch from the man's pocket. Although the thieves took to flight at once, pursuit followed swiftly, Jack being seized near Leicester House by a burly sergeant of the Guard. Having been handed over to the constables, he was locked up for the night in St. Ann's Round-house, Soho. On the following morning Edgworth Bess came to visit him and was detained also. Eventually both of them were taken before Justice Walters who, having heard evidence with regard to the Cook and Phillips robberies, committed them to the New Prison, Clerkenwell, a sort of chapel of ease for Newgate when that prison was full. Being regarded as man and wife, they were permitted to share the same cell.

Jack Sheppard Escaping from St. Giles's Round=House, April, 1724

From the drawing by Jack Sketch in *The History of Jack Sheppard*, 1839

The Prison-breaker.

IV.—The Prison-breaker.

The New Prison was a commodious building on the north-east side of Clerkenwell, adjoining the Bridewell, " a house of correction for disorderly persons," the wall of which served as part of its boundaries.[6] Determined that the slippery young thief should not repeat his performance at St. Giles's Round-house, Captain Geary, the Governor of the prison, loaded him with a pair of " double links and basils " about 14 lb. in weight, and had chosen the Newgate Ward as his cell because it was the strongest in the whole gaol. But the good man was a victim of the slack regulations in vogue in those times. Friends were allowed to see the prisoners, and since Jack's two exploits at St. Giles's Round-house had delighted every footpad in the town, lots of clever cracksmen were eager to come to his assistance. He had entered the New Prison on Wednesday, 20th May, and during the next four days all sorts of ingenious little saws and files were slipped into his hands by visitors.

Jack realised full well how important it was to obtain his freedom. Although he had only committed six felonies up to date, each of the six was a capital offence. There was the theft of two spoons at the " Rummer " Tavern; the mysterious disappearance of Mr. Bains's roll of fustian; Mr. Charles's silver plate; the two burglaries at Cook's and Phillips's; and, finally, the snatching of the gentleman's watch in Leicester Fields. All these transgressions, though inconsiderable in themselves and spread over twelve months, might be set out in indictments against him, and whether proven or not would lead his judges to regard him as an inveterate young criminal. The evidence against him was available at any moment. The fact that he had broken his apprenticeship would go against him. In the eyes of the indignant authorities his escape from St. Giles's Round-house had placed the coping-stone on his short career of crime.

He chose Sunday evening, 24th May, the fifth day of his imprisonment, as the appropriate moment for his effort to escape. As soon as the turnkeys had left him for the night, he proceeded to file through his fetters, having little difficulty in cutting the tough iron chains. To get out of the window, the next task that had to be accomplished, was a far more formidable one. The window was protected by an iron bar and by an oak beam 9 inches in thickness. After some strenuous sawing with his files, Jack succeeded in getting rid of the first obstacle,

---

[6] " History of Clerkenwell," by W. J. Pinks (1881), p. 183; " A New History of London," by John Noorthouck, p. 752.

Jack Sheppard.

but the beam resisted all his efforts until he hit upon a way to remove it. By boring it through with his gimlet, making a row of little holes close together, he weakened it at either end, so that at last he was able to drag it from its position. The way to liberty was now open, but the cell was on the top storey, 25 feet above the yard below. The buxom Bess, too, was also to be a passenger on the journey. She was Amazonian in build and very strong, so that when she and Jack quarrelled in their cups and fought one another, she could give as good as she received, and was able to beat her man severely until his superior endurance gave him the ultimate victory. But nature had not intended her to be a prison-breaker. Realising at once that he would have to take command all through, Jack ordered her to strip to her shift while he fashioned a rope out of her petticoats and their blankets. Then, fastening a stout strand around her waist, he persuaded her to crawl through the window and lowered her to the ground. Afterwards he tied the rope of petticoats to the broken beam and slid down into the yard below. It was now two o'clock in the morning and the day was Whit Monday.

Nevertheless, for the moment they had merely escaped from one prison to another. Surrounding the yard the wall of Clerkenwell Bridewell towered 22 feet high, topped by *chevaux-de-frise* of iron. At only one place did it seem vulnerable. The locks and bolts and bars of the great door suggested a scaling ladder, and by supplementing these footholds with his gimlets Jack managed to mount to the top of the gate, taking a ladder of sheets and blankets with him. The task of dragging up his corpulent paramour taxed his strength more than anything that he had yet attempted, for her feet kept slipping away from the slender supports, and he had to support her in mid-air until she regained her footing. Still, at length he had hauled her to the top and she was sitting in her shift, straddle-legged beside him on the wall. Attaching the petticoats and blankets rope to a spike, he showed her how she could slide down into the street, following her instantly as soon as she arrived in safety.

Later on this Whit Monday it became known publicly that Jack Sheppard, the young thief who had escaped from the Round-house, had accomplished the far more difficult feat of breaking out of the Newgate Ward in Clerkenwell New Prison, and the whole town wondered. The like had never been heard of. This stripling, only twenty-two years and three months old, had broken out of one of the strongest prisons in England. Although loaded with fetters and impeded by a female companion as well, he had taken her away with him in spite of her

Jack Sheppard, with Edgworth Bess. Escaping from the New Prison, Clerkenwell, 25th May, 1724

From the Drawing by George Cruikshank for Ainsworth's *Jack Sheppard*, 1839

The Prison-breaker.

bulk and immobility. No wonder that the underworld of London began to regard this redoubtable Jack Sheppard as the cleverest of them all.

V.—A Short Career of Crime.

Jack's next misdemeanour was a somewhat elaborate burglary at the house of Mr. Carter, a mathematical instrument maker in Wych Street, which was suggested to him by an apprentice named Anthony Lamb who was employed there. The intended victim was a master-tailor called Barton, a lodger in the house and a man in a good way of business. On 16th June, in the middle of the night, the disloyal apprentice admitted Jack and his comrade, a cooper of the name of Grace, who was sent up into Barton's bedroom with a loaded pistol, being instructed to shoot him should be wake up and attempt to give the alarm. Fortunately, however, for the tailor, he slept peacefully all the time. Jack had soon collected a considerable loot from trunks—cash, bonds, notes, and a few choice suits of clothes, the whole being valued at £300, whereupon the robbers departed by the street door just as they had arrived. Later they had no difficulty in disposing of their booty at an alehouse where the receivers were in the habit of visiting. The base Lamb was the only one to suffer for the crime. Being charged before a magistrate, he made a full confession, and at his trial was sentenced to transportation beyond the seas.

Jack now committed his most famous robbery, his victim being his benefactor, William Kneebone, the good-natured woollen draper near the New Church, St. Mary's, in the Strand. His boon companion was now Blueskin, a burly ruffian several years older than himself, but devoid of his resource and intrepidity. This time also he was accompanied by two assistants. It was Saturday, 12th July, 1724, and when Jack arrived with Blueskin and William Field it was just midnight and the Kneebone family had retired for the night. Cutting out two oak beams in the cellar window of the kitchen at the back of the house in Little Drury Lane, the thieves made their way into the shop upstairs. For no less than three hours they were ransacking the premises, decamping finally with over 100 yards of woollen cloth, together with various other articles, to the value of nearly £50. In the morning, when the robbery was discovered, Mr. Kneebone suspected Jack Sheppard at once, and was bitterly grieved at his ingratitude.

Jack Sheppard.

It was a robbery that the malefactor often must have regretted, for it proved to be the one that brought him to justice.

On 19th July, Jack and Blueskin took part in a small misdeed on the Hampstead road. They stopped a passing carriage, containing one woman, a lady's maid, and bringing the vehicle to a halt secured all the money she had about her, which was only half a crown. At first the footman at the back seemed likely to give trouble, but Jack cowed him at once by displaying his pistol.

On the following evening, the 20th, they committed a robbery which had far-reaching consequences. About nine o'clock at night a tipsy chandler, named John Pargiter, came reeling up to them near the Half-way House, Hampstead. Jack at once went through his pockets, but could only collect three shillings, while Blueskin dealt him a couple of lusty blows with the butt end of his pistol, which laid him in the ditch. Next day, when sober once more, the vainglorious chandler, in order to show that he had been overcome by formidable antagonists, protested that he had been robbed and beaten by a couple of soldiers. A little later, while showing the place where he had been maltreated to a party of farmers, it chanced that two Grenadier Guardsmen, Francis and Benjamin Brightwell, should pass along the road, and no sooner did the besotted Pargiter catch sight of them than he swore that they were the men who had robbed and assaulted him. He repeated his accusation before a magistrate, with the result that the Brightwells were committed to Newgate.

No charge could have been more outrageous, the Brightwell brothers being soldiers of exceptional character, and Benjamin, in addition, was a classical scholar of rare excellence. " I believe," said a clerical friend of his, " there is not such another grenadier in the universe." At their trial they were acquitted honourably, and there was much indignation that they had been put to such an ordeal. The wretched Pargiter became an object of universal contempt. Unfortunately, his mistake had tragic consequences. Benjamin Brightwell caught the gaol distemper in Newgate Prison and, although attended by Sir Hans Sloane, he never rallied, dying a few weeks later.

On the 21st July, Jack and Blueskin stopped a stage-coach, but their plunder was inconsiderable, for they only collected 22s. from one of the passengers, not venturing to detain the coach for long. As a highwayman, Jack Sheppard, in spite of his strength and courage, never made any mark at all. Previously, he had made a gallant attempt to ride the High Toby, hiring two horses at an inn in Piccadilly, and setting out with his satellite, armed with pistols, upon the Enfield

A Short Career of Crime.

Chase. Here they met a coach containing four well-dressed young ladies with two footmen to protect them, obviously a party that would well repay an attack; but although Jack was eager to call upon them to stand and deliver he was thwarted by the poltroonery of Blueskin, who pretended that his horse had to be refreshed.

The toils were now fast closing around the young carpenter. Bitterly incensed by the treatment he had received, Mr. Kneebone had taken counsel with the famous Jonathan Wild, the self-styled "Chief Thief-catcher in England." Nevertheless, it was no vain title, for Jonathan was a gallant, intrepid fellow, although the greatest scoundrel unhung, and was the most successful sleuth of them all. His courage and determination were undaunted. During the previous ten years it was scarcely possible to take up a newspaper without reading a paragraph recounting his prowess—

"On Monday Jonathan Wild, the thief-taker, apprehended a highwayman and brought him to Newgate . . . he is entitled to the first premium of £100 offered by the proclamation over and above what is granted by law."

"Jonathan Wild and one of the turnkeys from Newgate was drinking on horseback at the 'Three Foxes' in Holloway when Mr. May, a 'change broker was set upon by a single highwayman. Jonathan took into the road and fired a pistol at the highwayman, who got clean off."

"Two notorious highwaymen and housebreakers were taken a night or two ago by Jonathan Wild and are committed."

"Nine foot-robbers have been taken, and are committed, by the care of Jonathan Wild."

"The famous Jonathan Wild, going to Reading to the trial of the Blacks,[7] met a notorious street robber by accident whom he apprehended and brought to town."

He was the uncrowned king of Newgate Prison. Both felons and turnkeys trembled at his nod. It was in his power to order or defer the indictment of a malefactor. He seemed to know every rogue in London as well as the history of their lives, and could set a hand upon any of them at any time. Yet, there was another side to this picture. In secret Jonathan Wild was a receiver of stolen goods, keeping a sort of clearing-house for thieves' plunder, always ready to hand it over to the rightful owners upon payment of a fine, or, if no reward was offered for the lost property, he would have it sold in the open

---

[7] The Waltham Blacks: see "Newgate Calendar," by Knapp and Baldwin (1824), I, p. 187.

market. In this way he earned a considerable income in addition to his income as a detective. In the end, of course, he was found out, and ended his life at Tyburn.

Jonathan lost no time in letting loose his emissaries, very craftily going in search of the female of the species as being the easier to capture. And so it proved, for on 22nd July the baggage Bess was arrested in a brandy shop near Temple Bar and divulged the hiding place of her paramour. The next day Quilt Arnold, one of Wild's most trustworthy henchmen, found him at the house of Blueskin's mother in Rosemary Lane, and it would have gone hard with the adventurous Quilt had not the pistol which Jack presented at his breast flashed in the pan. Being now unarmed, he was overpowered in spite of his struggles, and before nightfall of this Thursday, 23rd July, he was lodged in his former cell in the New Prison. On the following morning, when taken before Justice Blackerby, he was committed to Newgate.[8]

It was on the next day, Saturday, 25th July, that his exploits were chronicled in the newspaper press for the first time. The following paragraph appeared in *The Daily Journal*, a sheet published by Thomas Warner:—

"Yesterday, one Shepheard, a notorious housebreaker who lately made his escape from the New Prison and had impeach'd his own brother, was committed to Newgate, having been retaken by Jonathan Wild. He is charged with several burglaries . . ."

It was just two months since his former escape, during which time he had accomplished two considerable housebreakings and three paltry thefts. So far, except for his achievements at the Round-house and the New Prison, he had shown himself a very ordinary criminal.

VI.—Newgate Prison.

In the days of Jack Sheppard the prison of Newgate was one of the most curious gaols in England. It consisted of the city gate that spanned Newgate Street—rebuilt in 1673 after the Great Fire of London—in conjunction with two spacious annexes, each four floors in height, which adjoined the gate on either side of the roadway. All these blocks were connected together on each storey by passages and staircases. The gate was a handsome structure, 60 feet high, adorned with pilasters and statues both on its eastern façade and on its west.

---

[8] Nathaniel Blackerby, died 21st April, 1742; House-keeper to the House of Lords, and J.P. for Middlesex.

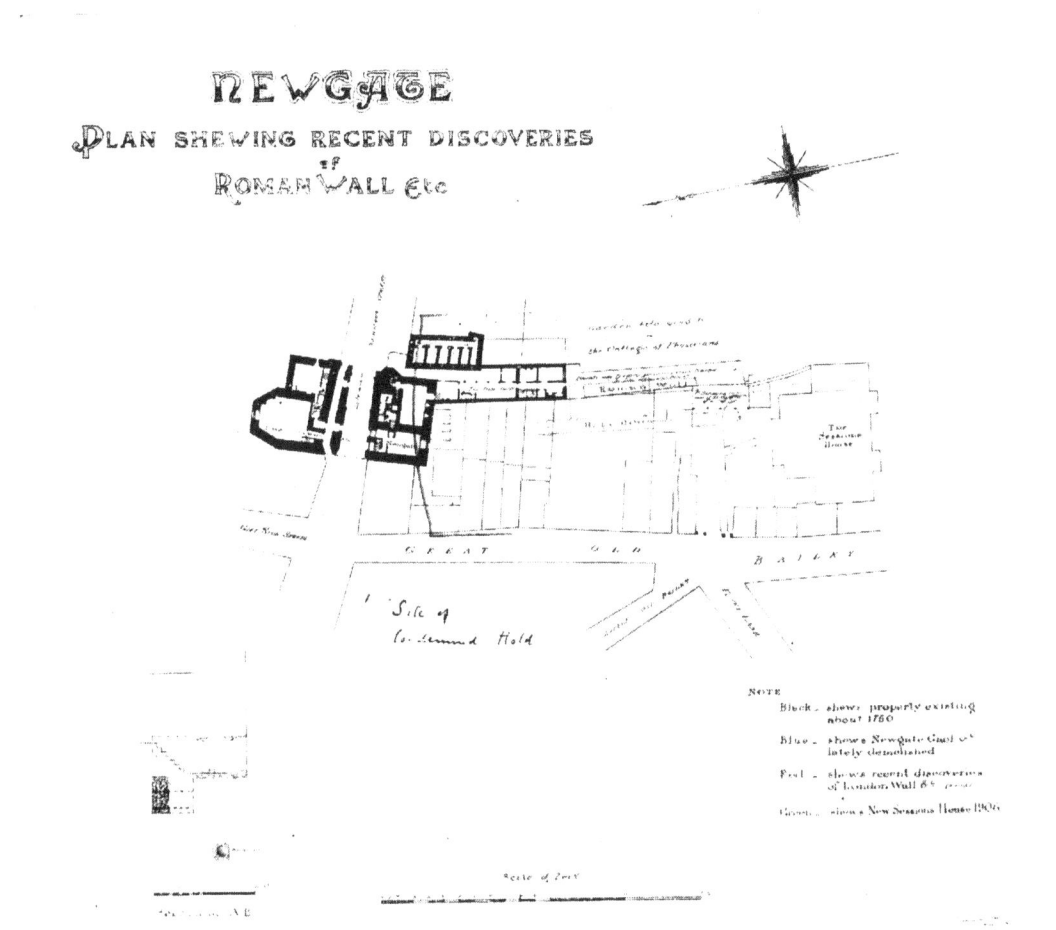

The Situation of Newgate Prison

Reproduced by permission of the Corporation of London

Newgate Prison.

One of these, representing Liberty, had the word "*Libertas*" carved on her hat and the figure of a cat lying at her feet, in allusion to the legend of Sir Richard Whittington.

Inside, the prison was a rabbit warren of cells and dungeons, there being half a dozen on each storey within the gate itself, but none of them was more than 20 feet in either length or breadth, for most of the larger wards were situated in the north and south annexes. The southern annexe had a frontage of little more than 7 yards in the Old Bailey, its principal façade, facing the wide open courtyard which surrounded the Sessions-house. Thus, the front of the prison seemed to be turned towards Ludgate Hill.

The main entrance, however, was through a door on the south side of Newgate Street, close to the archway of the gate, which led into a large apartment on the ground floor, known as the Lodge. This room, in addition to being the taproom of the prison, where very good beer, brandy, wine, and tobacco could be bought by the prisoners,[9] contained the entrance into the famous Condemned Hold. This cell, a dungeon 20 feet by 14, was situated alongside the wall of the gateway on the level of the street; for it had been originally the right-hand postern leading into the city. It was divided from the Lodge by a heavy door, on top of which was an aperture, protected by spikes, where prisoners could converse with their visitors. The condemned man had to pay eighteenpence for the privilege of coming down to the grille to talk to his friends.

The Condemned Hold was provided with a good fireplace and "a receptacle for necessary conveniency," and the upper part, where the prisoners slept, was boarded over with planks and fitted with ringbolts in case any were disorderly. The place was very dark, for the window, which looked out on to the street within the archway of the gate, was very small and had thick iron bars. Three years later, when the "new cells" were built at the north end of the Press Yard, this Condemned Hold was abolished, the vacant space being used for a staircase which can be seen in the plans of Newgate Prison after 1727.

On the top storey of all was the Chapel in the south-east angle of the gaol, where the capital convicts were brought for divine service twice every day, and, penned in a large pew containing the facsimile of a coffin, were admonished and browbeaten by the chaplain in his sermon on the Sunday morning before their execution. On the last

---

[9] Although only the debtors seem to have been entitled to this privilege, the felons usually got as much drink as they wanted, as long as they could afford to pay for it.

Jack Sheppard.

day of all they were taken up to the Chapel to receive the holy sacrament, after which they were led down to the Stone-hall on the first floor, where their irons were knocked off and the halters which were to hang them bound around their breasts. Then, descending to the Lodge, they were led through the prison door and put into the carts that were to convey them to Tyburn.

For several days before this fatal morning they had been kept in the dismal Condemned Hold, and during the previous night another torture was inflicted upon them. For the sexton of St. Sepulchre's Church always came within the gateway outside the window of their cell, ringing his bell, and delivered the following exhortation:—

"You prisoners that are within,
After wickedness and sin,

after many mercies shown, you are now appointed to die to-morrow in the forenoon, give ear and understand, that to-morrow Morning the greatest Bell of St. Sepulchre's shall toll for you in the form and manner of a passing Bell, as used to be tolled for those that are at the point of Death: To the end that all godly People, hearing that Bell, and knowing that it is for you going to your death, may be stirred up heartily to pray to God to bestow his Grace and Mercy on you whilst you live. I beseech you, for Jesus Christ's sake, to keep this Night in Watching and Prayer, to the Salvation of your Souls, while there is yet time and place for Mercy; as knowing to-morrow you must appear before the Judgment Seat of your Creator, there to give an account of all things done in this Life and to suffer eternal Torments for your Sins committed against him, unless, upon your hearty and unfeigned Repentance, you find Mercy, through the Merits, Death, and Passion of your only Mediator and advocate Jesus Christ, who now sits on the right hand of God to make Intercession for as many of you as patiently return to him."[1]

The best parts of the prison were in the Press Yard, an open space of 54 feet long and 7 feet broad, situated on the south-west of the gate, where there were "divers large spacious rooms, good air and light." Special fees were required for admission to this privileged sanctuary, being the perquisites of the Governor or Keeper. At this period the Keeper was one William Pitt, "citizen and grocer," who had been in office since 1707. Not long before he had been in disgrace with the authorities, having been suspected of conniving at the escape of a Jacobite prisoner. Upon an inquiry being held, he was found to be innocent and was reinstated.

---
[1] "History of London," by Wm. Maitland (1756), I, p. 26.

Newgate Prison in the Eighteenth Century

The Trial.

VII.—The Trial of Jack Sheppard.

Sessions were held by the King's Commission of Oyer and Terminer at Justice Hall in the Old Bailey eight times a year. The Court-house stood on the southern side of the prison, about 200 feet down Great Old Bailey, and was set back from the street in a large open space. The judges of the Court were the Lord Mayor, Aldermen that were past the chair, and the Recorder, always attended by both the Sheriffs and generally by one of the High Court judges. The edifice was a plain brick building, huge and menacing, without ornament or embellishment of any kind. Within, the Justice Hall was square and commodious, well-lighted by tall windows, and above the President's chair hung a figure of Justice with a drawn sword.

Jack's trial took place on the second day of the Sessions, Thursday, 13th August, 1724. No judge of the High Court attended the Recorder on this occasion. None of the criminals was sufficiently important for such a parade and all the offences were petty felonies. Sir Peter Delme, the Lord Mayor, was in his place upon the Bench[2] surrounded by his richly caparisoned Aldermen, while Sir William Thompson, the Recorder,[3] who was in charge of the proceedings, came into Court with Serjeant Raby, his deputy.[4] Bowing solemnly to counsel in the body of the Court, they took their seats among the Sheriffs and Aldermen. Then little Jack Sheppard, very pale and looking a mere boy, was placed in the huge dock in the centre of the Justice Hall.

Three indictments were proffered against the accused youth, who was described in each as John Sheppard of St. Martin's-in-the-Fields.

(1) He was indicted for breaking and entering the house of William Phillips and stealing divers goods on 14th February, 1724, in the night, but the evidence not being sufficient he was acquitted.

(2) He was indicted for breaking and entering the house of Mary Cook in the parish of St. Clement's Danes and stealing divers goods, on 5th February, 1724; but for want of sufficient evidence was likewise acquitted of this indictment.

(3) He was a third time indicted for breaking and entering the house of William Kneebone in the parish of St. Mary, Savoy, and stealing 108 yards of woollen cloth, two silver spoons, and other goods, on 12th July, 1724, in the night time.

---

[2] Sir Peter Delme, Knt., Alderman of Langhorn Ward, died 4th September, 1728.

[3] Sir William Thompson died 27th October, 1739.

[4] John Raby, serjeant-at-law, Recorder of Huntingdon, died 26th January, 1732.

Jack Sheppard.

No great official of the Crown appeared to prosecute. At the Sessions on this occasion the Proceedings of the King's Commission of Peace and Oyer and Terminer and Gaol Delivery of Newgate were left in the hands of the Old Bailey attorneys. After the Clerk of Arraigns had read the indictments, one of these would now rise and address the Recorder—

"May it please your lordship and you gentlemen of the jury I am counsel for the King against the prisoner at the Bar . . ."

And the Recorder would bow his acquiescence.

The jury in the box had been chosen from householders of the county, since the robbery at Kneebone's had been committed in the county of Middlesex. Men such as these were likely to make short shift with a burglar, and poor Jack's trial did not last for long. No counsel, of course, was allowed to appear in his defence. In law the judge was supposed to be counsel for all prisoners, it being his duty to protect them. No relaxation of this rule was made until long after the year 1724. So Jack was left naked to his enemies.

Very few witnesses appear to have been required.

WILLIAM KNEEBONE—The prisoner hath sometime since been my servant. On 12th July last about 11 o'clock at night I saw all my doors and windows made fast and then went to bed. I was called up about four in the morning and found my house broke open. The bar of my cellar window was cut, the bolts of my cellar door were drawn, and the padlock wrenched off; the shutters in my shop were broke, and 108 yards of woollen cloth, two silver spoons, and other things, were taken away. I presently suspected the prisoner, because he had lately committed some ill-actions in the neighbourhood, and acquainting Jonathan Wild with it, by his means the prisoner was apprehended and committed to the New Prison. I went to see him there and asked him how he could be so ungrateful as to rob me after I had shown him so much kindness. He confessed he had been very ungrateful in doing so, but said he had been drawn into it by ill-company, and then he gave a particular description of the manner of his breaking into my house.

[Kneebone was still feeling very sore and hurt at the treatment he had received from Jack Sheppard considering his charity towards him and his family. Still, it is improbable that he would have prosecuted him to the death unless pressure had been brought upon him by the authorities.]

JONATHAN WILD—The prosecutor came and told me that his house had been broken into and he had lost a large quantity of woollen

The Trial.

cloth. That he suspected the prisoner was concerned in the fact because he had committed several rogueries thereabouts and he desired me to inquire after the goods. I promised to do him all the service I could, and accordingly, understanding that the prisoner was acquainted with Joseph Blake, alias Blueskin, and William Field, I sent for Field, who coming to me I told him if he would make an ingenious confession I believed I could prevail with the Court to admit him as evidence. Then he discovered the prisoner and gave an account how some of the cloth they stole was disposed of; by which means the prisoner was apprehended and part of the cloth was found.

WILLIAM FIELD—The prisoner told me and Blueskin that he knew of a ken worth milling—that is, a house worth breaking—for he said there was something good to be got in it. And so he carried us to take a view of the prosecutor's house. Blueskin and I disapproved of the design, because we did not think it could easily be done, but the prisoner told us that it might be done with all the pleasure in life, for he had lived with the prosecutor and was acquainted with every part of the house and would undertake it himself if we would but stand where we were and give a good look-out. We agreeing to this, he cut the bar of the cellar and window and so got into the shop and brought out three pounds of cloth, which we carried away.

[Field was a base fellow, who was a thief and the associate of thieves, but, lacking the courage to make a successful robber, he acted usually as a receiver of stolen goods.]

Other witnesses deposed that when the prisoner was apprehended and carried before the justices he confessed the fact.

JACK SHEPPARD was now called upon to make his defence. Never lacking in courage he stuttered out what he had to say bravely, but he made no attempt either to deny or to extenuate his guilt in the matter of the robbery. Carried away by his resentment against the colleague who had "peached," he devoted his whole speech to the subject of Field and his character, declaring that he was an old offender himself, a seducer of unwary youths, and an encourager of all the fatal practices that procure their ruin. Finally, he denied that Field had been concerned in any way in the Kneebone robbery, but that Blueskin and he had told him the particulars from which he had concocted his evidence.[5]

Most people considered that his defence could not possibly have

---

[5] "Authentic Memoirs of the Life and Surprising Adventures of John Sheppard" (Joseph Marshall, 1724), p. 19. "The History of the Remarkable Life of John Sheppard" (John Applebee, 1724), p. 32.

Jack Sheppard.

been more weak, and when the jury retired few had any doubt as to what their verdict would be. They were not absent for long, and when they returned they declared that Jack Sheppard was guilty. Nothing more occurred on this day, and Jack was bustled out of Court by the turnkeys and taken along the covered passage by the Roman wall which connected the Sessions-house with the prison of Newgate.

Next morning, Friday, 14th August, he was led back to the Justice Hall. The Sessions were over and the Recorder was waiting to announce the doom of each of the convicted malefactors. When asked if he had anything to say why sentence of death should not be pronounced against him, Jack made one last frantic attempt to justify himself. He begged earnestly for transportation to the most extreme boundary of His Majesty's dominions, pleading youth and ignorance as the motive that had led him into crime. It was in vain. The common hangman had already tied his thumbs together with whipcord as well as those of the other capital felons, a barbarous custom that was continued for many years. Five of them were sentenced to death besides himself, four men and one woman, viz., Joseph Ward and Robert Colthorp for robberies on the highway; Anthony Upton for felony and burglary; Stephen Fowler for shop-lifting; and Frances Sands for stealing between £30 and £40 out of a club box. Nine felons were burned in the hand (four of them for marrying second wives while their first were living), and 31 ordered for transportation.[6]

VIII.—The First Escape from Newgate.

Jack was now a celebrity, talked about in the newspapers. In addition to the paragraph in *The Daily Journal* of 25th July, another had appeared a week later in the columns of *Applebee's Original Weekly Journal*, of which Daniel Defoe was editor, or, at least, chief contributor—

" Sheppard, the Notorious Housebreaker, who lately escaped from the New Prison and was retaken by Jonathan Wild and committed to Newgate, attempted to escape also from that Gaol a day or two ago; several saws and instruments proper for such a design being found about his bed. He is since confined in an Apartment called the Stone-

---

[6] This account of the Trial of Jack Sheppard is taken from the " Old Bailey Session Papers " (1716-1727) in the Inner Temple Library, and from " Select Trials at the Sessions-house in the Old Bailey," 1720-1724 inclusive. Printed for J. Wilford, 1734. Vol. I, p. 435. Brit. Mus. 6495, a.a.a. 14.

The First Escape from Newgate.

Room, kept close and sufficiently Loaded with Irons to prevent his designs for the future."[7]

The gaolers of Newgate were all very much on the alert, determined that the slippery young carpenter should not repeat his former achievement at the New Prison. For the moment, William Pitt, the keeper, was indisposed, but his second in command, one Bodenham Rouse, who had been a turnkey for nearly twenty-five years, was a reliable substitute. The under turnkeys—Messrs. Alston, Perry, Langley, and Ireton—were all incorruptible folk, incapable of accepting a bribe and too sagacious to be easily outwitted. At that time Newgate was supposed to have the most efficient staff of any prison in England.

Nevertheless, the Newgate officials could not have helped being relieved when they learned that in the Recorder's " report," which had been considered at a general meeting of the Council at Windsor on 22nd August, the name of Jack Sheppard was among the list of those ordered for execution. A few days later they must have anticipated an early termination of their responsibilities when the " dead warrant " arrived at the prison, appointing Friday, 4th September, as the day for the journey to Tyburn.[8] Jack Sheppard at last could be consigned to the Condemned Hold, where all those doomed to death passed their last few days on earth, and officialdom was able to breathe freely, convinced that they had got him safely held in the " stone jug " now.

In spite of his terrible dungeon and the imminence of the March to Tyburn his courage remained undaunted, nor did he ever seem depressed. All the time he was buoying himself up with dreams of escape, confident that he would be able to outwit his gaolers once more. When a pious friend, perhaps Wood or Kneebone, who came to visit him, reminded him that he should be thinking of his latter end, since his execution was fixed for the following Friday, Jack replied with the utmost gaiety—

" Yes, so my great Lord and Master says; but, by God, I'll do my best endeavours to make him a false prophet."

No kind friend managed to bring Jack any tools that might assist his escape, as was done at the New Prison; but there were eight other unhappy wretches with him in the Condemned Hold, and one of these,

---

[7] *Applebee's Original Weekly Journal*, Saturday, 1st August, 1724.

[8] The so-called " dead warrant " was merely the Recorder's " report," or list of names of the convicts who had been capitally convicted. Those struck out of the list had been reprieved; those included in the report were " ordered for execution."

Jack Sheppard.

Lumley Davis, who had been thwarted in his attempt at prison-breaking, was charitable enough to hand over his watch-springs, files, and saws to his fellow-prisoner. Jack came down to the hatchway of his cell on the morning that his benefactor was put into the cart to be taken to Tyburn, and celebrated the occasion by setting to work to file through one of the great iron spikes on the top of the doorway. On the next day, Saturday, 29th August, he made fine progress with his work, but he did nothing on the Sunday, fearing to be detected because of the crowds of visitors that passed through the Lodge. For it was in the Lodge, of course, that the doorway of the Condemned Hold was situated.

On the following day, 31st August, his "wife," Edgworth Bess, visited him, along with another of his doxies, who may have been Mistress Maggot, staying chatting with him at the hatch of the gate all the afternoon while he continued to file away at the stubborn spike. About six o'clock it was almost cut through, and at last, with the help of the women, he was able to break it off. Some of the turnkeys were drinking at a table at the far end of the Lodge,[9] but their view of the entrance to the Condemned Hold was obstructed by a projecting porch, which led into a passage that communicated with another part of the prison. And at that moment, oddly enough, they were talking about Jack Sheppard's wonderful escape at Clerkenwell.

As soon as the spike was broken off at the top of the door there was no reason for Jack to tarry in Newgate any longer.[1] It was an easy matter for him to squeeze his slender body through the narrow aperture—though it is a matter of dispute whether he went head first or feet first—and there was the stalwart Bess and her companion to catch him on the other side. He had dressed himself in a nightgown reaching to his ankles in order to conceal the fetters around his legs. Hobbling swiftly across the floor of the lodge with one of his women, he passed through the front door of Newgate into the street, being

---

[9] Mrs. Spurling, a plump widow, presided over the tap in the Lodge. Her husband, who had been head turnkey of Newgate, was shot dead by William Johnson, a butcher, in the courtyard of the Old Bailey Sessions-house in 1712.

[1] The original iron grille and stonework of the cell can now be seen in the Chamber of Horrors at Madame Tussaud's with the wax figure of Jack Sheppard. These portions of the old prison were purchased when Newgate was demolished in 1903, and they were re-erected stone by stone in the Waxwork Exhibition. At the same time Tussaud's purchased the old toll bell from Newgate, bearing the inscription—

"Ye people all who hear me ring,
Be faithful to your God and King."

All these relics escaped destruction in the great fire at Tussaud's in 1925.—S.M.E.

Jack Sheppard Escaping from the Condemned Hold in Newgate, 31st August, 1724

Frontispiece to *A Narrative of all the Robberies, Escapes, &c., of John Sheppard*, attributed to Daniel Defoe, 1724

The First Escape from Newgate.

picked up by a hackney coach that was in waiting at the top of the Old Bailey. Thus he disappeared into the night.[2]

Naturally, the newspapers marvelled at the wonderful escape, an event unprecedented in the history of the gaol, for no prisoner had ever before broken out of the Condemned Hold in the daytime under the very noses of the turnkeys. Sympathy was expressed for the officers of the prison, who were declared to be the "most careful, vigilant, and at the same time the most humane and gentleman-like of any in the kingdom." Not being able to lay hands on Jack, these same officials set Jonathan Wild on the track of Edgworth Bess, who was discovered by that efficient sleuth after a short search and lodged in Newgate.

IX.—A Short Spell of Freedom.

On 1st September Jack went in search of William Page, the son of a butcher in Clare Market, whom he describes as his "trusty comrade." Certainly Page proved himself a friend in need. Full of admiration for the marvellous escape from the Condemned Hold, he offered to give Jack all the help he could, buying him a blue frock and a woollen apron so that he could pass as a butcher's apprentice too, and suggested that he should go with him in hiding into the country. On the following morning the pair set out for Chipping Warden, in Northamptonshire, to visit some of Page's relatives who, he thought, would give them lodging for a while. The two young men were kindly received, but were expected to earn their keep by working on the farm, an obligation that did not meet with their fancy. After two or three days they decamped and trudged back to London, where they arrived on 8th September.

Towards dusk that evening Jack committed a characteristically impudent robbery. Passing down the Old Bailey in front of Newgate, he came into Fleet Street, where, noticing the shop of one Martin, a watchmaker, opposite St. Bride's Church, he broke the window and pillaged the tray of watches inside. Previously he had secured the door, so that the people in the shop would not pursue him, by fixing a gimlet in the doorpost and fastening the knocker to it with a piece of pack-thread.

Jack's two unlucky companions in the Condemned Hold had been hanged at Tyburn on 4th September, the day appointed for his execu-

---

[2] He was met by William Page, the butcher-boy. See pages 69-71, 193.

Jack Sheppard.

tion also; and on the following Monday a letter, supposed to have been written by John Sheppard to Jack Ketch on the fatal morning, appeared in *The London News*.[3] Obviously, the letter could not have been composed by him, its style betraying a journalistic pen.

> Sir,—I thank you for the favour you intended me this day. I am a gentleman and allow you to be the same. Fond Nature prompted. I followed. Oh, propitious minute! And to show you that I am in Charity I am now drinking your health and a *bon repos* to poor Joseph and Anthony.[4] I am gone a few days for the air, but design speedily to embark and this Night I am going upon a mansion for a supply. It's a stout Fortification, but what difficulties cannot I encounter, dear Jack. You find that Bars and Chains are but trifling obstacles in the way of
>
> Your Friend & Servant,
>
> JOHN SHEPHEARD.
>
> From my Residence in *Terra Australis incognita*.
> Friday, Sept. 4, 1724.
>
> P.S.—Pray my services to Mr. Or(dina)ry and Mr. Appl(e)bee.

Jack could read and write, but tags of Latin and French were beyond him.

The John Applebee mentioned in the postscript of this spurious letter, was the printer of *Applebee's Original Weekly Journal* and of T. Warner's *Daily Journal*, but the chief contributor to these and to others, too, was the famous Daniel Defoe, author of "Robinson Crusoe."[5] It is improbable that Jack Sheppard knew the printer, who no doubt was principally concerned in his shop, but it is not unlikely that he was well acquainted with the writer, whose duties must have brought him often to Newgate Prison. And if the letter to Jack Ketch was composed by Defoe himself—as it may have been—it is characteristic that he should have taken the opportunity of advertising his journal by mentioning the name of its printer. From this time onwards until the end of Jack Sheppard's life, Daniel Defoe appears to have taken the greatest interest in him.[6]

Jack now found that his old haunts in Drury Lane and the Seven Dials were too hot for him. Jonathan Wild was on his track, combing every rookery with characteristic intrepidity in search of the fugitive. So Jack moved out to Finchley Common, accompanied by the faithful Page, who foolishly declined to desert him, although he was no more

---

[3] 7th September, 1724.

[4] Joseph Ward and Anthony Upton, who were hanged on 4th September.

[5] John Applebee, printer, died in Bolt Court, Fleet Street, 20th January, 1750.

[6] "Daniel Defoe," by William Lee, I, pp. 383-389.

A Short Spell of Freedom.

use to him, and took refuge in a secluded cottage. Nevertheless the officials of Newgate soon got wind of him.

On Thursday morning, 10th September, the "big four" of them rode out to Finchley—Bodenham Rouse, Alston, Langley, and Ireton—dispersing themselves over the Common as soon as they arrived there, resolved to beat it thoroughly from end to end. It was not very long before their tactics succeeded. Jack and Page, who happened to be taking a walk along a hedge, dressed in their blue frocks and aprons, on the lookout for a solitary wayfarer whose pocket they could pick, were soon espied by Langley.

"Here's a stag," cried Jack, catching sight of the turnkey at the same instant, and, having warned his friend, he took to his heels. Page, however, was not so swift-footed and Langley overtook him. After which the whole company joined together in search of the more important fugitive who had disappeared in the fields.

Later in the morning their search took them to a farmhouse near Brown's Well on the Common, and, thinking this a likely place of refuge for the elusive Jack, they made a search of the outbuildings. It happened that Jack had taken shelter in an old stable, but he was like to have outwitted his pursuers once more, for no trace of him could be discovered until the quick-eyed farmer's daughter—mean girl, to have betrayed the poor fellow—caught sight of his toes sticking out of the hay in which he had buried himself. At first he was going to make a fight for it, but he saw at once that it would be of no avail, for his antagonists were all provided with pistols. So he allowed himself to be handcuffed and searched when two of the watches that he had filched from Martin's shop in Fleet Street were found under his armpits and a knife in his pocket. A hackney-coach had been brought from London, and about two o'clock in the afternoon Jack was brought back to the Old Bailey, where he was lodged in the Condemned Hold again, loaded with irons. The unfortunate William Page also was committed to Newgate.[7]

X.—Newgate Once More.

The authorities of the prison soon forgave Jack for the trouble that he had caused them, since no prisoner proved such a gold mine. Crowds of visitors, every one of whom had to pay an entrance fee,

---

[7] *Daily Post*, 11th September; *London News*, 14th September, 1724. "Select Trials" (1720-1724), I, p. 468. Brit. Mus. 6495, a.a.a. 14.

Jack Sheppard.

flocked to see him, and although the charge for admission was low, the small profits were counterbalanced by the quick returns. Sir Erasmus Philipps, Bart., notes in his diary—

"Saw in Newgate John Shepherd, the famous thief, who had escaped so often out of prison. Cost me three and sixpence to see the rascal."[8]

Several gentlemen visited him in the Condemned Hold on the evening of his capture, when he chatted with them most cheerfully, explaining to them how he had got out of the prison, telling them all his adventures subsequently. On the following Sunday he was carried up to Chapel, "loaden with irons and with an instrument called the Sheers on," and the attendance on this occasion was more numerous than had ever been known. And many of these paid to visit him in his cell afterwards.

All sorts of rumours were spread with regard to his fate. At first, it was reported that he was to be hanged immediately. Then it was alleged that he would have to be tried again because he had committed several robberies since his escape. Most people imagined that he would have a long respite, since both the Recorder and his deputy were enjoying themselves at Bath and not inclined to cut short their visit for the sake of hanging a thief. Finally, the truth became known. It was impossible that Jack's execution could take place until after the next Sessions, since it was necessary in law to prove that he was the same person who had been convicted at the Justice Hall on 13th August.

Meanwhile the parsons were revelling in the opportunities of trying to shrive the wicked young man. It chanced that the Rev. Thomas Purney, the Ordinary, was in a poor state of health, necessitating "retirement into the country,"[9] but he had a burly substitute in the Rev. Mr. Wagstaff, who appears to have loved a wrangle with Jack, the latter having shocked him at one of their early interviews by telling him that "there was neither lock nor key ever made that he should make any difficulty to open." Wagstaff declared that Jack was "an inhuman and barbarous thief and housebreaker," and treated him accordingly. In addition to Mr. Wagstaff, the Rev. Mr. Flood, chaplain of the Fleet, and the Rev. Mr. Hawkins, chaplain of the Tower, came to admonish the unlucky prisoner.[1]

---

[8] *Notes and Queries*, 2 series, XII, p. 392. Sir Erasmus Philipps, 5th Bart., economic writer, died 1743.

[9] Rep. 120, f. 263. Guildhall Record Office.

[1] Rev. — Flood, died in Fleet Prison, 2nd January, 1730. Rev. — Hawkins, chaplain to the Tower, died 12th June, 1736.

Newgate Once More.

Since his execution was no longer imminent, Jack was taken from the Condemned Hold and lodged in another part of the gaol. The cell chosen for him was one of the strongest in Newgate, a room called the Castle, 20 feet long and 10 feet broad, situated on the third floor of the Gate itself, the top storey but one. The only window, heavily protected by iron bars, looked westward towards Snow Hill. A great number of people of "tolerable fashion" still flocked to see him. In spite of his irons and the padlock which fastened his ankles to a staple in the floor, he was pleasant and cheerful still, turning everything into banter. He declared to Mr. Robbins, the City Smith, that whoever put the spikes on the Condemned Hold was an honest fellow, for a better piece of metal he had never wrought upon in his life, and told him that he had to thank him (Jack) for the job of setting up another.[2]

While Jack was in the Castle, the fate of his elder brother Thomas was finally decided. As far back as July he had been tried and convicted of the robbery at the house of Mary Cook, but the jury had brought him in guilty of a felony of only 39s., an offence not punishable by death. So he was cast for transportation. A few days before he was to sail, he begged for a last interview with his brother, but the request was refused, and they were allowed merely to see one another in Chapel at a distance. Eventually, unless the convict ship foundered at sea, Thomas Sheppard must have reached the West Indies or the American colonies, but what became of him there is unknown at present.

Meanwhile, Blueskin, who had been arrested for the robbery at Mr. Kneebone's, was also a prisoner in Newgate. Hitherto, he had been known only as a commonplace thief of no great pluck or ingenuity, but on the morning of his trial he committed a deed that has made him one of the celebrities of the Newgate Calendar. While waiting in the open space outside the Sessions-house, known as the bail-dock, Jonathan Wild came up and offered him a dram of brandy. Encouraged by this affability, Blueskin begged the great man to speak a word for him at his trial. Jonathan shook his head.

"I can't do that," he replied. "You are a dead man."

Infuriated by the cruel answer, Blueskin flung himself upon the thief-taker, resolved to kill him on the spot. Snatching a claspknife from his pocket, he seized Wild by the hair and cut his throat to the windpipe. Had he not been wearing a muslin stock, and if the blade

---

[2] John Robbins, City Smith, died 26th October, 1734.

had not been a blunt one, the wound would have been fatal. Fortunately for Jonathan, three skilful surgeons happened to be close at hand—Messrs. Dobbin, Martin, and Coletheart were their names according to the newspapers—who put in a number of stitches and saved his life.

Although Wild was unable to give evidence at the trial which took place in a few hours, the testimony of Kneebone, Quilt Arnold, and William Field, the informer, was sufficient to secure the conviction of Blueskin. At the end of the Sessions he was condemned to death.

During the few days that he was in the Condemned Hold after his recapture, Jack used to give the authorities much anxiety because of the number of prison-breaking implements that were discovered in his possession. One day it was a small file; another day it was two files, a chisel, and a hammer. When asked how these tools had come to him, he always flew into a rage, exclaiming—

"How can you? You always ask me questions like these."

The Rev. Mr. Wagstaff, who seems to have been a nosey person, was the discoverer invariably of these instruments, which he found in the seat of the chair or concealed in a Bible.

"One file is worth a hundred Bibles," snarled Jack in retaliation.

Even in the Castle he continued to rehearse a projected escape. On 7th October the turnkeys found him wandering about the room with his fetters clanking around his legs when they happened to enter suddenly when he did not expect them. It appeared that he had unlocked the great padlock that fastened his ankles to the staple in the floor with the help of a nail, thus being able to move about his cell as he chose. He had made an attempt to ascend the chimney, but although wide enough to allow him to creep up, an iron bar, fixed across it, made it impossible to climb very high. Angry at this breach of discipline, the officials proceeded to load him with heavier irons and a larger padlock, and in spite of his entreaties they fitted a pair of handcuffs around his wrists. Nevertheless, most of them must have considered that such precautions were superfluous, for the Castle was such a strongly built cell that it seemed impossible that any human creature could break out of it.

XI.—The Great Escape from Newgate.

The Sessions at the Old Bailey commenced on 14th October, and Jack knew full well that his escape would have to be accomplished during the next few days if it was ever to be made at all. Every one of the

The Great Escape from Newgate.

turnkeys now had his hands full. Dozens of prisoners had to be escorted to the Justice Hall each day and carefully guarded while being taken backwards and forwards and while they were being tried, for many of them were desperate ruffians who might run amok at any moment. It was during this period that the vigilance of the gaolers would be relaxed a little as far as those locked up in cells were concerned. Naturally they would conclude that a convict in the Castle—even though he were a Jack Sheppard—was safely enough caged.

About two o'clock on the afternoon of Thursday, 15th October, William Austin, one of the under-turnkeys, brought Jack Sheppard his dinner as usual. Captain Geary, the Keeper of the New Prison, looked in at the same time as well as one or two other officials, and they talked and joked with Jack, who was in a good humour. During the customary examination of his fetters and manacles Jack begged Austin to come and see him again that evening, a masterly stroke of audacity sure to lull any suspicion that might be lurking in the turnkey's mind. The man replied abruptly that he was too busy to pay another visit to the Castle till next morning, advising Jack to ask for anything he might want now since he would not have another chance of getting it that evening. Jack said he wanted nothing and proceeded to eat his dinner with a good appetite, while Captain Geary and the others kept him company.

It was nearly three o'clock when Austin and the visitors went away, leaving but two and a half hours of daylight, for the sun set soon after five o'clock. Jack lost no time in beginning his task, realising that he could not have a better opportunity for escape since he would never again be left undisturbed for such a long period. First of all he tried to rid himself of his handcuffs, succeeding at length after great difficulty. It is uncertain how he managed to take them off, for he has left no clear account of the matter, and, although he offered subsequently to give a demonstration of how it was done, officialdom refused to allow the exhibition. According to one theory, he merely squeezed his fingers together and slipped his hands through the rings after the fashion of the modern " handcuff king." Another version declares that he unfastened them by means of a nail or a pin.

His hands free, he went to work to remove the manacles that secured his feet, a far more formidable undertaking, since the fetters and the horse-padlock that bound him to the staple in the floor had been strengthened since his escapade of a few days previously. Eventually, he succeeded in opening the padlock with a nail, and after twisting the chain between his legs to and fro, exerting all his powerful

Jack Sheppard.

strength to burst it asunder, he broke one of the weaker links, releasing himself from the staple. Then, taking off his boots and stockings, he tied the end of each of the broken fetters firmly around his knees and calves by means of his stockings and garters to prevent them from dragging at his heels. For he was unable to unfasten the iron bands that encircled his ankles.

Knowing the structure of the gaol intimately, he was aware that it would be no advantage to break open the door of the Castle, since it would not lessen the number of the doors that he would have to unfasten before he gained the Leads, which was obviously the best route to take. Moreover, the large room, where the Master Debtors were confined, was situated immediately opposite across the passage on the same storey, so that the debtors would be sure to hear the noise that he was making if he began to smash open the door of his own cell.

The alternative, of course, was to escape up the chimney into the room above, in spite of the obstacle of the iron bar. Picking the mortar from between one of the bricks with one of the broken links of his fetters, Jack at last got the first brick loose after prodigious labour and forced it from its place. The iron bar was fixed across the chimney about 6 feet above the level of the floor, so a big hole had to be broken in the wall in order to reach it. Using the great horse-padlock as a battering-ram, Jack brought a rush of bricks and mortar crashing down around him, excavating in a little while an opening 3 feet in width and 6 feet high. There was a risk that the Master Debtors would hear the sound in their room across the passage, but even so, it was improbable that they would try to raise an alarm, or, if they did, that any of the turnkeys would take notice of it. When at last he had reached the bar, more than a cartload of debris was strewn at his feet.

He had now the tedious task of picking the bar from its place in the brickwork, but he succeeded after removing some of the bricks around it. Tearing it from the chimney, he found that it was an iron bar 2 feet 6 inches in length and 1 inch square, " a notable implement."[3] With such a weapon in his hands he now made swift progress. Climbing into the chimney, he worked his way as far as the ceiling and had little difficulty in smashing an entry into the room above. Tossing his bar on to the floor, he crept through the aperture.

The room in which he found himself was known as the Red-room,

---

[3] So Defoe makes him describe it in his pamphlet on Jack Sheppard.

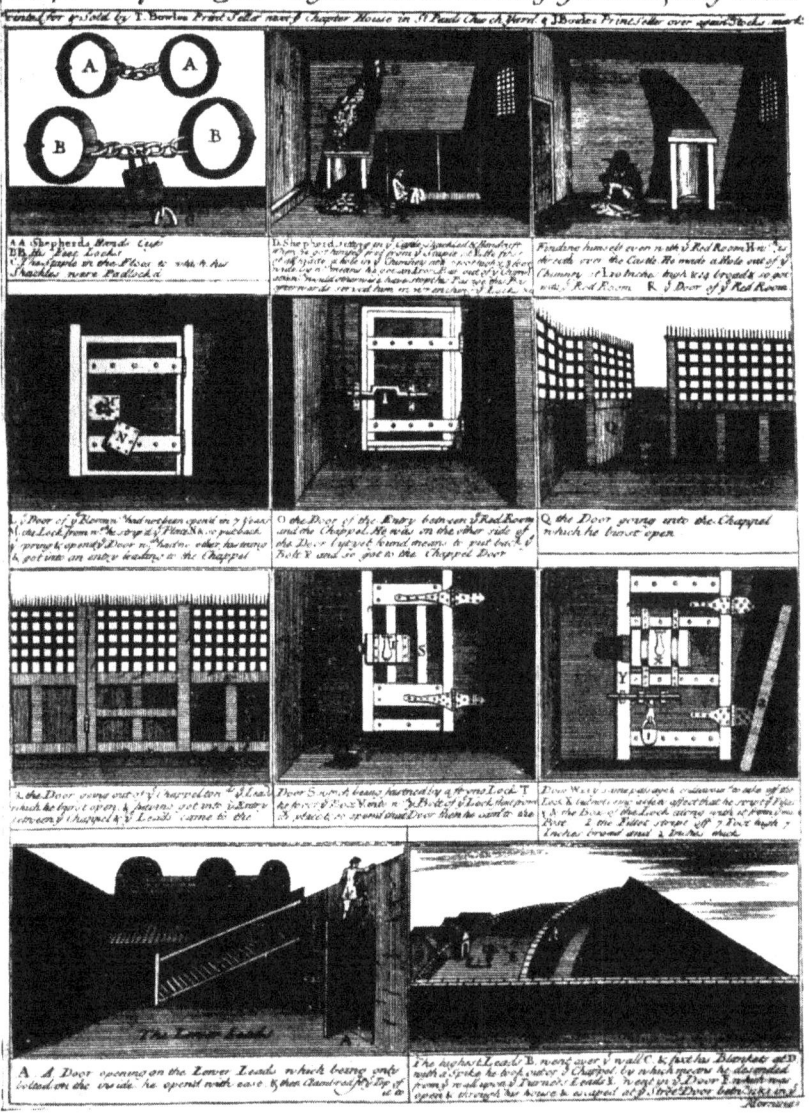

Jack Sheppard's Escape from the Castle in Newgate Prison,
15th October, 1724

The Great Escape from Newgate.

an apartment on the fourth floor of the gateway, 20 feet by 11, with a barred window facing Snow Hill and St. Sepulchre's Church, like the view from the Castle. It had been in disuse for eight years since the year 1716, when numbers of the Lancashire Jacobites were confined there. Making his way to the door, he examined how it was fastened. Fortunately, his foot struck against a large nail which he seized upon with delight, knowing what a useful tool it was. Night had now fallen and it was pitch dark. Subsequently the newspapers declared that he had been assisted by a full moon, which was untrue, for the moon was new, therefore rising and setting with the sun.[4]

The door of the Red-room was strong and had not been opened for seven years, but after removing a nut he forced aside the plate that covered the lockbox and in seven minutes had shot back the lock with his fingers. Pulling open the rusty door, he went out into the passage, turning to the left after walking past the top of the staircase that led to the lower storey, and 3 yards farther on came to another door that barred the entrance to the Chapel. On the right stood a large cell over the Master Debtors' quarters, on the left a " darkie "[5] for women, both out of use. There was no means of escape except through the door leading to the Chapel.

It was a strong door, and to Jack's consternation he could find neither lock nor keyhole when he ran his hands around it. He had now to rely solely upon his sense of touch, having neither tinder-box nor candle. In a moment or two he perceived that the door was bolted on the far side, and for a while he was puzzled how to get it unfastened. Then, feeling that there was a strip of wall-work all around it, he proceeded to break a hole on one side with his iron bar. It was an arduous task, for the wall was built of stone, but he made a breach at last large enough to pass his arm through and, pushing back the bolt, passed into the Chapel. The Master Debtors were in the room on the floor below, and he had made so much noise that he was sure they must have heard him.

The Chapel, which was situated in the south-east corner of the gaol, was a grim chamber, 34 feet by 30, divided into five pens for the various grades of prisoners, each pen being enclosed by partitions of wood and iron surmounted by a row of sharp spikes. The structure of the place was familiar to Jack, for he had sat in the condemned pew below the pulpit several times and listened to the lucubrations of

---

[4] Information from the Astronomer Royal, *cf. London News*, 19th October, 1724.

[5] A dark room.

Jack Sheppard.

Mr. Purney and Mr. Wagstaff, every foot of both sitting and standing room being occupied on these occasions. Groping his way from the passage whence he had come to the enclosure which surrounded the condemned pew, he felt for the entrance gate, which, having found, he burst open in a few minutes.

He was now in the centre of the Chapel and another partition similar to the first barred his progress. But he wasted no energy in forcing its gate open. Instead, he broke off one of the spikes that crowned the top with a blow of his bar and then climbed over. Taking the spike with him in case of further need, and descending a couple of steps, he came to the door that guarded the passage leading to the Leads.

It was the stoutest door of all that he had yet encountered, the lock being so strong that his efforts to pick it were unavailing, and for a while he believed that he would never succeed in opening it. For half an hour he toiled away in the dark, using the bar, the spike, and the nail in turn without making any impression, but, finally, he changed his tactics and began to attack the box itself instead of the keyhole. Very soon his patience was rewarded. By skilful leverage he forced the box from its place, eventually pushing it far enough aside to enable him to open the lock within. "And so," he declared subsequently, "I made the door my humble servant."

Six yards farther on at the very end of the passage he was stopped by another door, the sixth and the last of all. And it was by far the most formidable obstacle that he had met. For a moment, while his fingers examined it all over, his heart failed him, but the clock of St. Sepulchre's Church happened to strike eight o'clock, and, realising how much he had accomplished in the short space of five hours, his pluck came back to him. Again he felt the surface of the door from end to end, trying to hit upon a means to conquer it.

It was secured by a huge lockbox, bigger and stronger than any of those which he had undone, a box, too, that was plated with iron and clamped to the door with thick iron hoops. Beneath, a stout bolt was retained in its socket by a hasp which was fastened by a great padlock, and the door itself was strengthened further by four broad metal bands running across it. A broad iron fillet, reaching from top to bottom, overlapped the side on which the bolts were placed and held the door fast to the doorpost. As his fingers revealed these obstacles to him one by one, it seemed to him that there was little hope of overcoming them.

Concluding that neither the lock nor the bolt could be opened in

The Great Escape from Newgate.

reasonable time, he attacked the fillet with the ambitious object of shattering the door itself and ignoring its fastening. It was a tough piece of metal, 7 feet high, 7 inches broad, and 2 inches thick, which resisted his implements for a long time, but, at last, when he had forced his indispensable bar underneath it, he felt that it was yielding. In the end he wrenched it entirely from the doorpost, bringing both the box of the lock and the padlocked bolt away with it too, thus stripping the door of all its fastenings. It was a notable feat of strength, one that a less robust man might have toiled at in vain, all the more extraordinary, moreover, because it was performed in pitch darkness. Pushing open the door, he came to another door a few feet along the passage, but, being bolted on the inside, it checked his progress for only a few seconds.

Descending a couple of steps, he now found himself in the fresh air within a space on the roof known as the Lower Leads, 26 feet by 12, on the north-east corner of the gateway. Lofty walls rose around him on all sides. Obviously it was necessary to gain the Higher Leads in order to make his escape to any of the adjacent houses. The ascent to the Upper Leads proved an easy matter. Leaving the last door a little ajar, he clambered on top of it, and, balancing there for a moment on his hands and knees, he drew himself on to the roof above. Then, having scrambled across the tiles over the women-felons' ward, he reached the western side of the prison. He was on the summit of the northern annexe and, looking over the wall, he could see the roofs of the neighbouring houses, which stretched along Newgate Street as far as Giltspur Street, about 7 yards below.

Nothing now remained to be done except to lower himself to the roof immediately beneath him, but, in order to secure the materials for this purpose, it was necessary to go back to the Castle for his blanket. The return journey to his dungeon must have been an unpleasant ordeal, for he was amongst his enemies once more and at any moment a party of turnkeys might spring upon him from a doorway. Yet nothing of the sort happened. He was unmolested, arriving in the Castle on the third storey without mishap a few minutes after he had quitted the Higher Leads.

Everything was just as he had left it. There was the huge pile of bricks and mortar; the great hole gaping in the wall of the chimney; his padlock and manacles lying in a heap on the floor. Seizing his blanket from the barrack-bedstead, he climbed back again into the chimney. A moment later he had crept through the ceiling into the Red-room overhead. While groping his way along the pitch-dark passages and through the Chapel, the recollection of the six mighty doors that he had shattered must have filled his heart with pride as he went through them again one by one. There was the door of the Red-room from which he had stripped the lockplate; the door at the end of the corridor where he had pierced a hole in the wall to reach the bolt; the two doors in the Chapel which he had overcome so easily; the door that led out of the Chapel with its obstinate lockbox; and, finally, the sixth and last door in the passage leading to the Lower Leads, the terrific door with its bolts and boxes and hasps and padlock where he had stripped the fillet away from the doorpost and made all the mighty fastenings useless. Nothing happened to retard him while he was passing through these six doors again, and in a few minutes he found himself back on the Lower Leads. Scrambling up to the Higher Leads, he crossed the roof of the northern annexe and peered over the wall to find a suitable place for his descent.

It did not take him long to discover one. The streets were all lighted—the shops being open still—and he was able to see the roof of the house below him quite clearly. Fixing the spike from the Chapel firmly in the brickwork, he attached his blanket to it and slid down on to the slates. It was now nearly nine o'clock, so it had taken him almost six hours to make his escape. The one thing requisite to make the escape perfect was to get rid of the ends of the chains which were girded to his calves by his garters and stockings. If these were knocked off he was confident that he could evade re-arrest.

Fortunately, as he crept along the roofs overlooking Newgate Street he came to a garret window, the sash of which was open, so creeping through noiselessly he waited for awhile in the room within.[6] Hearing no noise, he descended two pairs of stairs until the sound of people talking in a room on the first storey made him pause on the second-floor landing. At the same moment his fetters gave a clank.

"Lord!" cried a woman's voice, "what was that?"

"Oh, perhaps the dog or the cat," replied a man, and no further notice was taken.

Alarmed by the incident, Jack crept upstairs again, and, taking refuge in the garret which he had first entered, he laid himself down on the bed to rest, utterly exhausted. Two hours later, feeling less tired, he ventured downstairs, realising that it was important that he should get away from the house before the family retired to their rooms. Pausing again on the second floor, he was glad to hear a

---

[6] It was the house of Mr. Bird, a turner, in Newgate Street.

Jack Sheppard Escaping from Newgate Prison, 15th October, 1724

The Great Escape from Newgate.

guest taking his leave from the company below; and, as soon as the man had been lighted to the front door by the maid, Jack rushed down the stairs as fast as he could and made his escape into the street.

It was now past twelve o'clock, but Jack made no haste now that he was out of doors, strolling along unconcernedly in order not to attract attention. Passing by St. Sepulchre's Watch-house, he bade the watchman good-morrow, and strolled down Snow Hill. Having crossed Fleet Bridge, he turned up Holborn Hill, walking past two more watch-houses at St. Andrew's Church and at Holborn Bars on his way, and made for the open fields along Gray's Inn Lane. At last, about two o'clock in the morning, when quite worn out, he came to an ancient cowhouse at the village of Tottenham, where he took refuge.

Flinging himself on the ground he fell asleep, but was awake again three hours later. He was in too great pain to sleep soundly, for his fetters had bruised and cut his ankles, which had become badly swollen. He was in much anxiety, too, for he knew that, if found in his chains, his identity might be discovered. Eagerly he counted the money in his pockets, ascertaining that he possessed between 40s. and 50s., the result of presents that he had received from visitors who came to visit him in the Castle. It was too risky to venture forth to buy tools, so he remained in his hiding-place all day. It poured in torrents from seven in the morning till nightfall, which raised his spirits since it was unlikely that any one would wander about the fields while the weather was so bad. He saw nobody all day.

XII.—Another Short Spell of Freedom.

When William Austin, the turnkey, entered Jack Sheppard's dungeon at eight o'clock in the morning of this memorable Friday, 16th October, 1724, no turnkey was ever more dumbfounded in the long history of the gaol. After one horrified glance at the wreckage on the floor, the man fled downstairs and rushing into the Lodge, he told his colleagues what had happened. In a few minutes all the officials of the prison were gathered in the Castle and the corridors outside. At first it was imagined that Jack could not have got out of the Red-room above, but that delusion was destroyed when a turnkey who had gone up to the fourth storey in advance of the others came back with the tidings that the door which had not been unlocked for seven years was standing wide open.

With growing amazement the company of gaolers followed the route

Jack Sheppard.

of Jack Sheppard's escape, marvelling at the havoc that he had wrought, fearful lest they should be called to account on a charge of negligence or connivance. Upon reaching the lower leads, all perceived how the rest of the escape had been accomplished. Later on, some of the turnkeys were sent on to the higher roofs and discovered the spike and the blanket fixed on the wall. It was estimated by an expert that it would cost £60 to repair the damage to the doors and brickwork.

William Pitt, the Keeper of the prison, and Bodenham Rouse, his second in command, were sorely distressed for a long time, convinced that they would be censured by the authorities.[7] During the course of the day, however, their spirits rose since crowds of visitors—well-to-do folk who could afford to pay an entrance fee—flocked to Newgate to see the marvellous handiwork of the great prison-breaker. They had a call of investigation also from the Sheriffs and their underlings, when they were required to give an explanation of all the details of the escape in order to show that Jack had no aider and abettor among the gaolers. Subsequently, they were summoned to the Sessions-house by the Lord Mayor and the Recorder, and examined at great length before they could satisfy the Bench that no one in Newgate was to blame in the matter. It was the system and not the staff that was at fault.

In *The Evening Post* of the same day an advertisement was published, offering a reward for Jack Sheppard's arrest, and scores of copies of the proclamation were distributed throughout the metropolis—

"John Sheppard did brake out of Newgate in the Night, between the 15th and 16th inst. of October with double irons on his legs and hand-cuffs on his hands, with a bright Horse-Lock under his other irons. He is about 22 years of age, about 5 feet 4 inches high, very slender, of a pale complexion, has an Impediment or Hesitation in his Speech, and did wear a Butcher's Blue Frock with a great coat over it and is a Carpenter or House Joyner by trade. Whoever will discover or apprehend him, so that he be brought to justice, shall have twenty guineas reward, to be paid by the Keeper of Newgate.

N.B.—If any person conceal him from justice (knowingly) since he has made his escape it is a felony and they will be prosecuted for the same."[8]

---

[7] William Pitt, "citizen and grocer," Keeper of Newgate, 1707-1732, died in his house in Newgate Street, 16th May, 1732.

[8] At the first glance it would appear that Jack went off with his handcuffs still on, but it would be absurd to imagine that he went away with a "horse-lock under his other irons." Obviously, the proclamation is merely giving a full description of the fetters that he was wearing in the Castle before his escape.

Another Short Spell of Freedom.

Throughout the whole of Friday Jack Sheppard remained hidden in his cowshed, listening to the rain pattering on the roof, thankful for the bad weather which was keeping away possible intruders. No one was likely to come rambling in the fields while the downpour continued. Soon after nightfall he issued forth, concealing his irons as best he could under the overcoat that he had carried with him from his cell, and walked into the little village of Tottenham, where he bought bread and cheese and beer at a small chandler's shop. His hunger being appeased, he slept soundly all night, remaining in his shelter the whole of Saturday until evening when he ventured forth again to buy provisions. Being unable to obtain a hammer, he could not rid himself of his fetters, but he beat them into the shape of a hoop with the help of a large stone in the vain hope that he might manage to slip his heels through.

During Sunday afternoon the owner of the shed happened to arrive, and was much alarmed when he set eyes upon the manacled felon.

"For God's sake, who are you?" he demanded.

"An unfortunate young man," replied Sheppard, "who has been sent to Bridewell about a Bastard-Child, not being able to give security to the Parish, and has made his escape."

The man retorted that it was a small fault, and he had done the same thing himself, remarking, nevertheless, as he walked away, that he did not like Jack's looks and cared not how soon he was gone.

Later in the afternoon a working-man happened to pass by, and, going out to accost him, Jack repeated his tale of the bastard child, ending up by offering the man twenty shillings for a smith's hammer and a punch. The fellow proved sympathetic and returned in a little while with the tools, so that Jack was able at last to knock off his fetters, which he gave to his benefactor as a remembrance along with the promised reward. Free from the unsightly chains and being able to put on his stockings once more, he set off at once to his haunts in London. The same evening he ate a good supper of roast veal in a cellar at Charing Cross.

The story of the escape was now all over the town. On the previous day (Saturday) the two principal daily newspapers—*The Daily Post* and *The Daily Journal*—had published short paragraphs, and the weekly ones—such as *Mist's Weekly Journal*, *Read's Weekly Journal*, and *Applebee's Original Weekly Journal*—had given brief accounts also. That in the latter newspaper naturally is the most descriptive, because in all probability it was written by Daniel Defoe. Apparently the writer had taken the greatest interest in Jack ever since his escape

Jack Sheppard.

from the Condemned Hold; and, realising what good "copy" he made, often came to visit him in his prison. Since the newspaper was known colloquially as "Applebee's Journal," it is a reasonable conjecture that Jack would regard its chief contributor as Mr. Applebee of Blackfriars. At least, that is how he is always made to address him in the tracts and in the paragraphs.[9]

During the next twenty-four hours Jack wandered from alehouse to alehouse, receiving fresh evidence every moment of his wonderful notoriety. All the town seemed to be discoursing about Sheppard. Most were making merry over his flight from Newgate. Street singers were singing ballads about him at every corner. Whenever a crowd collected, the people would be sure to be talking about him. For the moment he was the most famous person in the kingdom.

On Tuesday, 20th October, he hired a garret in Newport Market as a permanent lodging, sending for a "sober young woman," who for a long time past had been the real mistress of his affections, to keep him company. The fair one, whose name was Kate Cook, obeyed his summons at once, bringing her friend, Catherine Keys, to help to cheer his loneliness. Evidently this pair had supplanted Elizabeth Lyon and Mistress Maggot for some time; and in any case Bess was no use to him at the moment, being still locked up in prison.

During the next few days a letter from Jack to his mother appeared in *Parker's London News*, and two more to Mr. Applebee and to William Austin, the turnkey, were published in *Applebee's Original Weekly Journal*. Both newspapers protested that the actual documents could be inspected at their offices, but in spite of this declaration it is doubtful whether they were genuine. From time to time many alleged letters from Jack Sheppard were printed in the daily and weekly press, although there was no need for him to write them, and most were couched in a style which he could not possibly have assumed. To publish a spurious letter from some notoriety was the favourite device of the eighteenth century editor.

It was reported in the newspapers that Mrs. Sheppard, who seems to have been a worthy woman, paid a visit to St. James's Palace about this time to petition for a pardon for her son. Rumour declared also that "some Great Personage" was interested in the unhappy young man and induced to intercede on his behalf. Yet, though it was supposed that George I was much amused by his several escapes, insisting

---

[9] Daniel Defoe (1661-1731), author of "Robinson Crusoe" (1719) and "Moll Flanders" (1721). *Cf.* "Daniel Defoe," by William Lee, I, pp. 383-389. Mr. Lee was the first to discover the relationship between Sheppard and Defoe.

Another Short Spell of Freedom.

upon being shown all the prints and diagrams relating to them, there never was any suggestion that he would show mercy to the criminal.

While living with the two Kates in his garret, Jack is supposed to have committed one or two minor robberies, but nothing of importance happened until 29th October. Ever since his escape from Newgate he had been hoping to obtain some new clothes, being disgusted with the butcher-blue frock which William Page, the butcher's son, of Clare Market, had given to him two months previously before their visit to Chipping Warden. While casting his eyes about for a likely crib to crack, he lit upon the ideal one, a pawnbroker's shop—at the sign of the Four Balls—in Drury Lane belonging to brothers named Rawlins. There was an array of fashionable attire in the window that he could not resist.

The same night he broke into the premises, but the brothers, who were asleep in the next room, awoke while he was plundering the shop. Hearing them talking in frightened whispers, Jack pretended that he had not come alone, bawling at the top of his voice to an imaginary colleague to shoot the first man through the head that opened the door. Thus, terrifying the timid pawnbrokers into quiescence, he continued his pillage and decamped. His booty consisted of a new suit of black, a tie wig, a ruffled shirt, a silver-hilted sword, a gold watch, and a diamond ring. During the whole of the next day he strutted about in this attire, as fine a gentleman as could be seen in Drury Lane, heedless of the hue and cry after him.[1]

Still more greatly daring, he dined with his two women on the following afternoon at a tavern in Newgate Street, afterwards driving in a hackney-coach past the prison and through the arch of the gateway. It was the last day of October and he had been at liberty just over a fortnight. Going in the evening to the "Sheers" alehouse in Maypole Street, Clare Market, he sent for his mother, who lived hard by, and gave her a glass of brandy. Falling on her knees before him, the unhappy woman implored him to quit the country at once before he was recaptured. In order to appease her, Jack gave the promise that she required, and soon afterwards got up and left her.

Having several guineas in his pocket—part of the proceeds of the robbery at the pawnbrokers'—he wandered from one gin-house to another, drinking and standing treat in each. A volatile young woman, named Moll Frisky, had now attached herself to him, a friend of many months' standing like the two Kates. When it was nearing twelve o'clock, he

---

[1] The senior Rawlins died at his house in Long Acre on 28th July, 1763; *St. James's Chronicle.*

Jack Sheppard.

was seen outside a butcher's shop in Drury Lane, "cheapening" some ribs of beef, after which he went a few doors farther on, to Mrs. Campbell's, a chandler, where he sat drinking with Moll. Unluckily for him, he was seen and recognised by the potboy at the "Rose and Crown" across the street, who informed his master that Jack Sheppard was in the brandy-shop opposite. Being a Headborough of the district, the innkeeper sent at once for the watch and for a constable, upon whose arrival the tipsy Jack was apprehended and put into a hackney-coach.

Great crowds had assembled in Holborn while the coach was driving to Newgate, the rumour that Sheppard had been taken again having spread abroad, and Jack shouted to the people to come to his rescue.

"Murder," he vociferated; "help, for God's sake . . . Rogues . . . I am murdered and am in the hands of bloodhounds . . . Help for Christ's sake."[2]

None, however, interfered in his behalf and, soon after midnight, on Sunday, 1st November, he was brought back once more to Newgate, where he was lodged in the Middle Stone-room, a very strong dungeon "adjoining to the Castle." The fetters that were put upon him were tremendous, for he was doubly ironed on both legs, handcuffed and chained down to the ground with a chain running through his irons, which were fastened on each side of him. The weight of his manacles is said to have been 300 pounds. In order to prevent any possibility of escape a watch was kept on him day and night.

XIII.—Newgate Again.

During the next few days a great number of visitors flocked to the gaol to see the famous prison-breaker, many of them being noblemen and persons of distinction, and before the end of the week the keepers of Newgate had collected more than 200 guineas in entrance fees. Naturally, they soon forgave their troublesome guest for all the vexation that he had caused them, particularly as he was always merry and bright, notwithstanding his dreadful predicament. His cheap Cockney wit bubbled forth whenever any one came to pay him a visit.

"So you are Sheppard?" inquired a gentleman who called one morning.

"Yes, sir," retorted Jack. "I am the Shepherd and all the

---

[2] *Daily Journal*, 2nd November, 1724.

Newgate Again.

turnkeys here are my flock, and I cannot stir abroad but they are all at my heels baaing after me."

Another caller in banter gave him an invitation to dinner, which Jack accepted with laughter on the spot, saying that he would take an early opportunity of waiting on him. He seems to have buoyed himself up with the hope of another escape, which was the reason no doubt of his high spirits.

Once when Governor Pitt, encouraged by the massiveness of his prisoner's irons which he had just examined, remarked with a smile—

"It's your business to make your escape if possible, and mine to take care you shall not."

"Then let's both mind our own business," Jack replied instantly.

He was on the best of terms even with the numerous "divines," who were always waiting upon him, although actually he had no regard for them, declaring behind their backs that they were "all gingerbread fellows, and came rather out of curiosity than charity, and to form pamphlets and ballads out of his behaviour." The Rev. Thomas Purney, the Ordinary, a minor poet, who wrote "Pastorals in the Simple Manner of Theocritus," and was a protégé of White Kennet, Bishop of Peterborough, was still obliged to remain in the country owing to ill-health, so Jack never saw him, having again to content himself with Mr. Wagstaff, who was acting as deputy.[3]

It is strange that he remained on friendly terms with this clergyman, for besides being a truculent shriver, he, as already related, had ferreted out several files and saws that Jack had secreted both in the Condemned Hold and the Castle on the eve of his two previous escapes. His only expression of resentment was the reiterated catchphrase, which vexed the reverend gentleman intensely—

One file's worth all the Bibles in the world.

Before the end of the week officialdom had learned from the law officers what legal process would have to be adopted in order that Jack Sheppard's convictions might be confirmed. On Friday, 6th November, Holles, Duke of Newcastle, Secretary of State for the Southern Department, wrote to Sir Philip Yorke,[4] the Attorney-General, to give him formal instructions—

Whitehall, Nov. 6, 1724.

Sir,—His Majesty being informed of the 'extraordinary escapes that John Sheppard a Felon convict has twice made out of Newgate and how very dangerous a person he is, has commanded me to signify to you his pleasure that you

---

[3] Rev. Thomas Purney was Ordinary of Newgate, 1719-1727.
[4] Sir Philip Yorke, afterwards 1st Earl of Hardwicke.

Jack Sheppard.

do *forthwith* cause him, in the proper course of Law, to be brought before the Court of King's Bench to the end that execution may *without delay* be awarded against him: And that he may be the more securely kept His Majesty would have you move the Court that he may be remanded to Newgate to remain in Custody there until his execution.

I am, Sir,
Your most Humble Servant,
HOLLES NEWCASTLE.[5]

Mr. Attorney-General.[6]

The Attorney-General moved swiftly. On the following morning he made motion at the King's Bench Bar, Westminster, that John Sheppard might be brought before that Court to have "Execution of the Sentence of Death" awarded against him; whereupon their lordships ordered a writ of habeas corpus and a writ of certiorari for bringing the prisoner and the report of his conviction to Westminster. The advertisement of "Jack Sheppard's Funeral Ticket," which appeared in the newspapers on the same day, was a grim commentary.

XIV.—Jack's Second Appearance Before the Judges.

Tuesday, 10th November, was the day appointed for Jack's second trial. About half-past ten in the morning he was put into a hackney-coach at the door of the Lodge in Newgate Street, and, accompanied by the higher officials and a sufficient number of turnkeys, set out for Westminster. News that the famous criminal was to be brought before the judges had been noised abroad, so that many curious little crowds were assembled at various parts of the route. From Temple Bar onwards, where the crowd thickened, a large party of constables walked on either side of the coach. A vast multitude was assembled outside Westminster Hall, making the approach difficult.

Since the officials dared run no risk, Jack wore his fetters and handcuffs during the journey, but after entering the Hall they were removed before he was taken into the Court of King's Bench to face his judges. When the Attorney-General had stated the facts of the case, the record of Jack Sheppard's conviction for burglarly and felony at the Old Bailey Sessions was read to the Court, after which witnesses were called to give evidence that he was the identical malefactor who had received sentence of death. Jonathan Wild, who had not yet recovered from his wounds, was unable to appear, but Pitt and Rouse and others had no difficulty in satisfying the judges as regards identity.

---

[5] Thomas Pelham-Holles, 1st Duke of Newcastle (1693-1768).
[6] Addl. MSS. 36, 135, fo. 87.

Second Appearance Before the Judges.

This point having been established, Sir Philip Yorke moved that the execution should be speedy and a rule of Court made for Friday next.

Still as plucky as ever, Jack made a speech to the Bench, beseeching his judges to intercede with His Majesty for mercy, and desired that a copy of a petition which he had sent to the King might be read aloud. Permission being granted, the petition was read, but at its conclusion Jack was asked by the Court how he came to repeat his crimes in such an outrageous manner after his two escapes. In reply, he pleaded his youth and ignorance in extenuation, and, above all, his necessities. With a pathos that rings true he declared that, while he was wandering about, he had been afraid of every child and dog that looked at him, so closely was he pursued. He protested that he had no opportunity to obtain his bread in an honest way, and that he had prepared to leave the kingdom on the Monday after he was retaken at Drury Lane.

In reply to this appeal, he was told that the only way in which he could obtain clemency was by making " an ingenious discovery " of those who had aided and abetted him. Without a moment's hesitation he asserted solemnly that he had named all his accomplices in his robberies already, and that he had not had the least assistance from any person in his escapes—but God Almighty.

The President of the Court, one Mr. Justice Powys, a dull and pious old judge, was greatly shocked by what he stigmatised as profanity, reprimanding Jack severely for taking in vain the name of God.[7]

In order to prove that no accomplices were necessary to him, Jack informed the Court that if they would order his handcuffs to be put on, he by his art would take them off before their faces, but the Judges would not allow the exhibition.

Mr. Justice Powys then proceeded to deliver judgment, soon convincing the unhappy youth that no mercy could be expected. Although his career as a robber was little more than fifteen months' old, and his misdeeds had been trifling until the beginning of the year, the Judge spoke of him as if he had been the most brutal ruffian in the land. His various escapes, obviously, had hardened the hearts of all those in authority against him, causing them to magnify his offences. So Mr. Justice Powys continued to harangue at length upon the number and hideousness of Jack Sheppard's crimes, and, having given him admonitions suitable to his sad circumstances, pronounced sentence of death

---

[7] Sir Littleton Powys (1648?-1732). Appointed to the King's Bench 1700; retired 1726.

Jack Sheppard.

upon him. But the execution was not fixed as early as the Attorney-General had desired, being postponed until Monday, 16th November.[8]

An unusual incident occurred before Jack left Westminster Hall, for he was summoned to the Chancery Bar by the Lord Chancellor of England,[9] who was curious to see and talk with the famous prison-breaker. By an odd coincidence a committee of the Privy Council had just been appointed to investigate Lord Macclesfield's administration of the funds under his control, for the system which regulated them was a most vicious one and serious defalcations were suspected. In the end the Lord Chancellor was impeached in the House of Lords, and, although no penalty was inflicted, he was compelled to resign his office. The meeting between the thief and the culpable statesman was too good an opportunity for the satirist to neglect, and the following set of verses was published in a broadside all over the town :—

AN EPISTLE FROM JACK SHEPPARD TO THE LATE L(O)RD C(HANCE)LL(O)R OF E(NGLAN)D, WHO, WHEN SHEPPARD WAS TRY'D, SENT FOR HIM TO THE CHANCERY BAR.

> Since your Curiosity led you so far
> As to send for me to the Chancery Bar,
> To show what a couple of Rascals we are,
>   Which no Body can deny.
>
> Were your virtues and mine to be weighed in a Scale,
> I fear, honest Tom, that thine would prevail,
> For you broke through all laws while I only broke jail,
>   Which, etc.
>
> Yet something I hope to my merit is due,
> Since there ne'er was so barefaced a Bungler as you,
> And that I'm the more dext'rous rogue of the two,
>   Which, etc.
>
> We, who rob for a living, if taken, must die;
> Those who plunder poor Orphans pray answer me why
> They deserve not a rope more than Blueskin and I,
>   Which, etc.
>
> Tho' the Masters[1] were Rascals, that you should swing for 't
> Would be damnable hard, for your Lordship, in short,
> Was no more than the Jonathan Wild of the Court,
>   Which, etc.
>
> Excuse me the Freedom in writing to thee,
> For the World then allow'd they never did see
> A Pair so well match'd as your Lordship and Me.
> At thy present Disgrace, my Lord, never repine,
> For Fame rings of Nothing but thy Tricks and mine,
> And our Names will alike in all History shine,
>   Which no Body can deny.

---

[8] *Daily Journal*, 11th November, 1724.
[9] Thomas Parker, 1st Earl of Macclesfield (1666?-1732), Lord Chancellor 1718-25.
[1] *I.e.*, the Masters in Chancery.

Second Appearance Before the Judges.

When Lord Chancellor Macclesfield had satisfied his curiosity, Jack was remanded back to Newgate. By now the news of his trial had spread all over the town, so the return journey was made through an immense throng. Westminster Hall had never been so crowded since the trial of the Seven Bishops. A great multitude fought and jostled outside in Old and New Palace Yard. A constable was knocked down and had his leg broken. Many persons were crushed and wounded at the Hall gate. But a large retinue guarded the hackney-coach containing Jack and his gaolers, and he was taken to his prison without much difficulty. For the night he was lodged again in the Middle Stone-room, but on the next morning, when Blueskin and two others were taken away to Tyburn and hanged, he was placed in the Condemned Hold. At the moment there was only a single occupant, one Lewis Houssart, a French barber, condemned for the murder of his wife, in Swan Alley, Shoreditch.

XV.—In the Condemned Hold Once More.

Elaborate precautions had been taken to prevent a repetition of the former escapes. Since Jack Sheppard's escapade with Edgworth Bess and Mrs. Maggot, the hatchway on the top of the door of the Condemned Hold had been boarded up, convicts being permitted no longer to come down to the grille to talk to their friends. Nor was Jack free to wander up and down his narrow cell as hitherto. Instead, he was "stapled" to the floor and manacled with ponderous chains. Two men, who were relieved at intervals, remained on watch both night and day. No modern murderer was ever guarded more effectively.

It was on the Wednesday that he was cast into the Condemned Hold, and on the Monday he had to die. Since he was a youth of intelligence, one may be certain that his thoughts were full of bitter regrets as the dreary hours crept nearer to his doom. Not that he can have felt a pang because he had failed to plod along as a journeyman until his uncommon skill made him a master-joiner like the good Owen Wood. Such a humdrum existence was an impossible one for Jack Sheppard. But he may well have perceived that a career in the army or navy would have suited his craving for adventure, giving him, perhaps, the chance of advancement. Or, since a thief is always best employed in being set to catch a thief, he may have realised that he could have won success in the profession of Jonathan Wild. And he must have regretted most of all the insensate folly—the result of women and strong drink—that had caused him to neglect the chance

Jack Sheppard.

of leaving the country and seeking his fortune in a foreign land. There had been many opportunities following his three great escapes from prison.

Still, in spite of the gloom of his dungeon and the weight of his shackles, the condemned youth was full of mirth and high spirits. Although he must have known that prison-breaking was no longer possible, he appears to have been convinced that he might make a sensational escape at the last hour while on the march to Tyburn. With this hope burning in his breast, he looked forward to Black Monday with undaunted eyes. He had made the few essential preparations a few days beforehand.

An " abundance " of nobility and gentry visited him still, braving the horrors of the Condemned Hold. To gratify them, he described his life and adventures at full length, answering all their questions and keeping them amused with his Cockney banter. Before they left he implored them to intercede for him with the King, so that he might obtain the royal pardon on condition that he was transported for life. It does not appear, however, that a single one of these visitors made an effort to help the poor wretch. Nevertheless, the hope may have helped to keep up his spirits. His vanity, moreover, was piqued by the fuss that was made about him, which led him to believe that he would cheat the gallows in the end.

On Friday morning, only three days before the day on which he was to die, an unusual adventure befell him. For Sir James Thornhill, R.A., one of the most eminent portrait painters in the land, took a fancy to visit Newgate in order to " take a draught " of the most famous criminal of the century.[2] The picture was painted in the Condemned Hold, Jack sitting at a table beneath the barred window under the archway, dressed in the stylish black suit that he had stolen from the pawnbroker, and wearing his handcuffs on his wrists. The portrait became familiar to every one, for an excellent mezzotint was made of it by George White which was to be seen in the print-shops for many years afterwards.[3]

Besides being a faithful likeness of Jack Sheppard, the mezzotint has considerable historical value, since it gives an exact representation of the interior of the Condemned Hold—the only one that exists—showing what a dismal dungeon it was. It depicts Jack as a mere stripling, scarcely looking his twenty-two years, with a saucy pug-dog

---

[2] Sir James Thornhill (1675-1734). His daughter, Jane, married Hogarth in 1729.

[3] George White, engraver (1671-1732).

Jack Sheppard

From the painting by Sir James Thornhill, R.A., done in the Condemned Hold of Newgate Prison, 13th November, 1724

Engraved by G. White

In the Condemned Hold Once More.

face and great yearning eyes, eyes that have been saddened by the anticipation of eternity. But nothing in the portrait is more remarkable than the hands—broad, muscular hands with strong thick fingers, which taper, nevertheless, like the hands of the painter or musician. When Thornhill had " pencilled out the face," he showed the rough sketch to Jack, who objected that he was made to look too old, whereupon the artist altered it as it now stands.[4]

The incident was made the subject of a poem, which gained much popularity, the complete version appearing in the newspapers a few days after the portrait was finished.

TO SIR JAMES THORNHILL ON HIS PICTURE OF JOHN SHEPPARD.

> Sheppard is now secured at last:
> Thornhill has fixed the felon fast.
> Oft though he loosed himself before,
> The slippery rogue escapes no more.
>
> Thornhill, 'tis thine to gild with fame
> Th' obscure, and raise the humble name;
> To make the form elude the grave,
> And Sheppard from oblivion save.
>
> Tho' Life in vain the Wretch implores
> An exile on the farthest shores,
> Thy pencil brings a kind reprieve,
> And bids the dying robber live.
>
> This piece to latest time shall stand,
> And show the wonders of thy hand;
> Thus former Masters graced their name,
> And gave egregious robbers Fame.
>
> Apelles, Alexander drew,
> Cæsar is to Aurellius due,
> Cromwell in Lely's work does shine,
> And Sheppard, Thornhill, lives in thine.
>
> Thou, that to Churches dost impart,
> And hospitals, thy matchless art,
> Let prisons, too, thy bounty share,
> And Newgate boast thy Sheppard there.
>
> Still to behold him crowds shall sue;
> And hide from homicides the view,
> Lest fired by his daring soul,
> They loose their chains and break the Gaol.[5]

---

[4] *Daily Journal*, 14th November; *London Journal*, 14th November, 1724; " British Mezzotinto Portraits," J. Chaloner Smith, Pt. IV, div. I, p. 1585.
[5] *The British Journal*, 28th November, 1724.

Jack Sheppard.

During the next two days—Jack Sheppard's last two days on earth—the "divines" who attended him became more assiduous than ever. Mr. Wagstaff, the deputy-Ordinary, aided and abetted by his colleagues, Flood of the Fleet and Hawkins of the Tower, were to and fro in the Condemned Hold all day long in the hope of gleaning a new bit of gossip to help to swell a pamphlet or to serve as a newspaper paragraph. It was rumoured even that Mr. Purney himself intended to leave his rural retreat to come up to town to preach the "Condemned Sermon" in Newgate Chapel on Sunday morning; but, although it is true that the Ordinary published a sermon dealing with Sheppard and his sins, there is no evidence that he was well enough to deliver it in person.

The chapel was always filled with a curious crowd on the day of a "Condemned Sermon," and on Sunday, 15th November, 1724, it had never been so thronged before. Jack bore himself with meek resignation, listening to the service with attention, believing no doubt that in docility lay his best chance of obtaining a reprieve. No visitor seems to have come to see him on this his last day on earth, so his two warders and Houssart, the French barber, were the sole companions of the weary hours. And at midnight in the black darkness he had to endure the sexton with his clanging bell beneath the archway outside, and listen to the terrible exhortation—

"You prisoners that are within,
After wickedness and sin;
After many mercies shown, you are appointed to die on the morrow."
and so to the end of the dismal monologue.

XVI.—The March to Tyburn.

On the fatal morning, Monday, 16th November, 1724, the officers of Newgate did not hurry over their ritual unduly. It was not until nine o'clock that the turnkeys entered the Condemned Hold and carried Jack Sheppard up to the Chapel, where he heard prayers and the holy sacrament was administered. There is no mention of a meal being prepared for him, but it was usual to allow the convict to have both food and drink, and there is no reason to suppose that the rule was altered on this occasion.

Between ten and eleven o'clock Jack was brought down to the Press Yard. Apparently the Sheriffs, Messrs. Robert Baylis and Joseph Eyles, had no wish to be present, for Watson, the Under-Sheriff, came alone to make the formal demand for the body of the condemned man.

The March to Tyburn.

After taking a formal receipt, Bodenham Rouse handed his prisoner over, whereupon a journeyman-smith, who had been waiting hard by with block and hammer, began to knock off the young man's fetters.

Jack remained docile and tranquil while the chains about his ankles were being removed, stuttering forth the usual quips and cranks for the benefit of his gaolers, but as soon as his legs were free he demanded impatiently that his handcuffs should be taken off also. It was the custom to bind the arms to the side with stout ropes, as he knew well enough, but not usual to make the criminal wear his handcuffs. The Under-Sheriff, however, was obdurate, telling Jack jocosely that he was an imp of mischief whom it would be impossible to deliver safely at Tyburn unless he had irons on his wrists.

To every one's surprise Jack flew into a passion. When the official known as "the Knight of the Halter" advanced to bind around his breast the rope that was to hang him he made a fierce resistance, demanding angrily that his handcuffs should be removed. At last Under-Sheriff Watson became suspicious. Motioning to the turnkeys to hold the prisoner, he began to search him thoroughly in spite of his struggles. All at once he started back with a cry of pain and bleeding fingers. Between the lining of Jack Sheppard's waistcoat, near the button-holes, a sharp claspknife had been fastened, placed conveniently with the edge pointing outwards. And it was not until after a hard fight that the weapon was taken away.

While the unlucky Watson was having his hand bound up, Jack confided to his gaolers all the details of this new and last scheme of escape. Now that he had been balked in his design, he cast it from his mind absolutely, as was always his habit, nor did he bear any malice against those who had thwarted him. Laughingly he told the turnkeys as they paced the narrow Press Yard together that he had intended to leap out of the cart on the road to Tyburn, and that he was sure he would have succeeded but for the handcuffs. By leaning forward in his seat, he could have cut the rope binding his hands, which having accomplished, he was going to throw himself amongst the mob, confident that they would aid his flight by closing around him. The place selected for the escape was Little Turnstile in Lincoln's Inn Fields, where the narrow passage would have made pursuit difficult. Jack talked and joked about this lost chance as though he had another hope still of averting his doom, which indeed he had.

About half-past eleven the Under-Sheriff reappeared and signified to the officials that he was ready to proceed, so, a procession being formed, Jack was conducted from the Press Yard through the Middle

Jack Sheppard.

Ward and along the passage skirting the Condemned Hold into the Lodge. A crowd of "master debtors" had collected in both chambers to bid adieu to the poor little lad, for all were sorry for his sad fate. In the street outside the gate of the Lodge the City Marshal on horseback was arranging a company of peace-officers to walk at the head of the cavalcade to Tyburn, which was distant two miles from Newgate, and situated north of Hyde Park to the left of the Edgware Road.

The City Marshal placed himself at the head of his men and gave the signal to set out. Springing on to his horse the Under-Sheriff took the position next in order, a posse of constables coming after him. No Sheriffs being present, the Sheriff's coach was unnecessary, so that the open tumbril with the convict followed. In those days it was not etiquette for the hangman to enter the prison, so Jack first caught sight of him sitting on the driver's seat of the cart. Unfortunately it has not been ascertained who this hanging functionary was. In all probability it was either Banks, a bailiff, appointed in 1717, or one Richard Arnet, who apparently was his successor.[6] The Ordinary, or rather deputy Wagstaff, sat beside the felon in the cart. In the rear marched a few javelin-men and some constables on horseback. Since there was only one criminal the procession was a short one.

Proceeding across the space where Giltspur Street joins Newgate Street and the Old Bailey, the City Marshal led the way to the porch of St. Sepulchre's Church, where a halt was made. The deep bell was booming high above the heads of the crowd, while the sexton, smaller bell[7] in hand, delivered another solemn admonition from the steps of the porch similar to that which had disturbed Jack's slumbers on the previous night—

All good people pray heartily unto God for this poor sinner who is now going to his death and for whom the great bell doth toll.
You who are condemned to die repent with lamentable tears. Ask mercy of the Lord for the salvation of your soul through the merits of the death and passion of Jesus Christ, Who now sits on the right hand of God to make intercession for you, if you penitently return to Him.
        The Lord have mercy upon you.
        Christ have mercy upon you.

This ordeal was inflicted upon the criminal from a pious motive, a charitable Merchant-Taylor, named Richard Dow, having bequeathed an annual donation in his will for the purpose.

---

[6] "The Hangmen of England," by Horace Bleackley, pp. 39, 40.
[7] The original bell was discovered in a chest in the vestry of St. Sepulchre's in 1896, and is now preserved in the church.—S. M. E.

The March to Tyburn.

Usually, however, there were other more diverting incidents at the porch of St. Sepulchre's, for numbers of young girls nearly always contrived to find a place on the steps with nosegays in their hands to throw to the convict, and kind messages and kisses to cheer him on his way. Such diversions were some compensation to poor Jack for the recitative of the dour sexton. We are not told if any of his Kates or Moll Friskys had come to say farewell. Bess could not have done so, being still in prison. A moment later the procession had started again and St. Sepulchre's was left behind.

Bearing to the left, the City Marshal led the way down the steep slopes of Snow Hill, at the bottom of which the road again turned abruptly to the left, crossing the Fleet river over a narrow stone bridge on the right. Ascending Holborn Hill, the street broadened, and the constables were able to march more closely on either side of the cart in order to prevent any attempt at rescue. Here, the walls and steps of St. Andrew's Church, which rose high above the roadway, were covered with spectators. The crowd increased every moment now and the progress of the cortège became more slow.

Every one was sorry for poor Jack. The forlorn little figure with the great pathetic eyes, looking a mere lad in his teens, could not have been otherwise than an object of compassion had his crimes been infinitely more dastardly than they were. Such a gallant young fellow with his wonderful record of pluck and endurance seemed too splendid a spirit to end his life on Tyburn Tree. The people gazed with amazement at the slightly built form, so trim and dapper in his well-fitting suit of black, and marvelled that one apparently so fragile had accomplished those prodigious feats of strength. And when they perceived that he bore his head high and had a brave smile still on his pale face, although the Common Hangman rode with him in the cart and a dismal priest was croaking prayers for the dead in his ear, they pitied and admired him as none in his situation had ever been pitied and admired before. "His behaviour was modest," writes the reporter of *The London News*, "but his concern seemed less than could be expected from one under such fatal circumstances."

When passing New Turnstile, a pang of regret must have swept over him, for he would have perceived that, if he had worn a rope instead of handcuffs about his wrists, he might have severed it by fretting it against his knife, after which it was possible to have made his escape by leaping amidst the crowd. A little later an incident happened which the spectators did not understand. While going by the New Buildings near the Church of St. Giles's-in-the-Fields, a young

Jack Sheppard.

man pushed his way through the line of constables and, getting close to the cart, whispered something in Jack's ear which amused him so much that he laughed heartily. It may be that he had been told that there would be a rescue at the last moment at Tyburn itself.

In spite of the weary persistence of the chaplain, Jack continued to be quite amiable with him, listening politely to what he said and making answer now and then.

"I have now as great satisfaction at heart," he remarked in the course of the tedious journey, "as if I was going to enjoy an estate of £200 a year."

And Mr. Wagstaff was much gratified with the remark, without reflecting that it might merely have been said to propitiate him.

One occurrence on the way gave Jack infinite delight, for he was allowed to call upon Figg, the prize-fighter, whose house was on the route to Tyburn, at the sign of the "City of Oxford" in the Oxford Road, Marylebone Fields. The pugilist had been a visitor at the Middle Stone-room in Newgate, and Jack had promised to stop on the way to the Triple Tree and drink a farewell draught with him. When the procession stopped at his gate, Figg was waiting with a glass in his hands, a pint of warm sack with a toast in it, which Jack tossed off greedily, for he must have been chilled to the bone after the long drive in the open cart in the cold November weather.

All the district to the right of the Oxford Road was now open country, extending through Marylebone Fields to Hampstead, the spire of whose church crowned the high land on the horizon. In the distance at the top of the rise of the road there was now a clear view of the Triple Tree, a great triangular erection surmounted by three wide cross-bars upon each of which seven bodies could hang side by side. It was not far from the wall of Hyde Park, and there was a broad space all around where Edgware Road terminated. At one corner stood a large grand-stand with seats for spectators, each of which was filled to-day and had been occupied for a long time. An enormous multitude had been awaiting the arrival of the procession for many hours.

Riding forward, followed by his men, the City Marshal cleared an open space around the gallows, forming a double circle of constables and peace-officers to keep back the crowds. Then the hangman urged his horse, and, driving within the ring of custodians, brought the cart beneath one of the cross-bars.

The Triple Tree.

XVII.—The Triple Tree.

At first, when Jack beheld the Triple Tree and realised that he had come to the fatal place, the onlookers observed that " his countenance changed very much and he appeared very restless and uneasy." In all probability his distress was caused more by cold than by fear. Vanity had led him to make the long journey without a topcoat in a thin suit of clothes, so, in spite of Figg's pint of sack, he was chilled to the bone. In a little while, however, as he stood up in the cart and stammered forth confessions of his burglaries in response to the questions of Mr. Watson, who was curious to learn as much of Sheppard as he could, his pluck seemed to return, and he laughed and joked as heartily as ever.

No doubt he was regaining confidence when he reflected how easy it would be to cheat death still if his friends were adroit enough to follow his directions. Resuscitation often occurred after a man was hanged, and he expected that it would be possible in his case. He had given instructions that when his body was cut down from the gallows it should be wrapped in hot blankets and put into bed, after which he should be blooded copiously and friction used to bring back the circulation. By this means he hoped that it would be possible to bring him back to life again.[8] A house adjacent to Tyburn was bespoken for the experiment. Friends had assured him that he should not be allowed to hang for long, but should be cut down at once in spite of anything that constables or peace-officers should do to prevent it. Encouraged by those hopes, little Jack Sheppard bore himself bravely to the last.

Shortly after his arrival at the Triple Tree a curious incident happened. A week before an advertisement had appeared in all the newspapers announcing the second edition of " A Narrative of All the Robberies, Escapes, etc., of John Sheppard," written by himself and printed by John Applebee of Blackfryars. Jack had been holding the little pamphlet in his hands ever since leaving Newgate and, sending to the printer to come to the cart, he delivered it to him, desiring that it might be published forthwith as his last dying confession. Possibly the person summoned may have been Applebee himself, a man in the prime of life, who lived twenty-six years longer; but it has been suggested that it was actually Daniel Defoe, the author of the pamphlet in question. This seems highly improbable. Defoe was now sixty-three years of age, in a precarious state of health, and it is unlikely

---

[8] " Select Trials " (1720-24), vol. I, p. 445. Brit. Mus. 6495, a.a.a. 14.

Jack Sheppard.

that he would have trusted himself amongst a Tyburn crowd on a bleak November morning when Mr. Applebee had many gazetteers who would serve the purpose. No doubt the idea of the whole affair came from Defoe, who realised the value of the advertisement. The little book had a larger circulation than any of the " Lives " of Jack Sheppard, and naturally was by far the best written.[9]

At last the Rev. Mr. Wagstaff and Mr. Watson had satisfied their curiosity with regard to their prisoner. He had confessed that he had committed the robberies both at Mr. Phillips's and Mrs. Cook's, although for want of evidence the juries had acquitted him of both. He acknowledged also that he and Blueskin were guilty of the housebreaking at Kneebone's, again alleging perjury against Will Field, who, he declared, was not with them. All was now ready for the final scene.

Having come to an end of the customary prayers, the chaplain offered up a final benediction and then clambered down from the cart. The hangman, who was standing beside his victim, had tied the end of the halter to the cross-bar overhead, after which he slipped the noose over the young man's neck. With a low bow the Under-Sheriff intimated to the fellow to proceed with his work. Springing quickly to the ground, he went to his horse's head, and as Jack Sheppard was drawing down the handkerchief which had been bound across his forehead, the cart began to move away from beneath him. In another moment he was swinging from the beam at the end of the rope.

It is reported that he " died with great difficulty and was much pitied by the people," which implies that the poor creature was struggling for a long time while the life was slowly choked out of him. For he was one of the light-weights who always suffered most at the hands of Jack Ketch, and it must have been many minutes before oblivion came to him. But he was not allowed to hang for long. When he had been tied up for about a quarter of an hour, and the spasmodic movements of his limbs had scarcely ceased, a soldier sprang from among the crowd and, forcing his way through the ring of constables, cut the body down from the gallows. Scores followed in the wake of the ringleader, and Jack Sheppard was carried away on the shoulders of the mob. Sympathising, no doubt, with the criminal, the constables made no attempt to restrain the people.

Unluckily for Jack Sheppard, there were two contending parties among his friends. The few, who were anxious to attempt resuscitation, strove to get possession of the body so that they might bear it away

---

[9] " Daniel Defoe," by William Lee, I, pp. 387-9.

The Execution of Jack Sheppard at Tyburn, 16th November, 1724

From the Drawing by George Cruikshank for Ainsworth's *Jack Sheppard*, 1839

The Triple Tree.

to the house where hot bankets and a surgeon were awaiting it. The vast majority, however, knew nothing of these matters, being obsessed by a wholly different idea. As usual, most of the mob were under the impression that the surgeons intended to obtain Jack Sheppard's body for purposes of dissection and had laid most crafty plans to accomplish their project.

A large hearse had been standing a few yards outside the ring of constables ever since the arrival of the cortège at the Triple Tree, a hearse that had aroused suspicion from the first, the people believing that it was a device of the surgeons in order to carry off their prey to Surgeons' Hall. Furious at this apparent duplicity, the mob made a fierce attack upon the hearse and its attendants, pelting the driver from his seat with showers of stones and loosing the horses from the shafts. Then they broke up the vehicle and scattered the fragments over the road.

Yet it was all a mistake, and one not without its humorous side, for the hearse had been provided by the firm of John Applebee with the intention of giving Jack Sheppard a decent burial in St. Sepulchre's Churchyard, where a grave had been dug for him.[1] In return for the magnificent *réclame* to be provided for his pamphlet, Daniel Defoe had promised Jack to save him from the surgeons, hence the elaborate funeral arrangements at Tyburn. When the incident was noised abroad, journalistic rivals were intensely delighted at the Defoe-Applebee misadventure with their " Mourning Hearse."

Meanwhile, Jack Sheppard's body was being sadly bruised and battered, as scores of uproarious folk snatched it from one another, each and all striving to keep hold of it lest it should fall into the clutches of the surgeons. It was believed that there were signs of life when he was cut down, but soon it became evident that the mob was carrying along a corpse. Those who had prepared the arrangements for resuscitation dispersed regretfully when they perceived that nothing they could do was now of any avail. And all must have realised that Jack Sheppard had finished with all earthly affairs before he had been pulled to and fro by his rough partisans for ten minutes. " They killed him with kindness," wrote one of his chroniclers.

Finally, a few stalwart fellows got the body on their shoulders and set off along the Oxford Road towards London. Directed by some authoritative person, they made their way down Bond Street and up Piccadilly into Long Acre, where they deposited the dead malefactor

---

[1] *Daily Journal*, 18th November, 1724; *cf.* " Authentic Memoirs of John Sheppard " (Joseph Marshall), p. 69.

Jack Sheppard.

at the "Barley Mow" Tavern. The mob followed in dense array to make sure that their wishes were carried out. Soon, however, a sinister rumour spread from lip to lip. It was said that a bailiff had stolen the corpse, which he was hiding in his own house in Long Acre in order to sell it to Surgeons' Hall in the morning. Immediately, a fierce riot broke out. Infuriated by their defeat and determined that there should be no dissection if physical force could prevent it, the mob arose in great wrath and began to make attacks upon various houses in the neighbourhood in the hope that chance might reveal the missing body of Jack Sheppard. Volleys of brick and stones hurtled through the air from one end of Long Acre to the other. There were many broken heads when the rioters came to grips with the peace-officers.

At last the justices met together and sent an urgent message to the Savoy, begging for a party of the Prince's Guard in order to quell the tumult. Assistance was given speedily. A strong company of Foot-Guards was sent into Long Acre at once, and at the sight of their fixed bayonets the unruly became peaceful citizens again without delay. Three of the ringleaders—one of whom is said to have been a solicitor—were arrested on the spot and, being taken before the justices of the peace, were "bound over for the Sessions." The body of Jack Sheppard was delivered to a gentleman who had desired the care of it, promising that it should receive burial. The name of the man was not divulged. Possibly it was Defoe himself acting for the firm of Applebee, or it may have been the charitable William Kneebone, who had forgiven Jack long ago for robbing him and had been one of his most constant visitors at Newgate. At all events, whoever he was, his credentials had satisfied the magistrates.

It was thought best to postpone the interment of Jack Sheppard until the anger of the mob had cooled down, and it was therefore announced early in the afternoon that the ceremony would be performed in the evening. An elm coffin was sent to the "Barley Mow," in which the dead malefactor lay in state for the rest of the day, covered with a velvet pall. A military funeral awaited him. At ten o'clock the same evening when the cortège set out for St. Martin's-in-the-Fields, a line of Guardsmen marched on each side of the mourning coach in which the coffin was carried, with fixed bayonets and their muskets loaded with ball. But no disturbance occurred. In spite of the vast crowds the burial ground was reached without difficulty and the service proceeded without interruption, and the poor youth, who had lived such a short tempestuous life, was lowered to his rest. All the time the multitude looked on reverently, well content that Surgeons' Hall had been balked of its prey. The registers of St. Martin's-in-the-Fields confirm the fact that Jack Sheppard was buried in its churchyard before midnight on 16th November, 1724. Nearly a hundred and fifty years later, 1866, when the plot was dug up for the enlargement of the National Gallery, the workmen came across his coffin placed next to that containing the body of John Heriot, the philanthropist.[2]

XVIII.—The Criminal.

Poor little Jack Sheppard! His misdeeds have been magnified so often that it is excusable to try to exonerate him as much as possible. Over and over again he has been stigmatised unjustly as one of the most atrocious of criminals.

"This inhuman and barbarous thief and robber," declared Parson Wagstaff.

"A low-lived, drunken, and dirty blackguard," writes the fastidious Francis Place, "without any one thing but his ignorant impudence and the gross manners of the times in his favour."[3]

"Ainsworth dared not depict his hero as the scoundrel he knew him to be," said Thackeray, in a hostile criticism of Harrison Ainsworth's "Jack Sheppard." "He must keep his brutalities in the background."[4]

That Jack was a persistent little thief cannot be denied, but that his thievery was of large dimensions or his methods brutal is certainly untrue. In none of the robberies of which we have record does any force seem to have been used except in the case of the tipsy John Pargiter, when it was Blueskin who dealt the blows. Jack Sheppard was always ready to flourish his horse-pistol and make a great bluster in order to intimidate his victim, but never once does he appear to have hurt any one from whom he stole. In most instances the burglary was accompanied by a practical joke, as when he shouted to imaginary accomplices to guard a door or bade unarmed companions shoot if any one stirred. Robbery with violence was not one of Jack Sheppard's habits.

Actually, he was a most commonplace young thief. Scarcely more than a dozen thefts, many of them small ones, have been recorded

---

[2] "London Past and Present," by H. B. Wheatley and P. Cunningham, II, p. 478. The grave was in that portion of the churchyard attached to the Workhouse of St. Martin's-in-the-Fields, on the west side of the road.

[3] Place MSS. 27.826.

[4] "Harrison Ainsworth and his Friends," by S. M. Ellis, I, p. 371.

Jack Sheppard.

against him, and the value of his booty cannot have exceeded £500. The criminal career of no other famous malefactor has ever been so short. From first to last he was a robber for little more than twelve months. Had his fame rested upon his achievements as a burglar, he would not have earned a place in the Newgate Calendar. It is to his prowess, of course, as a prison-breaker that he owes the undeserved reputation of being a savage and unscrupulous marauder. It was imagined that the man who could make such havoc with the bolts and bars and manacles of strong prisons must be the superman of crime, an ogre among cracksmen.

Even had he stolen as much as Jonathan Wild and had been as brutal as Blueskin, the fate of poor Jack Sheppard was a hard one. In his day no great sympathy was spared for the youth who had to hang for a paltry theft, since, with inadequate police protection and the existence of a large criminal population, it was necessary to have draconic laws for the safeguarding of property, and the capital penalty undoubtedly was a great deterrent. But the people realised how unfair it was that a cruel cut-throat should have a speedy death, while a mere pickpocket should suffer slow strangulation; and so the pity of thousands went out to the little carpenter-boy when they watched his agony on Tyburn Tree. It was a common example of the injustice of the law. Certainly, the punishment was not commensurable with the crime in Jack Sheppard's case.

Jack had other sins besides house and prison-breaking. Fond of women and strong drink, he was prone to over-indulge in both predilections. In this respect, however, he was no worse than a great many eminent men of the period. If all who were as debauched as he were to receive equal condemnation, some of the most illustrious names of the century would lose their glamour. His temptations, too, were out of the common, since when he had rescued Edgworth Bess from the Round-House he became a hero amongst the flash sisterhood, who vied with each other for his favours. With Bess herself he seems to have become alienated soon after his escape from the Condemned Hold, which was ungrateful, considering how useful she had been to him.[5] Evidently he regarded her as the siren who had lured him on to crime.

"There is not a more wicked, deceitful, lascivious wretch living in England," he told Mr. Wagstaff, and always spoke of her as being the cause of his ruin.

---

[5] She was arrested on 1st September for assisting in Jack's escape, and kept in prison till 9th December, when she was discharged without bail, so he had no opportunity of meeting her again.

The Criminal.

It does not seem to be a fantastic idea that Jack Sheppard—who was only twenty-two years and eight months old at the time of his execution—had been the victim of a temptress.

Tippling does not appear to have been one of his persistent vices. Had he been a perpetual drunkard, he would never have attained a high skill in his profession, nor would his house-breakings have been accomplished so deftly. A chronic drinker would not have had the nerve or the resourcefulness to break out of prison in the masterly manner that he did. Most of his carousals occurred during periods of nervous excitement, to celebrate a successful robbery or to drive away care when he was dreading recapture.

To sum up, therefore, we find that both Thackeray and Francis Place were ignorant of the most essential details of Jack Sheppard's career. He was the Prince of Prison-Breakers, of course, but he accomplished nothing that was not mediocre (though it was always skilfully carried out) in his professional career as a burglar. No magnificent deed of daring lies to his credit such as Colonel Blood's attempt on the Crown Regalia, nor one even like Wesket's appropriation of Lord Harrington's guineas. Women like Jenny Diver or Elizabeth West were his superiors by far as a cut-purse. Although he could crack a crib like a master, the cribs he cracked were not the great mansions of the wealthy where well-filled bureaus and rich jewel-cases would have made the risk worth while, but they were the shops of small tradesmen in which the booty was inconsiderable. Never once was a burglary of Jack Sheppard planned on a large scale. In his drinking habits, too, he displayed a similar lack of discrimination. On the only two occasions on which there is a record of him getting drunk, he was arrested while he was tipsy. He was as great a mediocrity as a toper as a thief.

XIX.—His Posthumous Fame.

Francis Place acknowledges with reluctance that Jack Sheppard was the most notorious thief of the day, who, as late as the 'seventies of the eighteenth century, more than fifty years after his execution, was " spoken of and sung with applause."[6] The print-shops had " taken him " from the first, the mezzotint by George White, after Sir James Thornhill, being the most popular; but it was closely run by a line engraving in the Hogarth manner of Jack sitting in the Castle

---

[6] Addl. MSS. 27.826.

Jack Sheppard.

in his irons and handcuffs, which showed the great hole that he had made in the chimney wall.

A sermon which caused much amusement, delivered by a zealous parson soon after his death, indicates how his achievements had obsessed the minds of his contemporaries.

"Now, my beloved," said the priest, "what a melancholy consideration it is that men should show so much regard for the preservation of a poor perishing body, that can remain at most but a few years, and at the same time be so unaccountably negligent of a precious soul, which must continue to the age of eternity! O, what care, what pains, what diligence, and what contrivances are made use of for, and laid out upon, these frail and tottering tabernacles of clay: when, alas! the nobler part of us is allowed so very small a share of our concern, that we scarce will give ourselves the trouble of bestowing a thought upon it!

"We have a remarkable instance of this in a notorious malefactor, well known by the name of Jack Sheppard. What amazing difficulties has he overcome, what astonishing things has he performed, for the sake of a stinking, miserable carcass, hardly worth hanging! How dexterously did he pick the padlock of his chain with a crooked nail! How manfully did he burst his fetters asunder, climb up the chimney, wrench out an iron bar, break his way through a stone wall, and make the strong doors of a dark entry fly before him, till he got upon the leads of the prison; and then, fixing a blanket to the wall with a spike, he stole out of the Chapel; how intrepidly did he descend to the top of the turner's house, and how cautiously pass down the stair and make his escape at the street door!"

Another divine, inspired by the same imagery, exhorted his flock to "open the locks of their hearts with the nail of repentance; burst aside the fetters of lust; mount the chimney of hope; take from thence the bar of good resolution; break through the stone wall of despair; rise to the leads of Divine meditation; descend the stairs of humility, and so escape from the prison of iniquity and the clutches of that old executioner—the devil!"[7]

Many flash songs in praise of Jack's adventures were composed and sung after his great escape from Newgate, and another appeared in one of the newspapers on the morning of his execution, in which he is supposed to sing of his exploits—

---

[7] "William Harrison Ainsworth and His Friends," by S. M. Ellis, I, p. 355.

His Posthumous Fame.

> To the Hundreds of Drury I write,
> And to all my Filching Companions,
> The Buttocks who pad it all night,
> The Whores, the Thieves, and the Stallions.
> I then, who am now in the Witt,
> Does rattle my darbys with Pleasure,
> And laughs at the Cullies I've bit,
> For I have still store of their Treasure.
>
> Moll Frisky was here t'other night,
> And tipped me a quartern of Diddle,
> And swore she'd been damnably tight
> Upon Pritchard who plays on the fiddle.
> She snaffled his main, Poll, and Tail,
> For which she was rubb'd to the Witt, sir,
> And now the whore pads it in jail,
> And laughs at poor Pritchard she bit, sir.

and so on to the end of the five stanzas.[8]

The minstrelsy of Jack Sheppard is extremely voluminous.

"It was his personality even more than his prowess that caused Jack Sheppard to make so deep an impression on popular imagination. He had a cheery and impudent humour that appealed to the common folk, whose love for him grew fonder when they saw that he was always merry when everything seemed most black. Sharp of tongue and quick of wit, he was a typical specimen of the Cockney guttersnipe, and as such the great city of London took him to its heart. A morose slow-of-speech ruffian would never have gained the affection of the people, however many times he had broken out of the 'Stone Jug.' Jack's physique was also a help to his renown. A dapper fellow, such as he, subtle as a panther and with muscles of steel, was naturally the ideal hero of his particular feats of skill. In popular fancy he became the will-o'-the-wisp of crime."[9]

No criminal hitherto had rejoiced in so many pamphleteers. Ten tracts at least, giving an account of his life and adventures, were published (several of them before his execution) during October, November, and December, 1724, the one attributed to Daniel Defoe, entitled "A Narrative of All the Robberies, Escapes, etc., of John Sheppard," being the most notable by far. Although it is improbable, for reasons stated previously, that the great novelist ventured to Tyburn himself to receive a copy from Jack own's hands—in order to gull the public into supposing that it was the malefactor's autobiography—most

---

[8] *Daily Journal*, 16th November, 1724.
[9] "The Hangmen of England," Horace Bleackley, p. 45.

Jack Sheppard.

critics are agreed, from evidences of style and some little circumstantial evidence, that the pamphlet could only have been written by Defoe.[1] It contains an exciting description of Jack's great escape from Newgate; and it is possible that much of the information was communicated to the author by the criminal himself during their chats in prison. An advertisement in the newspapers[2] announces the second edition on 8th November, a week before Jack Sheppard's execution, and it reached eight editions altogether. The little book, nevertheless, is now exceedingly rare.

Another pamphlet, which bears the title "Authentic Memoirs of the Life and Surprising Adventures of John Sheppard," contains one of the most intimate biographies of the great prison-breaker that came from the press. It is illustrated by numerous quaint woodcuts, displaying the various incidents of Jack's escape. Many of these "Exact Representations" of his "Means of Escape," depicting the holes in the chimney and the various locks, bolts, and doors, that he broke through—which were published also on large folio sheets and sold separately—show in detail the whole progress of his escape. Thus, both in verse and prose and picture, all the chief incidents of his career were revealed to the public during his lifetime far more completely than those of any previous criminal. Before his death he had become a national hero. As stated above, the mezzotint fashioned by George White, after the canvas painted by Sir James Thornhill in the Condemned Hold, remained deservedly the most popular portrait of all; but it had a close rival in a line engraving in the Hogarthian style in which Jack is sitting in the Castle wearing his irons, the holes that he made in the chimney being shown in the background.

The first monograph of Jack Sheppard to appear in a compendium of Famous Trials is to be found in one of the earliest specimens of "The Newgate Calendar," entitled "Select Trials," printed for J. Wilford, St. Paul's Churchyard, in 1734. It contains one of the most excellent biographies of the criminal, forming the groundwork of all subsequent accounts in similar publications. It was copied in successive versions of "The Newgate Calendar"—"The Tyburn Chronicle" of 1768, and the Rev. John Villette's "Annals of Newgate" in 1776; and reappeared again in "The Newgate Calendar," by William Jackson and Knapp and Baldwin, and the "Celebrated

---

[1] "A Chronological Catalogue of the works of Daniel Defoe," William Lee, pp. 24, 25; "Daniel Defoe," William Lee, I, pp. 383-9; "Daniel Defoe," William Minto, pp. 127, 128.

[2] *Daily Journal*, 8th November, 1724.

His Posthumous Fame.

Trials" of George Borrow during the second and third decades of the nineteenth century.

In all these monographs the compiler seems to have no doubt with regard to the status of Jack Sheppard. He is an arch-criminal of the highest eminence and his escapes from Newgate are described in terms of awe! And it was as a superman that the readers of criminology continued to appraise him for a hundred years or more after his death. Then, in 1839, William Harrison Ainsworth, the novelist— who had already published " a best seller," " Rookwood," in which he had glorified Dick Turpin—put the coping-stone upon Jack Sheppard's fame by making him the hero of a romance which became " a best seller " also. Henceforth the name of Jack Sheppard remained a household word, and, thanks to the great *réclame* given him by Ainsworth, there was no danger of his achievements being forgotten. From this time onward he tops the Newgate Calendar, a greater figure even than Dick Turpin or Claude Duval.[3]

XX.—The Exploits of Jack Sheppard.

In the opinion of Jack Sheppard's contemporaries the escape from the Castle of Newgate was an almost superhuman exploit, which in all probability could have been accomplished by no other living man. They regarded its author as an abnormal craftsman, whose like had never been seen in the world before and never would be seen again. It is curious to speculate how far these people are right. Was Jack Sheppard indeed a superman and inimitable; or were there others, both then and since, who, given his opportunity and methods, would have been able to break out of the " Stone Jug " just as easily as he did?

Although Admirable Crichtons in any walk of life are rare specimens of humanity, it would be foolish to assume that Jack Sheppard's achievements are incomparable. It is certain that there are men to-day who could have done what he did. Records are made to be broken, and it does not follow that his are unassailable. Nevertheless, it is evident that a prison-breaker like Sheppard must have possessed rare and abnormal qualities. Such persons must always have been few in number. " Handcuff kings," who can juggle with manacles and free their hands from almost any kind of fetter by pliability of sinew and bone, astonish the public from time to time; and no doubt one of

---

[3] " The Hangmen of England," by Horace Bleackley, p. 46.

Jack Sheppard.

these modern prodigies could strip his wrists of his "darbies" as deftly as Jack himself. But when this was done there would still be the fetlocks about his legs to be broken, an operation that called for exceptional strength. In addition to being a "Handcuff King," the man who could shed his irons like Jack did in the Castle of Newgate must be as powerful a chain-breaker as Sandow or Samson, a combination of qualities that do not often exist together. Jack Sheppard was not only an accomplished juggler, but a "strong man" as well. That he was well aware of his dexterity is shown by his public boastings of what he could do "by his *art*," as he called it. He bragged about it in his dungeon to the visitors and turnkeys; he did the same to Justice Powys in the Court of King's Bench. Jack Sheppard left other evidence of his prowess in his cell. He plucked the iron bar from across the chimney with the help only of a broken link in his chain, an effort proving the strength of his fingers. He made a hole in the wall from which he removed a cart-load of brickwork. None but a very muscular man would have succeeded in breaking a way into the room above, even when freed of his fetters and left undisturbed by his gaolers.

Assuming that an apocryphal imitator made his escape from the Castle into the Red-room overhead as Jack Sheppard did—having stripped off his handcuffs and snapped his chains in a similar manner—he would find that he needed other qualities than those of the "handcuff king" and the "strong man" in order to gain his freedom. There were five strong doors—he leaped over a sixth in the Chapel—fastened by locks and bolts and padlocks of various strength, which barred his way to the roof. Abnormal muscular power, of course, was necessary to overcome many of these, so strongly were they secured, but still more essential was the skill of the journeyman-locksmith. To do what he did with four of the six doors, Jack Sheppard must have been a most dexterous locksmith indeed.

It must be remembered that he was working all the time in pitch darkness. So difficult was it to believe this, that one of the newspapers declared that he had been assisted in his labours by the light of the moon, a statement obviously untrue, since the moon was a new moon and rose and set with the sun, that is to say about 6.30 a.m. and 5 p.m. It was his knowledge of the mechanism of the lock-box that enabled him to pick each of them open as he did. It was his wonderful sense of touch that guided his fingers in their work. It is all a question of pure handicraft, but a very exceptional handicraft even in a first-class housebreaker. To resemble Jack Sheppard, a criminal would have to be a "handcuff king" and a "strong man" and a most exceptional

The Exploits of Jack Sheppard.

"cracker of cribs" rolled into one. Fortunately for the safety of the public, few such prodigies have plied their art since 1724.

Others have won renown as a prison-breaker since his day—like Casanova and Mr. Winston Churchill—and there were many audacious escapes from prison both in England and Germany during the Great War, but they have lacked the artistry of the escape from Newgate on 15th October, 1724. All other escapes from Newgate, and there were many such during the eighteenth century, seem to have been puerile efforts that showed no imagination, owing any success they obtained to some fortuitous circumstances. It is not possible to discover any labour that is comparable with that of Jack Sheppard. He must remain for all time the Prince of Prison-Breakers.

Jack Sheppard.

EPILOGUE.

Jack Sheppard in Literature and Drama.

By S. M. ELLIS.

In that Epistle which a satirist of 1724 imagined Jack Sheppard writing to the Earl of Macclesfield, the Lord Chancellor who had the curiosity to interview the young thief, occur the lines—

> Fame rings of Nothing but thy Tricks and mine,
> And our Names will alike in all History shine.

The world has long since forgotten that particular Lord High Chancellor of England and his "Tricks," but the name of Jack Sheppard is almost as famous to-day as when he was alive and performing those marvellous "Tricks" which enabled him, a heavily manacled felon, to escape from the formidable prisons of Clerkenwell and Newgate. Thousands of people who have never heard of Lord Macclesfield are familiar with the career of Jack Sheppard by means of romance, picture, and play. Even the doubtless incomplete bibliography of works relating to Jack Sheppard, which is appended to this Epilogue, numbers some 100 entries, and I doubt if any Lord Chancellor can rival that amount of reference: whereby it would seem that the petty thief is greater than the Head of the Law. For the enduring fame of Jack Sheppard is the more remarkable by reason of the fact that he was simply a commonplace little robber: he was never a murderer, and not even a picturesque highwayman. His robberies were committed in small houses and shops, mainly in the Drury Lane district, petty thefts of fustian, clothes, and some stray pieces of silver: he did not attempt the great houses of the aristocrats, for he would not have cared for personal conflicts with the watchmen and the athletic legs of the running footmen of milord: he was poles asunder from the designs of an archthief, such as Blood who aimed at the Crown Jewels of England. And yet he is the most celebrated criminal in the annals of English crime: he proudly wears the Newgate Garland and takes precedence before his two nearest competitors for the Hempen Crown—Dick Turpin and Claude Duval, despite the fact that these rivals possessed all the

In Literature and Drama.

superior advantages of the romantic concomitants of the highwaymen, the gayest minions of the moon who ever took "the air upon the heath at eventide," with their splendid cloaks and plumed hats, their great boots and holster pistols, their magnificent horses which reared and pawed the air and whose thundering hooves heralded the approach of rapine to the terror-stricken passengers in the slow coach caught on the lonely moor. All this was High Romance, as painters and countless writers have testified.[1] Duval was gallant in both senses of the word, as his epitaph at St. Paul's Church, Covent Garden, once recorded—

> ... For all
> Men he made stand, and Women he made fall;
> The second Conqueror of the Norman Race,
> Knights to his Arms did yield, and Ladies to his Face;
> Old Tyburn's glory, England's blustering thief,
> Du-Vall the Ladies' Joy, Du-Vall the Ladies' grief.

Dick Turpin, too, had his meed of feminine admiration, and was the originator of a school of romantic fiction and allusion second only in importance and length to that of Jack Sheppard. Yet Jack Sheppard, who boasted no horses or ornate horse-pistols or other picturesque trappings, won his way to immortality with just a file, a rusty nail, and a bar wrenched from a chimney; for it is not the small burglaries he committed in the short course of his criminal career, which only lasted a little over a year, but his marvellous exploits as a prison-breaker that have appealed alike to the imagination of his contemporaries and of posterity for over two hundred years. Further, at the time of his execution and all through the after years there has been a keen regret for his untimely end entertained by all acquainted with the facts. He was only twenty-one when, in 1723, as a carpenter's apprentice, he fell in with bad company and perpetrated his first theft—a couple of silver spoons—to satisfy the demands of the prostitute, Edgworth Bess, to whom he, afterwards, attributed his ruin. Other robberies followed, and it was for stealing "108 yards of woollen cloth, two silver spoons, and other things," that he was sentenced to

---

[1] As Lecky truly says in his "History of England in the Eighteenth Century": "The early Hanoverian period has, indeed, probably contributed as much as any other portion of English history to the romance of crime. The famous burglar, John Sheppard, after two marvellous escapes from Newgate, which made him the idol of the populace, was at last hanged in 1724. The famous thief-taker, Jonathan Wild, after a long career of crime, being at last convicted of returning stolen goods to the rightful owner without prosecuting the thieves, which had lately been made a capital offence, was executed in the following year, and was soon after made the subject of a romance by Fielding. The famous highwayman, Dick Turpin, was executed in 1739."

Jack Sheppard.

death and slowly strangled out of life at the age of twenty-two. "To make the punishment fit the crime" was an unknown doctrine in the eighteenth century. Most crimes were capital then, but Jack Sheppard's offences seem the most inadequate of all for such dire retribution. To-day, when petitions are numerously signed for the reprieve of the most cruel of condemned murderers and young women who dispatch their illegitimate babies are treated as heroines, poor Jack would have been almost eligible for the Juvenile Courts and discharged with a few words of admonition: at the worst, he would have been sentenced at the Old Bailey to a short term of imprisonment. It was his ill-fortune to be born out of time, when his abilities, pluck, endurance, agility, strength, humour, and happy disposition that could overcome all difficulties never found their right use but were diverted to a wrong course. There was no one to counsel and direct him after his first step on the broad road which led to destruction. He would have made a splendid soldier or sailor, and might well have become one of those gallant adventurers and dauntless explorers in foreign lands who have added glory and power and other peoples' property and possessions to their native country in the guise of "Empire Builders."

At the outset of his life, after the Workhouse School period, Jack was simply a typical little Cockney guttersnipe, audacious and cheeky, possessed of a remarkable flow of lingo and bad language, with a restless, prank-playing disposition that inevitably led to trouble once he had run wild. This type of London boy has been unchanging for centuries, particularly in the district of St. Giles's and Seven Dials. Jack's grandsons might have been the thieving boys of Fagin depicted by Dickens in "Oliver Twist," when the gallows had ceased to be the punishment for crimes such as theirs. The next generation held horses' heads and turned somersaults in the mud for the coppers of the "swells" driving to the races; and the type still survives, despite county schools and Boy Scouts, in the urchins with soot-blackened faces and indigenously blackened hands, who levy toll for days previous to 5th November without even the pretence of the feeblest simulacrum of poor Guido Fawkes. "Spare a copper fer the guy" is the authentic echo from the boys of Gay's "Trivia, or the Art of Walking the Streets of London," in 1715, wherein he pictures the shoe-blacks as the "Black Youth," and "Sophrosunius" tells how "the 'prentice speaks his disrespect by an extended finger": though it would seem that making "a long nose" is no longer a prevalent vulgar habit with the gamin of the town as it certainly was thirty years ago.

Jack Sheppard was a boy of the streets and of the common people,

In Literature and Drama.

and so it came about that even in those hard and callous times, when the mob was accustomed to witness the penalty of death for nearly all minor crime, as well as major, his untimely fate moved every spectator to regret and indignation, for he was a gallant youth who had no fear of death, and his slight figure, smooth, round face, and great, wistful childish eyes, made him seem much younger than his actual age. This popular sympathy at once found expression in the ballads and pamphlets that appeared almost before the breath had left his tortured body, for " he died with great difficulty and was much pitied by the people." Thus in one of these ephemera he is imagined to say in his " Dying Speech "—

> Like Doctor Faustus, I my Pranks have play'd,
> (By Contract with his Master long since made)
> Like him liv'd gay, and revell'd in delight,
> Drank all the Day, and Whor'd the livelong Night.
> To raise my Name above all Rogues in Story
> I've made Chains, Bolts, and Bars fly all before me :
> But, heark, the Dismal Sound ! the Clock strikes One !
> The Charm is broke, and all my Strength is gone :
> The Dragon comes, I hear his Hideous Roar :
> Farewel, my Friends, for now Poor JACK's no more.

Another writer provided

" An Epitaph designed for John Sheppard's Tomb-Stone (whenever the Carver shall finish it) propos'd to be erected in Tyburn Road : in Imitation of the memorable Monument at Calais "—

> Stay, Traveller, stay, and this Inscription read :
> View well this Funeral Urn, and then proceed.
> Here the World's Wonder, the Great SHEPPARD lies :
> Cartouch himself did never France surprise
> With half such bold exploits, or Robberies.
> He, whom no Gaol could hold, no Chains make fast,
> By Death's Superior Bands is tam'd at last;
> Within this Narrow Prison's kept secure;
> From this Stone-Room he will escape no more;
> Hard Fate ! at Tyburn's Triple-Tree he swung . . .[2]

---

[2] Ballads were sung also in the streets at the time Jack Sheppard was making his wonderful escapes, and in these effusions much fun was made of the discomfiture of his jailers. In the " Narrative . . . of John Sheppard," which purported to be " Publish'd at the particular Request of the Prisoner," Jack relates that after his great escape from Newgate : " I came to a cellar at Charing-Cross, and refresh'd very comfortably with roast veal, etc., where about a dozen people were all discoursing about Sheppard, and nothing else was talk'd on whilst I staid amongst them. I had tyed an Handkerchief about my Head, tore my woollen Cap in many places, as likewise my Coat and Stockings, and look'd exactly like what I designed to represent, a Beggar-Fellow. The next day I took shelter at an Ale-house of little or no trade, in Rupert Street, Piccadilly. The Woman and I discours'd much about Sheppard. I assur'd her it was impossible for him to escape out of the Kingdom, and that the Keepers would have him again in a few Days. The Woman wish'd that a Curse might fall on those who should betray him. I continued there till the Evening, when I stept towards the Hay-market, and mixt with a Crowd about two Ballad-Singers, the Subject being about Sheppard. And I remember the Company was very merry about the Matter."

Jack Sheppard.

There can be no doubt that Jack Sheppard's short and fateful career suggested to Hogarth the idea for his great series of pictures entitled "Industry and Idleness" (1747), for Jack Idle, the Bad Apprentice, is drawn physically very like Jack Sheppard and in the same way pursues his course to Tyburn Tree by reason of bad companions, wine, and women. There is every probability that Hogarth[3] visited Jack Sheppard in Newgate when he was made a public exhibition prior to his execution. The great painter, "whose pictur'd Morals charm the mind," causes Jack Idle to commit a murder, the ultimate crime Jack Sheppard never was guilty of, but in other respects the analogy is preserved, for both youths traced their doom to "a common Prostitute." Jack Sheppard said of Edgworth Bess at the last, when he regarded her as the temptress who had lured him to ruin, "A more wicked, deceitful, and lascivious Wretch, there is not living in England. She has prov'd my bane." His story, of course, is the stock model of the boy who goes to the bad through evil companions, wine, and women, leading to utter ruin and the gallows. But there is much more in Jack Sheppard's actual life-story than this grim application of the text "As a man sows," for it alone would not have given him his posthumous and lasting fame: countless youths have shared his retributive fate but not his celebrity. No, it was his pluck and endurance, the strength of his slight body, which accomplished those marvellous escapes from prisons without the aid of tools and light, the pathos of his short life so horribly ended in agony, and this fate so cruel for a boy who had never taken another person's life—these are the memories that have girt his history with regret and pitiful romance. There were human qualities in him which in a more merciful age might have won compassion in exquisite expression phrased by a poet like Mr. A. E. Housman, who has so often voiced sympathy for hot youth cut off by infringement of the laws of man—

> The sure, the straight, the brave,
> The hearts I lost my own to,
> The souls I could not save . . .
>
> There sleeps in Shrewsbury jail to-night,
>   Or wakes, as may betide,
> A better lad, if things went right,
>   Than most that sleep outside.

---

[3] Hogarth in 1724 was, apparently, still living near Newgate. He was born in Smithfield in 1697, and after his father's death in 1718 at Long Lane, in the parish of St. Bartholomew's, William Hogarth is assumed to have remained there with his mother and sisters for some years longer.

In Literature and Drama.

> And naked to the hangman's noose
> The morning clocks will ring
> A neck God made for other use
> Than strangling in a string.
>
> And sharp the link of life will snap,
> And dead on air will stand
> Heels that held up as straight a chap
> As treads upon the land.

Jack Sheppard's contemporaries could not have expressed their feelings thus, but they realised there was something decidedly wrong in his fate, and even before he was dead they set about preserving his fame and aspect for far posterity. As he lay under sentence of death in Newgate, the most celebrated Court painter of the time, Sir James Thornhill, came and set up his easel in the Condemned Hold and painted the famous portrait of the young criminal, showing, chained, the strong, sensitive hands which had made matchwood of chains and locks and bars, and the large, appealing eyes, a portrait which has circulated ever since in the form of countless fine engravings and rough prints.[4] As I have already indicated, there were numerous ballads and broadsheets published, lamenting Jack's fate, as well as pamphlets purporting to relate his history and adventures. Two of these pamphlets are believed to have been written by Defoe. Horace Bleackley deals with Defoe and Jack Sheppard in this book, so I need do no more than point out the picturesqueness of word and phrase which characterises these early narratives of 1724. How clearly is Defoe's hand evident in such a passage as this which relates Jack's movements after his first escape from Newgate—

Having now got clear of his Prison, he took Coach disguis'd in a Nightgown at the corner of the Old Bailey, along with a Man who wait'd for him in the Street (and is suppos'd to be Page the Butcher) ordering the Coachman to drive to Black-Fryers Stairs, where his Prostitute gave him the Meeting, and they three took Boat, and went a Shoar at the Horse-Ferry at Westminster, and at the White-Hart they went in, Drank, and stay'd some time; thence they adjourn'd to a Place in Holbourn, where by the help of a saw he quitted the Chains he had brought with him from Newgate; and then like a Freeman took his Ramble through the City and came to Spittle-Fields, and there lay with Edgworth Bess.

---

[4] It does not appear to be known where the original portrait by Thornhill now is, or even if it still survives. G. A. Sala stated that when in Washington he saw, in the bar-parlour of a tavern off Pennsylvania Avenue, the portrait of a young man in eighteenth century costume which was said to be the picture in question. Mr. Charles Gordon, in his "Old Time Aldwych and Neighbourhood," relates that a newspaper of 1845 mentioned a Mr. Smith, proprietor of the "Hope" tavern in Blackmoor Street, Clare Market, as the owner, at one time, of Thornhill's portrait of Jack Sheppard and another of his mother (a picture of very doubtful authenticity). Mr. Smith sold the pair for ninety-seven guineas to Mr. Merivale, of Gray's Inn. In removing the portrait of "Mrs. Sheppard" from its frame, below the moulding were found seven guineas and a number of copper coins of the period. Coins were also discovered within the framework of the other picture, together with papers and documents relating to the Jacobite rising of 1745.

Jack Sheppard.

William Page, the butcher-boy mentioned above, was the "trusty comrade" of Jack Sheppard, but not a criminal. He was the son of a respectable butcher in Clare Market, but his unswerving devotion to Jack never failed, and is one of the few beautiful things in the narrative of a life that knew no other faithful and disinterested friend. It was Page who, after this particular escape, provided Jack and himself with two new blue butchers' smocks and, so garbed, took him down to Northamptonshire, where some relatives of Page's received and entertained them most kindly, "the People lying from their own bed to Accommodate them." But the two youths could not subsist away from London long, and on their return the narration of how they were apprehended on Finchley Common again furnishes an example of Defoe's vivid and pictorial prose—

On Thursday, the 10th of September, a posse of Men, both of Spirit and Conduct, furnish'd with Arms proper for their Design, went for Finchley, some in a Coach and Four, and others on Horseback. They dispers'd themselves upon the Common aforesaid, in order to make their View, where they had not been long e're they came in Sight of SHEPPARD in Company of WILLIAM PAGE, habited like two Butchers in new blue Frocks, with white Aprons tuck'd round their Wastes. Upon Sheppard's seeing Langley, a Turnpike at Newgate, he says to his Companion Page, "I see a Stag." Upon which their Courage dropt; knowing that now their dealing way of business was almost at an End; however to make their Flight as secure as they could, they thought it adviseable to take to a Footpath, to cut off the pursuit of the Newgate Cavalry; but this did not prove most successful, Langley came up with Page (who was hindermost) and Dismounting with Pistol in Hand, commands Page to throw up his Hands, which he trembling did, begging for Life, desiring him to Fisk him (viz., search him), which he accordingly did, and found a broad Knife and File; having thus disarm'd him, he takes the Chubb along with him in quest of the slippery Eel, Sheppard; who had taken Shelter in an old Stable, belonging to a Farm-House; the pursuit was close, the House invested, and a Girl seeing his Feet as he stood up hid, discover'd him. Austin, a Turnkey, first attach'd his person, Langley seconded him, Ireton, an Officer, help'd to enclose, and happy was the hindermost in this great Enterprise . . . And now having gain'd their Point, and made themselves Masters of what they had often endeavoured for, they came with their Lost Sheep to a little House on the Common that sold Liquors, with this Inscription on the Sign, "I have brought my Hogs to a fair Market"; which our two unfortunate Butchers under their then unhappy circumstances had too sad Reason to apply to themselves. Sheppard had by this time recover'd his Surprize, grew calm and easy, and desir'd them to give him Brandy, they did, and were all good Friends and Company together . . .

Jack Sheppard would never incriminate William Page, though pressed to do so, for he was grateful to this one good boyhood's friend —" he carefully guarded himself against uttering any thing that might affect him, peremptorily declar'd him Innocent of that (Robbery), as

In Literature and Drama.

well of being privy to his Escape, and said, that he only out of Kindness, as being an old Companion, was resolv'd to share in his Fortunes after he had Escap'd."[5]

Jack Sheppard had been dead only twelve days when the first of the many stage plays written around his name and fame was produced. This was "Harlequin Sheppard," by John Thurmond, and it may be presumed that Colley Cibber had a hand in the production on 28th November, 1724, at Drury Lane, for he was one of the triple managers of the theatre, the other two being Barton Booth and Robert Wilks. This curious pantomime " in Grotesque Characters " made a jest of death and the gallows, and the illustration in the published version of the play shows Jack Sheppard as a bearded man, heavily manacled, wearing the traditional dress of Harlequin with the additions of a ruff and sombrero. The drama had aroused expectations by the promise of " New scenes Painted from the Real Places of Action," but it proved to be a poor show of no merit. Its principal interest now is in a canting song which is quoted in J. S. Farmer's " Musa Pedestris," the best work dealing with the " flash chaunts " of thieves, for it foreran by over a century the famous " flash " song written by Ainsworth for " Rookwood " and sung in the dramatised versions of his " Jack Sheppard "—" Nix my doll, palls, fake away." In " Harlequin Sheppard " Frisky Moll warbled—

From Priggs that snaffle the Prancers strong,	*Steal horses.*
To you of the Peter lay,	*Carriage thieves.*
I pray now listen awhile to my Song,	
How my Boman he hick'd away.	*Fancy man.*
	Obstacles in Newgate.
He broke thro' all Rubbs in the Whitt,	
And chiv'd his Darbies in twain;	
But Filing of a Rumbo Ken	*Breaking into a pawnbroker's.*
My Boman is snabbled again.	*Nabbed and imprisoned.*
I, Frisky Moll, with my Rum Coll	*Good man.*
Would Grub in a Bowzing Ken:	
But ere for the Scran he had tipt the Cole,	*Refreshments paid.*
The Harman he came in.	*Constable.*
A Famble, a Tattle, and two Popps	*Ring, watch, and pistols.*
Had my Boman when he was ta'en:	
But had he not Bowz'd in the Diddle shops,	*Gin shops.*
He'd still be in Drury Lane.	

---

[5] It does not seem to be recorded what fate or penalty was awarded to William Page for his assistance in Jack Sheppard's escape. He must not be confused with a later William Page, a highwayman, who was executed in April, 1758.

There was also a John Shepherd, a forger and highway robber, executed in November, 1786, whose " Trials and Escapes " is erroneously catalogued at the British Museum Library under the heading of the more famous Jack Sheppard.

Another John Shepherd figures in " The Newgate Calendar " as an incendiary who was imprisoned in 1808 for the burning of Rochdale Prison.

Jack Sheppard.

This canting song was written by John Harper, a clever actor from the Fairs of Bartholomew and Southwark who had won praise for his character performances of Falstaff and Sir Wilfull Witwoud, and as Sir Epicure Mammon in "The Alchemist" at Drury Lane in 1721. He was also good as booby squires, and was "a jolly, facetious low comedian," with an excellent singing voice, so he was entirely suited as the first of Blueskins on the stage, for this was the part he enacted in "Harlequin Sheppard." Like his great successor in the rôle of Blueskin, Paul Bedford, he had a popular song in the piece, set to the tune of "Packington's Pound," the words being attributed to Swift[6]—"Newgate's Garland," written in commemoration of how Jonathan Wild's throat was actually cut by the real Blueskin a few weeks before. There were six verses in this style, sung by the jovial Harper—

> Ye Fellows[7] of Newgate, whose Fingers are nice
> In Diving of Pockets or cogging of Dice,
> Ye Sharpers so rich, who can buy off the Noose,
> Ye honest poor Rogues who die in your Shoes.
>   Attend and draw near,
>   Good news ye shall hear,
> How Jonathan's Throat was cut from Ear to Ear;
> How Blueskin's sharp Knife hath set you at ease,
> And every Man round me can rob as he please.

There were ten scenes in "Harlequin Sheppard," the first six showing the incidents associated with Jack's escape from Newgate, and the remaining four dealing with his subsequent adventures. When the curtain rose, Jack Sheppard was discovered in the Castle at Newgate, seated in his chair (which also in fact served as his only "bed"), loaded with fetters and padlocked to the ground. The orchestra plays a plaintive air, the while Jack is wrapped in deep thought. Presently he finds a small nail lying near him, and with this he unlocks the padlock which holds his chains to the staple in the floor. Being now at liberty, he scrambles up the chimney, but his progress is stopped by the iron bar. At this moment some of the turnkeys appear and he is caught *in flagrante delicto*. The gaolers pounce upon him, drag him back to his chair, and load him with much heavier chains. Once more he is fastened securely (as they believe) to the staple, and the turnkeys depart. Shortly after, one of them returns, carrying a large pie, which he leaves for Jack's supper. The "musick" now changes

---

[6] See later page 202.
[7] Gallants in the version printed in Swift's "Miscellanies," 1727.

Jack Sheppard's First Appearance on the Stage, showing him as Harlequin Sheppard

From the Frontispiece to *Harlequin Sheppard*, by John Thurmond, 1724, as performed at Drury Lane Theatre, 28th November

In Literature and Drama.

to a lively air. Opening the pie, Jack takes out a set of housebreaking tools, and sets to work to free himself. First he loosens his wrist-manacles with his teeth, and these undone, he twists asunder one of the chains that secure his legs. Able now to move about, he ties up his fetters to his waist with his garters, and once more attacks the bar in the chimney. In due course he makes a breach in the masonry, and escapes. It is after this that his friend, William Page, the butcher-boy of Clare Market, makes his one and only appearance on any stage, for Jack, having escaped " thro' the Cieling, gets on the Top of the House, and throws down the Tyles upon the People below. . . . The Scene changes to Clare Market, and discovers a Butcher's Shop. Sheppard comes in very merry, and goes to purchase some of the Meat. Sheppard and the Butcher go off together."

But even this presentation of affectionate comradeship could not save the play so ill written, and " Harlequin Sheppard," according to one of its critics, " was dismissed with a universal hiss. . . . If Sheppard had been as wretched and silly a rogue in the world as the ingenious and witty managers have made him upon the stage, the lower gentry, who attended him to Tyburn, would never have pitied him when he was hanged." Messrs. Colley Cibber, Wilks, and Booth were duly caricatured for their blunder by Hogarth in his cartoon, " A Just View of the British Stage, or Three Heads are better than One. Scene Newgate, by MD-V-TO " (Mr. Devoto was the scene-painter at Drury Lane), 1725.

Some three years after Jack Sheppard's execution, Gay was writing " The Beggar's Opera," and its origin, according to a statement by Pope, was that " Dr. Swift had been observing once to Mr. Gay what an odd pretty sort of thing a Newgate Pastoral might make." They had been discussing a recent pastoral, a ballad opera called " The Gentle Shepherd," which had won much success in 1725. Perhaps Shepherd made them think of Sheppard, and Swift had written already about Blueskin and Jonathan Wild.[8] So Jack Sheppard can claim to be a predisposing cause of " The Beggar's Opera," for he had made Newgate and the Triple Tree the most engaging topics of the time. Macheath escapes from Newgate, and one of his gang is called " Crook-finger'd Jack," while the whole paraphernalia of " The Beggar's Opera," with its cells and fetters and gallows, its pickpockets and fences, its strumpets and boozing ladies, is a refurbishing of the

---

[8] See pages 72 and 202.

Jack Sheppard.

properties of Jack Sheppard.[9] Further, the success of "The Beggar's Opera" in 1728 caused the resuscitation of a play entitled "The Prison Breaker, or the Adventures of John Sheppard," which had been intended for production at the theatre in Lincoln's Inn Fields in 1725, but the scheme was abandoned, owing perhaps to the failure of "Harlequin Sheppard." The farce, however, was published in 1725, and it is quite likely that Gay obtained from it some of his ideas and details for "The Beggar's Opera." After the first run of the latter piece concluded, Thomas Walker (1698-1744), the original Macheath, obtained "The Prison Breaker" and converted it into "The Quaker's Opera," which he produced in 1728 at Lee's and Harper's[10] Theatrical Booth at Bartholomew Fair. Walker, though a big, heavy man of thirty, insisted on playing the part of the slight stripling Jack Sheppard. As in "The Beggar's Opera," songs were set to old popular tunes. Here, as "Tipling John," appeared the air now known as "The Vicar of Bray." Jack Shepard (*sic*) had many songs to sing: thus of Newgate—"The Whit"—

> And when we come unto the Whit
>   Our Darbies to behold,
> Our Lodging is on the bare ground,
>   And we bouze the Water cold:
> But as I've lived to come out again,
>   If the merry Old Roger I meet
> I'll tout his Muns and I'll snabble his Poll
>   As he Pikes along the Street.
> At St. Martin's, St. Giles's, we shall have burial still
>   And here the Bowman's Prig stands Buff,
> And the Pimps have miss'd their Will.

In another chanson he voices his philosophy of life—

> Of all the gay Enjoyments
>   That can be valu'd rare
> None gives such sweet Employments
>   As Women Fine:

---

[9] In his "Jack Sheppard," in the scene where Sir James Thornhill, Hogarth, and Gay visit Jack in Newgate, Ainsworth causes two of the characters to talk thus—

"An idea has just occurred to me," said Gay, "which Jack's narrative has suggested. I'll write an opera, the scene of which shall be laid altogether in Newgate, and the principal character shall be a highwayman. I'll not forget your two mistresses, Jack . . . my opera shall have no music except the good old ballad tunes."

Said Hogarth: "I've an idea as well as you, grounded in some measure upon Sheppard's story. I'll take two apprentices, and depict their career. One, by perseverance and industry, shall obtain fortune, credit, and the highest honours; while the other, by an opposite course and dissolute habits, shall eventually arrive at Tyburn."

[10] John Harper, the actor who played Blueskin in "Harlequin Sheppard" at Drury Lane in 1724. See *ante*, page 72.

In Literature and Drama.

> To them and Wine
> Most men incline
> And think it charming Duty :
>   But he's a Slave,
>   A sneaking Knave,
> That is not fir'd with Beauty.
> Then drink about brave Fellows
> And make the Welkin ring,
> We'll kiss and clasp each lively lass,
>   And jovially we'll sing.

But at the end he discovers the vanity of such pleasures, and in his last song before going to the scaffold Jack mournfully sings—

> Farewell each vicious Pleasure,
> I've indulged you above Measure,
> Farewell Gaming, Drinking, Swearing,
> Farewell Raking, Thieving, Daring!
> To each Vice a long Adieu . . .
>   After Sentence
>   Late Repentance.

After his execution, there is a most unseemly chorus of truculent joy—

> Let us Rejoyce, Revenge and Justice assume their Seat,
> Vice shall be punished and Virtue and Virtue again be great . . .
>   Sing and Rejoyce with a General Voice.

In the original version of "The Prison Breaker" the author regarded poor Jack in a much more forgiving manner and pleaded for him in the "Prologue Intended to be Spoken by Mr. Hulett, Written by Mr. Leigh"—

> Our Author—Fools not being in Vogue—
> This Night his Heroe makes a Pilf'ring Rogue.
> One who had Wit his Gaolers to deceive,
> And sign, for two short Months, his own Reprieve.
> Whatever Locks his Master-key essay'd,
> As soon as touch'd, both open'd and obey'd.
> Oh! what a Delight the dex'trous Rogue might prove
> Had he a Master-Key to Locks of Love . . .
> Such was the Youth of whom our Muse doth sing,
> Who took for these Exploits a decent Swing . . .
> The Heroe whom this Night her Colours paint
> Is but Low Life, and all her Drawings faint.
> Let him be therefore in your Censures spar'd,
> To execute him twice will be too hard :
> On the World's Stage he has his Doom receiv'd,
> Show Mercy here, and let him be Repriev'd.

Jack Sheppard.

The dialogue of "The Prison Breaker" is on the broad lines of the period. Thus when a sanctimonious Quaker, who visits Jack in prison, says: "Well, I have done with thee, thou Eldest Son of Satan: Look to him, Friends:" Sheppard replies: "Do you go home, and look to the Whore of thy Bosom, thou Sanctify'd Cuckold." The characters in the play comprise—

>Sheppard.
>Jonathan Wile (sic).
>Coax-Thief, a public-house keeper.
>Blunder, an Irishman.
>Dr. Anatomy, a dissector.
>A Quaker.
>A Welsh Lawyer.
>Rust and Careful, two gaolers.
>File, Nym, Hempseed, Bulk, four thieves.
>Mrs. Coax-Thief.
>Mrs. Poor-Lean.

In addition to these "The Quaker's Opera" provided the characters of

>Mrs. Frisky.
>Mrs. Huckabout.
>The Lawyer's Maid.
>Tommy Padwell, the boy.
>Women of the Town.

Within a year after Jack Sheppard's death a few short memoirs of him were published (see Bibliography, page 128), "The History of the Lives of Jonathan Wild, Joseph Blake, and John Sheppard," in particular, being of great interest by reason of the free, contemporary language in which it is narrated.

Next appeared the clever "Imaginary Conversation" between Jack Sheppard and Julius Cæsar, which forms the fourth appendix of this volume, reprinted from *The British Journal* of 4th December, 1725, and without doubt written by one of the leading satirists of the time, though, unfortunately, the name of the author has not been traced. Possibly the subject and style of this ironical pasquin suggested to Fielding the idea for his own superlative essay in satire, "The History of the Life of the late Mr. Jonathan Wild the Great," which he probably wrote in 1740-42.[1] Certainly Jack Sheppard may claim his share in the origins of this work, for Fielding's aim in

---

[1] It was first published in his "Miscellanies," 1743.

In Literature and Drama.

the first place had been to tilt with his armoury of irony against the hero-worship accorded by the public to the romantic criminals of his century, and, as this work has demonstrated, none of the band had been so notorious and lamented, after death, as Jack. Indeed, it would seem, Jack Sheppard is directly introduced as "Fireblood," one of Wild's gang, thus—

> The name of this youth, who will hereafter make some figure in this history, being the Achates of our Æneas, or rather the Hephæstion of our Alexander, was Fireblood. He had every qualification to make a second-rate GREAT MAN; or, in other words, he was completely equipped for the tool of a real or first-rate GREAT MAN ... This youth, who was esteemed the most promising of the whole gang, Wild often declared to be one of the prettiest lads he had ever seen, of which opinion, indeed, were most other people of his acquaintance.

One might fancy that Fielding when writing this passage had just previously been reading the work I mention above, "The History of the Lives of Jonathan Wild, Joseph Blake, and John Sheppard" (1725), where occur these words: "Sheppard was the darling of the mob, and the favourite of Jonathan, who was heard to say that the day he was hang'd that he had not left his Fellow behind him."

In 1734 was published an early biography of Jack Sheppard, based on the actual facts of his life, in a collection of "Select Trials," printed for J. Wilford. This was the foundation of the subsequent accounts in "The Bloody Register," "The Tyburn Chronicle," and the various editions of "The Newgate Calendar," which were issued during the second half of the eighteenth century and the first thirty years of the nineteenth century, and in the "Celebrated Trials" by George Borrow, 1825. Some chap-books, also on these lines, followed, and then in 1839 came "The Great Resuscitation," by means of William Harrison Ainsworth's fine romance, "Jack Sheppard," which in the course of one year, by reason of its immediate and tremendous popularity, materially aided by George Cruikshank's superb illustrations, had triple publication in the form of serial in "Bentley's Miscellany," in three volumes (3000 copies of the first edition were sold in one week alone), and in weekly parts, to which was added the vast *réclame* of the theatre; for no less than nine dramatised versions of the story were produced in 1839-40, and Ainsworth's "little burglar," as he said, "became the lion of the day." So once again, Jack Sheppard, now one hundred and fifteen years after his shameful death, was the topic of almost every tongue, strutted the dramatic boards (this time with unprecedented success), and formed the subject of comment by many of the most famous writers of the day, who were moved to notice him as a very topical matter, while others employed

Jack Sheppard.

their pens in either praising or blaming Ainsworth for his choice of a hero from Newgate. The "ayes" of praise had it, and even fifty years later 12,000 copies of "Jack Sheppard" were sold within five years. Nearly a century later this romance goes on selling and is still widely read, and with its numerous illicit progeny of imitations is, as Charles Kent truly said, "the most hydra-headed of romances and the very phœnix of literature."

Ainsworth deserved his great success and could afford to disdain the attacks made upon him on "moral grounds" and from critics with axes to grind on a whetstone not free from bias. For he had written his story on the Hogarth model; it is entirely moral and points one moral throughout—the path of vice and wrong-doing leads only to the gallows; and as he said years later: "I never had the remotest intention of holding vice up to admiration. If I have done so, I believe Hogarth to be equally culpable." It is true that he threw a romantic glamour over his merry sinners; but that has ever been the prerogative of the greatest of poets, novelists, dramatists, and even of some historians. It was the cruder and very realistic presentation of his characters on the stage that caused some obloquy to Ainsworth in an age which, though intensely interested in the Social Evil, as it was called, and entirely aware of the scandalous state of its Haymarket at night, could not tolerate any allusions to such low topics in its romantic fiction or on its stage. Ainsworth had not in any way stressed in his story the immoral character of Jack Sheppard's relations with Edgworth Bess and Poll Maggot, but in the theatre it was made very clear that they were "Women of the Town." Such ladies are received with acclaim and laughter in modern revivals of "The Beggar's Opera" and in "Bitter-Sweet," but the critical attitude in 1839 was very different. Hence the outcry in certain quarters that "Jack Sheppard" was a corrupter of youth and caused divers "errand-boys" and young clerks to take to petty theft, strong drink, and intercourse with light ladies, leading to worser crimes and murder. If any such youths were so beguiled, it was through the stage versions of the romance, for in those days of apprenticeship and low wages they could not have afforded twenty-five shillings for the book or even a shilling each for a number of serial parts. But criminals are not often made by books and plays: they are in the main the product of heredity and early environment. Though human nature, and particularly the human boy, is imitative, it can be but seldom that a boy embarks definitely on a criminal career entirely from the stimulus of what he has read or seen on a stage: the influence of the modern

In Literature and Drama.

" shocker " film is another matter, for there vice is glorified and the heel-dogging hangman does not often fulfil his retributive office at the end, as he does in the novels of The Newgate School of Fiction. In " The Decay of Lying " Oscar Wilde makes an interesting comment on this alleged influence for evil of fiction—

> As it is with the visible arts, so it is with literature. The most obvious and the vulgarest form in which this is shown is in the case of the silly boys who, after reading the adventures of Jack Sheppard or Dick Turpin, pillage the stalls of unfortunate old apple-women, break into sweet-shops at night, and alarm old gentlemen who are returning home from the City by leaping out on them in suburban lanes, with black masks and unloaded revolvers. This interesting phenomenon, which always occurs after the appearance of a new edition of either of the books I have alluded to, is usually attributed to the influence of literature on the imagination. But this is a mistake. The imagination is essentially creative, and always seeks for a new form. The boy-burglar is simply the inevitable result of life's imitative instinct. He is Fact, occupied as Fact usually is, with trying to reproduce Fiction, and what we see in him is repeated on an extended scale throughout the whole of life.

This is the usual Wildean paradox, but there is a truth in it, though in his allusion to " Jack Sheppard " he was thinking of the cheap imitations of Ainsworth's story. However, in 1839, two of Ainsworth's friends, Thackeray and Forster, from reasons of personal pique, chose to say in print that, in their opinions, the influence of his romantic resuscitation of The Hero of Newgate was pernicious, or at any rate not salutary! Forster wrote in *The Examiner*: " Bad as we think the morals, we think the puffs even more dangerous . . . public morality and public decency have rarely been more endangered than by the trumpeted exploits of ' Jack Sheppard.' "[2] Upon which Ainsworth commented: " Forster's article has been perfectly innocuous, and has done no harm whatever here. In fact ' Jack ' is carrying everything before him. . . . They are bringing him out at half the theatres in London." *That* was the trouble with Forster. He could never tolerate that his idol, Dickens, should be surpassed and eclipsed. The sales of " Jack Sheppard " had exceeded those of " Oliver Twist," and there were no stage versions of " Oliver Twist " filling " half the theatres in London." It was quite illogical for Forster to make this protest and at the same time avoid mention of the fact that Dickens was one of the band of The Newgate Novelists, for it is clearly the case that he wrote " Oliver Twist," that is to say the Fagin and Bill Sikes portions, in emulation of the earlier criminal romances of " Paul Clifford," by Bulwer, and " Rookwood," by Ainsworth, for these had

---

[2] See later page 106.

Jack Sheppard.

proved to be very popular and successful. The "morals" of Bill Sikes are worse than Jack Sheppard's (who was never a murderer), and on the stage the murder of Nancy would be—and has been—as horrible as that of Mrs. Wood; it needs no argument to prove that an actual demonstration on the stage or in a film of how Fagin's pupils learned to pick pockets would be of much greater injury to youthful morals than anything Ainsworth ever wrote or any scene of his put upon the stage. And if contemporary evidence is wanted that Dickens was regarded as a principal exponent of the Newgate School of Novels, it can be found in *Punch*, even then, in his infancy, a criterion of popular feeling. Here, in 1841, is Mr. Punch's " Literary Recipe " for " A Startling Romance," combining the ingredients of " Jack Sheppard " and " Oliver Twist "—

Take a small boy, charity, factory, carpenter's apprentice, or otherwise as occasion may serve—stew him well down in vice—garnish largely with oaths and flash songs—boil him in a cauldron of crime and improbabilities. Season equally with good and bad qualities—infuse petty larceny, affection, benevolence, and burglary, honour and housebreaking, amiability and arson—boil all gently. Stew down a mad mother—a gang of robbers—several pistols—a bloody knife. Serve up with a couple of murders—and season with a hanging match.

N.B.—Alter the ingredients to a beadle and a workhouse—the scenes may be the same, but the whole flavour of vice will be lost, and the boy will turn out a perfect pattern. Strongly recommended for weak stomachs.

So much for Forster. Dickens himself in those days was quite content to be classed with the Newgate Novelists; and when, in the preface to the fifth edition of " Rookwood," Ainsworth referred to Sam Weller's ballad, " Bold Turpin vunce on Hounslow Heath," and added, " Mr. Dickens, with his wonderful knowledge of London life and character, and unequalled powers of delineation, has done more for the metropolis in ' The Pickwick Papers ' and in ' Oliver Twist ' than Paul de Kock, in all his works, has done for Paris," Dickens was delighted and gratefully wrote to thank Ainsworth for " your flattering and kind-hearted mention of myself. . . . if the weather had been finer I intended riding out to tell you how warmly I felt it, and how much sincere delight your friendship affords me." And it may be supposed that in the course of one of their conversations, around the library fire at Kensal Lodge, Ainsworth provided Dickens with the name for his Bill Sikes, when discussing the figures of The Newgate Calendar, for there was an actual James Sykes, a violent ruffian known as " Hell and Fury," a friend of Blueskin and Jack Sheppard, the same who by his treacherous impeachment of the latter caused Jack's arrest and imprisonment in St. Giles's Round-House.

In Literature and Drama.

And the two friends with Forster (who was first introduced to Dickens by Ainsworth at Kensal Lodge during the previous year) projected a visit together to Newgate in 1837, as this still existing letter proves—

48 Doughty Street,
Wednesday morning.

My dear Ainsworth,

I do not exactly remember whether I reminded Forster to tell you that I shall expect you to dine with me on Tuesday, after we have been to Newgate. This is to give notice that I shall expect you.

My dear Ainsworth,
Ever faithfully yours,
Charles Dickens.

William Harrison Ainsworth, Esqre.

Now for Thackeray. Moved by the vast success of "Paul Clifford," "Rookwood," "Oliver Twist," and "Jack Sheppard," he wrote his not very obvious satire of "Catherine"—"to counteract the injurious influence of some popular fictions of that day, which made heroes of highwaymen and burglars, and created a false sympathy for the vicious and criminal." His story appeared in *Fraser's Magazine* during 1839-40, and he took for his subject Catherine Hayes, an actual murderess from The Newgate Calendar, who was burned alive after conviction for *petit treason*, that is the murder of her husband, whose head was cut off and thrown into the Thames. A bizarre feature of the case was that the head was recovered from the river by the authorities and placed on a pole reared in the churchyard of St. Margaret's, Westminster, for the purposes of identification. This was in the year 1726, the Jack Sheppard decade, and, accordingly, Thackeray starts off with some rather pedestrian irony—

Though it may be said, with some considerable show of reason, that agreeably low and delightfully disgusting characters have already been treated, both copiously and ably, by some eminent writers of the present (and, indeed, of future) ages; though to tread in the footsteps of the immortal FAGIN requires a genius of inordinate stride, and to go a-robbing after the late though deathless TURPIN, the renowned JACK SHEPPARD, or the embryo[3] DUVAL, may be impossible, and not an infringement, but a wasteful indication of ill-will towards the eighth commandment; though it may, on the one hand, be asserted that only vain coxcombs would dare to write on subjects already described by men really and deservedly eminent; on the other hand, that these subjects have been described so fully, that nothing more can be said about them; on the third hand (allowing, for the sake of argument, three hands to one figure of speech), that the public

---

[3] An allusion to Ainsworth's promises, in the prefaces to the fourth and fifth editions of "Rookwood," that he would commemorate in romantic fiction, in addition to Turpin, both Jack Sheppard and Claude Duval. But the intention with regard to Duval was not carried out at the time, though he appeared many years later in "Talbot Harland" (1870).

Jack Sheppard.

has heard so much of them, as to be quite tired of rogues, thieves, cut-throats, and Newgate altogether; though all these objections may be urged, and each is excellent, yet we intend to take a few more pages from the "Old Bailey Calendar," to bless the public with one more draught from the Stone Jug (this, as your ladyship is aware, is the polite name for her Majesty's prison of Newgate):—yet awhile to listen, hurdle-mounted, and riding down the Oxford Road, to the bland conversation of Jack Ketch, and to hang with him round the neck of his patient, at the end of our and his history. We give the reader fair notice, that we shall tickle him with a few such scenes of villainy, throat-cutting, and bodily suffering in general, as are not to be found, no, not in ——; never mind comparisons, for such are odious. . . . In sooth, I can never pass Cumberland Gate without a sigh, as I think of the gallant cavaliers who traversed that road in old time. Pious priests accompanied their triumphs; their chariots were surrounded by hosts of glittering javelin-men. As the slave at the car of the Roman conqueror shouted, "Remember thou art mortal!" before the eyes of the British warrior rode the undertaker and his coffin, telling him that he too must die! Mark well the spot . . . Here stood Tyburn.

He then proceeds to tell the tale of Catherine Hayes with, at times, some very good burlesque imitations of the style of Ainsworth—

At this moment the moon, which had been hidden behind Westminster Abbey, rose above the vast black mass of that edifice, and poured a flood of silver light upon the little church of St. Margaret's, and the spot where the lovers stood. On a sudden Max's face assumed a look of the most dreadful surprise and agony. He stood still, and stared with eyes starting from their sockets; he stared upwards, at a point seemingly above Catherine's head. At last he raised up his finger slowly, and said, "Look, Cat,—*the head—the head!*" Then uttering a horrible laugh, he fell down grovelling among the stones, gibbering and writhing in a fit of epilepsy. Catherine started forward and looked up. She had been standing against a post, not a tree—the moon was shining full on it now; and on the summit, strangely distinct, and smiling ghastly, was a livid human head.

Excellent, too, is the précis of the scene-setting and "props" of such an episode as Ainsworth's great description of the Murder on the Thames on the night of the tremendous Storm of 26th November, 1703, when Thackeray makes one of the men thrust "forward his halberd (seven feet long, richly decorated with velvet and brass nails, and having the City Arms, argent, a cross gules, and in the first quarter a dagger displayed of the second)"—but at times he forgot he was writing a burlesque, and his narrative reaches the full flavour of a serious Newgate Novel; his presentment of the youthful villain, Master Tommy Billings, and that lad's doxy, Polly Briggs, was in every way as "pernicious" and "vicious" for Victorian "errand-boys" as the exploits of Jack Sheppard and Edgworth Bess.[4] So, if he

---

[4] At the end of "Catherine" Thackeray observes that he had had the good fortune to read some newspaper critiques of the tale which abused it as "one of the dullest, most vulgar, and immoral works extant. It is highly gratifying to

In Literature and Drama.

seriously expected that his "satire" would kill the public taste for the Newgate School of Fiction, he soon discovered his error, and his object—if he had one beyond writing an entertaining story—failed, for, in Thackeray's own words, "When the public went on reading the works which I had intended to ridicule, 'Catherine' was, in a word, a failure, and is dead with all its heroes." But he was wrong: "Catherine" is not dead, and it was not a failure in the final literary sense, for he had a curious tale to tell and he told it remarkably well with a full detail of its grim and bizarre horror. It remains one of the most interesting of his lesser works, and his interest in Catherine Hayes has its part in Thackeray's biography. For, as is well known, in the last number of "Pendennis" he again referred to her, in company with Bluebeard and George Barnwell, suggesting that she and "the greatest criminals and murderers . . . had some spark of human feeling, and found some friends," and that the Irish press of the time, most ridiculously and ignorantly, thereupon chose to protest that he was wantonly insulting a young Irish singer, Catherine Hayes (1825-61), who had by this date, 1850, become known as a charming vocalist and was about to make her London début as Lucia at Her Majesty's Theatre to the Edgardo of Sims Reeves. It is quite likely, however, that the Hibernian newspaper writers made their mistake intentionally as a means of "getting one back" on Thackeray for some of his unflattering comments in his "Irish Sketch Book," published in 1843. Anyhow *The Freeman's Journal* said Thackeray had "damned himself to everlasting infamy"; that he was "the hugest humbug ever thrust on the public"; and that he was "The Big Blubberman," an epithet which seems to have forestalled the elegancies of modern American slang. The *Mail* and the *Packet* joined in, and Thackeray was foolish enough to reply to them at great length in *The Morning Chronicle* of 12th April, 1850. But far worse than the newspaper pricks was the conduct of an irate Irishman named Briggs who wrote to inform Thackeray that he would thrash him for his insult to the Womanhood of Ireland, and for that purpose took lodgings opposite to the novelist's house in Young Street, Kensington. Possibly Mr. Briggs imagined there was some implication that the strumpet,

---

the author to find such opinions are abroad, as they convince him that the taste for Newgate literature is on the wane, and that when the public critic has right down undisguised immorality set before him, the honest creature is shocked at it, as he should be, and can declare his indignation in good round terms of abuse. The characters of the tale *are* immoral, and no doubt of it; but the writer humbly hopes the end is not so." But the writer does not point out that "Jack Sheppard" and "Oliver Twist" have an equally moral end with vice punished and Jack Ketch triumphantly exercising the arts of Ketchcraft!

Jack Sheppard.

Polly Briggs, in the story of "Catherine," was an ancestress of his own. However, Thackeray thought discretion to be the best course, so he called on his expected assaulter and after explanations was able to convince him that the Catherine Hayes (1690-1726) he had written about and alluded to was a foul murderess who had been burned alive just a hundred years before the other Catherine Hayes, the singer, was born.

Possibly because he was piqued that his "Catherine" did not put the Newgate Novels out of fashion, Thackeray launched later this year (1840) a further attack on Ainsworth and "Jack Sheppard" in the form of two critical articles concerning George Cruikshank and Henry Fielding which appeared respectively in *The Westminster Review* for June and in *The Times* of 2nd September, wherein he voiced the most illogical and inconsistent opinions imaginable. Comparing Ainsworth with Fielding, he wrote: "Ainsworth dared not paint his hero as the scoundrel he knew him to be. He must keep his brutalities in the background . . . and so he produces a book quite absurd and unreal, and infinitely more immoral than anything Fielding ever wrote." It is obvious here that Thackeray was not acquainted with the real facts of Jack Sheppard's life, for, as this work has demonstrated, Jack was not such a very alarming "scoundrel"— merely a petty thief. The "brutalities" he committed were all recorded by Ainsworth, who even exaggerated the case against his hero, for he makes him be present at the murder of Mrs. Wood by Blueskin, an incident, of course, which never occurred, and was merely one of Ainsworth's fictional introductions for the purposes of a romance. But when Thackeray considers the "infinitely immoral" life-story of this "brutal" young "scoundrel" as recorded by the glorious pencil of Cruikshank, he finds it worthy of the highest praise, so much so, that "it seems to us that Mr. Cruikshank really created the tale, and that Mr. Ainsworth, as it were, only put words to it." Thus regarded, crimes become delightful: "The Robbery in Willesden Church" is "a piece of artistical workmanship"; "The Escape from Willesden Cage" is "excellent"; the "Burglary in Wood's House" "has not less merit"; "The Murder of Trenchard" has "terrible vigour"; and "Jack's Escape from Newgate" exudes "reality and poetry." But nothing is said about the "immorality" of presenting such incidents as murders and robberies and whores in a bousing-ken with all the glamour of "artistical workmanship" and "poetry"—no abuse of the artist for not daring to "paint his hero as the scoundrel he knew him to be." However, neither literary nor artistic criticism

Lord John Russell as Jack Sheppard

Cartoon by H. S. Henning in *Punch*, 11th December, 1841

Reproduced by permission of the Proprietors of *Punch*

In Literature and Drama.

was Thackeray's forte, and it is more entertaining to turn to one of his humorous allusions to "Jack Sheppard" in the first days of *Punch*. He is writing about The Boy Jones who had the peculiar mania of secreting himself in Buckingham Palace, and on three occasions in March, 1841, was discovered near the Queen's bedroom. "In-I-go Jones"—as Lady Sandwich wittily dubbed him—was sent to sea, after Dickens had interested himself in the youth's future, and Thackeray in his best Jeames de la Pluche style provides "The Boy Jones's Log"—

At see, on board the ship, Apollo . . .

Halass! sir, the wicktim of that crewel blewbeard, Lord Melbun, who got affeard of my rising poplarity in the Palass, and as sent me to *see* for my *peeping*, though, heaven nose, I was acktyated by the pewrest motiffs in what I did. The reel fax of the case is, I'm a young man of an ighly cultiwated mind and a very ink-wisitive disposition, wich naturally led me to the use of the *pen*. I ad also been in the abit of reading *Jak Sheppard*, and I may add, that I O all my eleygant tastes to the perowsal of that faxinating book. O! wot a noble mind the author of these wollums must have!—What a frootful inwention and fine feelings he displays!—what a delicat weal he throws over the piccadillys of his ero, making petty larceny lovely and burglarly butiful. However, I don't mean now to enter into a reglar crickitism of this egxtrornary work, but merely to observe. when I read it fust I felt a thust for literrerry fame spring up in my buzzem; and I thort I should to be an orthor. Unfortinnet delusion.— that thort has proved my rooin. It was the *bean* of my life and the destroyer of my *pease*. From that moment I could think of nothink else; I neglekted my wittles and my master; and wanderd about like a knight-errand-boy who had forgotten his message. Sleap deserted my lowly pillar, and, like a wachful shepherd, I lay awake amongst my flocks . . .

And so on for a couple of columns. But *Punch* gave "Jack Sheppard" his best advertisement and compliment when it borrowed George Cruikshank's inimitable design of Jack carving his name on the beam for a principal cartoon (11th December, 1841) depicting Lord John Russell, then Leader of the Opposition, as an unruly apprentice, causing worry to Peel, the Premier (in the guise of Wood, the carpenter), on the question of tariffs and the uncertainty of what his relations with O'Connell might be in the near future.[5] It was this same picture of Jack Sheppard carving his name on the beam which was used on the bill-posters of some of the versions of the story at the theatres, and there were many other publicity aids and allusions in contemporary papers and books. Sir Theodore Martin in *Tait's Edinburgh Magazine*, 1841, was the writer of ten pieces, appearing under the generic title of "Flowers of Hemp, or the Newgate Garland," satirising the popular delight in "Jack Sheppard" and the criminal

---

[5] See later page 107.

Jack Sheppard.

romances of Bulwer, Dickens, and G. W. M. Reynolds. Thus, in "The Faker's New Toast"—

>Come all ye jolly covies, vot faking do admire,
>And pledge them British authors who to our line aspire;
>Who, if they were not gemmen born, like us had kicked at trade,
>And every one had turned him out a genuine fancy blade,
>   And a trump.
>
>'Tis them the boys as knows the vorld, 'tis them as knows mankind,
>And vould have picked his pockets too, if Fortune (vot is blind)
>Had not, to spite their genius, stuck them in a false position,
>Vere they can only write about, not execute their mission,
>   Like a trump.
>
>If they goes on as they've begun, things soon will come about,
>And ve shall be the upper class, and turn the others out;
>The laws ve'll execute ourselves, and raise their helevation,
>That's tit for tat, for they'd make that the only recreation
>   Of a trump.
>
>But *ketch* us! only vait a bit and ve shall be their betters;
>For vitch, our warmest thanks is due unto the men of letters,
>Who, good 'uns all, have showed us up in our own proper light,
>And proved us prigs for glory, and all becos its right
>   In a trump.
>
>'Tis ve as sets the fashion: Jack Sheppard is the go,
>And every vord of "Nix my dolls" the finest ladies know;
>And ven a man his fortin'd made, vy, vot d'ye thinks his vay?
>He does vot ve used to do—he goes to Botany Bay.
>   Like a trump.
>
>Then fill your glasses, dolly pals, vy should they be neglected,
>As does their best to helewate the line as ve's selected?
>To them as makes the Crackman's life the subject of their story,
>To Ainsvorth, and to Bullvig, and to Reynolds be the glory,
>   Jolly trumps.

Another of these ballads, wickedly burlesquing the beautiful old song, "She wore a wreath of roses," described a lady such as Edgworth Bess in a bousing-ken—

>She wore a rouge like roses, the night when first we met,
>Her lovely mug was smiling o'er mugs of heavy wet;
>Her red lips had the fullness, her voice the husky tone,
>That told her drink was of a kind where water is unknown.
>I saw her but a moment, yet methinks I see her now,
>With the bloom of borrowed flowers upon her cheek and brow.
>
>A pair of iron darbies, when next we met she wore,
>The expression of her features was more thoughtful than before;
>And standing by her side was he who strove with might and main
>To sooth her leaving that dear land she ne'er might see again.
>I saw her but a moment, yet methinks I see her now,
>As she dropped the judge a curtsey, and he made her a bow . . .

In Literature and Drama.

There was also a parody of Wordsworth's lines to Milton—

> Great men have been among us,—names that lend
> A lustre to our calling—better none :
> Maclaine, Duval, Dick Turpin, Barrington,
> Blueskin, and others, who called Sheppard friend.

"Flowers of Hemp" were the cause of a famous collaboration, for, struck by their amusing gift of parody, Professor W. E. Aytoun communicated with Theodore Martin, and in due course the two writers produced "The Bon Gaultier Ballads," published in 1845, wherein Jack Sheppard again was mentioned. It was this constant allusion to Jack plus the crude realism of his presentment at the theatres which caused the storm of "moral" objection to burst over Ainsworth's head, making him the scapegoat for all the alleged evils resulting from the writings of the Newgate Novelists, for, as he was the most popular and successful of the quartette, the attack was mainly directed at him. Yet, as Laman Blanchard pertinently asked: "Why did not the outcry break out when the housebreaker first broke out amidst public plaudits? Why was it silent for a whole twelvemonth? As the story month by month developed, not an audible objection was raised in the most fastidious coterie. . . . The prison-breaker's popularity became all at once an offence . . . because low people began to run after him at the theatres." So it was, a "cry" was raised, and the chronicler of the Hero of Newgate was considered thereby to be unsuitable for membership of the Athenæum Club! Lady Blessington was very anxious for her handsome favourite to join that ponderous institution, and her influence with the leading men of the day would, no doubt, have defeated the malcontents at the election, but Ainsworth declined to be nominated. He wrote to Lady Blessington—

> After all, your kind exertions on my behalf, in respect to the Athenæum, were thrown away,—or rather, I was unwilling to avail myself of them, having been given to understand that I should meet with formidable opposition from a hostile party, whom I must term the Anti-Jack-Sheppardites; and have thought it better to let things take their course, and withdraw, though I have since been informed the strength of the enemy was greatly overrated, and that I should have come off victorious, had I done otherwise. I do not regret the step I have taken . . . I am deeply sensible of your kindness and shall ever consider myself largely your debtor.

Truly, as a contemporary writer observed, the history of Ainsworth's "Jack Sheppard" is a chapter in the history of London manners of the nineteenth century. The Pecksniffs of the time attacked him, but he had the defence of the talented. Barham, the author of

Jack Sheppard.

"The Ingoldsby Legends," wrote: "We are all here delighted with 'Jack'"; and in another letter he makes allusion to the proposed publication of the book near 16th November, the date of Jack Sheppard's execution: "As to 'Jack,' I am delighted to find he is so soon to come out in a collected form, though I shall miss his monthly visit much. . . . By the way, so curious or rather felicitous a coincidence of date as the 16th offers should not be lost sight of in the *advertisement*. . . . I shall be truly rejoiced to see you dancing your hornpipe by and bye 'out of fetters.'" Francis Mahony, the learned Jesuit, "Father Prout," would write to Ainsworth to ask if Jack Sheppard had "so monopolised your thoughts that you forget us? Yet ought you to have learnt from the old play that the cry of 'MURDER! RAPE! ROBBERY!' is not complete without the finishing touch of 'THE JESUITS!'" Sir Theodore Martin (the future biographer of the Prince Consort) found "Jack Sheppard" "full of nature and happy observation, and a fidelity in minute touches of feeling and description that reminds me of your friend Dickens"; and H. W. Pickersgill, R.A., declared "your 'Jack Sheppard' one of the most powerful and best-written works I have ever read." Still, there *was* the "cry," raised by John Forster and Thackeray, in the first place, and as Ainsworth said (ten years later)—

The book was run down in certain quarters because it was thought necessary to run down the writer . . . Some persons, to serve their own purposes, got up a "cry" against me, but with whom my quarrel is now arranged . . . I really believe the romance to be harmless—as harmless at least as "Oliver Twist" and "Paul Clifford." I have never compared the last edition of "Oliver Twist" with the first; but I suspect there are considerable alterations to fit it for the scrupulous reader.

The point of view of these "scrupulous readers" of the first decade of the Victorian era (for it must be borne in mind that the Newgate Novelists were in spirit and taste products of the latitude of the Regency, even if they overlapped, at times, into the reign of William IV) was well put by the famous Miss Mitford, for the irresistible "Jack Sheppard" broke into even the maiden shrines of "Our Village." She wrote—

I have been reading "Jack Sheppard," and have been struck by the great danger, in these times, of representing authorities so constantly and fearfully in the wrong; so tyrannous, so devilish, as the author has been pleased to portray it in "Jack Sheppard," for he does not seem so much a man, or even an incarnate fiend, as a representation of power—government or law, call it as you may—the ruling power. Of course, Mr. Ainsworth had no such design, but such is the effect; and as the millions who see it represented at the minor theatres

William Harrison Ainsworth

A cartoon by W. J. Welch (about 1870)

By courtesy of Mr. Alfred E. Dillon

In Literature and Drama.

will not distinguish between now and a hundred years back, all the Chartists in the land are less dangerous than this nightmare of a book, and I, Radical as I am, lament any additional temptations to outbreak, with all its train of horrors. Seriously, what things these are—the Jack Sheppards, and Squeerses, and Oliver Twists, and Michael Armstrongs—all the worse for the power which, except the last, the others contain, grievously the worse. My friend, Mr. Hughes, speaks well of Mr. Ainsworth. His father was a collector of these old robber stories, and used to repeat the local ballads upon Turpin, etc., to his son, as he sat upon his knee; and this has perhaps been at the bottom of the matter. A good antiquarian, I believe him to be, but what a use to make of the picturesque old knowledge.

On the other hand, John Timbs, the learned antiquarian, highly praised Ainsworth's use and design of "the picturesque old knowledge" and said: "None but a master could have produced such a work out of such materials." And even *Punch*, who often was sharply personal in his allusions to Ainsworth, observed of "Jack Sheppard": "The pen that recorded his adventures played like a sunbeam about him," and pointed out that the morals of this romance were on an entirely different plane to the host of imitations generated by its vast success. These imitations were indeed a host, and they continue to appear still. I have noted some of these in my bibliography, but it would be impossible and needless to trace all the descendants of "Jack Sheppard," for many of them are poor, rickety children only worthy of repudiation by the alleged ancestor. Mr. Osbert Sitwell, in his recent Note on "Charles Dickens," asserts that Dickens was (particularly with "Oliver Twist")

the originator of the modern "thriller," the father—and a parent how much more lively and entertaining than his children!—to Sherlock Holmes and all the numerous subsequent tales of crime detected through coincidence or by means of consummate ability, and then punished with a striking and enviably appropriate justice.

I agree with the latter part of this diagnosis, but not with the first six words: the originator of the modern "thriller" was undoubtedly Ainsworth, for he was in the field with "Rookwood" long before Dickens adopted crime for his subject, and, as I have demonstrated in this work, the criminal portions of "Oliver Twist" were written to a great extent in imitation of his friend's very successful style, with some recollection also of the earlier "Paul Clifford," by Bulwer.

Of the immediate and direct plagiarisms of Ainsworth's "Jack Sheppard," the most audacious was an anonymous production which was rushed out before the close of the eventful year, 1839, that had witnessed the birth of the original. It was entitled "The History

Jack Sheppard.

of Jack Sheppard: His Wonderful Exploits and Escapes," and was the most brazen imitation of Ainsworth's story and characters; his incidents and his "flash" songs were flagrantly paraphrased. When novelty was attempted, the result became absurd. Thus, in this work the heroine was Edgworth Bess, and she is amusingly translated from the Amazon strumpet of fact into an innocent and fragile milkmaid of fifteen, with flaxen hair, dazzling white skin, and eyes of clear blue: "Her mouth was small, with ripe rosy lips compressed as if withdrawing into their own odorous bower, and gave, perhaps, a stronger promise of innocence and modesty than was conveyed even by her retiring look and somewhat downcast lids. Her figure was *petite* and seemingly fragile." If poor Edgworth Bess in life could have known of this remarkable apotheosis that was destined for her a hundred years later, even the purlieus of Drury Lane would have been shaken by the force and velocity of her sanguinary comments. The clever illustrations to "The History of Jack Sheppard" were supplied by "Jack Sketch," an ingenious pun combining the idea of an artist and Jack Ketch, the hangman, and they, too, imitated the style and subjects of George Cruikshank's plates for Ainsworth's romance.[6] This piracy had a remarkable success, and when "a new and improved edition, having long been imperatively called for by the public," was issued by another publisher in 1845, the work was re-entitled " The Life and Adventures

---

[6] The law of copyright at this date apparently provided no redress for such flagrant piracy; and I have not found that either Ainsworth or Cruikshank took any steps in the matter. They had suffered a similar complimentary appropriation of their ideas at the hands of one, Henry Downer Miles, who produced an imitation of "Rookwood," with rough woodcuts, which he entitled "Dick Turpin." His piracy seems to have been eminently successful, for in the fourth edition, which appeared in 1845, the preface states that 20,000 copies had been sold to date: even a second-rate "Ride to York" had power to attract in view of Ainsworth's *tour de force* of writing. But Mr. Miles never mentioned Ainsworth there-anent, though he had borrowed most of his incidents for "The Ride," and stated that his narrative was based on "the scarce and curious itinerary entitled 'The Roads of England and Wales,' by J. Ogilby, 1719." He quoted learnedly from other antiquarian authorities, from the "Parliamentary Journal" and Henry Fielding, for his period data, but he omitted to explain why three of his fictional characters bore the same names as three of the people in "Rookwood"—Ralph, Reginald, and Elinor! H. D. Miles seems to have had apt facility for following another writer's success. Thus, when in the early part of 1838 "Memoirs of Joseph Grimaldi," edited by "Boz," sold 1700 copies in the first week of publication, Mr. Miles came out that same year with his "The Life of Joseph Grimaldi, With Anecdotes of his Contemporaries." Perhaps he was the protesting gentleman mentioned by Forster in connection with Dickens's editing of Grimaldi. H. D. Miles was also the author of "The Fratricide" and of "Claude Du Val," a romance of the days of Charles the Second, published in 1850. He also translated the romances of Sue in 1846, and wrote on Pugilism.

The most preposterous plagiarism Ainsworth ever endured was a catchpenny "version" of his "Tower of London" (1840), entitled "Legend of the Tower," by "J. H. Hainsworth," published in parts by Edward Lloyd, 44, Holywell Street, 1840.

In Literature and Drama.

of Jack Sheppard," by Lincoln Fortescue, Esq., which I imagine was a *nom de plume*. He was a writer of some skill and reading, with a pleasing gift for mordantly humorous comment, as when, alluding to Blueskin's youthful addiction to playing marbles, he says the boy had " a very fine collection of ' taws ' and ' alleys,' which, with other inferior marbles, he had, Elgin-like, acquired, wherever he had found them, without being at all particular about the means." The author advanced the audacious statement that this version of Jack Sheppard's life story was based on the criminal's direct confession to the Ordinary of Newgate Prison, the Reverend Mr. Wagstaff (mentioned in Bleackley's narrative), and that Mr. Wagstaff sold this " Confession," " which I had obtained by virtue of my holy office," together with many other particulars, for fifty guineas to a publisher of the time, who curiously enough did not utilise his " find." So it devolved on " Lincoln Fortescue, Esq.," over a century later, " for reasons not now necessary to explain," to give to the world for the first time the narrative " which will form its own comment."

Edgworth Bess is also the heroine, with Jack Sheppard as hero, of " Blueskin," an anonymous work published 1867-8, now extremely scarce and much sought for by reason of its numerous and remarkable illustrations by R. Prowse. The tale does not follow facts, although Jonathan Wild, Quilt Arnold, Sir James Thornhill, and other actual people are introduced, for after a horrific description of the hanging of Sheppard, a mysterious German scientist obtains the body and in his laboratory restores Jack to life. Later, Wild is hanged, and eventually Jack Sheppard, Blueskin, and Edgworth Bess (who proves to be an heiress !) sail " for some foreign land." " Blueskin " was written by Edward Viles, author also of the famous " Blood," " Black Bess, or the Knight of the Road," 1867-8, a story of Dick Turpin.

Of " Charley Wag, the New Jack Sheppard," possibly written by G. A. Sala, and other tales which presented Jack as a mid-Victorian figure, I make some mention in the Bibliography. Over thirty years elapse, and then in 1899 we come to the best of the later versions of Jack Sheppard's story, " When Rogues Fall Out," by Joseph Hatton, the only author of the long line who had borrowed from Ainsworth's romance to express his acknowledgments. Hatton said in his preface : " I am greatly indebted to Harrison Ainsworth's ' Jack Sheppard.' " And so were all the others, and even more so were the producers of the stage versions of the book, for they made a great deal of money ; but owing to the faulty laws of copyright Ainsworth could claim none of it. To-day his theatrical royalties would have been immense, for

Jack Sheppard.

no other author can have had the experience of nine versions of his story running almost simultaneously in the theatres of London. During October and November, 1839, productions of "Jack Sheppard" were put on at the Adelphi, Sadler's Wells, the Surrey, the Victoria, Garrick, the City of London, the Pavilion, the Queen's, while, at Christmas, Drury Lane staged the drama in the form of a pantomime. Yet only one manager, G. B. Davidge, of the Royal Surrey Theatre, condescended to send a little conscience-money to the author. It was but £20, and he got his money's worth back in the form of a testimonial letter from Ainsworth stating that he had witnessed a rehearsal of the play and was satisfied that it would "furnish a complete representation of the Principal Scenes of the Romance." This letter was printed on the programmes preceded by the Management's long dissertation "To the Public" on the morals of this play, in the course of which it was pronounced—

> As Fielding has chosen "Jonathan Wild" as his "great man" to barb the keenest shafts of irony against crime, so do we think Mr. Ainsworth has, in an entirely different and more popular way, selected his ruffian victim, Jack Sheppard, to demonstrate that . . . depravity, however covered by bravado, is sure to entail compunction and punishment . . . See Cruikshank's inimitable procession of Sheppard to Tyburn; the buffoonery, the riot, the orgies, the triumph of Sin, the incitement to rapine and bloodshed; and compare them with the sad and solemn administration of the law, the change effected within a century; and say whether the upholding of the past to censure is not calculated to expedite the further improvement of the future! In fine, Jack Sheppard is
>
> To all an example—to none a pattern,
>
> and an ignominious death is the just reward of an atrocious life. The touches of remorse and repentance, with which it has pleased Mr. Ainsworth to invest his closing career are worthy of much commendation, not only as finishing the humanity of his conception, but as doing homage to the invincible principles of conscience and retribution.

Well, well, poor Jack! However, the dramatic fare which followed was far more lively, judging from the fact that here at this theatre was seen the drama of "The Devil's Daughter, or Hell's Belles." The "New and Singularly Graphic, Melodramatic, and Panoramic Adaptation of Jack Sheppard," adapted by J. T. Haines, author of "My Poll and My Partner Joe," was produced on 21st October, 1839: the hero was played by a man, E. F. Saville, and his costume is described with one of the old tinselled portraits of the time: "The youthful miscreant is depicted full length in full fig, with the famous shaped cap (?) bearing a complete armoury. A pistol in each hand, two more in belt, and sheathed sword at side. Silk doublet, rest of costume and armoury heavily tinselled, top boots." Jonathan Wild was acted

In Literature and Drama.

by "Handsome" John Neville (father of Henry Neville, the well-known actor), and others in the cast included—

Mrs. Sheppard,	Mrs. Henry Vining.
Mrs. Wood,	Miss Martin.
Winifred Wood,	Miss Chartley.
Edgworth Bess,	Mrs. Lewis.
Lady Trafford,	Miss Grant.
Sir Rowland Trenchard,	Mr. Dale.
Mr. Kneebone,	Mr. Heslop.
Owen Wood,	Mr. W. Smith.
Marvel, the hangman,	Mr. Henry.
Blueskin,	Mr. Cullen.
Thames Darrell,	Mr. Laws.

E. F. Saville was the brother of Helen Faucit (who married Sir Theodore Martin) and Mrs. Henry Vining was the mother of Mrs. John Wood.

The version at the Queen's Theatre, Tottenham Street, was also produced on Monday, 21st October, 1839, and here Miss Rogers played Jack Sheppard. Mr. H. Howard was Jonathan Wild, while Blueskin and Mrs. Sheppard were respectively enacted by Mr. and Mrs. J. Parry, with Mr. Roy as Thames Darrell.

The first London theatre to get out with a version of "Jack Sheppard" was the Pavilion, Whitechapel Road, on 17th October, 1839, where W. or "Cock-Sparrow" Rogers was in control, when an actor named Henry Hughes (father of the better-known performer, Mrs. Gaston Murray) played the principal rôle. W. Rogers himself took the part of Blueskin, J. R. Williams was the Jonathan Wild, and as Thames Darrel (sic) Mr. Gardner sang "Bright, Bright Wine" and "My Childhood's Happy Home"—"composed expressly for him by Alexander Lee, Esq." The rest of the music was by M. Corri. This adaptation of "Jack Sheppard" was written by Thompson Townsend, author of "John Stafford," "The Post Captain," etc.; but, true to the traditions of misplaced aspirates in vogue with East-end Cockneydom, the programmes of this production announced it as based on "Mr. Hainsworth's popular tale." Hard on its heels came the production at "Queen Wictoria's Own Theayter"—the Old Vic—where the adaptation was done by William T. Moncrieff, an energetic hack playwright of the time, who eventually died a pensioner at the Charterhouse in 1843. The Reverend R. H. Barham, author of "The Ingoldsby Legends," relates in his diary on 17th October, 1839—

Went with W. Harrison Ainsworth to call on Mr. Moncrieff, author of the forthcoming version of "Jack Sheppard" for the Victoria Theatre. Moncrieff

Jack Sheppard.

was quite blind, but remarkably cheerful. He gave us in detail the outline of the plot as he had arranged it, all except the conclusion, which had not as yet been published in the novel, but which Ainsworth promised to send him. Moncrieff, in a very extraordinary manner, went through what he had done, without having occasion to refer to any book or person, singing the songs introduced, and reciting all the material points of the dialogue. He adverted to his literary controversy with Charles Dickens respecting the dramatic version of "Nicholas Nickleby," which he declared he would never have written had Dickens sent him a note to say it would be disagreeable to him.

Miss Baylis's predecessor at this date, Mrs. Beverley, was also an energetic lady. She was great at advertisement and on the playbills of "Jack Sheppard" the manageress pointed out to "the crowded audiences that every night fill the Victoria Theatre to the very ceiling" that

At the Victoria Theatre alone can the romance of "Jack Sheppard" be seen completely represented. The public is now fearlessly challenged to decide if in its present most ASTONISHING AND ELECTRICAL Representation of the GREAT HURRICANE on the river Thames, during the night of the 26th Nov., 1703, the Artists of the Theatre have not equalled and even surpassed all previous efforts of a like nature.

Mr. Harding played Jack, Mr. "Brayvo" Hicks was the Jonathan Wild, Mr. and Mrs. Howard were respectively Blueskin and Mrs. Sheppard, while Miss George as Edgworth Bess had a new song composed for her by Mr. S. Nelson, "My Love is a Rover."

The City of London Theatre, in Bishopsgate Street, also produced its version on Monday, 21st October, 1839, with Miss Vincent as Jack Sheppard—the clever melodramatic actress who won fame as Susan Hopley in "The Vicissitudes of a Servant Girl," and was proclaimed at the Victoria Theatre as "the only acknowledged heroine of domestic drama." As a child she had played with Macready as the boy Albert in "William Tell."

At the Garrick Theatre, in Leman Street, Whitechapel (destroyed by fire in 1846), under the management of Gomersal and Conquest, there was given an adaptation of "Jack Sheppard" by Charles Webb:

Jack Sheppard,	James Bennett.
Thames Darrell,	E. Gomersal.
Blueskin,	M. Gomersal.
Jonathan Wild,	J. T. Johnson.
Winifred Wood,	Clara Conquest.

On 26th December, 1839, Drury Lane produced for its annual pantomime, "Harlequin Jack Sheppard, or The Blossom of Tyburn Tree," with the characters assigned or metamorphosed thus—

In Literature and Drama.

Master Jack Sheppard,	Master Daffy Screecherly.
Jack Sheppard,	Mr. Oxberry.
Afterwards Harlequin,	Mr. Howell.
Jonathan Wild,	
Afterwards Clown,	Mr. Jefferini.
Blueskin,	
Afterwards Pantaloon,	Mr. Asbury.
Poll Maggot,	Mr. King.
Afterwards Columbine,	Miss Frood.
Edgworth Bess,	Mr. A. Richardson.
Mrs. Sheppard,	Mr. Yarnold.
Hogarth,	Mr. Fenlon.
Gay,	Mr. Melville.

The opening scene of this extravaganza was in Mrs. Sheppard's apartment in Wych Street. For The Interior of Newgate there was an "Awful Incantation." As topicality had to be introduced, in view of the approaching marriage of the youthful Queen Victoria with Prince Albert, the final scene of "The Blossom of Tyburn Tree" displayed the exterior of Buckingham Palace—"The Temple of Hymen. *Vivat Regina!*"

The actor who played Jack Sheppard was no doubt William Henry Oxberry (1808-52), who after an unsuccessful season as manager of the English Opera House (1833-7) had returned to the stage. He was also author of plays and burlesques. The Clown, Jefferini, who according to *The Sunday Times* was "dull beyond belief," was really named Jeffreys, the proprietor of a tobacconist's shop, known as "The Little Snuff-box," in Garnault Place, Clerkenwell, and his portrait adorned for many years the exterior sign board of the "Clown" tavern, St. John's Street Road. Jefferini was a very tall man, and the sight of his long legs disappearing through the windows and traps of the pantomime scenes made him the delight of the children of his period. On one occasion he fell and sustained a severe internal injury, which could not be cured and caused him acute agony to the end of his life—" his facial contortions, which excited roars of laughter from the audience, were only a vent for the tortures the poor fellow in motley suffered from internal pain consequent on his leaping and dancing."

It was one hundred and fifteen years and one month after the production of the former "Harlequin Sheppard" at Drury Lane on 24th November, 1724, that jest was once again made of a tragic theme at the Premier Theatre, so public manners and tastes had not greatly changed in the course of a century.

Richardson's Show would not be behind in the race, so "Jack Sheppard," as in "The Quaker's Opera" one hundred and eleven

Jack Sheppard.

years earlier, once more strutted it outside and inside a booth. Richardson's Show must always have its spectre, so the ghost of Mrs. Sheppard appeared to her hapless son in the condemned cell in this version. But we must pass on to the most celebrated production of "Jack Sheppard," at the Adelphi Theatre on 28th October, 1839, where we shall

> See Jack Sheppard, noble stripling, act his wondrous feats again,
> Snapping Newgate's bars of iron like an infant's daisy-chain,

as Bon Gaultier wrote in the cadences of "Locksley Hall," burlesqued as "The Lay of the Lovelorn." This version of Ainsworth's tale was done by J. B. Buckstone, later to be a celebrated humorous actor and manager of the Haymarket Theatre for twenty-three years, and, as the story faithfully followed the original, its tremendous success was assured.[7] It ran until Christmas at the original showing, and was frequently revived during the next two decades.[8] At the outset it drew crowds owing to the remarkable impersonations of Jack and Blueskin by, respectively, Mrs. Keeley and Paul Bedford. Two of the minor parts were raised to prominence by the clever character actors who presented them; Edward Wright, with his humour as Shotbolt, the gaoler, and F. H. Yates (the manager of the Adelphi Theatre and the father of Edmund Yates), who made a sinister figure of the snuffling Jew, Abraham Mendez. Yates also played Sam, the one-eyed sailor, and Gay, the poet. The other parts " of the unparalleled 'Jack Sheppard' and grand spectacle" were assigned thus—

Jonathan Wild,	Mr. Lyon.
Owen Wood,	Mr. Wilkinson.
Thames Darrell,	Mr. E. H. Butler.
(Later the part was taken by J. F. Saville.)	
Sir Rowland Trenchard,	Mr. Maynard.
Kneebone,	Mr. H. Beverley.
Mrs. Wood,	Mrs. Fosbroke.
Winifred Wood,	Miss Allison.
Mrs. Sheppard,	Miss M. Lee.
Poll Maggot,	Mrs. Nailer.
Edgworth Bess,	Miss Campbell.
Hogarth,	Mr. Cullenford.
Rachel,	Miss E. Honner.

---

[7] It was printed in Webster's "National Acting Drama."

[8] During December, 1839, there was a double Ainsworth bill at the Adelphi, for "Jack Sheppard" was followed each night by a version of his "Crichton": "Taken from W. H. Ainsworth, Esq.'s popular Historical Romance, entitled 'The Admirable Crichton,' a Grand Chivalric Drama adapted by Mr. E. Stirling called 'The Knight of the Dragon and the Queen of Beauty.'" F. H. Yates played Henri de Valois, and Edward Wright was Chicot the Jester. Mrs. Fosbroke was Queen Catherine de Medici, and Miss Allison the Marguerite de Valois.

Mrs. Keeley as Jack Sheppard at the Adelphi Theatre, 1839

In Literature and Drama.

Mrs. Keeley at this date was a mature lady of thirty-four years, and it is curious that she should have had a predilection then for playing such parts as Jack Sheppard and Smike and Oliver Twist, for she did not in the least look like a real boy, and she had behind her a long record of brilliant soubrette successes in comedy and farce; also she had played Nerissa to the Shylock of Charles Kemble, and had sung in light opera, in " Rosina," and as Polly in " The Beggar's Opera "; she sang the Mermaid's Song from " Oberon " before the composer, Weber, so well that he patted her on the head and said, " Mine child, dat song vill do." Her singing voice was of value in " Jack Sheppard," and she was so sprightly and vivacious, and acted so well, that the absurdity of the lines of her female figure adapted to the wiry stripling Jack was overlooked in the pleasure aroused by her performance. As one of the critics said: " Nothing could be more exquisite than Mrs. Keeley's acting; the naïveté, the assurance, the humour, and the boldness of Sheppard were excellently delineated; the slang was given without the least admixture of vulgarity." Henry Neville told me " she was a little too fat for a boy, but her dramatic power and pathos were marvellously convincing "; he was a boy when he saw her in " Jack Sheppard," and when he was supposed to be in bed and asleep he used to slide down a pipe outside his window and slip off to the Adelphi—a very adventurous proceeding, for he lived in a lonely house, " Melrose," at Kennington, which was surrounded by a large garden and orchard. Mr. Serjeant Ballantine, another young admirer of Mrs. Keeley in this rôle, recorded nearly half a century later: " How well I remember her charming little figure upon the stool in Jack's workshop, and her sweet voice singing the naughty sentiment contained in the words, ' and I'll carve my name on the dungeon stone ' "—

> When Claude du Val was in Newgate thrown,
> He carved his name on the dungeon stone;
> Quoth a dubsman, who gazed on the shattered wall,
> " You have carved your epitaph, Claude du Val,
>   With your chisel so fine, tra la! "
>
> Du Val was hanged, and the next who came
> On the self-same stone inscribed his name;
> " Aha! " quoth the dubsman with devilish glee,
> " Tom Waters, *your* doom is the triple tree!
>   With your chisel so fine, tra la! "
>
> Full twenty highwaymen blithe and bold,
> Rattled their chains in that dungeon old;
> Of all that number there 'scaped not one
> Who carved his name on the Newgate stone,
>   With his chisel so fine, tra la!

Jack Sheppard.

Mrs. Keeley entirely deserved the praise and success that were awarded her as Jack Sheppard, for her rendering was the result of much study, genuine hard work, and considerable expenditure of physical energy. She had visited Newgate and seen the scenes of Jack's exploits, and talked with prisoners and gaolers; she planed real chips from the wood in the carpenter's shop scene and really carved her name on the beam, for which purpose the stage carpenters used to lend her their best tools; she wore real locked handcuffs for the Great Escape, and squeezing her hands from these was a painful process, she said. "I came down to the front, in full blaze of the footlights, so that the audience might fully judge." Her wrists and knuckles were often bruised, and after the strenuous climbing of the chimney, she used to stagger off the stage completely exhausted and collapse into the arms of a man specially stationed in the wings to prevent her from falling. "It was a very exhausting piece for me—so much so that I remember on one occasion falling asleep on a sofa between the acts, and they only just managed to rouse me in time for the raising of the curtain." On another night she fell heavily from a ladder and broke an ankle. For all these exertions and excitements Mrs. Keeley received only £20 a week, for the inflated salaries of to-day were undreamed of by the brightest "stars" of 1839. But she had her reward in the applause and affection of her audiences, "who followed her every movement with rapt attention," the while "young eyes sparkled as Jack carved his name on the cross-beam" and broke his fetters and escaped so dashingly from Newgate. At every performance "Nix my dolly, pals, fake away" was uproariously encored, this being the famous canting song Ainsworth had written in "Rookwood" and which was now transferred, in a shortened form, to the stage versions of "Jack Sheppard," with music composed by George H. Buonaparte Rodwell, who was also author of "Old London Bridge" (1849) and other romances in the style of Ainsworth—

In the box of the Stone Jug I was born	*Cell in Newgate.*
Of a hempen widow the kid forlorn.	
Fake away.	*Go on.*
My noble father as I've heard say	
Was a famous merchant of capers gay.	*Dancing master.*
Nix my dolly, palls (*sic*), fake away.	*Nothing, go on, comrades, work or thieve away.*
The knucks in quod did my school-men play	*Thieves in prison.*
And put me up to the time of day.	
Fake away.	
No dummy hunter had forks so fly,	*Pickpocket's forefingers.*
No knuckler so deftly could fake a cly.	*Pick a pocket.*
Nix my dolly, palls, fake away.	

Paul Bedford and Mrs. Keeley singing "Nix my dolly, pals, fake away" in "Jack Sheppard" at the Adelphi Theatre, 1839

Drawn on the spot by George Cruikshank

In Literature and Drama.

But my nuttiest lady one fine day
To the beaks did her gentleman betray.
    Fake away.
And thus was I bowled out at last,
And into the Jug for a lag was cast.   *Transportation.*
Nix my dolly, palls, fake away.

But I slipp'd my darbies one morn in May   *Fetters.*
And gave to the dubsman a holiday.   *Turnkeys.*
    Fake away.
And here I am, palls, merry and free,
A regular rollocking Romany.
Nix my dolly, palls, fake away.[9]

Towards the end of the last verse Mrs. Keeley, Paul Bedford, Mrs. Nailer, and Miss Campbell would dance to the tune—just as they are seen in the sketch opposite, which Cruikshank drew from the life one uproarious night at the Adelphi in the long ago. This was the popular song of the day, sung and whistled by every one, while "Fake away" was a catchword among all classes. As Sir Theodore Martin records—

"Nix my dolly" ... travelled everywhere, and made the patter of thieves and burglars "familiar in our mouths as household words." It deafened us in the streets, where it was as popular with the organ-grinders and German bands as Sullivan's brightest melodies ever were in a later day. It clanged at midday from the steeple of St. Giles, the Edinburgh Cathedral. (A fact. That such a subject for cathedral chimes, and in Scotland, too, could ever have been chosen will scarcely be believed. But my astonished ears often heard it)[10]; it was whistled by every dirty guttersnipe, and chanted in drawing-rooms by fair lips, little knowing the meaning of the words they sang.

And there was Barham's friendly allusion in "The Ingoldsby Legends"—in "The Lay of St. Aloys"—

Your cracksman, for instance, thinks night-time the best
To break open a door, or the lid of a chest ...
Nought is waking—Save Mischief and "Faking,"
And a few who are sitting up brewing or baking:

With the added footnote to "Faking"—

"Nix my dolly, pals, *Fake* away!"—words of deep and mysterious import

---

[9] In its original form in "Rookwood" there were 41 lines of verse apart from the refrain, which then had some difference in spelling, "Nix my doll, palls, fake away." Ainsworth had made an intensive study of the argot of thieves, and many of their cant terms he found in a slang dictionary at the end of "The Memoirs of James Hardy Vaux," a criminal returned from transportation.

[10] See Martin's "On Hearing 'Nix my dolly' ... played by the Bells of St. Giles Cathedral." (In "Flowers of Hemp.")

Jack Sheppard.

in the ancient language of Upper Egypt, and recently inscribed on the sacred standard of Mehemet Ali. They are supposed to intimate, to the initiated in the art of Abstraction, the absence of all human observation, and to suggest the propriety of making the best use of their time—and fingers.

There were political parodies, too, of this all-pervading song, as when Sir Robert Peel introduced his Bill in 1842 for the imposition of an income tax of 7d. in the pound (happy days!) his opponents sang, "Quick, my Tory pals, Tax Away." No wonder that Cruikshank would write to Ainsworth, " Go on, my boy, FAKE AWAY."

Almost equally popular in the theatre and outside was the drinking song in " Jack Sheppard," set to music by Rodwell, and sung at the Adelphi in his own inimitable style by that prince of port-wine comedians, " Glorious Paul Bedford "[11]—an earlier Baron Ochs—whose jovial red face and mellow voice were exactly suited to this ballad, which Ainsworth had adapted for Blueskin in a free lyrical translation from one of the " *Vaux-de-Vire* " of Olivier Basselin—

> Jolly Nose! the bright rubies that garnish thy tip
>   Are dug from the mines of Canary,
> And to keep up their lustre I moisten my lip
>   With hogsheads of claret and sherry.
>   Jolly Nose!
>
> Jolly Nose! He who sees thee across a broad glass
>   Beholds thee in all thy perfection,
> And to the pale snout of a temperate ass
>   Entertains the profoundest objection.
>   Jolly Nose! Jolly Nose!
>
> For a big-bellied glass is the palette I use,
>   And the choicest of wine is my colour;
> And I find that my nose takes the mellowest hues,
>   The fuller I fill it—the fuller.
>   Jolly Nose! Jolly Nose! . . .

The fame of Paul Bedford's " Jolly Nose " was heard and seen far and wide. He tells in his " Reminiscences " how, when suffering from hoarseness, he took medical advice: " The doctor advised me to inhale the floating vapour. I did so for a long time. ' Now,' said he, ' try your voice,' and I began chanting that pathetic ballad, ' Jolly

---

[11] Paul Bedford had a famous catchword: " I believe you, my boy." Clement Scott, who saw him in his later years, said Bedford did not strike him as being funny, as his humour was of the solemn, mirthless variety; but such a curious criticism would rule out the claims of many famous comedians in the style of Robson and Alfred Lester.

Paul Bedford, as Blueskin, singing "Jolly Nose" in "Jack Sheppard" at the Adelphi Theatre, 1839

From the contemporary Music-Front of the song

In Literature and Drama.

Nose.' At that moment the bell in the adjoining apartment rang; the doctor disappeared, and on entering the room the occupant said, ' Ah! ah! I know who my neighbour is! It is Jolly Nose Paul! Will you, doctor, ask him to oblige me by singing the song through?' At the request I complied, and my admiring friend in the next room was none other than Prince Louis Napoleon." Many years later at the Shakspere Tercentenary Musical and Dramatic Fête, held at the Agricultural Hall, Islington, in 1864, Paul Bedford warbled " Jolly Nose " to an audience of some 20,000, the song being, presumably, selected for its Falstaffian qualities. Before commencing to sing, Paul addressed his hearers thus: " My fostering and encouraging friends, I will breathe forth the result of a dream, dreamed by that inspired and immaculate bard, William Shakspere." The vision of the poet proved to be of Bardolph and his " Jolly Nose." His " address was greatly enjoyed," Bedford adds, and the vinous ballad was " vociferously redemanded by the admiring crowd," the members of which were, doubtless, more eager to partake of their subsequent similar refreshments than to witness the crowning of the Colossal Tercentenary Bust of the Bard, executed by Charles Bacon, by persons symbolising Tragedy and Comedy.

The fame of the Adelphi version of " Jack Sheppard " has eclipsed the records of the other contemporary productions, though it is strange that so few references to the play at Sadler's Wells survive, for this adaptation, written by Thomas Greenwood, seems to have been excellent and on more serious lines of vraisemblance in the physical aspects of the chief character. Jack Sheppard was played by a young man of thirty, R. W. Honner, who had become lessee of Sadler's Wells the year before; but previously he had won distinction as a ballet dancer and, consequently, he was possessed of the agility and élan so necessary for the actor who achieves success in this arduous rôle. His version, produced on the same night as the Adelphi show, on Monday, 28th October, 1839, was later published in Cumberland's series of plays, and his programmes asserted it was " allowed by all to be the best and most dramatic . . . the House being each night literally thronged with the most Numerous and Respectable Audiences that ever graced the walls of a Theatre." Jack was rescued at the end, and at the outset the orchestra played a " New Medley Overture, consisting of popular airs from ' The Beggar's Opera.' " In the earlier scenes, when Jack was an urchin of thirteen, the lessee's wife, Mrs. R. W. Honner, formerly Miss Maria Macarthy, now aged twenty-seven, was his impersonator, her husband taking over the rôle for the second two acts after Jack

Jack Sheppard.

had come of age. Miss Pincott (Mrs. Alfred Wigan) played Thames Darrell when he, too, was thirteen; Miss Richardson was the Mrs. Sheppard, Mr. Williams the Owen Wood, Mr. C. Montgomery the Blueskin, while H. Hall, the good old-time actor, as Jonathan Wild appropriated the song of "Jolly Nose" to another tune composed by J. B. Blewitt. Some fine lithographic portraits of Honner as Jack together with two of his actors, H. Hall and C. Montgomery, represent him as a thin, wiry man,[1] and it seems probable that he was one of the best of the countless Jack Sheppards, though he is now forgotten, for he died early, in 1852, at the age of forty-three. Honner was the son of a solicitor, so it is amusing that he should have excelled in the acting of criminal plays. His "Jack Sheppard" proving very successful, on 20th September, 1841, he put on at Sadler's Wells another Newgate drama, "Jack Ketch, or a Leaf from Tyburn Tree," by George Almar, wherein Honner as Ketch presented a boy apprentice of robbers who became a Knight of the Post and finally the Public Executioner. The Common Hangman was played by Mr. Williams, and Mrs. Honner was in the principal female part. One of the scenes was grimly remarkable— A Rope Walk on the banks of the Thames, near Execution Dock.

Before the various London productions of "Jack Sheppard" in October, 1839, there was an earlier version in September at the Theatre Royal, Sheffield, written by T. H. Lacy, who himself appeared as Jack, with P. Rae as Jonathan Wild and W. Johnson as Blueskin. Ainsworth's story was not completed until October.

Brighton saw at least three productions of "Jack Sheppard." At the Theatre Royal on 25th November, 1839, was given a version by H. P. Grattan, who acted Thames Darrell, while C. Hill, the manager of the house, played Blueskin to the Jack Sheppard of his wife. J. Bradshaw was Wild. On 13th August, 1852, under his own management, Henry Farren was Blueskin to the Jack of Miss Louisa Howard. On 24th September, 1857, in J. B. Johnstone's version at the Theatre Royal, Miss Thirlwall played the youthful Jack, George Melville taking over the rôle in the later acts.

On 12th November, 1853, at the Bowery Theatre, New York, there was a hashed version of "Jack Sheppard" by Miss Leah Goldstein, who took the part of Mrs. Sheppard; Mrs. Yeomans appeared as Jack; Mr. Hamblin as Wild; and Mr. Stevens as Blueskin.

In 1867, a Jack Sheppard play entitled "The Knights of Tyburn,

---

[1] These lithographic portraits of the actors named can be seen in a collection, preserved at the British Museum, relating to Sadler's Wells Theatre, volume 6, the press-mark being Crach. I. Tab. 4-5.b.

In Literature and Drama.

or London in 1715," was given at Niblo's Garden, but it only ran for three nights, and the theatre was demolished on Boxing Day of that year.

Mrs. Keeley, despite advancing years, continued to regard Jack Sheppard as her particular rôle and property. She appeared in a revival at the Haymarket on 6th September, 1852. The middle-aged but indomitable matron had recently suffered a severe accident, but she duly bounded on to the carpenter's bench, and to the stool on that, to carve her name on the beam as in the glorious nights thirteen years agone, and *The Times* records: "Mrs. Keeley has recovered from her severe accident and appeared last night in the popular melodrama of ' Jack Sheppard.' She was received with enthusiastic applause." Paul Bedford was again her Blueskin, and there was an excellent Jonathan Wild in the person of S. Emery, with O. Smith, Miss Laura Honey, and Miss Ellen Chaplin (the younger Mrs. Fitzwilliam) also in the cast. Three years later, Mrs. Keeley, now aged nearly fifty, revived the play at Sadler's Wells in May, 1855, this being the interregnum between the eleventh and twelfth seasons of Samuel Phelps. At first Paul Bedford was Blueskin, but four days later an actor named Barrett was playing the part with G. F. Edgar as Jonathan Wild. On 5th May Miss Mary Keeley was billed as Jack, she being Mrs. Keeley's elder daughter and the wife of Albert Smith, the well-known novelist and entertainer; but a few days later in the month the intrepid and ever-youthful mother was once again " the noble stripling, snapping Newgate's bars of iron like an infant's daisy-chain," for as her faithful *Times* put it: " Mrs. Keeley is in the ascendant, and ' Jack Sheppard,' so often denounced as the cause of West-end wickedness, threatens the moral purity of Islington." By 1858 Mrs. Keeley seems to have realised she must resign her favourite part to another, for at the revival of the play this year at the Surrey Theatre (whither the Adelphi company migrated during the rebuilding of their own theatre) Mrs. John Billington appeared as Jack, while Paul Bedford was seen yet once again as Blueskin, now at the age of sixty-six. Undoubtedly these veterans " lagged superfluous " as they essayed to repeat the splendid successes of their prime when the years said " No! " Though of course Mrs. Keeley retained immense vitality until her death at the age of ninety-four, for her last appearance as an actress was made when she was eighty-four.

These mature presentations of Jack Sheppard by Mrs. Keeley set an unhappy fashion, for, as she finally let her rivals seize her sceptre of the iron bar, even more mature and far stouter ladies decided that *this* was the suitable rôle for exhibiting their talents and

Jack Sheppard.

adipose figures. The crowning absurdity seems to have been reached in the person of an actress whom Weedon Grossmith related he had the melancholy pleasure of seeing as Jack. She was a very comely lady of forty-five or so—Weedon Grossmith himself found the part of Jack Sheppard too arduous for his strength when he was a year younger—she was short and plump, and seemed to experience a vast deal of difficulty in climbing down from an upper window of the prison in an escape scene; in fact, she would never have accomplished this feat without the assistance of Blueskin (who had no business to be on the spot). He took her by the hand, guided her descent, and helped her along gracefully, as if he were conducting her to her brougham. This same lady, when Wild called Jack a liar, earned the warm approval of the gallery by replying at the top of her " refaned " feminine voice: " Jack Sheppard was a thief, but he never told a lie." All these absurdities began to bring the old drama into disrepute. Sometimes the absurdities were accidental, as on that famous occasion in the old theatre at Brighton, on 28th March, 1853, when Henry Farren, the father of Nellie Farren, was taking his benefit on the eve of his departure for St. Louis, where he was to die seven years later while still a young man. " Jack Sheppard " was the last piece played, and the lights grew dimmer and dimmer as the inadequate gas supply failed. Consequently the *entr'actes* grew longer and longer, and in the morning of the night of the benefit the play was still proceeding as gaily as it could as lamp after lamp went out. The orchestra left at midnight. At two o'clock in the morning the execution of Sheppard took place amid almost total Cimmerian darkness, but by that time nearly all the audience had departed.

Another Jack Sheppard, in the person of Miss Vyvyan, once, during the course of a performance, advanced to the footlights in tears and informed the audience that she was too upset to continue, as the Jonathan Wild of the play, who was also the treasurer of the company, had decamped with the night's receipts and all the cash in hand; this actor had evidently studied to his own advantages the treacherous character of the Great Thief-taker as adapted to a cash-taker in the manner he is presented in Fielding's satire. Mr. Alfred Nelson related that when he was playing in " Jack Sheppard " at Ballarat, in 1856, two mysterious men took up a position in the wings one night. At the fall of the curtain, they stepped on to the stage and arrested the actor who had played the part of Jonathan Wild on a charge of burglary.

There was a version of " Jack Sheppard " in French, the work of Dennery and Bourget, produced in Paris on 7th July, 1857, at the

In Literature and Drama.

Porte St. Martin Theatre. It contained many absurdities. " Sir " William Hogarth paints Jack's portrait in Newgate and procures for him an interview with the King, George the First, who pardons the young criminal because he has saved the life of Thames Darrell and thereby preserved an ancient title, that of Comte de Chatillon, the heir whereof is Thames. When Ainsworth witnessed a performance of this play, he was convulsed with laughter, which became almost hysterical at the sight of a gauze curtain stretched across the stage to simulate a London fog, for the title of the piece was " *Les Chevaliers du Brouillard.*" Jack was played by Madame Marie Laurent, and Ainsworth, in reply to a query from Charles Hervey, thus determined the respective merits of the two leading female exponents of the rôle—

> I can say—without a moment's hesitation—that, as a whole, I preferred Mrs. Keeley's " Jack Sheppard " to that of Madame Marie Laurent, though there were particular points in which the admirable French actress far excelled the other. But both pleased me so much that I scarcely like to institute a comparison between them. Madame Marie Laurent's was undoubtedly a more vigorous conception of the part—but I cannot give the palm to her.

Ainsworth, of course, was a life-long victim of " sex-appeal," and consequently never seems to have perceived that from an artistic point of view only a young male actor could possibly present the character of Sheppard in a realistic manner; so the author, like most of the other men of his generation, accepted the " male impersonator," with all its unpleasant implications, as a pleasant convention. We of to-day cannot laugh at them, for we still preserve the absurdities of female " principal boys " in pantomime, of girls as Siebel in the opera of " Faust," and as Octavian in " *Der Rosenkavalier* " (most improper in all senses of the word is the opening love-scene of this great opera!), of married ladies as Peter Pan, the boy who would not grow up!; and we encouraged the lamentable spectacle of the aged Bernhardt tottering as Hamlet and a boy Napoleon—which altogether lacked the risible qualities that cheered the performances of *embonpoint* Jack Sheppards.

In 1840, when Mrs. Keeley went on tour with " Jack Sheppard " in Dublin an extraneous event affected the success of the production. She relates:

> The very night we opened, Courvoisier's confession was published. In this he says that the first idea of crime which he ever had came to him while he was witnessing the play of " Jack Sheppard " at the Adelphi, and he had been really led into cutting Lord William Russell's throat through that play. That settled our business, for although we fulfilled every night of our engagement, I remember the houses were very poor.

Ireland, of course, being a country that holds murder in extreme

Jack Sheppard.

abhorrence, could not be expected to tolerate the stage murders of Mrs. Wood and Sir Rowland. Courvoisier's alleged assertion gained currency, for it is alluded to in Mahony's heavy and obscure satire, "The Cruel Murder of Old Father Prout," an attack on Ainsworth by his former friend, the quarrel commencing by Father Prout professing to be grieved by Ainsworth's descent from the scholarly "Crichton" to the criminal "Jack Sheppard"—

> But Prout, who had misgivings of the "gentle Sheppard's" razor,
> Calmly deferred doffing his beard till Bentley came or Fraser,
> For he had read his several tales of severing bone and muscle
> (So had the late Courvoisier, who killed Lord William Russell).

Lord William Russell, when seventy-two years of age, had been murdered in his own bedroom at 14, Park Lane, on 5th May, 1840, by his valet, B. F. Courvoisier. The criminal made several "confessions" after arrest, and in one of these he was said to have alleged that the first idea of his fatal act came to him after a perusal of "Jack Sheppard." He does not seem to have stated that it was Ainsworth's story he had read, but the general impression of the public was that he meant that book. Ainsworth was highly indignant, and in *The Times* of 7th July, 1840, appeared a letter from him protesting against a statement in the paper that Courvoisier had said "He wished he had never seen the work." Ainsworth continued—

> I have taken means to ascertain the correctness of the report, and I find it utterly without foundation. The wretched man declared he had neither read the work in question nor made any such statement. A Collection of Trials of Noted Malefactors (probably "The Newgate Calendar") had indeed fallen in his way, but the account of Jack Sheppard contained in this series had not particularly attracted his attention. I am the more anxious to contradict this false and injurious statement because a writer in *The Examiner* of Sunday last, without inquiring into the truth of the matter, has made it the groundwork of a most violent and libellous attack upon my romance.[2]

---

[2] In *The Examiner* of 28th June, 1840, it was written, no doubt by John Forster again, for reference is made to his earlier hostile review of "Jack Sheppard" in this paper (see *ante*, page 79)—

"In Courvoisier's second confession, which we are more disposed to believe than the first, he ascribes his crimes to the perusal of that detestable book, 'Jack Sheppard'; and certainly it is a publication calculated to familiarise the mind with cruelties and to serve as the cut-throat's manual, or the midnight assassin's *vade-mecum*, in which character we now expect to see it advertised. Curious it is that the very words used by Courvoisier, in describing the way in which he committed the murder—'I drew the knife across his throat'—are to be found in the horrid book alluded to, in Blueskin's murder of Mrs. Wood. The passage is this . . .

"In an article in reprobation of the book in *The Examiner* of Nov. 3, 1839, the passage is quoted, and this comment made upon it. If ever there was a publication that deserved to be burnt by the hands of the common hangman it is 'Jack Sheppard.'"

In Literature and Drama.

Two days later there was published in *The Times* the following letter :—

> Sir,—I observe in your journal of this morning a letter signed " W. Harrison Ainsworth " denying that Courvoisier had asserted that the idea of murdering his master was first suggested to him by a perusal of the romance of " Jack Sheppard." I think it my duty to state distinctly that Courvoisier did assert to me that the idea of murdering his master was first suggested to him by a perusal of the book called " Jack Sheppard," and that the said book was lent to him by a valet of the Duke of Bedford.
>
> Your obedient servant,
> William Evans,
> Sheriff of London and Middlesex.
>
> July 7th, 1840.

But once again there is no proof that the murderer had said it was Ainsworth's book he had read; and it is not likely that even a ducal valet would expend twenty-five shillings for a copy, though it is possible such a person may have " borrowed " Ainsworth's romance from the library of his Grace of Bedford, who was the nephew of Lord William Russell. The murdered man was also the uncle of Lord John Russell, who was to figure as Jack Sheppard in the cartoon in *Punch* some eighteen months later, so perhaps there was some *arrière-pensée* in the artist's mind in addition to the (now) rather obscure political significance of the picture.[3]

Courvoisier's " confessions " were quite worthless, for as *The Times* of 27th June had truly observed—

> It seems pretty clear that no credit can be given to any statement which has hitherto been made by this wretched culprit, except as regards the fact of the murder itself; but it would be idle to speculate on the motives of a mind so manifestly perverted.

Still, he may have read Ainsworth's " Jack Sheppard," just as he may have read of the murder of Sisera by Jael in the Bible and the numerous bloody murders in Shakspere, but an author cannot be held responsible for the workings of a perverted mind. Mrs. Keeley said it was seeing the performance at the Adelphi Theatre of " Jack Sheppard " which led Courvoisier to the gallows, but the broadsheet sold in the streets and around the scaffold at his execution, " The Lament of Francis Courvoisier," to be sung to the tune of " Bank of Primroses," and garnished with a fine woodcut of the felon swinging

---

[3] See *ante*, page 85.

Jack Sheppard.

from the beam, transferred the credit to the stage version at the Royal Surrey Theatre—

> To the Surrey for to see Jack Sheppard
>   To beguile the time I went one night,
> But I little thought that fatal evening
>   That it would all my prospects blight.
>
> Alas! that night has proved my ruin,
>   In innocent blood I have my hands imbued,
> I was unworthy of such a master,
>   Who to me was always kind and good.
>
> For a whole week I planned the murder,
>   It engaged my mind by day and night,
> I felt no remorse, but like a demon
>   It seemed to me a source of great delight.

After this catchpenny "confession" the Lord Chamberlain took fright and for many years regarded "Jack Sheppard" as a terrible drama unworthy of his ægis and the very prompt-book for the grocer's-boy to reach the gallows. Licence to perform plays of that name was now to be refused; but it was only at the minor theatres that the ban was enforced, and, even then, the managers circumvented the edict by putting on Jack Sheppard plays under other titles, such as "The Boy Burglar," "The Young Housebreaker," and so on. For some strange reason, Buckstone's version, as played at the Adelphi, was smiled upon by the Lord Chamberlain, although, as already related, Mrs. Keeley thought this was the theatre where Courvoisier obtained his "idea" for cutting the throat of his master. When Mrs. Keeley revived "Jack Sheppard" at the Haymarket in September, 1852, the play-bills contained this notice—

The Public is respectfully requested to Notice that the Version at this Establishment (which has never been interdicted, and therefore not now re-licensed) is the Only One that was written by J. B. Buckstone, Esq., and Licensed by the Lord Chamberlain. This statement is rendered necessary by the numerous unlicensed imitations that have been acted under the same title, and in which scenes and situations have been presented to the Audience that, however harmless when followed by the context in reading the novel, were deemed unfit for delineation on the stage. In the present adaptation all objectionable passages are carefully expunged, and whilst every care is taken to illustrate the striking incidents of the Drama, the most scrupulous may rest assured that in "adorning the tale" the great end of Dramatic Representation—"to point a moral"—has not been forgotten.

So matters went on for several years. In 1868, on 13th July, the East London Theatre came out with a full-blooded melodramatic

In Literature and Drama.

version of the old tale, "Jonathan Wild, or the Storm on the Thames," by H. Young, which utilised the exciting episodes Ainsworth, in his finest and most vivid writing, had entwined with the historic Great Storm of November, 1703, in Epoch the First of "Jack Sheppard." But Jack Sheppard could not appear under his own name, and consequently was called "Charley Ives." In 1870 (the year is not printed on the yellow bill, adorned with a fine cut of Jack Sheppard's fetters being struck off before his execution), S. Lane of "Britannia, The Great Theatre, Hoxton," proclaimed:

UNRIVALLED ATTRACTION!
UNPARALLED PROGRAMME!
UNEQUALLED NOVELTY!

Wednesday, May 11th.

For the benefit of Miss Eliza Clayton, and last night but three of her engagement previous to her Provincial Tour.

The performance will commence with a new Adaptation by Miss Eliza Clayton of Harrison Ainsworth's Novel in Four parts, entitled THE TWO APPRENTICES, OR INDUSTRY AND IDLENESS.

Idle Jack, surnamed Idleness,	Miss Eliza Clayton.
(As played by her above 280 Nights with the greatest success).	
Thames, surnamed Industry,	R. Leslie.
Sir Rowland,	W. Richardson.
Kneebone,	E. Harding.
Wood,	J. Parry.
Blueskin (with song of "Nix My Dolly, Pals")	G. Bigwood.
Wild,	J. Reynolds,
Quilt Arnold,	J. Pitt.
Mendez,	E. Elton.
Joan Sheppard (Mrs.),	Miss J. Coveney.
Mrs. Wood,	Mrs. W. Newham.
Winifred,	Miss A. Downing.
Pollo,	Miss L. Rayner.
Bess,	Miss Henmann.

After "The Two Apprentices," Miss Eliza Clayton enacted Richmond to the Richard III of Miss Henderson in Shakspere's play, with "The Fight at Bosworth Field." And the evening concluded with "Miss Clayton's highly successful comedy," "The Red Lamp," in which she appeared as Constance Reeks. Actresses certainly worked hard in those days.

Perhaps these resuscitations suggested to a professional humorist of the day (he was the leading writer of extravaganzas and the words for musical plays) that the story of Jack Sheppard was now in the traditional collection of England and therefore fit subject for burlesque. So at the Royal Strand Theatre on 10th September, 1870, was produced

Jack Sheppard.

an absurd travesty of the old drama entitled " The Grand Hurly-Burlyesque, The Idle 'Prentice, A Tyburnian Idyll of High-Low Jack and his Little Game," written by H. B. Farnie, remarkable for " all the talents " of subsequently famous people who were in the cast—

Little Jack,	Jenny Lee.
Mrs. Sheppard,	Edward Terry.
Master Wood,	H. J. Turner.
Winifred Wood,	Kate Santley.
Jonathan Wild,	Eleanor Bufton.
Thames Darrell,	J. P. Burnett.
Sir Rowland,	Amy Sheridan.
Lady Trafford,	Mrs. Raymond.
Poll Maggot,	Miss Metcalf.
Edgworth Bess,	Miss E. Rose.
and	
Blueskin,	Harry Paulton.[4]

As *The Daily Telegraph* critic rightly surmised, the Lord Chamberlain had excluded the objectionable title of Sheppard from the Strand play-bill,[5] " but ' The Idle 'Prentice ' is simply the prohibited piece in a travestied form," and lacking Ainsworth's final moral of retribution, for this burlesque was a wild perversion of the Hogarthian model: Jack was everything that was gallant and worthy of emulation, but Thames was a milksop, played as a grotesque by J. P. Burnett, no doubt on the same lines as Mr. Ernest Thesiger presented George Barnwell in recent times at the Lyric, Hammersmith. Jenny Lee, " saucy and smart," must have been the youngest performer who ever enacted Jack Sheppard, for she was but twelve years old at this date. Curiously enough, she was destined to marry her Thames Darrell just mentioned, J. P. Burnett, and it was he who later wrote the stage version of " Bleak House " wherein Jenny Lee was to achieve her great success as Jo, the crossing-sweeper—" He wos wery good to me, he wos." Fifty-five years hence Jenny Lee was herself to die in poverty, alone, and almost friendless, her husband and daughter dead and her son killed in the recent war. Eleanor Bufton (who twelve years before had played Regan to the Lear of Charles Kean), at the

---

[4] For the particulars of this programme, and of several others mentioned in this history, I am indebted to the collection of play-bills and other matter relating to the Theatre formed by Mrs. Gabrielle Enthoven, O.B.E., and now in the Victoria and Albert Museum.

[5] By the courtesy of the present Lord Chamberlain I have inspected the original manuscript of " The Idle 'Prentice," which was submitted in August, 1870, before the licence was granted for the production of the piece, and throughout the name of Sheppard has been heavily erased by pencil.

In Literature and Drama.

Strand, was a new kind of Jonathan Wild, a female Mephistopheles, " A Gentleman in Black," in a suit of " shining black silk," in contrast to Amy Sheridan, as Sir Rowland, " who displayed her imposing figure in a glittering garb of white satin and silver trimmings," while Bella Goodall " in dazzling blue satin trowsers danced innumerable hornpipes to the frantic delight of the gallery." Kate Santley sang with great piquancy. This was Harry Paulton's first appearance in London, and he made a vast success with his Blueskin, who was transformed into a modern policeman and vented a popular song, " I'll run you in." While Edward Terry as the Widow Sheppard— " I'm a lovely widdy "—converted into an Irishwoman, with a pipe and apple-stall, had a wild song beseeching her volatile " ginger-beer not to ' fly ' until a customer comes by." Poor Mrs. Sheppard! That sad widow who had endured so much and suffered the grief of seeing both her sons go to ruin, one to transportation and the other to the gallows, how little she could have conceived in life that her name would live on for more than two centuries and her tragic experiences become the properties of romancers and dramatists, and she herself a stock figure on many stages. At one extreme of literary licence, Ainsworth bestowed on her aristocratic descent and caused her to die by her own hand after a period of insanity in Bedlam; and at the other extreme, Farnie and Edward Terry presented her as a comic harridan, one of the earliest examples, if not the originator, of the music-hall and pantomime dame as played by broad male comedians of the school of Herbert Campbell, Dan Leno, Fred Emney, and George Robey. But Mrs. Sheppard, Owen Wood, Blueskin, Edgworth Bess, Mr. Kneebone, and the rest of Jack Sheppard's circle have been dragged at the heels of his procession to Tyburn for all time and had bestowed upon them an abiding notoriety by reason of the countless actors and actresses who have impersonated them upon the stage, for if Jack Sheppard had never existed or had been, like his father and grandfather and great-grandfather before him, a simple, honest carpenter, all these people he knew would have lived their little lives, died, and been entirely forgotten before the close of the eighteenth century. As it is, they are a recurring feature in the history of the British Stage.

" The Idle 'Prentice " at the Strand in 1870 was very successful, for it ran until just before Christmas, over three months,[6] and even

---

[6] During the run of " The Idle 'Prentice," on the other side of the Strand at the Gaiety Theatre there was a season of " The Beggar's Opera " with Constance Loseby as Polly and Beverley as Macheath.

Jack Sheppard.

then the last night was announced as only " for the present." The piece was also sent on a provincial tour, under the title of " Little Jack Sheppard " in defiance of the still nervous Lord Chamberlain, who, however, in view of the piece being absurd burlesque, took no action. This company was also remarkable for its talents. One would have liked to have seen Lottie Venne as Jonathan Wild. Rose Massey played Jack and Charles Groves was Blueskin, G. W. Anson being also in the play, which formed the after-piece to Robertson comedy. Farnie's travesty was revived as " Little Jack Sheppard, or The Idle 'Prentice," at the Royal Surrey Theatre in May, 1880, with Polly Randall as Jack and Kate Newton as Jonathan Wild. Arthur Williams took over the exuberances of Mrs. Sheppard, and Blueskin was enacted by Harry Nicholls, who must have been one of the most jovial exponents of that bibulous rascal.

In December, 1872, Madame Marie Laurent, inspired by Mrs. Keeley's former defiance of Time, revived at the Gaîeté Theatre, Paris, " *Les Chevaliers du Brouillard,*" fifteen years after her original impersonation of Jack Sheppard. Her new company included Adèle Page as Mrs. Sheppard. The revival was successful, so a version in English was written by " F. Boyle," who, I understand, was John Oxenford, and, entitled " Old London," it was produced at the Queen's Theatre in Long Acre on 5th February, 1873, with never a hint of Jack Sheppard in the title; for the Lord Chamberlain was more terrified and terrifying than ever, so Jack masqueraded as Dick Wastrell. All the other characters had their names changed too for the purposes of this foolish make-believe, which indeed deserved its alternative title of " The Knights of the Fog "—

Dick Wastrell (Jack Sheppard),	Miss Stewart (as the boy).
	Henrietta Hodson (as the youth).
Velvet Grawl (Jonathan Wild),	J. Nelson.
Old Nollekins (Blueskin),	W. Belford.
Mr. Smiles (Owen Wood),	J. Vollaire.
Sir Randolph Brand (Sir Rowland),	F. Kilpack.
Stephen Wyvern (Thames Darrell),	H. Neville.

But all these devices were vain. Soon after the curtain went up, an enthusiastic gentleman in the gallery gave vent to his feelings and bawled out, " Why, blast me! if it isn't ' Jack Sheppard '! " And then there was great fun as the audience welcomed again their old friend from the past. As Clement Scott, who was present, says : " The gallery and pit ruthlessly tore off the mask. Stalls and boxes chuckled when they thought how the Lord Chamberlain sought to cajole

In Literature and Drama.

them with his Old London and Dick Wastrell... The situations have stood the test of time, and they succeeded once more in rousing pit and gallery." The scenery was effective, particularly the set showing Old London Bridge and on one of its slimy buttresses the dare-devil young hero left for dead with the tide rising. The Newgate scene, too, was good, though a foolish " addition " was Mrs. Sheppard tearing up blankets to form a rope for her son's escape. According to Scott, the actors were not good, with the exception of Henrietta Hodson who played Dick, or Jack, remarkably well, with intelligence and tact, though she was too refined and suggested more the idea of Claude Duval. Miss Hodson, who was the wife of Henry Labouchere, politician and journalist and controller of the Queen's Theatre, acted this part at the age of thirty-two, and what her appearance was like can be seen in a portrait entitled " Jack Sheppard Redivivus," by Alfred Bryan, in the *Entr'acte* of 3rd May, 1873. " Old London " ended at the Queen's on 29th April, but reopened at the Standard on 3rd May.[7]

Imitation is always the bane of theatrical managers, and consequently " Old London " caused the management of the Adelphi Theatre to rush out a re-presentation of their old success, " Jack Sheppard," under the direction of Edward Stirling, as in 1839. This was accomplished on 22nd March. But the Lord Chamberlain—probably he was a new one—no longer shed the full light of his partial face upon the Adelphi version as he had done in the days when Mrs. Keeley enacted Jack. For now, in 1873, J. B. Buckstone had to rewrite his adaptation, eviscerate it of any full-blooded qualities that might offend, give it a new title and rechristen all the characters with names bereft of immoral associations, and present it with the piteous apology: " This is the only form in which the escapades of the popular hero of Ainsworth's romance are allowed to be acted on the stage, its representation having been specifically sanctioned by the Lord Chamberlain." Buckstone's version could no longer claim exemptions, for the Examiner of Plays was adamant, and these changes *must* be made. The Lord Chamberlain, in his capacity of custodian of public morals, was making what proved to be his last attempt to prohibit Jack Sheppard's appearance on the stage in the guise of a hero. The result of all this hanky-panky was " The Stone Jug," " Adapted by J. B. Buckstone from the celebrated

---

[7] There was also a provincial production of " Old London " in 1873 at the Bristol New Theatre Royal. Another play of this name, " Old London," by Arthur Shirley and W. M. Tilson, was produced at the Queen's Theatre, Manchester, on 25th July, 1891, and at the Marylebone Theatre, London, on 29th August, 1892. Jack Sheppard under his own name and not as Dick Wastrell.

Jack Sheppard.

Novel of 'Jack Sheppard,' by Harrison Ainsworth," with the following weirdly named cast—

Robert Chance: The Idle Apprentice (Jack Sheppard),	Miss Hudspeth (Mrs. Edmund Phelps).
Richard Riverside (Thames Darrell),	Mr. A. C. Lilly.
The Marquis de Chatillon (father to Richard),	Harwood Cooper.
Sir Neville Montague (Sir Rowland),	J. G. Shore.
Benjamin Bevel (Owen Wood),	B. Egan.
Butler Buckhurst (Kneebone),	F. Roland.
Sampson Savage, a Thief-taker (Jonathan Wild),	James Fernandez.
Jim, alias "Purpleface" (Blueskin),	Augustus Glover.
Ken Kennedy (Master of the Mint),	R. Romer.
Mrs. Chance (Mrs. Sheppard),	Miss Marston-Leigh.
Mrs. Bevel (Mrs. Wood),	Mrs. Addie (Fanny Hamilton).
Millicent Bevel (Winifred Wood),	Miss M. Howard.
Sally,	Miss Phillips (possibly Kate Phillips).

Poor Edgworth Bess and Poll Maggot, being too immoral for stage whitewash, were snuffed out entirely. The result was feeble and only endured for a fortnight, for as Clement Scott observed of this production nearly a quarter of a century later, the producers " might as well have sold bottles of ginger-beer as champagne. There is a bouquet of flavour about 'Jack Sheppard' as there is in the fruit of the vine. . . . Fortunately for a peace-loving community, the School Board Epoch has removed from the public mind unhallowed fears of 'Jack Sheppard.' We have passed the stage when the Life and Adventures of that engaging house and prison-breaker fluttered the Lord Chamberlain's heart and gave active occupation to red tape."[8] So it was, "The Stone Jug" of 1873 was the last of the disguised Jack Sheppard plays, and when next Jack reappeared it was under his own name, at the Surrey Theatre, on 15th May, 1880, that same Surrey Theatre where just forty years before Courvoisier, according to his bogus "Lament," had seen the same play and was thereby led to cut the throat of Lord William Russell. Here, in 1880,

---

[8] The persistence and penetration of Jack Sheppard's story is remarkable. Less than thirty years ago a friend of mine when staying at Cancale, near St. Malo, witnessed a performance, in French, of course, of a village play entitled "Petit Jean Sheppard." It was acted entirely by fisher boys, of ages ranging from twelve to nineteen, and was staged in a disused church in the Vieux Place, which made a good setting for the dungeons and fetters of Newgate. Four of the characters were described as Scotch men and wearing the national dress of their country—oilskins and sou'westers. When the actors were asked subsequently why the national costume took this protective form, the answer was: "Because it was always raining there."

In Literature and Drama.

as previously related, there was a revival of H. B. Farnie's burlesque, "Little Jack Sheppard, or The Idle 'Prentice."

Five years later there was a famous burlesque, "Little Jack Sheppard," produced at the Gaiety Theatre on 26th December, 1885. John Hollingshead, the manager, had made a speciality for some years of trimming and keeping bright the sacred lamp of burlesque, and, accordingly, he commissioned a new travesty of the tale the stage had represented for over a century and a half. The "book," in rhyming couplets, was written by William Yardley, "Bill of the Play," a briefless barrister, good cricketer, and Bohemian journalist, and H. Pottinger Stephens, a Jewish journalist, much esteemed on *The Daily Telegraph*, according to the late H. G. Hibbert, "because he could write about social functions like a gentleman, and did not get tangled among the titles." The attractive music was composed by Meyer Lutz, Arthur Cecil, Hamilton Clarke, and Florian Pascal. There were thus six cooks for making the broth, but far more conducive to its fame were the waiters, so alert and talented, who dispensed it across the footlights—

Jack Sheppard,	Nellie Farren.
Blueskin,	David James.
Thames Darrell,	Tillie Wadman.
Mrs. Sheppard,	Harriet Coveney.
Winifred Wood,	Marion Hood.
Polly Stanmore,	Sylvia Grey.
Sir Rowland,	E. J. Odell.
Kneebone,	Willie Warde.
Edgworth Bess,	Bessie Sansen.
Owen Wood,	M. Guise.
Captain Cuff,	Emily Duncan.
Kitty Kettleby,	Miss Eunice.
Mendez,	Frank Wood.
and	
Jonathan Wild,	Fred Leslie.

It was a brilliant company, and at its head flamed Nellie Farren, the most popular "star" of burlesque and musical extravaganza of all time. She received £100 a week, considered a stupendous salary in those days, and certainly a good advance on the £15 or £20 a week which Mrs. Keeley had been paid for her rendering of Jack forty-six years earlier.[9] She was the legitimate successor of Mrs. Keeley in

---

[9] The octogenarian Mrs. Keeley witnessed more than once a performance of "Little Jack Sheppard." She was loud in her praise of Nellie Farren and Fred Leslie, but she "did not consider that the piece was altogether worthy as a clever travesty."

Jack Sheppard.

comedy parts, and, as was the case with her predecessor, she was a mature lady of thirty-seven when she played Jack Sheppard and did not in the least degree look like a boy and Jack least of all boys.[10] But again talent, high spirits, infectious gaiety, and restless agility triumphed and made her performance a delight and one of the most successful she ever presented, for in her case it was personality that carried her to the heights, despite advancing age and the absence of any particular beauty of face and form. Nellie Farren was neither boy nor girl on the stage in her greatest performances, but a kind of sexless *espièglerie*—for there was no " sex-appeal " in her deserved fame—brought her into line with Puck and the mischievous sprites of Thalia. Entirely Puck-up-to-date was her presentation of Jack as a cheeky Cockney guttersnipe, full of tricks and mischief, as exemplified in her first song, which incidentally commenced with two lines from the original " Nix my dolly, pals, fake away "—

> In a box of the Stone-Jug I was born,
> Of a hempen widow the kid forlorn,
> My baby rags were tattered and torn.
> On the Fifth of November I used to shy
> My crackers right in the policeman's eye,
> While I shouted " Hullo! another Guy! "
> To be merry I still contrive-o.

Nellie Farren did not contrive to be merry in her own life much longer. In a little over five years more her stage career was terminated by ill-health, and she died in 1904, at the age of fifty-six. In 1898 she had a wonderful " Benefit " at Drury Lane, when her " Gallery Boys " assembled in great strength to cheer and do her honour : " They hungered for just one sound of that voice of hers—that peculiar, well-known, beloved cockney voice, London in every timbre and fibre—and when it came it gave the mighty audience the first great thrill of the day. As she spoke there was a ' silence that was felt,' and when, in the never-to-be-forgotten accents of the street Arab, she smiled and said, ' Thank ye, sir,' tears rushed up unbidden to thousands of eager, loving eyes."[11] The " Gallery Boys " of " Our Nellie " cannot all be dead, and it is strange that there does not seem to be even one to remember her now and place a spray of roses or a sprig of rosemary

---

[10] H. G. Hibbert stated, in " A Playgoer's Memories," that Nellie Farren had played Jack Sheppard in her earlier life in a serious version of the play at the Victoria Theatre, where she was succeeded in the rôle by Mrs. Frederick Wright, but 1 have not seen programmes of these performances, which were presumably about 1863-64.

[11] Clement Scott in *The Daily Telegraph*.

Nellie Farren as Little Jack Sheppard at the Gaiety Theatre, 1885-6
Photograph from Rischgitz Studios

In Literature and Drama.

on her neglected grave in desolate Brompton Cemetery, where she lies forgotten, the cheers all silent, the once brilliant lights all out.

With her, in " Little Jack Sheppard," Fred Leslie achieved a great success. He was a young actor, whose real name was Hobson, the son of a military outfitter at Woolwich. He had lately been playing Rip Van Winkle in the provinces, and both Hollingshead and George Edwardes afterwards claimed the perspicacity for engaging him for the Gaiety company in place of the recreant Edward Terry, who had betaken himself elsewhere. Leslie had a brief and meteoric career, for his early death in 1892, at the age of thirty-seven, was an irreparable loss to the theatre; preceded, as it was, by the collapse in health of Nellie Farren, the twin calamity caused the end of burlesque, which was succeeded by musical comedy. Consequently " Little Jack Sheppard " has a pathetic interest, for in it these two unrivalled artistes last played together at the heights of their powers. Fred Leslie combined refinement with the grotesque, and his Jonathan Wild must have been a very remarkable blend of the melodramatic and the artistic— " A Jonathan Oscar Wilde," as one critic suggested. His admirers still remember some of his comic " business " in this part—how he wore gloves with detachable fingers, which he would peel off one by one and cast upon the stage with exaggerated rage, and how he would cool his fury by a miniature snowstorm, which he threw over himself from his snuff-box. Burlesques meant the wildest of puns, and Fred Leslie brought the house down one night with an impromptu. J. L. Toole was present in a box: Leslie picked up something from the stage : " Ah ! " said he, " a good old file here—another Jail (J. L.) Tool(e) ! " He had a popular song—

> And yet all the while I've a manner and style
> Which I flatter myself must please,
> The things that I say bring Barons to bay,
> And Duchesses down on their knees.
> I am ready and smart with my hand on my heart,
> And the agony duly piled ;
> In the popular craze of bygone days
> I'm Jonathan Oscar Wild.

But the great song in " Little Jack Sheppard " was sung by the unctuous comedian, David James, famous for ever as Perkyn Middlewick in " Our Boys." On the first night of " Little Jack Sheppard," as he stepped upon the stage, Nellie Farren called out, " Brightest of ' Our Boys ' ! " To which, amid a roar of cheers, the immortal ex-butterman retorted with his famous catch-phrase, " Yer 'and, Guv'ner, yer 'and." David James was the Blueskin, and seated in an arm-

Jack Sheppard.

chair on a high table, smoking a church-warden pipe (as did Paul Bedford before him), he sang to the company in the Thieves' Kitchen, the assembled crowd of footpads and their strumpets joining in the chorus to the mellow tune of " Botany Bay "—

> Now, all my young Dookies and Duchesses,
> Take warning from what I've to say;
> Mind all is your own as you toucheses,
> Or you'll find us in Botany Bay,
> Singing,
> >   Too-ral-li, ooral-li, addity,
> Likewise
> >   Too-ral-li, ooral-li-ay,
> Equally so
> >   Too-ral-li, ooral-li, addity,
> Not forgetting
> >   Too-ral-li, ooral-li-ay.
>
> Farewell to old England for ever,
> Farewell to my rum culls as well,
> Farewell to the well-known Old Bailee,
> Where as I used for to cut such a swell.
>
> Chorus.[1]

---

[1] In "Musa Pedestris" (1896) by J. S. Farmer, Appendix II, it is stated that in "Janet Pride" "(revived by Charles Warner at the Adelphi Theatre in the early eighties) was sung the following, here given from memory"—

> Farewell to old England, the beautiful.
> Farewell to my old pals as well,
> Farewell to the famous Old Ba-i-ley (Whistle),
> Where I used for to cut sich a swell.
> Ri-chooral, ri-chooral, Oh!!!
>
> (Four more verses before "The Morrell.")
>
> Now all you young wi-counts and duchesses
> Take warning by wot I've to say,
> And mind all your own wot you touches is (Whistle),
> Or you'll jine us in Bottiny Bay. Oh!!!
> Ri-chooral, ri-chooral, ri-addiday,
> Ri-chooral, ri-chooral, iday.

In the original manuscript of "Janet Pride," which I have seen by the kind permission of the present Lord Chamberlain, the song in question does not occur. This first production of the play was licenced for 5th February, 1855, at the Adelphi Theatre, being a version of an old French drama, "*Marie Jeanne, ou la Femme du Peuple.*" Madame Céleste played the heroine. It was revived at the opening of the Princess's Theatre on 1st August, 1874, when Ben Webster appeared in his old part of Richard Pride. The third revival, mentioned by Mr. Farmer, was on 1st August, 1881, at the Adelphi Theatre, with Charles Warner as Richard Pride, H. Proctor as Black Jack, Miss Gerard as the heroine, while F. W. Irish and Clara Jecks were also in the cast. It is of course possible that the "Botany Bay" song, or something of the kind, was introduced into "Janet Pride" (for one of the scenes was laid in the Old Bailey, said to have been the first faithful and realistic representation on the stage of a Court of Justice): but it seems more probable that Mr. Farmer was confusing the song with that sung, with almost identical words, by David James in "Little Jack Sheppard" at the

In Literature and Drama.

Thus did David James in 1885 link up with John Harper as Blueskin in 1724 singing Swift's "Newgate's Garland"—"Ye Fellows of Newgate . . . and every man round me can rob as he please."

E. J. Odell, who played Sir Rowland at the Gaiety, was the ancient man who lived on to 1928, when he died a "Brother" at the Charterhouse, aged ninety-four, and who, according to the stories of his fellow-members at the Savage Club, must have been one of the rudest and most disagreeable of the human species. "Little Jack Sheppard" ran for nearly eight months—a long period for those days—when it was succeeded by "Dorothy," in September, 1886. Eight years later it was revived owing to the following circumstance.

There was produced on 12th March, 1894, at the Standard Theatre, "Old London Bridge in the Days of Jack Sheppard and Jonathan Wild," with this cast—

Jack Sheppard,	Nellie Lauraine.
Thames Darrell,	Emily Spiller.
Jonathan Wild,	Harold Hilliard.
Blueskin,	Lloyd Turrow.
Sir Rowland,	Edward Chester.
Lady Trafford, Mrs. Sheppard,	Ethel Arden.
Winifred Wood,	Rose Moncrieff.

This Jack was a vehement one, and Clement Scott wrote in *The Daily Telegraph*—

Jack with all his faults has ever been represented as a lad with a heart. He stands, therefore, on the stage not as a professional outlaw, but as the wronged child, with a touch of the devout desperado.

This critic was always interested in the various Jack Sheppard plays, and so he went on to suggest to the manager of the Gaiety Theatre

---

Gaiety Theatre in 1885. There were undoubtedly earlier versions of the words, as for instance those of a song well-known in Rutland and Wiltshire.

> Come all you young men of learning good,
>   A warning take by me.
> I'll have you quit night-walking,
>   And shun bad company . . .
> Or else you'll rue the day,
> And you will be transported
>   And go to Botany Bay.

The tune of this folk-song was used by Cecil Sharp in Granville-Barker's production of Hardy's "Dynasts" for the "Trafalgar" song. The very different tune of the "Botany Bay" song at the Gaiety was adapted by Meyer Lutz from another old melody.

Jack Sheppard.

that he should revive "Little Jack Sheppard." The advice was taken and the burlesque once more appeared on 11th August, 1894, but with only two of the original actors, Willie Warde and Frank Wood, who had been in the cast of eight years before—

Jack Sheppard,	Jessie Preston.
Jonathan Wild,	Seymour Hicks.
Blueskin,	Charles Danby.
Kneebone,	William Warde.
Owen Wood,	E. W. Royce.
Sir Rowland,	W. Cheesman.
Winifred Wood,	Ellaline Terriss.
Thames Darrell,	Amy Augarde.
Edgworth Bess,	Violet Monckton.
Mrs. Sheppard,	Lizzie Collier.
Poll Stanmore,	Florence Levey.
Captain Cuff,	Ethel Earle.
Shotbolt,	Maud Sutherland.
Little Gog and Magog,	Misses Raynor and Rossell.
Kittie Kettleby,	Georgina Preston.

But, alas! this time it was a failure and only ran for six weeks, for the taste of the public for burlesque was dead. Jessie Preston and her sister were recruits from the Halls. As Jonathan Wild, Seymour Hicks had one of his first important parts in London; he was extremely good and made false prophets of those who said he could never wear the mantle of Fred Leslie. Ellaline Terriss was delightful, as ever; but there were the memories of their great predecessors to contend with. As Miss Terriss tells, in her book of Recollections, of the first night—

What made the entire night like a subscription dance in a cemetery was the fact that Fred Leslie and David James both being dead, and that very lamp of burlesque, Nellie Farren, a hopeless cripple, all their friends who remembered their inimitable performances in the original production some nine years previously, came round between the acts to offer congratulations with streaming eyes and sobbed out: "Ah! dear old Fred." "And I remember, too, what James did so clearly." "And Nellie, who will ever forget her?" "Oh! how wonderful they all were," and so on, and so on, and so on.

It was in 1894 also that charming Kate James appeared as a dashing Jack Sheppard on the music halls, singing:

I'm the shade of Jack Sheppard, descending you know,
From the rackety times of the gay long ago,
I was King of the Dials and Lord of the Mint,
The theme of adventures that folk cannot print,
I always was ready when fun should begin
To give a smart hussy a chuck 'neath the chin.
Or I'd rid a man neatly of gold he had piled,
Smart thanks to the teaching of Jonathan Wild.

In Literature and Drama.

Chorus. Then here's to the fame of Jack Sheppard,
    Here's to the madcap boy,
Burglar and pride of the Ladies,
    Their prey and their readiest toy.
Idol of days when the people
    To the hardiest villain would bow,
Dark days that are dead—
    Do you think the world is better now

(Ending with the usual 4th verse of pathos.)

Let me paint a final picture,
Jack, with clasped and twitching hands,
At the funeral of his mother
In old Willesden churchyard stands.
In heart-broken stupor
He scarce hears friend Blueskin's warning, "Fly!
Jonathan Wild is here!" Then Jack sobs:
"Leave my mother's grave, not I!
Let them take me!" Wild has seized him!
Till the dreadful finish wait:
"I'll not struggle, for my mother's grave I will not desecrate."
Vile thief-taker Wild but mocks him,
Drags him off in brutal glee:
"Drive on lads! Hurrah for Newgate!
Half-way house for Tyburn Tree!"
Chorus.

Four years later saw the most ambitious production of all the Jack Sheppard plays, at the New Pavilion Theatre, Mile End, under the direction of Isaac Cohen. This "New Sensational Drama" was written by Joseph Hatton on the commission of Weedon Grossmith in 1896. Grossmith thought, and so did his friends, that he bore a strong resemblance in face and figure to Jack Sheppard, and both had the same short black hair. There *was* a likeness, as may be seen in the portrait of Weedon Grossmith as Jack Sheppard in the actor's book of reminiscences, "From Studio to Stage," and if he had been twenty instead of over forty the resemblance would, doubtless, have been more striking. He had long been interested in the historic youth, and he wanted to enact him on the stage as he actually was—not "the romantic milksop of Sheppard of the Stage generally played by a woman . . . it is amazing that this rough blackguard should ever have been played by one of the gentler sex." He explained his ideas of what he wanted to Joseph Hatton, who after an intensive study of criminology and the Sheppard Era was empowered to present the real, pale-faced, and agile hero of Newgate—

For a whole year I instructed Hatton in crime and criminals, and I never saw a man so thoroughly steeped in the knowledge of it. I gave two years of my life to that play, and couldn't count the number of cases of champagne that

Jack Sheppard.

were consumed at my old house at Canonbury during the very many pleasant dinners and lunches there while we were discussing crime in connection with Jack Sheppard. I am sure I never entered into anything so earnestly and ambitiously as I did in that play.

In two years' time all was ready, and with scenery painted by Bruce Smith and costumes designed by Percy Macquoid (the first work of the kind he did), the opening performance took place on 9th April, 1898. Sir Henry Irving arrived " early to assist, and received a right royal reception " (J. L. Toole was present on the last night). Here is the cast—

Jack Sheppard,	Weedon Grossmith.
Thames Darrell,	Herbert Sleath.
Blueskin,	Charles Groves.
Jonathan Wild,	Julian Cross.
Sir Rowland,	Ronald Bayne.
Edgworth Bess,	V. St. Lawrence.
Winifred Wood,	May Palfrey (Mrs. Weedon Grossmith).

Charles Groves, the Blueskin, had played that part *en burlesque* in the provincial company of " The Idle 'Prentice " twenty-eight years previously. Julian Cross as Wild gave " a fine and serious performance "; and the creation of Jack Sheppard was " entirely worthy of Mr. Grossmith and his reputation." These were the verdicts of Clement Scott, who, as I have already intimated, was deeply interested in the theatrical history of Jack Sheppard. To this production at the Pavilion Theatre he devoted two closely printed columns in *The Daily Telegraph* of 11th April, 1898, in the course of which he recalled earlier versions he had seen of the story, and said—

Mr. Hatton and Mr. Cohen, with their artistic assistants, have striven to do for Harrison Ainsworth what Gillray and Rowlandson and George Cruikshank did for Pierce Egan. They have snatched " Jack Sheppard " from the travesty-mongers and restored him to his lawful place in the ranks of the legitimate drama.

Weedon Grossmith undoubtedly gave a most virile and artistic performance, for Joseph Hatton, when the play was converted into a novel, " When Rogues Fall Out," rightly dedicated it to the actor " in recognition of Artistic Effort to Impersonate on the Stage ' the real Jack Sheppard.' " And John Coleman thought that Weedon Grossmith would never require another part, so admirably was he suited as Jack, and that the play would go on interminably in the provinces. The sad truth is that " Jack Sheppard " only ran for three weeks and ended for ever on 30th April, 1898. It is a biting commentary on public appreciation of true art that a drama, which was immensely successful when aided by the factitious cleverness of middle-aged women, such

In Literature and Drama.

as Mrs. Keeley and Nellie Farren, absurdly aping a boy, was a dead failure when presented in a serious, sincere, and realistic manner by a first-rate actor, equipped both mentally and physically to give vraisemblance to the creation. Weedon Grossmith was bitterly disappointed at the failure of all his efforts, study, and hard work. It had been intended that the run at the Pavilion should merely be a trial one, and that the piece would in due course be transferred to a large West-end theatre, when financial backing was promised by the "Boxing" Marquis of Queensberry, George Singer of Coventry, and a clergyman who remains nameless! But the collapse at the Pavilion ruined all plans; later on, either a large theatre or capital was unavailable, and, finally, when both might be had, Weedon Grossmith realised he no longer possessed the youth and strength essential for the part of Jack. So ended many bright hopes.

It was strange, at any rate, that the play did not run longer in Mile End, where so many criminals and "Rippers" are supposed to dwell. Isaac Cohen, the manager of the Pavilion, knew all Whitechapel and numbered most of its thieves among the patrons of his theatre. He was robbed of a valuable presentation watch. He complained of his loss one night from the stage before the curtain went up, and his Gallery-ites shouted back to him: "It wasn't us, sir; but we'll get the watch back for yer, Guv'nor." And they did. The stolen article was returned to Cohen a few days later, which was quite in the tradition of the methods of Jonathan Wild.

The East End had another glimpse of Jack Sheppard a year later, 1899, when "Jack Sheppard, or the Burglary at the Grange," was put on at the Bow Palace of Varieties.

At the Victoria, Broughton, was produced on Monday, 8th May, 1911, "The New Jack Sheppard," with the following cast:—

Jack Sheppard,	William Melvyn.
Jonathan Wild,	C. D. Pitt.
Largo, the hunchback,	A. Britton.
Sir Neville Montague,	C. Russell.
Blueskin,	C. R. Roberts.
Winifred Wood,	Cora Patey.
Mrs. Sheppard,	Cissie St. Elmo.

This play took fresh liberties with poor Mrs. Sheppard. As the heiress of the Montague (Trenchard in Ainsworth) estates, Jonathan Wild is resolved to marry her. She eventually dies from fright of his violence. Wild is drowned in the river by Largo, who then commits suicide in the same handy stream, while Jack Sheppard "throws his

Jack Sheppard.

sword after them, and so buries the past life," for he has already received the King's Pardon.

Finally, we come to the latest representation of " Jack Sheppard " at the Elephant and Castle Theatre, London, on 30th April, 1928. This piece, which ran for some weeks, the last performance taking place on Saturday, 2nd June, appropriately synchronised with the end of the old theatre, for this was the last production before its demolition: fifty-five years before it had opened with another version of " Jack Sheppard," and the same drama was put on there on 27th November, 1886. The piece as played in 1928 was written by Matt Wilkinson and followed the traditional lines of the original plays, though both actors and audiences were, apparently, more thin-skinned than their predecessors of 1839, for the following notice appeared in the papers—

Sidney Barnard announces that, in deference to numerous requests, he has discarded the coffin on which Jack Sheppard sits when on his last journey to Tyburn. Members of the Elephant cast have, it seems, expressed their immense relief afforded them by its departure.

This cast of sensibility was as follows:—

Jack Sheppard,	Peter Spagnoletti.
Thames Darrell,	Keith Beer.
Jonathan Wild,	J. Edwards Martin.
Blueskin,	Norman Leyland.
Owen Wood,	H. Ryeland Leigh.
Sir Rowland,	Bernard Benoliel.
Mrs. Wood,	Lillian Drake.
Winifred Wood,	Nancy Poultney.
Edgworth Bess,	Dorothy Mead.
Poll Maggot,	Nellie Hook.
Lady Trafford, Mrs. Sheppard,	Cecily Davies.

Peter Spagnoletti was one of the best of Jack Sheppards—perhaps the best of all—for, as far as I know, he was the only young actor who has ever played the strenuous part at the right age, twenty, and consequently his was a performance of boyish vim and agility, high spirits, yet with the right hint at times of that wistful pathos which was so essential a quality of the original, while his short, slight figure was entirely in the picture of Jack Sheppard's physical aspect. Norman Leyland sang " Jolly Nose " with the gusto of the traditional Blueskin. Miss Dorothy Mead, an energetic lady in the style of the Halls, gave an excellent conception of Edgworth Bess, vivid and voluptuous like the original, and her " introduced " song, " I am what I am, and I don't care a damn," was very popular. While Miss Lillian Drake, as Mrs.

Peter Spagnoletti as Jack Sheppard at the Elephant and Castle
Theatre, May, 1928

Copyright Photograph by Claude Harris, 122 Regent Street, W.1

In Literature and Drama.

Wood, when murdered most realistically by Blueskin, vented the most petrifying death-screech ever heard upon the stage: it was a wonderful piece of acting, and a century ago would have brought into action a whole crop of budding Courvoisiers from the New Kent Road.

As I have already pointed out, Jack Sheppard never was a murderer, and for that matter, Blueskin the actual never murdered Mrs. Wood. That incident was one of Ainsworth's dramatic additions, just as he introduced various scenes at Willesden and caused Jack Sheppard to be buried in the churchyard there. But in verity Jack Sheppard was never in Willesden for the purposes of theft, so far as we know, or burial; neither did his old master live at Dollis Hill, nor Mrs. Wood suffer murder at that pretty red-tiled Neasden farmstead. Ainsworth wielded a picturesque but powerful pen, and he so entwined fact and fiction that he has caused to trip later writers who have superficially dealt with this subject. Thus in *The Daily Telegraph* of 8th April, 1898, there was an article entitled "Last London Landmark of Jack Sheppard." The writer assumed an *ex cathedra* air of omniscience. He spoke of the "misguided pen of Harrison Ainsworth," but proceeded to accept as fact whatever romantic additions that writer had made to the life of Jack Sheppard, who, he goes on to say, generally selected "Finchley, Willesden, and Dollis Hill for his fields of adventure"! He also accepted Ainsworth's perversion that Jack's father had been executed at Tyburn, whereas that entirely respectable man had died early when his children were very young. Mrs. Sheppard was a widow, but never "the hempen widow" as portrayed by her countless stage impersonators of both sexes.

In 1907 a correspondent in *Notes and Queries* stated that Ainsworth had restored the grave of Jack Sheppard in Willesden Churchyard sixty years ago (1847). There was, it is true, a John Sheppard buried there in 1559, and Ainsworth may have put his tomb in repair for conscience sake, because in 1839, when half London came out to look at the wooden monument—two posts supporting a plank—which the novelist had imaginatively described as marking Jack's grave, the ancient sexton of Willesden cut off and sold little pieces of the wood to souvenir-hunters, his own fortune increasing as the wood-work decreased. As related earlier in this work, Jack Sheppard was buried in the graveyard of the Workhouse of St. Martin's-in-the-Fields, where his bones were discovered in 1866; the human remains from this spot were reinterred at Brookwood Cemetery, Surrey.

Ainsworth placed various scenes of his romance in Willesden for the reason that in "Jack Sheppard" he was writing what he called "another specimen of the *novela picaresca*." A picaresque novel sug-

Jack Sheppard.

gests vagabondage and the open road, so obviously he could not keep his characters to the Strand and Newgate. Rural scenes being necessary, Ainsworth naturally described those at Willesden, where he lived at the time he was writing and which was then a lovely sylvan district. Thus it came about that the locality obtained the name of " The Jack Sheppard Country." Ten years later Maclise wrote to Forster: " I certainly told them you were at a picturesque cottage in a green lane somewhere in the country of Jack Sheppard . . . in pastoral Willesden."

Probably no houses actually associated with Jack Sheppard still exist, though several were standing less than forty years ago. Owen Wood's dwelling and the courts off Wych Street, so well known to Jack, were swept away in 1900-03 when the Strand was widened and Aldwych built.[2] The " Black Jack " Tavern was demolished in 1896. It stood in Portsmouth Street; and a man, who was still living in the early part of the nineteenth century, had in his youth seen Jack Sheppard drop from an upper window of this house into the street when escaping on one occasion from Jonathan Wild and his myrmidons.[3] The " Black Lion " Tavern in Newton Street, where Jack first went to ruin with Edgworth Bess, stood until 1880. A rookery in Fulwood's Rents was mentioned in the Police Courts in December, 1905, as a dangerous human rabbit-warren off Holborn, and it was stated that its big fireplace had served as a means of escape for Jack Sheppard. That tradition has not been authenticated, but it is quite likely that the large kitchen of this house, 36 feet long, was such a one as depicted by Dickens as the Thieves' Kitchen in " Oliver Twist," for as these houses in Fulwood's Rents had communicating basements there was easy means of escape when arrest threatened. In 1907 a house described as " Jack Sheppard's " in the Mint, Southwark, was pulled down, but the associations of Jack and his mother with this district are the creation of Ainsworth.

So it is, there is scarcely a tangible relic of Jack Sheppard left. It is over two hundred years since he and his black crape mask and his iron bar vanished from the mortal scene, but he still lives on, vivid and visible, by the power of the pen and the scenes and spoken word of the theatre. There is some truth in Defoe's apothegm that Jack was " a Creature something more than Man, a Protoeus, Supernatural."

---

[2] Two fine mantelpieces from the house believed to have been occupied by Owen Wood were purchased by Mr. Walter T. Spencer, who had them placed in his residence, Grange House, Shanklin. Mr. Spencer had also purchased an old beam from Wych Street on which was carved " Jack Sheppard," but this was later claimed by the local authorities: where it is now I have not been able to discover.

[3] See " Last London Landmark of Jack Sheppard " (which it was not), *The Daily Telegraph*, 8th April, 1898.

Wych Street

From a drawing by J. H. Shepheard, 1853, in the British Museum

BIBLIOGRAPHY OF JACK SHEPPARD.

I.

CONTEMPORARY NEWSPAPERS (1723-4).

1. *The Original Weekly Journal.* A Whig newspaper, printed and sold by John Applebee, a little below Bridewell in Blackfriars. Probably the best of its kind, for Daniel Defoe was a principal contributor. Applebee died in Bolt Court, Fleet Street, 20th January, 1750.

2. *The Weekly Journal, or Saturday's Post.* August-November, 1724. A Tory newspaper, printed and published in Great Carter Lane by Nathaniel Mist, a notorious marplot, who was sentenced to the pillory and three months' imprisonment for "scandalous" reflections on George I. He died in 1737.

3. *The Weekly Journal, or British Gazetteer.* A Whig newspaper, printed and published by J. Read.

4. *The Daily Journal.* A Tory daily newspaper, published by John Applebee, along with his *Original Weekly Journal*, but printed by T. Warner.

5. *The British Journal.* A daily newspaper printed by T. Warner. The verses "To Sir James Thornhill on his picture of Jack Sheppard" were in the issue for 28th November, 1724, and "A Dialogue between Julius Cæsar and Jack Sheppard" appeared on 4th December, 1725.

6. *The Daily Post.* Printed by C. Meere in the Old Bailey.

7. *The London Journal.* A Whig newspaper, printed by W. Wilkins.

8. *The Daily Courant.*

9. *Parker's London News.* Published on Monday, Wednesday, and Friday. "The Letter to Jack Ketch" was in the issue for 7th September, and in October, 1724, appeared the apochryphal "Letter from Jack Sheppard to his Mother."

10. *The Dublin Gazette.*

There is a complete file of *Applebee's Weekly Journal* in the Bodleian Library, Oxford. That in the Newspaper Room at the British Museum is imperfect. In all the above newspapers there are innumerable paragraphs about Jack Sheppard, which throw much light upon his adventures.

II.

TRACTS AND BIOGRAPHIES.

CONTEMPORARY AND EARLY NINETEENTH CENTURY.

1. "The History of the remarkable Life of John Sheppard," containing a particular account of his many Robberies and Escapes . . . London: Printed and Sold by John Applebee in Black Fryers, J. Isted at the Golden Ball near Chancery Lane in Fleet Street, and the Booksellers of London and Westminster. (Price One Shilling. Published 19th October, 1724.)

Jack Sheppard.

William Lee, the biographer of Defoe, had no hesitation in assigning this tract to the author of "Robinson Crusoe." With greater caution the late Thomas Seccombe, in "The Dictionary of National Biography," under "Jack Sheppard," attributed it to "one of Mr. Applebee's garreteers."

2. "A Narrative of all the Robberies, Escapes, &c. . . . of John Sheppard," giving an Exact description of the Manner of his Wonderful Escape from the Castle at Newgate, and the Methods he took afterward for his Security. Written by himself during his Conefinement in the Middle Stone-Room, after his being retaken in Drury Lane. To which is Prefix'd A true Representation of his escape from the Condemn'd Hold, curiously engraven on a Copper Plate. The whole Publish'd at the Particular Request of the Prisoner. The Third Edition. London: Printed and Sold by John Applebee a little below Bridewell Bridge, in Black Fryers. 1724. Price Six Pence.

Probably this tract was written by Daniel Defoe.

3. "A Narrative of all the Robberies, Escapes, &c., of John Sheppard." Giving an Exact description of the manner of his Wonderful Escape from the Castle of Newgate . . . Dublin, 8vo. 1724.

4. "Authentic Memoirs of the Life and Surprising Adventures of John Sheppard," who was executed at Tyburn, November 16th, 1724. By way of Familiar Letters from a Gentleman in Town to his Friend in the Country. The Second and Correspondent Edition. Adorn'd with a Variety of Copper Cuts. London: Printed for Joseph Marshall at the Bible in Newgate Street, 1724. Price Bound 1s.

5. "Harlequin Sheppard." A Night Scene in Grotesque Characters as it is performed at the Theatre Royal in Drury Lane. By John Thurmond, dancing Master. With new scenes Painted from the Real Places of Action. To which is prefixed an Introduction, giving an account of Sheppard's Life. With a curious Frontispiece representing Harlequin Sheppard. London: Printed and Sold by J. Roberts in Warwick Lane and A. Dodd at the Peacock without Temple Bar. 1724. Price 6d.

6. "Sheppard in Egypt, or News from the Dead." 5th Edition. 1724.

7. "The Life and Adventures of Jack Sheppard executed at Tyburn." London, 1724.

8. "The History of the Remarkable Life of John Sheppard," Being a particular Account of his many Robberies and Escapes, was "to be had at the Printing Offices in Stamford." About 1724.

9. "The History of the Lives of Jonathan Wild, Thief Taker, Joseph Blake, alias Bleuskin, Footpad, and John Sheppard, Housebreaker," Giving a full and Exact Account of Jonathan's being Crown'd King of the Gypsies . . . as also a true Relation of the Pranks Jack Sheppard played and of his being Retaken. Taken from several Papers found since Jonathan's Death with Letters and Private Confessions to Friends never yet published. The Third Edition: London. Printed for Edw. Midwinter at the Three Crowns and Looking Glass in St. Paul's Churchyard. N.D. (1725?).

There is a quaint portrait of each of the three criminals, and at the end is the Canting Dictionary of Jonathan Wild.

10. "The Prison Breaker, or the Adventures of John Sheppard." A Farce as Intended to be acted at the Theatre Royal in Lincoln's-Inn-Fields . . . London: Printed for A. Moore near St. Paul's. MDCCXXV.

Bibliography.

This work was reproduced, with additions and new songs written or arranged by John Watts, as

"The Quaker's Opera," as it is Perform'd at Lee's and Harper's Great Theatrical Booth in Bartholomew Fair. With the Musick prefix'd to each Song. London: Printed for J. W.; and Sold by J. Roberts in Warwick Lane; A. Dodd, at the Peacock without Temple Bar; and E. Nutt and E. Smith at the Royal Exchange. 1728. Price 1s.

The copy at the British Museum (82 c. 48) bears the signature of "Thos. Walker," the actor who played the part of Jack Sheppard in the opera.

11. "An Epistle from Jack Sheppard to the late L . . D C . . . . . LL . R of E . . . . . D, who when Sheppard was try'd, sent for him to the Chancery Bar."

A broadside ballad of eleven verses in triple rhyme, set to the tune of "Which no Body can deny." Folio. 1725.

12. "A Dialogue between Julius Cæsar and Jack Sheppard." This appeared in *The British Journal*, Saturday, 4th December, 1725, a daily newspaper printed by T. Warner.

13. "La Vie et Les Vols du fameux Jean Sheppard," qui fut exécuté le 5 Decembre (*sic*) dernier à Londres. Avec une exacte Relation des moyens surprenants qu'il employa pour s'évader des prisons, et entr'autres des formidables Cachots de Newgate. Traduit de l'Anglois d'après la sixième édition. Amsterdam: Chez Guillaume Barents, Libraire sur le Vooburgwal, vis-à-vis le Nieuwe-Straat. MDCCXXV.

14. "Select Trials" . . . at the Sessions House in the Old Bailey. From the year 1720-1724 inclusive. London: Printed for J. Wilford behind the Chapter House in St. Paul's Churchyard. 1734. Vol. I, pp. 433-6, 440-5.

Press Mark. British Museum: 6495 a.a.a. 14.

15. "The Bloody Register." A Select and Judicious Collection of the Most Remarkable Trials . . . From the year 1700 to the year 1764 inclusive. London: Printed for E. and M. Viney in Ivy Lane, near Paternoster Row . . . MDCCLXIV.

Fifty pages are devoted to "Memoirs of the Life and Surprizing Exploits of Jack Sheppard, convicted of Burglary."

16. "Geschichte zweyer berüchtigten Strassenräuber Johann Sheppard" . . . Aus dem Englischen und Französischen ubersetzt . . . Dritte Auflage pp. 126. Frankfurt und Leipzig. 1765.

With a fine engraving of Johann Sheppard and a companion leaving a building in order to enter a waiting coach. River beyond under a dark sky with crescent moon: a most romantic picture.

17. "The Tyburn Chronicle, or Villainy Displayed." From the year 1700 to the Present Time. London: T. Cooke at Shakespeare Head in Paternoster Row. 1768. Four volumes. Vol. II, p. 97.

18. "The Annals of Newgate." By the Rev. Mr. Villette, Ordinary of Newgate, and Others. London, 1776. Four volumes. Vol. I, p. 253.

19. "The Criminal Recorder." 1804. Four volumes. Vol. II, pp. 365-377.

20. "The Newgate Calendar." By William Jackson. 1818. Vol. I, pp. 392-410.

21. "Portraits of Remarkable Persons from the Revolution in 1688." By James Caulfield. 1819. Vol. II, pp. 158, 167.

Jack Sheppard.

22. "The Newgate Calendar Improved." By George Theodore Wilkinson. Manchester: Published by J. Gleave, Deansgate, 1819. Vol. I, pp. 301-314. With an engraving of Thornhill's portrait of Jack Sheppard.

23. "The Newgate Calendar." By Andrew Knapp and William Baldwin. 1824-1828.

24. "Celebrated Trials." By George Borrow. London: Printed for Geo. Knight and Lacey, Paternoster Row. 1825. In six volumes. Vol. III, pp. 375-389.

25. "Der Neue Pitaval." Leipzig: Brockhaus. 1845. "John Sheppard" in Vol. 8, 30 pages. Contains German translation of No. 12, *ante*.

III.

PLATES.

1. "Jack Sheppard's Three Fatal Stages." This is an engraved plate, measuring 9½ by 14 inches, of contemporary date, probably 1724. There are three designs, with verses below:

A. *Going to Westminster Hall.*

> John Sheppard through these various
> Scenes has past,
> Been taken, 'scaped, retaken, tryd and Cast
> And at Westminster Ordered to appear,
> His final Charge and Dreadfull Doom to hear.

B. *Remanding back to Newgate.*

> His Sentence past, and he ordained to Die,
> He was sent back to Prison Instantly.
> And from that time in Newgate forced to stay,
> Loaded with Irons, till the fatal Day.

C. *Place of Execution.*

> To Close the Scene of all his Actions he,
> Was brought from Newgate to the fatal Tree.
> And then his Life resigned, his race is run,
> And Tyburn ends what wickedness begun.

I am indebted to the Reverend Montague Summers for the description of this rare plate, the only known copy of which is preserved in a folio volume of miscellaneous engravings at the Bodleian Library (Press Mark: Gough Maps. 46. fo. 230).

2. "Green's Diorama in *Jack Sheppard*." London: J. K. Green, 34, Lambeth Square, New Cut. Price Halfpenny. Sold by J. Redington, 208, Hoxton Old Town. This production was issued in single sheets, No. 3, published 26th December, 1839, shows a company of mounted men, presumably escorting Jack Sheppard to Execution.

IV.

MANUSCRIPTS.

1. State Papers domestic (1724). Bundle 56, f. 129. Public Record Office.
2. Add. MS. 36, 135, f. 87.
3. Add. MSS. 27, 826. MSS. of Francis Place.
4. Gaol delivery Rolls, Newgate (1724), Westminster Guildhall.
5. Registers of St. Dunstan's Church, Stepney.

Bibliography.

V.
LATER PUBLICATIONS, INCLUDING ROMANCES.

1. "The Life and Adventures of Jack Sheppard," the Notorious Housebreaker, With a Particular Account of his Extraordinary Prison Escapes. Reprinted from an Authentic History compiled shortly after his Execution at Tyburn. [Woodcut.] Published by C. Strange, Paternoster Row . . . and sold by all venders (sic) of Periodicals. Eight Pages. Price One Penny. Part of a series called The Universal Pamphleteer. No date (1820-30?).

2. "The Life and Exploits of Jack Sheppard," A Notorious Housebreaker and Footpad. Thomas Richardson, Derby; Simpkin Marshall and Co., London; S. Horsey, Portsea, and all other Booksellers. Price sixpence. Twenty-four pages. Green paper covers. No date (1829-30?).

3. "The Life of Jack Sheppard," A Notorious Housebreaker and Footpad. London: Printed for T. and J. Allman, 55, Great Queen Street, Lincoln's Inn Fields, 1829. With a coloured plate.

4. Bysh's Edition. "The Life of Jack Sheppard," A Notorious Housebreaker and Footpad. London: J. Bysh, 8, Cloth Fair, West Smithfield. No date (1830?).

Stated to be "Embellished with four coloured engravings." But the copy at the British Museum has one folding coloured plate with five scenes, the characters wearing dress of Mr. Pickwick's style.

5. "Jack Sheppard," A Romance, by William Harrison Ainsworth, was first issued serially in "Bentley's Miscellany," January, 1839, to February, 1840. With twenty-seven illustrations by George Cruikshank.

First book edition: "Jack Sheppard." A Romance. By W. Harrison Ainsworth, Esq., Author of "Rookwood" and "Crichton." With (27) Illustrations by George Cruikshank. In Three Volumes. London: Richard Bentley, New Burlington Street. 1839 (October). There are also two woodcuts by Cruikshank and a portrait of Ainsworth by R. J. Lane. Dark green cloth, yellow end papers. Tall medium crown octavo.

The most valuable form of this romance is in the Fifteen Weekly Shilling Parts which were published in 1840 by Bentley, and printed by T. Brettell, Rupert Street, Haymarket. These have the 27 illustrations by George Cruikshank and Lane's portrait of Ainsworth. The buff covers have a modified design of the plate "The Name on the Beam," and the actual title simulates the uneven way in which "Jack Sheppard" was carved on the beam. A good set of the Parts is now worth £100, though the original price was but 15s. A later rough issue of "Jack Sheppard," with Cruikshank's illustrations, in forty-four Penny Numbers by Henry Vickers, Angel Court, Strand, is also a very scarce work, dating from 1858. There have been very many editions of "Jack Sheppard" in other years, and it may safely be concluded that this romance has always been available in print, in some form or other, for what is now (1933) a period only six years short of a century.

6. "The History of Jack Sheppard: His Wonderful Exploits and Escapes." A Romance Founded on Facts. With Original Illustrations from Drawings by Jack Sketch. [A design of fetters, etc.] London: John Williams, 49, Paternoster Row, and 43, Aldersgate, 1839. Marble-paper boards, half-front in green leather. There are ten illustrations and a rough reproduction of Sir James Thornhill's portrait of Jack Sheppard.

Jack Sheppard.

This was the first of the audacious imitations of Ainsworth's romance, using many of his scenes and characters, and it was brought out later in the same year that witnessed the birth of his "Jack Sheppard," 1839.

Second Edition: "The Life and Adventures of Jack Sheppard." By Lincoln Fortescue, Esq., New Edition with numerous additions. Illustrated with twelve plates. "Truth is stranger than fiction."—Byron. London: James Cochrane, 128, Chancery Lane, 1845. Brown cloth boards, with pictorial designs in gold on the spine. This edition is not in the British Museum, and I am indebted to Mr. Walter T. Spencer, of 27, New Oxford Street, London, for the use of a copy and also for other interesting matter in his collection relating to Jack Sheppard.

7. "The Life and Adventures of Jack Sheppard, Dick Morris, William Nevison, and Sawney Beane," Notorious Thieves and Highwaymen. Manchester: Published and sold by William Willis and all Booksellers. 1839. With an engraving by J. Stephenson of "Jack Shepherd" (sic) breaking out of prison.

8. "The Life and Adventures of Jack Sheppard." [Woodcut.] J. Wrigley, Miller Street, Manchester. With six quaint woodcuts. Eight pages. Green paper covers. No date (1840?).

9. "The Life and Surprising Exploits of Jack Sheppard." The cover has the variation: Printed by S. & J. Keys, Devonport. "The Life and Adventures of Jack Sheppard." Eight pages. Blue paper cover, with picture. There are five other lurid woodcuts with the characters dressed in the style of Mr. Mantalini. No date (1840?).

10. "The Life and Surprising Exploits of that Notorious Housebreaker and Footpad Jack Sheppard," containing his wonderful Escapes from Newgate and other Prisons. To which is added his own Account of Himself as he left it in Manuscript for Publication. London: Printed and sold by J. Bailey, 116 Chancery Lane, and may be had of most booksellers. Price Sixpence.

With a frontispiece in colours.

11. "Jack Sheppard," by Obadiah Throttle. In One Volume. "In a box of the Stone Jug I was born, Of a hempen widow the kid forlorn, Fake Away." W. H. Ainsworth. London: Published at No. 11 Catharine Street, Strand. (1839-40.)

Illustrated with crude woodcuts.

12. "Life of Jack Sheppard the Housebreaker." London: Glover, Water Lane, Fleet Street. 1840.

In the Illustrated Library of Romance. This work was one of the frank imitations of Ainsworth's tale.

13. "Jack Sheppard" for the Juvenile Drama and Toy Theatre, running to about 48 sheets, was adapted from "the new and singularly graphic, melodramatic, and panoramic adaptation of 'Jack Sheppard'" by J. T. Haines, produced at the Royal Surrey Theatre on 21st October, 1839.

This work was issued in 1840 by Green and Slee, who originally had their Theatrical Print Warehouse at 5, Artillery Lane, Bishopsgate. The Reverend Montague Summers states that T. K. Green (1790-1860) is believed to have been the first publisher of plays for performance with toy theatres, his earliest imprint being dated February, 1811.

14. "The Life and Surprising Exploits of Jack Sheppard." Otley: Printed and published by William Walker.

Bibliography.

Another edition was issued by Fairburn, 110, Minories, with four illustrations in colours.

15. "Life and Singular Adventures of Jack Sheppard." London: Printed for G. Bladon, at 3, Paternoster Row. Price Eighteenpence.

16. "The Life and Exploits of Jack Sheppard," The Notorious Housebreaker and Footpad. Sydney: Printed, published, and sold by Edmund Mason, George Street South. Price Sixpence. Twenty-two pages. On the pink paper cover is "The Original Edition." No date (1845?).

17. "The Life of Jack Sheppard," The Notorious House and Gaol Breaker. Newcastle-on-Tyne: Bowman, Publisher, Nun's Lane. Price One Penny. Twenty-four pages. Woodcut on cover of a drinking-bar of the period 1840-50. No date (1850?).

18. "Charley Wag, The New Jack Sheppard," A New and Intensely Exciting Real Life Romance. Illustrated by R. Prowse. London: United Kingdom Press, 28, Brydges Street, Strand. 1860-1861. Published in Penny Numbers with green covers. Also issued in Monthly Parts. The Advertisement observes: "In this work . . . will be found the most graphic and reliable pictures of hitherto unknown phases of the Dark Side of London Life . . . rendered in stern, truthful language by one who has studied, in all its blackest enormity, the doings of secret crime."

Mr. Montague Summers thinks it possible this work was by G. A. Sala, and states that the late G. R. Sims committed himself to the assertion that "The two worst books I ever knew were 'Charley Wag' and 'The Woman with Yellow Hair.'" Mr. Sims would presumably have been even more shocked by "Fanny White and her Friend, Jack Rawlings," A Romance of a Young Lady Thief and a Boy Burglar, by the Author of "Charley Wag." With Twenty-one Original Illustrations. London: George Vickers, Angel Court, Strand, N.D. (1865?).

The origin of the name "Charley Wag" in this connection is not known. It was in use before 1860, the date of "The New Jack Sheppard," for there was a character of that name in the extravaganza of "The Seven Champions of Christendom," by J. R. Planché, produced at the Lyceum Theatre on 9th April, 1849. St. George (played by Miss Kathleen Fitzwilliam) had in attendance on him Charley Wag, Esq., enacted by Charles Mathews, who sang a number—

"In a jingling, chiming, crambo rhyming,
Pattery, chattery, what can it mattery
Charley Wag sort of a song"——

exemplifying the metre and triple rhyme so coolly appropriated in later years by W. S. Gilbert.

19. "Edgeworth Bess, or Shephard in Danger," No. 2 of The Blueskin Series issued by Robert M. de Witt: New York, No. 13, Frankfort Street, 1867. Each number complete. 100 pages. Price 25 cents.

The same publisher produced The Black Bess Series, The Claude Duval Series, The Nightshade Series, and the Jonathan Wild Series, No. 8 in the last named being "The Bleeding Phantom, or Wild in Fetters," in pictorial boards, 1867.

20. "The Real Life and Times of Jack Sheppard." Complete Edition. One Shilling. Beautifully Illustrated with Woodcuts. London: Newsagents' Publishing Company, 147, Fleet Street. No date (1866-8?).

This account is much copied from Ainsworth's romance, with scenes in Willesden, a place with which Sheppard had no association in reality.

Jack Sheppard.

21. "Blueskin," A Romance of the Last Century. By the Author of "Black Bess, or the Knight of the Road." With one hundred and fifty-seven Original Illustrations. London: E. Harrison, Salisbury Square, Fleet Street. No date (1867-8).

The author of this long book of 753 chapters, with 1259 pages of double columns in smallest type, was Edward Viles. The illustrations by R. Prowse are most remarkable and have caused this work to be much sought after by collectors of "Fierce Novels," as the old "Bloods" and "Shockers" are now called. But "Blueskin" is an exceedingly scarce book, and only four copies have been noted, one of these selling for £20. A perfect copy is in the collection of Mr. Montague Summers, who, apropos of the fact that Jack Sheppard is the hero of this book which does not bear his name on the title-page, has observed to me—

From 1839 onwards there were well-nigh innumerable romances and stories of the cheaper kind with Jack Sheppard as hero. The fact that his adventures were considered to have been so immoral an influence caused many of these books to be published surreptitiously, and the works connected with the "Sheppard Saga" are the rarest of these very scarce "Bloods" and "Shockers." The most important is "Blueskin." There was a series, "Jack Sheppard in France"; "Jack Sheppard in Italy"; "Jack Sheppard in America" (Red Indians); "Jack Sheppard in Spain" (Brigands): but these are late, about 1880-1890, and poor stuff. I fancy "Tyburn Dick," the Boy King of the Highwaymen, a Hogarth House romance, gave the adventures of Jack Sheppard's son. Jonathan Wild appears in the romance. Tyburn Dick's mother is a lady of bluest blood, and in the end he inherits vast estates. There are other Jack Sheppard romances. Sometimes the name is changed entirely (I suppose because "Jack Sheppard" was so dangerous) and he becomes "Bob Chance" as in "A Boy Burglar."

"Blueskin" was issued first in penny weekly parts, and with No. 95 was "presented gratis an authentic full-length portrait of Jack Sheppard. Observe. This portrait is beautifully printed in colours and has been copied from the painting by Sir James Thornhill."

Edward Viles's second and even more successful romance, "Black Bess, or the Knight of the Road," which had a circulation of two million copies a week in 1867 and was dramatised, was written concurrently with "Blueskin," for a notice in the latter work states: "Now publishing by the author of 'Blueskin' an Intensely Interesting Life of Dick Turpin entitled 'Black Bess, or the Knight of the Road.' With No. 107 will be presented a faithful full-length portrait. Observe. The portrait is beautifully printed in colours and has been copied from the print in the Library of the British Museum." There were 254 penny numbers of "Black Bess," which consequently was appearing during a period of nearly five years, but before its serial completion the story was published in book form by E. Harrison, Salisbury Court, Fleet Street, with the Preface dated 18th March, 1868.

This prolific Edward Viles was, presumably, the writer of the same name who collaborated with F. J. Furnivall in "The Fraternity of Vacabondes" (1869) and "The Rogues and Vagabonds of Shakspere's Youth."

Another Dick Turpin "Blood," now much sought after by collectors for its fine plates in colour, is "The Blue Dwarf: A Tale of Love, Mystery, and Crime. Introducing many Startling Incidents in the Life of that Celebrated Highwayman, Dick Turpin." By Percy B. St. John. London: Hogarth House, Bouverie Street,

Bibliography.

E.C. No date, but presumably published about 1875. The author wrote considerably under the influence of Ainsworth, and many years earlier Percy Bolingbroke St. John (1821-89) had dedicated his book, "The Trapper's Bride," A Tale of the Rockies, 1845, to W. H. Ainsworth, "in very sincere admiration of your genius."

22. "When Rogues Fall Out." A Romance of Old London. By Joseph Hatton. London : C. Arthur Pearson, Limited, Henrietta Street, W.C. 1899.

Dedicated to Weedon Grossmith "In Token of a Life-long Friendship and in Recognition of Artistic Effort to Impersonate on the Stage 'the real Jack Sheppard.'"

Frontispiece of Edgworth Bess, Ellaline Wood, and Dolly Cooke. Maroon covers. This story was later issued by the same publisher in yellow paper covers bearing an illustration of Jack Sheppard escaping from prison.

23. "Jack Sheppard" Tales were a series published in Penny Numbers during 1904-5-6 by The Aldine Publishing Company, 1-2-3, Crown Court, Chancery Lane, E.C. Numbers 1 to 24 are at the British Museum, and at the end of No. 24 is the notice that "25-28 of the 'Jack Sheppard' Tales will be announced in due course." Each number contained a complete tale with illustrations and was bound in pictorial coloured paper-covers. Although crude, these stories provide much exciting, mysterious, and ghostly incident; and the topographical descriptions of old London and the adjacent country are well done in the style of G. W. M. Reynolds, one very dramatic episode being the removal of the bodies of some malefactors from the gibbets that stood in the marshlands of the Thames east of the City.

24. "A New Jack Sheppard." By Ernest Treeton. Author of "The Instigator," "The Saving of Christian Sergison," "The Goring Mystery," etc., etc. London : George Routledge and Sons, Limited, Broadway House, Ludgate Hill. 1906. Price Six pence, in paper covers with picture of men in a boat on the river near old London Bridge. This book uses scenes and characters, such as Thames Darrell, from Ainsworth's romance.

25. "The Adventures of Jack Sheppard." A stirring Story of the Wonderful Escapades of the Most Amazing Boy in History, by A. C. Marshall, forming Numbers 1-13 of the "Black Bess" Library, 1921. London : George Newnes, Southampton Street. "Jack Sheppard at Bay" (The Sequel Serial), by A. C. Marshall, forming Numbers 14-24 of the "Black Bess" Library, 1922. London : George Newnes. Price 2d. With Illustrations by Glossop.

26. "Jack Sheppard." The Notorious Highwayman. Printed and Published by E. Lane, 21, South Street, Islington, N.1. Eight pages in pink covers with picture, and three other illustrations by D. Taylor.

This brochure was sold outside the Elephant and Castle Theatre at the time "Jack Sheppard" was performed there during the early summer of 1928—over two hundred years after the death of Jack Sheppard.

VI.

MISCELLANEOUS.

1. "The Dictionary of National Biography." Memoir written by Thomas Seccombe.

2. "Encyclopædia Britannica."

Jack Sheppard.

3. "Notes and Queries," 2 Series, XII, p. 392; 8 Series, pp. 77, 81, 264; 10 Series, VIII, p. 452; IX, pp. 56, 173.

4. "London Past and Present," Wheatley and Cunningham. I, p. 407; II, pp. 388, 478; III, pp. 111, 190, 415.

5. "The History of the Press Yard." A. Moor, St. Paul's Churchyard, 1717.

6. "An Accurate description of Newgate." London: T. Warner, 1724.

7. "Old Bailey Sessions Papers," 1716-1727: Inner Temple Library.

8. "The Historical Register," 1724. Pp. 38, 49.

9. "The Political State of Great Britain," T. Cooper, Paternoster Row, 1724. XXVIII, pp. 388-9, 392, 516.

10. "Lives of the Most Remarkable Criminals." Three volumes. John Osborn, at the Golden Ball, in Paternoster Row. 1735.

11. "A Biographical History of England," being a continuation of the Rev. J. Grainger's work by the Rev. Mark Noble, 1806. III, pp. 474, 475.

12. "The Retrospective Review," 1823. VII, pp. 273-278.

13. "The Terrific Register." 1825. Vol. I, pp. 757-62.

14. "William Ainsworth and Jack Sheppard" (a comparison with Fielding). *Fraser's Magazine*, February, 1840.

15. "Flowers of Hemp, or the Newgate Garland," by Bon Gaultier. *Tait's Edinburgh Magazine*, 1841. Pp. 215-23. The same, p. 249: "On Reading Ainsworth's 'Jack Sheppard.'"

16. "Daniel Defoe," by William Lee. J. C. Hotten. 1869. I, pp. 383-9.

17. "A Chronological Catalogue of the Works of Daniel Defoe," by William Lee. J. C. Hotten. 1869, pp. 24, 25.

18. "The Chronicles of Crime," by Camden Pelham. 1887. I, pp. 38-50.

19. "Daniel Defoe," by William Minto. 1902. Pp. 127-8.

20. "The History of Newgate" and "Mysteries of Police and Crime," by Major Arthur Griffiths. Cassell and Co.

21. "The Old Bailey and Newgate," by Charles Gordon, p. 123.

22. "Tyburn Tree," by Alfred Marks, pp. 230-4.

23. "The Hangmen of England," by Horace Bleackley. Chapman and Hall. Pp. 40-6, 47, 49, 79, 120, 217, 256, 260.

24. *Punch*. Vol. I, 7th August, 1841, p. 39—"A Startling Romance"; p. 46—"The Boy Jones's Log." 11th December, 1841, p. 259—Cartoon of Lord John Russell as Jack Sheppard. 18th December, 1841, p. 276—"Literary Intelligence." Vol. II, p. 68—"The Literary Gentleman"; p. 98—"Felons as they are and Felons as they ought to be: Jack Sheppard."

25. "A History of Clerkenwell," by W. J. Pinks. 1881. Pp. 183, 184, 355.

26. "History of the Stage," by W. R. Chetwood. 1749. P. 228.

27. "Biographia Dramatica." 1812. II, p. 283; III, p. 181.

28. "A Book of Scoundrels," by Charles Whibley, pp. 143, 157, 167, 179.

29. "British Mezzotinto Portraits," by J. C. Smith. 1883. Pt. IV, div. I, p. 1585.

30. Song. "Jack Sheppard." Words by Richard Morton. Music by George Le Brunn. Sung by Kate James. Published by Francis, Day, and Hunter (1894).

31. "William Harrison Ainsworth and His Friends," by S. M. Ellis. London: John Lane, The Bodley Head. Two volumes. 1910. Vol. I, chapters X and XI.

The History of His Life.

THE

HISTORY

Of the remarkable LIFE of

JOHN SHEPPARD,

CONTAINING

A particular Account of his many

ROBBERIES and ESCAPES.

Viz.

His robbing the Shop of Mr. Bains in White-Horse-Yard of 24 Yards of Fustian. Of his breaking and entering the House of the said Mr. Bains, and stealing in Goods and Money to the Value of 20 £. Of his robbing the House of Mr. Charles in May Fair of Money, Rings, Plate, &c. to the Value of 30 £. Of his robbing the House of Mrs. Cook in Clare-Market, along with his pretended Wife, and his Brother, to the Value of between 50 and 60 £. Of his breaking the Shop of Mr. Phillips in Drury-Lane, with the same Persons, and stealing Goods of small Value. Of his entering the House of Mr. Carter, a Mathematical Instrument Maker in Wytch-street, along with Anthony Lamb and Charles Grace, and robbing of Mr. Barton, a Master Taylor who lodged therein, of Goods and Bonds to the Value of near 300 £. Of his breaking and entering the House of Mr. Kneebone, a Woollen-Draper, near the New Church in the Strand, in Company of Joseph Blake alias Blewskin and William Field, and stealing Goods to the Value of near 50 £. Of his robbing of Mr. Pargiter on the Highway near the Turnpike, on the Road to Hampstead, along with the said Blewskin. Of his robbing a Lady's Woman in her Mistress's Coach on the same Road. Of his robbing also a Stage Coach, with the said Blewskin, on the Hampstead Road. Likewise of his breaking the Shop of Mr. Martin in Fleet-street, and stealing 3 silver Watches of 15 £ Value.

ALSO

A particular Account of his rescuing his pretended Wife from St. Giles's Round-House. Of the wonderful Escape himself made from the said Round-House. Of the miraculous Escape he and his said pretended Wife made together from New-Prison, on the 25th of May last. Of his surprizing Escape from the Condemn'd Hold of Newgate on the 31st of August: Together with the true manner of his being retaken; and of his Behaviour in Newgate, till the most astonishing and never to be forgotten Escape he made from thence, in the Night of the 15th of October. The Whole taken from the most authentick Accounts, as the Informations of divers Justices of the Peace, the several Shop-keepers above-mention'd, the principal Offices of Newgate and New Prison, and from the Confession of Sheppard made to the Rev. Mr. Wagstaff, who officiated for the Ordinary of Newgate.

LONDON: Printed and Sold by John Applebee in Black-Fryers, J. Isted, at the Golden-Ball near Chancery-Lane in Fleet-street, and the Booksellers of London and Westminster. (Price One Shilling.)
Published October 19th, 1724.

Jack Sheppard.

THE

HISTORY

Of the remarkable LIFE of

JOHN SHEPPARD, &c.

TO THE

CITIZENS

OF

LONDON AND WESTMINSTER.

GENTLEMEN,

Experience has confirm'd you in that everlasting Maxim, that there is no other way to protect the Innocent, but by Punishing the Guilty.

Crimes ever were, and ever must be, unavoidably frequent in such populous Cities as yours are, being the necessary Consequences, either of the Wants, or the Depravity, of the lowest part of the humane Species.

At this time the most flagrant Offences, as Burning of Dwellings; Burlaries, and Highway Robberies abound; and Frauds, common Felonies, and Forgeries are practic'd without Number; thus not only your Properties, but even your very Lives are every way struck at.

The Legislative Power has not been wanting in providing necessary and wholesome Laws against these Evils, the executive part whereof (according to your great Privileges) is lodged in your own Hands: And the Administration hath at all times applyed proper Remedies and Regulations to the Defects which have happen'd in the Magistracy more immediately under their Jurisdiction.

Through the just and salutary Severities of the Magistrates, publick excessive Gaming has been in a manner Surpress'd; and some late Examples of divine Vengeance have overtaken certain of the most notorious lewd Prostitutes of the Town, which together with the laudable endeavours of the great and worthy SOCIETIES, has given no small check to that enormous and spreading Vice.

But here's a Criminal bids Defiance to your Laws and Justice, who declar'd and has manifested that the Bars are not made that can either keep him OUT, or keep him IN, and accordingly hath a second time fled from the very BOSOM OF DEATH.

His History will astonish! and is not compos'd of Fiction, Fable, or Stories plac'd at York, Rome, or Jamaica, but Facts done at your Doors, Facts unheard of, altogether new, Incredible, and yet Uncontestable.

He is gone once more upon his wicked Range in the World. Restless Vengeance is pursuing, and Gentlemen 'tis to be hop'd that she will be assisted by your Endeavours to bring to Justice this notorious Offender.

THE

LIFE

OF

JOHN SHEPPARD, &c.

This John Sheppard, a Youth both in Age and Person, tho' an old Man in

The History of His Life.

Sin; was Born in the Parish of Stepney near London, in the Year 1702, a Son, Grandson, and great Grandson of a Carpenter : His Father died when he was so very Young that he could not recollect that ever he saw him. Thus the burthen of his Maintenance, together with his Brother's and Sister's, lay upon the Shoulders of the Widow Mother, who soon procured an Admittance of her Son John into the Work-House in Bishopsgate-street, where he continued for the space of a Year and half, and in that time received an Education sufficient to qualifie him for the Trade his Mother design'd him, viz. a Carpenter : Accordingly she was recommended to Mr. Wood in Witch-street near Drury-Lane, as a Master capable of entertaining and instructing her Son: They agreed, and Bound he was for the space of seven Years; the Lad proved an early profficient, had a ready and ingenious Hand, and soon became Master of his Business, and gave entire Satisfaction to his Masters Customers, and had the Character of a very sober and orderly Boy. But alas unhappy Youth! before he had compleated six Years of his Apprenticeship, he commenced a fatal Acquaintance with one Elizabeth Lyon, otherwise call'd, Edgworth Bess, from a Town of that Name in Middlesex where she was Born, the reputed Wife of a Foot Soldier, and who lived a wicked and debauch'd Life; and our young Carpenter became Enamour'd of her, and they must Cohabit together as Man and Wife.

Now was laid the Foundation of his Ruin; Sheppard grows weary of the Yoke of Servitude, and began to dispute with his Master; telling him that his way of Jobbing from House to House, was not sufficient to furnish him with a due Experience in his Trade; and that if he would not set out to undertake some Buildings, he would step into the World for better Information. Mr. Wood a mild, sober, honest Man, indulg'd him; and Mrs. Wood, with Tears, exhorted him against the Company of this lewd Prostitute : But her Man prompted and harden'd by his HARLOT, D—n'd her Blood, and threw a Stick at his Mistress, and beat her to the Ground. And being with his Master at Work at Mr. Britt's the Sun Ale-house near Islington, upon a very trivial Occasion fell upon his Master, and beat and bruised him in a most barbarous and shameful Manner. Such a sudden and deplorable Change was there in the Behaviour of this promising young Man. Next ensued a neglect of Duty, both to God and his Master, lying out of Nights, perpetual Jarrings, and Animosities; these and such like, were the Consequences of his intimacy with this she Lyon; who by the sequel will appear to have been a main load-stone in attracting of him up to the fatal Tree.

Mr. Wood having Reason to suspect, that Sheppard had robb'd a Neighbour, began to be in great Fear and Terror for himself. And when his Man came not Home in due season at Nights bar'd him out; but he made a mere jest of the Locks and Bolts, and enter'd in, and out at Pleasure; and when Mr. Wood and his Wife have had all the Reason in the World to believe him Lock't out, they have found him very quiet in his Bed the next Morning, such was the power of his early Magick.

Edgworth Bess having stol'n a Gold Ring from a Gentleman, whom she had pick'd up in the Streets, was sent to St. Giles's Round-house; Sheppard went immediately to his Consort, and after a short Discourse with Mr. Brown the Beadle, and his Wife, who had the Care of the Place, he fell upon the poor old Couple, took the Keys from them, and let his Lady out at the Door in spight of all the Out-cryes, and Opposition they were capable of making.

About July 1723, He was by his Master sent to perform a Repair, at the

Jack Sheppard.

House of Mr. Bains, a Peice-Broker in White-Horse-Yard; he from thence stole a Roll of Fustian, containing 24 Yards, which was afterwards found in his Trunk. This is supposed to be the first Robbery he ever committed, and it was not long e're he Repeated another upon this same Mr. Bains, by breaking into his House in the Night-time, and taking out of the Till seven Pounds in Money, and Goods to the value of fourteen Pounds more. How he enter'd this House, was a Secret till his being last committed to Newgate, when he confess'd that he took up the Iron Bars at the Cellar Window, and after he had done his Business, he nailed them down again, so that Mr. Bains never believed his House had been broke; and an innocent Woman a Lodger in the House lay all the while under the weight of a suspicion of committing the Robbery.

Sheppard and his Master had now parted, ten Months before the expiration of his Apprenticeship, a woeful parting to the former; he was gone from a good and careful Patronage, and lay expos'd to, and comply'd with the Temptations of the most wicked Wretches this Town could afford as Joseph Blake, alias Blewskins, William Field, Doleing, James Sykes, alias Hell and Fury, which last was the first that betray'd and put him into the Hands of Justice, as will presently appear.

Having deserted his Masters Service, he took Shelter in the House of Mr. Charles in May-Fair, near Piccadilly, and his Landlord having a Necessity for some Repairs in his House, engag'd one Mr. Panton a Carpenter to Undertake them, and Sheppard to assist him as a Journeyman; but on the 23d of October, 1723, e're the Work was compleat, Sheppard took Occasion to rob the People of the Effects following, viz. seven Pound ten Shillings in Specie, five large silver Spoons, six plain Forks ditto, four Tea-Spoons, six plain Gold Rings, and a Cypher Ring; four Suits of Wearing Apparel, besides Linnen, to a considerable value. This Fact he confess'd to the Reverend Mr. Wagstaff before his Escape from the Condemn'd Hold of Newgate.

Sheppard had a Brother, nam'd Thomas, a Carpenter by Profession, tho' a notorious Thief and House-breaker by Practice. This Thomas being committed to Newgate for breaking the House of Mrs. Mary Cook a Linnen-Draper, in Clare-street, Clare-Market, on the 5th of February last, and stealing Goods to the value of between 50, and 60 £., he impeach'd his Brother John Sheppard, and Edgworth Bess as being concerned with him in the Fact; and these three were also Charg'd with being concern'd together, in breaking the House of Mr. William Phillips in Drury-Lane, and stealing divers Goods, the Property of Mrs. Kendrick a Lodger in the House, on the 14th of the said February: All possible endeavours were us'd by Mrs. Cook, and Mr. Phillips, to get John Sheppard and Edgworth Bess Apprehended, but to no purpose, till the following Accident.

Sheppard was now upon his wicked Range in London, committing Robberies every where at Discretion; but one Day meeting with his Acquaintance, James Sykes, alias Hell and Fury, sometimes a Chair-man, and at others a Running Foot-man. This Sykes invited him to go to one Redgate's, a Victualling-house near the Seven Dials, to play at Skettles, Sheppard comply'd, and Sykes secretly sent for Mr. Price a Constable in St. Giles's Parish, and Charg'd him with his Friend Sheppard for the Robbing of Mrs. Cook, &c. Sheppard was carried before Justice Parry, who order'd him to St. Giles's Round-house till the next

The History of His Life.

Morning for farther Examination: He was Confin'd in the Upper part of the Place, being two Stories from the Ground, but e're two Hours came about, by only the help of a Razor, and the Stretcher of a Chair, he broke open the Top of the Round-house, and tying together a Sheet and Blanket, by them descended into the Church-yard and Escap'd, leaving the Parish to Repair the Damage, and Repent of the Affront put upon his Skill and Capacity.

On the 19th of May last in the Evening, Sheppard with another Robber named Benson, were passing thro' Leicester-fields, where a Gentleman stood accusing a Woman with an attempt to steal his Watch, a Mobb was gathered about the Disputants, and Sheppard's Companion being a Master, got in amongst them and pick'd the Gentleman's Pocket in good earnest of the Watch; the Scene was surprizingly chang'd from an imaginary Robbery to a real one; and in a moment ensued an Out-cry of stop Thief, Sheppard and Benson took to their Heels, and Sheppard was seiz'd by a Serjeant of the Guard at Leicester House, crying out stop Thief with much earnestness. He was convey'd to St. Ann's Round House in Soho, and kept secure till the next morning, when Edgworth Bess came to visit him, who was seiz'd also; they were carried before Justice Walters, when the People in Drury-Lane and Clare-Market appeared, and charged them with the Robberies aforemention'd: But Sheppard pretending to Impeach certain of his Accomplices, the Justice committed them to New-Prison, with intent to have them soon removed to Newgate, unless there came from them some useful Discoveries. Sheppard was now a second time in the hands of Justice, but how long he intended to keep in them, the Reader will soon be able to Judge.

He and his MATE were now in a strong and well guarded Prison, himself loaded with a pair of double Links and Basils of about fourteen pounds weight, and confined together in the safest Appartment call'd Newgate Ward; Sheppard conscious of his Crimes, and knowing the Information he had made to be but a blind Amusement that would avail him nothing; he began to Meditate an Escape. They had been thus detained for about four Days, and their Friends having the Liberty of seeing them, furnish'd him with Implements proper for his Design, accordingly Mr. Sheppard goes to work, and on the 25th of May being Whitson Monday at about two of the Clock in the Morning, he had compleated a practical breach, and sawed off his Fetters, having with unheard of Diligence and Dexterity, cut off an Iron Bar from the Window, and taken out a Muntin, or Bar of the most solid Oak of about nine inches in thickness, by boring it thro' in many Places, a work of great Skill and Labour; they had still five and twenty Foot to descend from the Ground; Sheppard fasten'd a Sheet and Blanket to the Bars, and causes Madam to take off her Gown and Petticoat, and sent her out first, and she being more Corpulent than himself, it was with great Pain and Difficulty that he got her through the Interval, and observing his directions, she was instantly down, and more frightened than hurt; the Phylosopher follow'd, and lighted with Ease and Pleasure; But where are they Escap'd to? Why out of one Prison into another. The Reader is to understand, that the New Prison and Clerkenwell Bridewell lye Contiguous to one another, and they are got into the Yard of the latter, and have a Wall of twenty-two Foot high to Scale, before their Liberty is perfected; Sheppard far from being unprepared to surmount this Difficulty, has his Gimblets and Peircers ready, and makes a Scaleing Ladder. The Keepers and Prisoners of

Jack Sheppard.

Both Places are a sleep in their Beds; he Mounts his Bagage, and in less than ten Minutes carries both her and himself over this Wall, and compleats an entire Escape. Altho' his Escape from the Condemn'd Hold of Newgate, has made a far greater Noise in the World, than that from this Prison hath, It has been allow'd by all the Jayl-Keepers in London, that one so Miraculous was never perform'd before in England; the broken Chains and Bars are kept at New Prison to Testifie, and preserve the Memory of this extraordinary Event and Villain.

Sheppard not warn'd by this Admonition, returns like a Dog to his Vomit, and comes Secretly into his Master Wood's Neighbourhood in Witch-street, and concerts Measures with one Anthony Lamb, an apprentice to Mr. Carter a Mathematical Instrument-maker, for robbing of Mr. Barton a Master Taylor; a Man of Worth and Reputation, who Lodg'd in Mr. Carter's House. Charles Grace, a graceless Cooper was let into the Secret, and consented, and resolved to Act his Part. The 16th of June last was appointed, Lamb accordingly lets Grace and Sheppard into the House at Mid-Night; and they all go up to Mr. Barton's Appartment well arm'd with Pistols, and enter'd his Rooms, without being disturb'd. Grace was Posted at Mr. Barton's Bedside with a loaded Pistol, and positive Orders to shoot him through the Head, if in case he awak'd. Sheppard being engag'd in opening the Trunks and Boxes, the mean while. It luckily happen'd for Mr. Barton, that he slept Sounder than usual that Night, as having come from a Merry-making with some Friends; tho' poor Man little Dreaming in what dreadful Circumstances. They carried off in Notes, and Bonds, Guineas, Cloaths, Made and Unmade, to the value of between two and three Hundred Pounds; besides a Padesuoy Suit of Cloaths, worth about eighteen or twenty Pounds more; which having been made for a Corpulent Gentleman, Sheppard had them reduc'd and fitted for his own Size and Wear, as designing to Appear and make a Figure among the Beau Monde. Grace and Sheppard, having disposed of the Goods at an Ale-house in Lewkenors Lane (a Rendezvous of Robbers and Ruffians)[1] took their Flight, and Grace has not been since heard of. Lamb was apprehended, and carried before Justice Newton, and made an ample Confession; and there being nothing but that against him at his Tryal, and withal, a favourable Prosecution, he came off with a Sentence of Transportation only. He as well as Sheppard has since confirm'd all the above particulars, and with this Addition, viz. That it was Debated among them to have Murder'd all the People in the House, save one Person.

About the latter End of the same Month, June, Mr. Kneebone, a Woollen-Draper near the New Church in the Strand, receiv'd a Caution from the Father of Anthony Lamb, who intimated to Mr. Kneebone that his House was intended to be broke open and robb'd that very Night. Mr. Kneebone prepar'd for the Event, ordering his Servants to sit up, and gave Directions to the Watchman in the Street to observe his House: At about two in the Morning Sheppard and his Gang were about the Door, a Maid-Servant went to listen, and heard one of the Wretches say, D—n him, if they could not enter that Night, they would another, and would have 300 £ of his, (meaning) Mr. Kneebone's Money. They

---

[1] Noted also for its houses of ill-fame. In Dryden's "The Wild Gallant" (1663) there is mention of a procuress whose "lodgings are in Lucknor's Lane." Also in Lewkenor's Lane lived Mr. Summers, a Thief Catcher, "the man that wrote against the impiety of Mr. Rowe's plays." The lane is now Charles Street.—S.M.E.

The History of His Life.

went off, and nothing more was heard of them till Sunday the 12th Day of July following, when Joseph Blake, alias Blewskins, John Sheppard, and William Field (as himself Swears) came about 12 o'Clock at Night, and cut two large Oaken-Bars over the Cellar-Window, at the back part of the House in Little-Drury-Lane, and so entered; Mr. Kneebone, and his Family being at Rest, they proceeded to open a Door at the Foot of the Cellar-Stairs, with three Bolts, and a large Padlock upon it, and then came up into the Shop and wrench'd off the Hasp, and Padlock that went over the Press, and arriv'd at their desir'd Booty; they continu'd in the House for three Hours, and carry'd off with them One Hundred and eight Yards of Broad Woollen Cloth, five Yards of blue Bays, a light Tye-Wig, and Beaver-Hat, two Silver Spoons, an Handkerchief, and a Penknife. In all to the value of near fifty Pounds.

The Sunday following, being the 19th of July, Sheppard and Blewskins were out upon the Hampstead Road, and there stopt a Coach with a Ladies Woman in it, from whom they took but Half-a-Crown; all the Money then about her; the Footman behind the Coach came down, and exerted himself; but Sheppard sent him in hast up to his Post again, by threat of his Pistol.

The next Night being the 20th of July, about Nine, they Robb'd Mr. Pargiter, a Chandler of Hampstead, near the Halfway-House: Sheppard after his being taken at Finchley was particularly examin'd about this Robbery. The Reverend Mr. Wagstaff having receiv'd a Letter from an unknown Hand, with two Questions, to be propos'd to Sheppard, viz. Whether he did Rob John Pargiter, on Monday the 20th of July, about Nine at Night, between the Turnpike and Hampstead; How much Money he took from him? Whither Pargiter was Drunk, or not, and if he had Rings or Watch about him, when robb'd? which, Request was comply'd with, and Sheppard affirm'd, that Mr. Pargiter was very much in Liquor, having a great Coat on; neither Rings on his Fingers or Watch, and only three Shillings in his Pocket, which they took from him, and that Blewskins knock him down twice with the Butt-end of his Pistol to make sure Work, (tho' Excess of drink had done that before) but Sheppard did in kindness raise him up as often.

The next Night, July 21, they stopt a Stage-Coach, and took from a Passenger in it, Twenty-two Shillings, and were so expeditious in the Matter, that not two Words were made about the Bargain.

Now Mr. Sheppard's long and wicked Course seemingly draws towards a Period. Mr. Kneebone having apply'd to Jonathan Wild, and set forth Advertisements in the Papers, complaining of his Robbery. On Tuesday the 22d of July at Night Edgworth Bess was taken in a Brandy-shop, near Temple-Bar, by Jonathan Wild; she being much terrify'd, discover'd where Sheppard was: A Warrant was accordingly issued by Justice Blackerby, and the next Day he was Apprehended, at the House of Blewskins' Mother, in Rose-Mary-Lane, by one Quilt, a Domestick of Mr. Wild's, though not without great opposition, for he clapt a loaded Pistol to Quilt's Breast, and attempted to shoot him, but the Pistol miss'd fire; he was brought back to New Prison, confin'd in the Dungeon; and the next Day carried before Justice Blackerby. Upon his Examination he Confess'd the three Robberies on the Highway aforemention'd, as also the Robbing of Mr. Bains, Mr. Barton, and Mr. Kneebone, he was committed to Newgate, and at the Sessions of Oyer and Terminer, and Goal delivery, holden at the Old-Baily, on the 12th, 13th and 14th of August, he was try'd upon three several Indictments, viz. First for breaking the House of William Phillips.

Jack Sheppard.

John Sheppard, of the Parish of St. Martin in the Fields, was indicted for breaking the House of William Phillips, and stealing divers Goods, the 14th of February last. But there not being sufficient Evidence against the Prisoner, he was acquitted.

He was also indicted a Second Time, of St. Clement Danes for breaking the House of Mary Cook, the 5th of February last, and stealing divers Goods: But the Evidence against the Prisoner being defficient as to this Indictment also, he was acquitted.

He was also indicted the Third Time, of St. Mary Savoy, for breaking the House of William Kneebone, in the Night-Time, and stealing 108 Yards of Woollen Cloth, the 12th of July last. The Prosecutor depos'd, That the Prisoner had some Time since been his Servant, and when he went to Bed, the Time mention'd in the Indictment, about 11 a-Clock at Night, he saw all the Doors and Windows fast; but was call'd up about four in the Morning, and found his House broke open, the Bars of a Cellar-Window having been cut, and the bolts of the Door that comes up Stairs drawn, and the Padlock wrench'd off, and the Shutter in the Shop broken, and his Goods gone; whereupon suspecting the Prisoner, he having committed ill Actions thereabouts before, he acquainted Jonathan Wild with it, and he procur'd him to be apprehended. That he went to the Prisoner in New Prison, and asking how he could be so ungrateful to rob him, after he had shown him so much Kindness? The Prisoner own'd he had been ungrateful in doing so, informing him of several Circumstances as to the Manner of committing the Fact, but said he had been drawn into it by ill Company. Jonathan Wild, depos'd, The Prosecutor came to him, and desir'd him to enquire after his Goods that had been stolen, telling him he suspected the Prisoner to have been concern'd in the Robbery, he having before committed some Robberies in the Neighbourhood. That inquiring after him, and having heard of him before, he was inform'd that he was an Acquaintance of Joseph Blake, alias Blewskins, and William Field: Whereupon he sent for William Field, who came to him; upon which he told him, if he would make an ingenuous Confession, he believ'd he could prevail with the Court to make him an Evidence. That he did make a Discovery of the Prisoner, upon which he was apprehended, and also of others since convicted, and gave an Account of some Parcels of the Cloth, which were found accordingly. William Field depos'd, That the Prisoner told him, and Joseph Blake, that he knew a Ken where they might get something of Worth. That they went to take a View of the Prosecutor's House, but disprov'd of the Attempt, as not thinking it easy to be perform'd: But the Prisoner perswaded them that it might easily be done, he knowing the House, he having liv'd with the Prosecutor. That thereupon he cut the Cellar Bar, went into the Cellar, got into the Shop, and brought out three Parcels of Cloth, which they carried away. The Prisoner had also confest the Fact when he was apprehended, and before the Justice. The Fact being plainly prov'd, the Jury found him guilty of the Indictment.

Sentence of Death was pronounc'd upon him accordingly. Several other Prosecutions might have been brought against him, but this was thought sufficient to rid the World of so Capital an Offender: He beg'd earnestly for Transportation, to the most extream Foot of his Majesty's Dominions; and pleaded Youth, and Ignorance as the Motive which had precipitated him into the Guilt; but the Court deaf to his Importunities, as knowing him, and his repeated Crimes

The History of His Life.

to be equally flagrant, gave him no satisfactory Answer: He return'd to his dismal Abode the Condemn'd Hold, where were Nine more unhappy Wretches in as dreadful Circumstances as himself. The Court being at Windsor, the Malefactors had a longer Respite than is usual; during that Recess, James Harman, Lumley, Davis and Sheppard agreed upon an Escape, concerted Measures, and provided Instruments to make it effectual; but put off the Execution of their Design, on Account the two Gentlemen having their hopes of Life daily renewed by the favourable Answers they receiv'd from some considerable Persons; but those vanishing the day before their Execution, and finding their Sentence irreversible, they two dropt their hopes, together with the Design, they form'd for an Escape, and so in earnest prepar'd to meet Death on the Morrow, (which they accordingly did.) 'Twas on this Day Mr. Davis gave Sheppard the Watch Springs, Files, Saws, &c. to Effect his own Release; and knowing that a Warrant was Hourly expected for his Execution with Two others, on the Friday following; he thought it high time to look about him, for he had waited his Tryal, saw his Conviction, and heard his Sentence with some patience; but finding himself irrespitably decreed for Death, he could sit passive no longer, and on the very Day of the Execution of the former; whilst they were having their Fetters taken off, in order for going to the Tree, that Day he began to saw, Saturday made a progress; but Sunday omitted, by Reason of the Concourse in the Lodge: Edgworth Bess having been set at Liberty, had frequent Access to him, with others of his Acquaintance. On Monday the Death Warrant came from Windsor, appointing that he, together with Joseph Ward, and Anthony Upton should be Executed on the Friday following, being the 4th of September. The Keepers acquainted him therewith, and desir'd him to make good use of that short Time. He thank'd them, said he would follow their Advice, and prepare. Edgworth Bess, and another Woman had been with him at the Door of the Condemn'd Hold best part of the Afternoon, between five and six he desir'd the other Prisoners, except Stephen Fowles to remain above, while he offer'd something in private to his Friends at the Door; they comply'd, and in this interval he got the Spike asunder, which made way for the Skeleton to pass with his Heels foremost, by the Assistance of Fowles, whom he most ungenerously betray'd to the Keepers after his being retaken, and the Fellow was as severely punish'd for it.

Having now got clear of his Prison, he took Coach disguis'd in a Night Gown at the corner of the Old Baily, along with a Man who waited for him in the Street (and is suppos'd to be Page the Butcher) ordering the Coachman to drive to Black-Fryers Stairs, where his prostitute gave him the Meeting, and they three took Boat, and went a Shoar at the Horse-Ferry at Westminster, and at the White-Hart they went in, Drank, and stay'd sometime; thence they adjourn'd to a Place in Holbourn, where by the help of a Saw he quitted the Chains he had brought with him from Newgate; and then like a Freeman took his Ramble through the City and came to Spittle-Fields, and there lay with Edgworth Bess.

It may be easy to imagine what an alarm his Escape gave to the Keepers of Newgate, three of their People being at the farther End of the Lodge, engag'd in a Discourse concerning his wonderful Escape from New-Prison, and what Caution ought to be us'd, lest he should give them the slip, at that very Instant as he perfected it.

Jack Sheppard.

On Tuesday he sent for William Page an Apprentice to a Butcher in Clare-Market, who came to him, and being Pennyless, he desir'd Page to give him what Assistance he could to make his way, and being a Neighbour and Acquaintance, he comply'd with it; but e're he would do any thing, he consulted a near Relation, who as he said, encourag'd him in it; nay, put him upon it, so meeting with this Success in his Application to his Friend, and probable an Assistance in the Pocket, he came to Sheppard having bought him a new blue Butchers Frock, and another for himself, and so both took their Rout to Warnden in Northamptonshire, where they came to a Relation of Page's, who receiv'd and Entertain'd them kindly, the People lying from their own Bed to Accommodate them. Sheppard pretending to be a Butcher's Son in Clare-Market, who was going farther in the Country to his Friends, and that Page was so kind as to Accompany him; but they as well as their Friend became tir'd of one another; the Butchers having but one Shilling left, and the People poor, and Consequently unable to Subsist two such Fellows, after a stay of three or four Days, they return'd, and came for London, and reach'd the City on Tuesday the 8th of September, calling by the way at Black-Mary's-Hole, and Drinking with several of their Acquaintance, and then came into Bishopsgate street, to one Cooley's a Brandyshop; where a Cobler being at Work in his Stall, stept out and Swore there was Sheppard, Sheppard hearing him, departed immediately. In the Evening they came into Fleet-street, at about Eight of the Clock, and observing Mr. Martin's a Watchmakers Shop to be open, and a little Boy only to look after it: Page goes in and asks the Lad whether Mr. Taylor a Watchmaker lodg'd in the House? being answer'd in the Negative, he came away, and Reports the Disposition of the Place: Sheppard now makes Tryal of his old Master-peice; fixeth a Nail Peircer into the Door post, fastens the Knocker thereto with Packthread, breaks the Glass, and takes out three Silver Watches of 15 £ value, the Boy seeing him take them, but could not get out to pursue him, by reason of his Contrivance. One of the Watches he Pledg'd for a Guinea and Half. The same Night they came into Witch-street, Sheppard going into his Masters Yard, and calling for his Fellow 'Prentice, his Mistress heard, knew his Voice, and was dreadfully frightened; he next went to the Cock and Pye Ale-House in Drury-Lane, sent for a Barber his Acquaintance, drank Brandy and eat Oysters in the view of several People. Page waiting all the while at the Door, the whole Neighbourhood being alarm'd, yet none durst attempt him, for fear of Pistols, &c. He had vow'd Revenge upon a poor Man as kept a Dairy-Cellar, at the End of White-Horse-Yard, who having seen him at Islington after his Escape, and engag'd not to speak of it, broke his Promise; wherefore Sheppard went to his Residence took the Door off the Hinges and threw it down amongst all the Man's Pans, Pipkins, and caus'd a Deluge of Cream and Milk all over the Cellar.

This Night he had a narrow Escape, one Mr. Ireton a Sheriffs Officer seeing him and Page pass thro' Drury-Lane, at about Ten o'Clock pursu'd 'em, and laid hold of Page instead of Sheppard, who got off, thus Ireton missing the main Man, and thinking Page of no Consequence, let him go after him.

Edgworth Bess had been apprehended by Jonathan Wild, and by Sir Francis Forbes one of the Aldermen of London, committed to the Poultry-Compter, for being aiding and assisting to Sheppard in his Escape; the Keepers and others terrify'd and purg'd her as much as was possible to discover where he was,

The History of His Life.

but had it been in her Inclination, it was not in her Power so to do, as it manifestly appear'd soon after.

The People about the Strand, Witch-street and Drury-Lane, whom he had Robb'd, and who had prosecuted him were under great Apprensions and Terror, and in particular Mr. Kneebone, on whom he vow'd a bloody Revenge; because he refus'd to sign a Petition in his behalf to the Recorder of London. This Gentleman was forc'd to keep arm'd People up in his House every Night till he was Re-taken, and had the same fortify'd in the strongest manner. Several other Shop-keepers in this Neighbourhood were also put to great Expence and Trouble to Guard themselves against this dreadful Villian.

The Keepers of Newgate, whom the rash World loaded with Infamy, stigmatiz'd and branded with the Title of Persons guilty of Bribery; for Connivance at his Escape, they and what Posse in their Power, either for Love or Money did Contribute their utmost to undeceive a wrong notion'd People. Their Vigilance was remarkably indefatigable, sparing neither Money nor Time, Night nor Day to bring him back to his deserv'd Justice. After many Intelligences, which they endeavour'd for, and receiv'd, they had one which prov'd very Successful. Having learnt for a certainty that their Haunts was about Finchley Common, and being very well assur'd of the very House where they lay; on Thursday the 10th of September, a posse of Men, both of Spirit and Conduct, furnish'd with Arms proper for their Design, went for Finchley, some in a Coach and Four, and others on Horseback. They dispers'd themselves upon the Common aforesaid, in order to make their View, where they had not been long e're they came in Sight of SHEPPARD in Company of WILLIAM PAGE, habited like two Butchers in new blue Frocks, with white Aprons tuck'd round their Wastes.

Upon Sheppard's seeing Langley a Turnpike at Newgate, he says to his Companion Page, I see a Stag; upon which their Courage dropt; knowing that now their dealing way of Business was almost at an End; however to make their Flight as secure as they could, they thought it adviseable to take to a Foot-path, to cut off the pursuit of the Newgate Cavalry; but this did not prove most successful, Langley came up with Page (who was hindermost) and Dismounting with Pistol in Hand, commands Page to throw up his Hands, which he trembling did, begging for Life, desiring him to Fisk him, viz. (search him,) which he accordingly did, and found a broad Knife and File; having thus disarm'd him, he takes the Chubb along with him in quest of the slippery Eel, Sheppard; who had taken Shelter in an old Stable, belonging to a Farm-House; the pursuit was close, the House invested, and a Girl seeing his Feet as he stood up hid, discover'd him. Austin a Turnkey first attach'd his Person, Langley seconded him, Ireton an Officer help'd to Enclose, and happy was the hindermost who aided in this great Enterprise. He being shock'd with the utmost Fear, told them he submitted, and desir'd they would let him live as long as he could, which they did, and us'd him mildly; upon searching him they found a broad Knife with two of the Watches as he had taken out of Mr. Martin's Shop, one under each Armpit; and now having gain'd their Point, and made themselves Masters of what they had often endeavoured for, they came with their Lost Sheep to a little House on the Common that sold Liquors, with this Inscription on the Sign, I have brought my Hogs to a fair Market; which our two unfortunate Butchers, under their then unhappy Circum-

Jack Sheppard.

stances, had too sad Reason to apply to themselves. Sheppard had by this time recover'd his Surprize, grew calm and easy, and desir'd them to give him Brandy, they did, and were all good Friends, and Company together.

They adjourn'd with their Booty to another Place, where was waiting a Coach and Four to Convey it to Town, with more Speed and Safety; and Mr. Sheppard arriv'd at his old Mansion, at about two in the Afternoon. At his a-lighting, he made a sudden Spring; He declar'd his Intention was to have slipt under the Coach, and had a Race for it; he was put into the Condemn'd Hold, and Chain'd down to the Floor with double Basels about his Feet, &c. Page was carried before Sir Francis Forbes, and committed to the same Prison for Accompanying and aiding Sheppard in his Escape. The prudence of Mr. Pitt caus'd a Separation between him and his Brother the first Night, as a Means to prevent any ensuing Danger, by having two Heads, which (according to our Proverbial Saying) are better than one.

The Joy the People of Newgate conceiv'd on this Occasion is inexpressible, Te Deum was Sung in the Lodge, and nothing but Smiles, and Bumpers, were seen there for many Days together. But Jonathan Wild unfortunately happen'd to be gone upon a wrong Scent after him to Sturbridge, and Lost a Share of the Glory.

His Escape and his being so suddenly Re-taken made such a Noise in the Town, that it was thought all the common People would have gone Mad about him; there being not a Porter to be had for Love nor Money, nor getting into an Ale-house, for Butchers, Shoemakers, and Barbers, all engag'd in Controversies, and Wagers, about Sheppard. Newgate Night and Day surrounded with the Curious from St. Giles's and Rag-Fair, and Tyburn Road daily lin'd with Women and Children; and the Gallows as carefully watch'd by Night, lest he should be hang'd Incog. For a Report of that nature obtain'd much upon the Rabble; In short, it was a Week of the greatest Noise and Idleness among Mechanicks that has been known in London, and Parker and Pettis, two Lyricks, subsisted many Days very comfortably upon Ballads and Letters about Sheppard. The vulgar continu'd under great Doubts and Difficulties, in what would be his Case, and whether the Old Warrant, or a New One must be made for his Execution, or a New Tryal, &c., were the great Questions as arose, and occasion'd various Reasonings and Speculation, till a News Paper, call'd the Daily Journal set them all to Rights by the Publication of the Account following, viz. 'J. Sheppard having been Convicted of Burglary, and Felony, and received Sentence of Death, and afterwards Escap'd from Newgate; and being since Re-taken; we are assur'd that it must be prov'd in a Regular, and Judicial way, that he is the same Person, who was so Convicted and made his Escape, before a Warrant can be obtain'd for his Execution; and that this Affair well be brought before the Court at the Old Baily the next Sessions.' This was enough; People began to grow calm and easy and got Shav'd, and their Shoes finish'd, and Business returned into its former Channel, the Town resolving to wait the Sessions with Patience.

The Reverend Mr. Wagstaff, who officiated in the absence of the Ordinary, renew'd his former Acquaintance with Mr. Sheppard, and examin'd him in a particular manner concerning his Escape from the Condemn'd Hold: He sincerely disown'd, that all, or any, belonging to the Prison were privy thereto; but related it as it has been describ'd. He declar'd that Edgworth Bess, who

The History of His Life.

had hitherto pass'd for his Wife, was not really so : This was by some thought to be in him Base, and Ungenerous in that, as she had Contributed towards his Escape, and was in Custody on that Account, it might render her more liable to Punishment, than if she had been thought his Wife; but he endeavour'd to acquit himself, by saying, that she was the sole Author of all his Misfortunes; That she betray'd him to Jonathan Wild, at the time he was taken in Rosemary-Lane; and that when he was contriving his Escape, she disobey'd his orders, as when being requir'd to attend at the Door of the Condemn'd-Hold by Nine, or Ten in the Morning to facilitate his Endeavours, she came not till the Evening, which he said, was an ungrateful Return for the care he had taken in setting her at Liberty from New-Prison; and thus Justify'd himself in what he had done, and said he car'd not what became of her.

He was also Examined about Mr. Martin's Watches; and whether Page was privy to that Robbery; he carefully guarded himself against uttering any thing that might affect him, peremptorily declar'd him Innocent of that, as well as of being privy to his Escape, and said, that he only out of Kindness, as being an old Companion, was resolv'd to share in his Fortunes after he had Escap'd.

He was again continually meditating a second Escape, as appear'd by his own Hardiness, and the Instruments found upon him, on Saturday the 12th, and Wednesday the 16th of September, the first Time a small File was found conceal'd in his Bible, and the second Time two Files, a Chisel and an Hammer being hid in the Rushes of a Chair; and whenever a Question was mov'd to him, when, or by what Means those Implements came to his Hands; he would passionately fly out, and say, How can you? you always ask me these, and such like Questions; and in a particular manner, when he was ask'd, Whether his Companion Page was an Accomplice with him, either in the affair of the Watches, or any other? (he reply'd) That if he knew, he would give no direct Answer, thinking it to be a Crime in him to detect the Guilty.

It was thought necessary by the Keepers to remove him from the Condemn'd-Hold to a Place, call'd the Castle, in the Body of the Goal, and to Chain him down to two large Iron Staples in the Floor; the Concourse of People of tolerable Fashion to see him was exceeding Great, he was always Chearful and Pleasant to a Degree, as turning almost every thing as was said into a Jest and Banter.

Being one Sunday at the Chapel, a Gentleman belong to the Lord Mayor, ask'd a Turnkey, Which was Sheppard, the Man pointed to him? Says Sheppard, yes Sir, I am the Sheppard, and all the Goalers in the Town are my Flock, and I cannot stir into the Country, but they are all at my Heels Baughing after me, &c.

He told Mr. Robins, the City Smith, That he had procur'd him a small Job, and that whoever it was that put the Spikes on the Condemn'd-Hold was an honest Man, for a better piece of Metal, says he, I never wrought upon in my life.

He was loth to believe his frequent Robberies were an Injury to the Publick, for he us'd to say, That if they were ill in one Respect, they were as good in another, and that though he car'd not for Working much himself, yet he was desirous that others should not stand Idle, more especially those of his own Trade, who were always Repairing of his Breaches.

When serious, and that but seldom, he would Reflect on his past wicked Life. He declar'd to us, that for several Years of his Apprenticeship he had an utter abhorrence to Women of the Town, and us'd to pelt them with Dirt

Jack Sheppard.

when they have fell in his way; till a Button-Mould-Maker his next Neighbour left off that Business, and set up a Victualling-house in Lewkenhors-Lane, where himself and other young Apprentices resorted on Sundays, and at all other Opportunities. At this House began his Acquaintance with Edgworth Bess. His Sentiments were strangely alter'd, and from an Aversion to those Prostitutes, he had a more favourable Opinion, and even Conversation with them, till he Contracted an ill Distemper, which, as he said, he cur'd himself of by a Medicine of his own preparing.

He inveigh'd bitterly against his Brother Thomas for putting him into the Information, for Mrs Cook's Robbery, and pretended that all the Mischiefs that attended him was owing to that Matter. He acknowledg'd that he was concern'd in that Fact, and that his said Brother broke into his Lodgings, and stole from him all his Share and more of the acquir'd Booty.

He oftentimes averr'd, that William Field was no ways concern'd in Mr. Kneebone's Robbery; but that being a Brother of the Quill; Blewskin and himself told him the particulars, and manner of the Facts, and that all he Swore against him at his Tryal was False, and that he had other Authority for it, than what came out of their (Sheppard and Blewskin) Mouths, who actually committed the Fact.

And moreover, that Field being acquainted with their Ware-house (a Stable) near the Horse-Ferry at Westminster, which Sheppard had hir'd, and usually resposited therein the Goods he stole. He came one Night, and broke open the same, and carried off the best part of the Effects taken out of Mr. Kneebone's Shop.

Sheppard said he thought this to be one of the greatest Villanies that could be acted, for another to come and Plunder them of Things for which they had so honourably ventur'd their Lives, and wish'd that Field, as well as his Brother Tom might meet with forgiveness for it.

He declar'd himself frequently against the Practice of Whidling, or Impeaching, which he said, had made dreadful Havock among the Thieves, and much lamented the depravity of the Brethren in that Respect; and said that if all were but such Tight-Cocks as himself, the Reputation of the British Thievery might be carried to a far greater height than it had been done for many Ages, and that there would then be but little Necessity for Jaylors and Hangmen.

These and such like were his constant Discourses, when Company went up with the Turnkeys to the Castle to see him, and few or none went away without leaving him Money for his Support; in which he abounded, and did therewith some small Charities to the other Prisoners; however, he was abstemious and sparing enough in his Diet.

Among the many Schemes laid by his Friends, for the preserving himself after his Escape, we were told of a most Remarkable one, propos'd by an ingenious Person, who advis'd, that he might be Expeditiously, and Secretly convey'd to the Palace at Windsor, and there to prostrate his Person and his Case at the Feet of a most Gracious Prince, and his Case being so very singular and new, it might in great probability move the Royal Fountain of unbounded Clemency; but he declin'd this Advice, and follow'd the Judgment and Dictates of Butchers, which very speedily brought him very near the Door of the Slaughter-house.

On the 7th of September, the Day as Joseph Ward, and Anthony Upton were

The History of His Life.

Executed, there was publish'd a whimsical Letter, as from Sheppard, to Jack Ketch, which afforded Diversion to the Town, and Bread to the Author, which is as followeth, viz.

SIR,

I Thank you for the Favour you intended me this Day: I am a Gentleman, and allow you to be the same, and I hope can forgive Injuries; fond Nature prompted, I obey'd, Oh, propitious Minute! and to show that I am in Charity, I am now drinking your Health, and a Bon Repo to poor Joseph and Anthony. I am gone a few Days for the Air, but design speedily to embark; and this Night I am going upon a Mansion for a Supply; it's a stout Fortification, but what Difficulties can't I encounter, when, dear Jack, you find that Bars and Chains are but trifling Obstacles in the way of your friend and Servant.

JOHN SHEPPARD.

From my Residence in
Terra Australi incognito.

P.S. Pray my Service to Mr. Or—di—y and to Mr. App—ee.

On Saturday the 10th of October, Anthony Lamb, and Thomas Sheppard with 95 other Felons were carried from Newgate on Shipboard for Transportation to the Plantations; the last begg'd to have an opportunity given him of taking his final Leave of his Brother John; but this was not to be Granted, and the greatest Favour that could be obtain'd, was that on the Sunday before they had an Interview at the Chapel, but at such a distance, that they neither saluted, or shook Hands, and the Reason given for it, was that no Implements might be convey'd to Sheppard to assist him in making an Escape.

This Caution seem'd to be absolutely necessary, for it appear'd soon after that Sheppard found Means to release himself from the Staples to which he was Chain'd in the Castle, by unlocking a great Padlock with a Nail, which he had pickt up on the Floor, and endeavour'd to pass up the Chimney, but was prevented by the stout Iron Bars fix'd in his way, and wanted nothing but the smallest File to have perfected his Liberty. When the Assistants of the Prison, came as usual with his Victuals, they began to examine his Irons; to their great Surprize they found them loose, and ready to be taken off at Pleasure. Mr. Pitt the Head Keeper, and his Deputies were sent for, and Sheppard finding this Attempt entirely frustrated, discover'd to them by what means he had got them off; and after they had search'd him, found nothing, and Lock'd and Chain'd him down again: He took up the Nail and unlock'd the Padlock before their Faces; they were struck with the greatest Amazement as having never heard, or beheld the like before. He was then Hand-Cuff'd, and more effectually Chain'd.

The next Day, the Reverend Mr. Purney, Ordinary of the Place, came from the Country to visit him, and complain'd of the sad Disposition he found him in, as Meditateing on nothing, but Means to Escape, and declining the great Duty incumbent upon him to prepare for his approaching Change. He began to Relent, and said, that since his last Effort had prov'd not Successful, he would entertain no more Thoughts of that Nature, but entirely Dispose, and Resign himself to the Mercy of Almighty God, of whom he hop'd still to find forgiveness of his manifold Offences.

He said, that Edgworth Bess and himself kept a little Brandy-shop together

Jack Sheppard.

in Lewkenhors-Lane, and once sav'd about Thirty Pounds; but having such an universal Acquaintance amongst Thieves, he had frequent calls to go Abroad, and soon quitted that Business, and his Shop.

On Friday the 2d, of October his old Confederate Joseph Blake alias Blewskin, was apprehended and taken at a House in St. Giles's Parish by Jonathan Wild, and by Justice Blackerby committed to Newgate. William Field who was at his Liberty, appearing and making Oath, that Blewskin together with John Sheppard and himself, committed the Burglary and Felony in Mr. Kneebone's House, for which Sheppard was Condemn'd.

The Sessions commencing at the Old Bailey on Wednesday the 14th of October following, an Indictment was found against Blewskin for the same, and he was brought down from Newgate to the Old Bailey to be Arraign'd in order to his Tryal; and being in the Yard within the Gate before the Court: Mr. Wild being their Drinking a glass of Wine with him, he said to Mr. Wild, You may put in a word for me, as well as for another Person? To which Mr. Wild reply'd, I cannot do it, You are certainly a dead Man, and will be tuck'd up very speedily, or words to that effect: Whereupon Blewskin on a sudden seiz'd Mr. Wild by the Neck, and with a little Clasp Knife he was provided with he cut his Throat in a very dangerous Manner; and had it not been for a Muslin Stock twisted in several Plaits round his Neck, he had in all likelyhood succeeded in his barbarous Design before Ballard the Turnkey, who was at Hand, could have time to lay hold of him; the Villain triumph'd afterwards in what he had done, Swearing many bloody Oaths, that if he had murder'd him, he should have died with Satisfaction, and that his Intention was to have cut off his Head, and thrown it into the Sessions House Yard among the Rabble, and Curs'd both his Hand and the Knife for not Executing it Effectually.

Mr. Wild instantly had the Assistance of three able Surgeons, viz. Mr. Dobbins, Mr. Marten, and Mr. Coletheart, who sew'd up the Wound, and order'd him to his Bed, and he has continu'd ever since, but in a doubtful State of Recovery.

The Felons on the Common side of Newgate, also animated by Sheppard's Example, the Night before they were to be Shipt for Transportation, had cut several Iron Bars assunder, and some of them had saw'd off their Fetters, the rest Huzzaing, and making Noises, under pretence of being Joyful that they were to be remov'd on the Morrow, to prevent the Workmen being heard; and in two Hours time more, if their Design had not been discover'd, near One Hundred Villians had been loose into the World, to have committed new Depredations; nothing was wanted here but Sheppard's great Judgment, who was by himself in the strong Room, call'd the Castle, meditating his own Deliverance, which he perfected in the manner following.

On Thursday the 15th of this Instant October, at between One and Two in the Afternoon, William Austin, an Assistant to the Keepers, a Man reputed to be a very diligent, and faithful Servant, went to Sheppard in the strong Room, call'd the Castle, with his Necessaries, as was his Custom every Day. There went along with him Captain Geary, the Keeper of New Prison, Mr. Gough, belonging to the Gate-house in Westminster, and two other Gentlemen, who had the Curiosity to see the Prisoner, Austin very strictly examined his Fetters, and his Hand-Cuffs, and found them very Safe; he eat his Dinner and talk'd with his usual Gayety to the Company: They took leave of him and wish'd

The History of His Life.

him a good Evening. The Court being sitting at the Old Bailey, the Keepers and most of their Servants were attending there with their Prisoners: And Sheppard was told that if he wanted any thing more, then was his Time, because they could not come to him till the next Morning: He thank'd them for their Kindness, and desir'd them to be as early as possible.

The same Night, soon after 12 of the Clock Mr. Bird who keeps a Turners-shop adjoyning to Newgate, was disturb'd by the Watchman, who found his Street Door open, and call'd up the Family, and they concluding the Accident was owing to the Carelessness of some in the House, shut their Doors, and went to Bed again.

The next Morning Friday, at about eight Mr. Austin went up as usual to wait on Sheppard, and having unlock'd and unbolted the double Doors of the Castle, he beheld almost a Cart-load of Bricks and Rubbish about the Room, and his Prisoner gone: The Man ready to sink, came trembling down again, and was scarce able to Acquaint the People in the Lodge with what had happen'd.

The whole Posse of the Prison ran up, and stood like Men depriv'd of their Senses: Their surprize being over, they were in hopes that he might not have yet entirely made his Escape, and got their Keys to open all the strong Rooms adjacent to the Castle, in order to Trace him, when to their farther Amazement, they found the Doors ready open'd to their Hands; and the strong Locks, Screws and Bolts broken in pieces, and scatter'd about the Jayl. Six great Doors (one whereof having not been open'd for seven Years past) were forc'd, and it appear'd that he had Descended from the Leads of Newgate by a Blanket (which he fasten'd to the Wall by an Iron Spike he had taken from the Hatch of the Chapel) on the House of Mr. Bird, and the Door on the Leads having been left open, it is very reasonable to conclude he past directly to the Street Door down the Stairs; Mr. Bird and his Wife hearing an odd sort of a Noise on the Stairs as they lay in their Bed, a short time before the Watchman alarm'd the Family.

Infinite Numbers of Citizens came to Newgate to behold Sheppard's Workmanship, and Mr. Pitt and his Officers very readily Conducted them up Stairs, that the world might be convinc'd there was not the least room to suspect, either a Negligence or Connivance in the Servants. Every one express'd the greatest Surprize that has been known, and declar'd themselves satisfy'd with the Measures they had taken for the Security of their Prisoner.

One of the Sheriffs came in Person, and went up to the Castle to be satisfy'd of the Situation of the Place, &c. Attended by several of the City Officers.

The Court being sat at the Sessions-House, the Keepers were sent for and Examin'd, and the Magistrates were in great Consternation, that so horrid a Wretch had escap'd their Justice. It being intended that he should have been brought down to the Court the last Day of the Sessions, and order'd for Execution in two or three Days after; if it appear'd that he was the Person Condemn'd for the breaking Mr. Kneebone's House, and included in the Warrant for Execution, &c.

Many of the Methods by which this miraculous Escape was effected, remain as yet a Secret; there are some indeed too Evident, the most reasonable Conjecture that has hitherto been made, is, that the first Act was his twisting and breaking assunder by the strength of his Hands a small Iron Chain, which

Jack Sheppard.

together with a great Horse Padlock, (as went from the heavy Fetters about his Legs to the Staples) confin'd him to the Floor, and with a Nail open'd the Padlock and set himself at Liberty about the Room: A large flat Iron Bar appears to have been taken out of the Chimney, with the Assistance whereof 'tis plain he broke thro' a Wall of many Foot in Thickness, and made his way from the Castle into another strong Room Contiguous, the Door of it not having been open'd since several of the Preston Prisoners were Confin'd there about seven Years ago: Three Screws are visibly taken off of the Lock, and the Doors, as strong as Art could make them, forc'd open. The Locks and Bolts, either wrench'd or Broke, and the Cases and other Irons made for their Security cut assunder: An Iron Spike broke off from the Hatch in the Chapel, which he fix'd in the Wall and fastn'd his Blanket to it, to drop on the Leads of Mr. Bird's House; his Stockings were found on the Leads of Newgate; 'tis question'd whether sixty Pounds will repair the Damage done to the Jayl.

It will perhaps be inquir'd how all this could be perform'd without his being heard by the Prisoners or the Keepers; 'tis well known that the Place of his Confinement is in the upper part of the Prison, none of the other Felons being Kept any where near him; and 'tis suppos'd that if any had heard him at Work, they would rather have facilitated, than frustrated his Endeavours. In the Course of his Breaches he pass'd by a Door on his Left belonging to the Common-Side Felons, who have since Curs'd him heartily for his not giving them an opportunity to kiss his Hand, and lending them a favourable lift when his Hand was in; but that was not a Work proper for Mr. Sheppard to do in his then Circumstances.

His Fetters are not to be found any where about the Jayl, from whence 'tis concluded he has either thrown them down some Chimney, or carried them off on his Legs, the latter seems to be Impracticable, and would still render his Escaping in such Manner the more astonishing; and the only Answer that is given to the whole, at Newgate, is, That the Devil came in Person and assisted him.

He undoubtedly perform'd most of these Wonders in the darkest part of the Night, and without the least Glimpse of a Candle; In a word, he has actually done with his own Hands in a few Hours, what, several of the most skilful Artists allow, could not have been acted by a number of Persons furnish'd with proper Implements, and all other Advantages in a full Day.

Never was there any thing better Tim'd, the Keepers and all their Assistants being obliged to a strict Attendance on the Sessions at the Old Bailey, which held for about a Week; and Blewskin having confin'd Jonathan Wild to his Chamber, a more favourable opportunity could not have presented for Mr. Sheppard's Purposes.

The Jaylors suffer'd much by the Opinion the ignorant Part of the People entertain'd of the Matter, and nothing would satisfie some, but that they not only Conniv'd at, but even assisted him in breaking their own Walls and Fences, and that for this Reason too, viz. That he should be at Liberty to instruct and train up others in his Method of House-Breaking; and replenish the Town with a new set of Rogues, to supply the Places of those Transported beyond Sea.

This is indeed a fine way of Judging; the well-known Characters of Mr. Pitt, and his Deputies, are sufficient to wipe of such ridiculous Imputations; and 'tis a most lamentable Truth, that they have oftentimes had in their Charge Villains of the deepest Die; Persons of Quality and great Worth, for

The History of His Life.

whom no Entreaties, no Sums how large soever have been able to interfere between the doleful Prison, and the fatal Tree.

The Officers have done their Duty, they are but Men, and have had to deal with a Creature something more than Man, a Protoeus, Supernatural, Words cannot describe him, his Actions and Workmanship which are too visible, best testifie him.

On Saturday the 17th, Joseph Blake, alias Blewskin, came upon his Tryal at the Old Bailey: Field gave the same Evidence against him, as he had formerly done against Sheppard; and the Prisoner making but a trifling Defence, the Jury found him Guilty of Burglary and Felony. The Criminal when the Verdict was brought in, made his Obeysances to the Court, and thank'd them for their Kindness.

It will be necessary that we now return to the Behaviour of Mr. Sheppard, some few Days before his last Flight.

Mr. Figg the famous Prize Fighter coming to see him, in NEWGATE, there past some pleasant Raillery between them; and after Mr. Figg was gone, Sheppard declared he had a Mind to send him a formal Challenge to Fight him at all the Weapons in the strong Room; and that let the Consequence be what it would, he should call at Mr. Figg's House in his way to Execution, and drink a merry Glass with him by way of Reconciliation.

A young Woman an Acquaintance of his Mother, who wash'd his Linnen and brought him Necessaries, having in an Affray, got her Eyes beaten Black and Blue; says Sheppard to her, How long hast thou been Married? Replyes the Wench, I wonder you can ask me such a Question, when you so well know the Contrary: Nay, says Sheppard again, Sarah don't deny it, for you have gotten your CERTIFICATE in your Face.

Mr. Ireton a Bailiff in Drury-Lane having pursued Sheppard after his Escape from the Condemn'd-Hold with uncommon Diligence; (for the safety of that Neighbourhood which was the chief Scene of his Villainies) Sheppard when Re-taken, declar'd, he would be even with him for it, and if ever he procur'd his Liberty again, he would give all his Prisoners an ACT OF GRACE.

A Gentleman in a jocose way ask'd him to come and take a Dinner with him, Sheppard reply'd he accepted of the Invitation, and perhaps might take an opportunity to wait on him; and there is great Reason to believe he has been as good as his Word.

He would complain of his Nights as saying, It was dark with him from Five in the Evening, till Seven in the Morning; and being not permitted to have either a Bed or Candle, his Circumstances were dismal; and that he never slept but had some confus'd Doses, he said he consider'd all this with the Temper of a Philosopher.

Neither his sad Circumstances, nor the seldom Exhortations of the several Divines who visited him, were able to divert him from this ludicrous way of Expression; he said, They were all Ginger-bread Fellows, and came rather out of Curiosity, than Charity; and to form Papers and Ballads out of his Behaviour.

A Welch Clergyman who came pretty often, requested him in a particular Manner to refrain Drinking; (tho' indeed there was no necessity for that Caution) Sheppard says, Doctor, You set an Example and I'll follow; this was a smart Satyr and Repartee upon the Parson, some Circumstances consider'd.

When he was visited in the Castle by the Reverend Mr. Wagstaff, he put

Jack Sheppard.

on the Face only of a Preparation for his End, as appear'd by his frequent Attempts made upon his Escape, and when he has been press'd to Discover those who put him upon Means of Escaping, and furnish'd him with Implements, he would passionately, and with a Motion of striking, say, ask me no such Questions, one File's worth all the Bibles in the World.

When ask'd if he had not put off all Thoughts of an Escape and Entertain'd none but those of Death, would Answer by way of Question, not directly, whether they thought it possible, or probable for him to Effect his Release, when Manacled in the manner he was. When mov'd to improve the few Minutes that seem'd to remain of his Life; he did indeed listen to, but not regard the Design and Purport of his Admonition, breaking in with something New of his own, either with respect to his former Accomplices, or Actions, and all too with Pleasure and Gayety of Expression.

When in Chapel, he would seemingly make his Responses with Devotion; but would either Laugh, or force Expressions (when an Auditor of the Sermon) of Contempt, either of the Preacher, or of his Discourse.

In fine, he behav'd so, in Word, and Action (since re-taken) that demonstrated to the World, that his Escape was the utmost Employ of his Thoughts, whatever Face of Penitence he put on when visited by the Curious.

AN ACCOUNT OF SHEPPARD'S Adventures of five Hours immediately after his Escape from Newgate, in a Letter to his Friend.

DEAR FRIEND!

Over a Bottle of Claret you'll give me leave to declare it, that I've fairly put the Vowels upon the good Folks at Newgate, i. o. u. When I'm able, I may, or may not discharge my Fees, 'tis a Fee-simple, for a Man in my Condition to acknowledge; and tho' I'm safe out of Newgate, I must yet have, or at least, affect, a New Gate by Limping, or turning my Toes in by making a right Hand of my Feet. Not to be long, for I hate Prolixity in all Business: In short, after Filing, defileing, Sawing, when no Body Saw. Climbing (this Clime in) it prov'd a good Turner of my Affairs, thro' the House of a Turner. Being quite past, and safe from Estreat on Person or Chattels, and safe in the Street, I thought Thanks due to him who cou'd Deliver hence; and immediately (for you must know I'm a Catholick) to give Thanks for my Deliverance, I step't amongst the Grey-Fryers to come and joyn with me, in saying a Pater-Noster, or so, at Amen-Corner. The Fryers being Fat began to Broil, and soon after Boild up into a Passion to be disturb'd at that time of Night. But being got Loose and having no Time to Lose, I gave them good Words, and so the Business was done. From thence I soon slip'd through Ludgate but was damnably fearful of an Old Bailey always lurking thereabout, who might have brought me to the Fleet for being too Nimble, besides, I was wonderfully apprehensive of receiving some unwelcome Huggings from the W...n there; therefore with a step and a stride I soon got over Fleet ditch, and (as in Justice I ought) I prais'd the Bridge I got over. Being a Batchelor, and not being capable to manage a Bridewell you know. I had no Business near St. Brides, so kept the right hand side, designing to Pop into the Alley as usual; but fearing to go thro' there, and harp too much on the same String, it gave an Allay to my Intention, and on I went to Shoe-Lane end, but there meeting with a Bully Hack of the Town, he wou'd have shov'd me down, which my Spirit resenting,

The History of His Life.

tho' a brawny Dog, I soon Coller'd him, fell Souse at him, then with his own Cane I strapp'd till he was force to Buckle too, and hold his Tongue, in so much he durst not say his Soul was his own, and was glad to pack of at Last, and turn his Heels upon me: I was glad he was gone you may besure, and dextrously made a Hand of my Feet under the Leg-Tavern; but the very Thoughts of Fetter-Lane call'd to mind some Passages, which made me avoid the Passage at the end of it, (next to the Coffee House you know) so I soon whip'd over the way, yet, going along, two wooden Logger-heads at St. Dunstan's, made just then a damn'd Noise about their Quarters, but the sight of me made perfectly Hush in a Minute; now fearing to goe by Chance-a-wry-Lane, as being upon the Watch my self, and not to be debarr'd at Temple Bar; I stole up Bell-Yard, but narrowly escap'd being Clapper-claw'd by two Fellows I did not like in the Alley, so was forc'd to goe round with a design to Sheer-off into Sheer-Lane, but the Trumpet sounding at that very time, alarm'd me so, I was forc'd to Grope my way back through Hemlock-Court, and take my Passage by Ship-Yard without the Bar again; but there meeting with one of our trusty Friends, (all Ceremonies a-part) he told me under the Rose I must expect no Mercy in St. Clement's Parish, for the Butchers there on the Back on't would Face me, and with their Cleavers soon bring me down on my Marrow Bones; you may believe I soon hasten'd thence, but by this time being Fainty and nigh Spent, I put forward, on seeing a Light near the Savoy-Gate, I was resolv'd not to make Light of the Opportunity, but call'd for an hearty Dram of Luther and Calvin, that is, Mum and Geneva mix'd; but having Fasted so long before, it soon got into my Noddle, and e'er I had gone twenty steps, it had so intirely Stranded my Reason, that by the time I came to Half-Moon-Street end, it gave a New-Exchange to my Senses, and made me quite Lunatick.

However, after a little Rest, I stole down George Passage into Oaf-Alley in York-Buildings, and thence (tho' a vile Man) into Villiers-Street, and so into the Strand again, where having gone a little way, Hefford's-Harp at the Sign of the Irish-Harp, put me a Jumping and Dancing to that degree, that I could not forbear making a Somerset or two before Northumberland-House. I thought once of taking the Windsor Coach for my self John Sheppard, by the Name of Crook—but fearing to be Hook'd in before my Journey's End, I stept into Hedge-Lane, where two Harlots were up in the Boughs (it seems) Branching out their Respects to one another, through their Windows, and People beginning to gather thereabout, I ran Pelmel to Piccadilly, where meeting, by meer Chance a Bakers Cart going to Turnham-Green, I being not Mealy Mouth'd nor the Man being Crusty I wheel'd out of Town.

I did call at Hammersmith, having no occasion directly. I shall stay two or three Days in that Neighbourhood, so, if you Direct a Letter for Mr. Sligh Bolt, to be left with Mrs. Tabitha Skymmington at Cheesewick, it's Safety will Bear Water by any Boat, and come Current, with the Tyde to

Dear BOB.
Yours from the Top
of Newgate to the Bottom

J. SHEPPARD.

P.S. If you see Blewskin, tell him I am well, and hope he receiv'd my last—I wou'd write by the Post if I durst, but it wou'd be, certainly Post-pon'd

Jack Sheppard.

if I did, and it would be stranger too, to trust a Line by a Stranger, who might Palm upon us both and never Deliver it to Hand.

I send this by a Waterman, (I dare trust) who is very Merry upon me, and says he wou'd not be in my Jacket.

Saturday Octob. 17, 1724.

We shall conclude with what had been often observ'd by many Persons to Sheppard; viz. That it was very Imprudent in him to take Shelter in the City, or the adjacent Parts of it, after his Escape from the Condemn'd Hold; and withal to commit a Capital Offence, almost within Sight of Newgate, when his Life and all was in such Danger. His Reply was general, viz. That it was his Fate: But being ask'd a particular Reason for his not taking a longer Rout than the City, and the Neighbouring part; pleaded Poverty as his Excuse for Confinement within those Limits; at the same time urging, that had he been Master at that time of five Pounds, England should not have been the Place of his Residence, having a good Trade in his Hands to live in any populated Part of the World.

FINIS.

ERRATA.

In Page 3, 1.22, line 4, read this Eminence of Guilt, instead of to the fatal Tree. (Page 139, line 35, of this volume.)

A Narrative of the Robberies, &c.

A

NARRATIVE

Of all the

Robberies, Escapes, &c.

OF

JOHN SHEPPARD:

Giving an Exact Description of the manner of his wonderful Escape from the Castle at Newgate, and of the Methods he took afterward for his Security.

Written by himself during his Confinement in the Middle Stone-Room, after his being retaken in Drury-Lane.

To which is Prefix'd,

A true Representation of his Escape from the Condemn'd Hold, curiously engraven on a Copper Plate.

The whole Publish'd at the particular Request of the Prisoner.

The Sixth Edition.[1]

LONDON:
Printed and Sold by John Applebee, a little below Bridewell-Bridge, in Black-Fryers. 1724.

(Price Six Pence.)

JOHN SHEPPARD'S

NARRATIVE

OF HIS

LIFE and ACTIONS, &c.

As my unhappy Life and Actions have afforded Matter of much Amusement to the World; and various Pamphlets, Papers, and Pictures relating thereunto are gone abroad, most or all of them misrepresenting my Affairs; 'tis necessary that I should say something for my self, and set certain intricate Matters in a true Light; every Subject, how unfortunate or unworthy soever, having the Liberty of publishing his Case. And it will be no small Satisfaction to me to think that I have thoroughly purg'd my Conscience before I leave the World, and made Reparation to the many Persons Injur'd by me, as far as is in my poor Power.

---

[1] The second edition of this pamphlet advertised on November 8th, 1724.

Jack Sheppard.

If my Birth, Parentage, or Education will prove of Service or Satisfaction to Mankind, I was born in Stepney Parish, the Year Queen Anne came to the Crown; my Father a Carpenter by Trade, and an honest industrious Man by Character, and my Mother bore and deserved the same. She being left a Widow in the early Part of my Life, continued the Business, and kept my self, together with another unfortunate Son, and a Daughter, at Mr. Garrett's School near Great St. Hellen's in Bishopsgate Parish, till Mr. Kneebone a Woollen-Draper in the Strand, an Acquaintance, regarding the slender Circumstances of our Family, took me under his Care, and improv'd me in my Writing and Accompts, himself setting me Copies with his own Hand; and he being desirous to settle me to a Trade, and to make my Mother easy in that Respect, agreed with Mr. Owen Wood, a Carpenter in Drury-Lane, to take me Apprentice for Seven Years, upon Condition that Mr. Kneebone should procure Mr. Wood to be employ'd in performing the Carpenter's Work, &c. at a House at Hampstead, which he did accordingly, and upon that and no other Consideration was I bound to Mr. Wood.

We went on together for about six Years, there happening in that Time what is too common with most Families in low Life, as frequent Quarrels and Bickerings. I am far from presuming to say that I was one of the best of Servants, but I believe if less Liberty had been allow'd me then, I should scarce have had so much Sorrow and Confinement after. My Master and Mistress with their Children were strict Observers of the Sabbath, but 'tis too well known in the Neighbourhood that I had too great a Loose given to my evil Inclinations, and spent the Lord's Day as I thought convenient. It has been said in Print that I did beat and bruise my Master Mr. Wood in a most barbarous and shameful manner at Mr. Britt's, the Sun Ale-House at Islington, and that I damn'd my Mistress's Blood, and beat her to the Ground, &c. These Stories have been greatly improved to my Disadvantage. Mr. Wood cannot but remember how hard I wrought for him that Day at Islington, what Refreshment was offer'd to my Fellow-Servant and my self; the Cause of that unhappy Quarrel is still fresh in my Memory: And as for that of my Mistress, when Elizabeth Lyon and her Husband, a Soldier, were quarrelling together in Mr. Wood's Yard, I bid them be gone, and threw a small Lath at Lyon, which might fall on my Mistress, but she received no Harm as I know of, and if she did, I am sorry for it.

After all I may justly lay the Blame of my Temporal and (without God's great Mercies) my Eternal Ruin on Joseph Hind, a Button-mould Maker, who formerly kept the Black Lyon Ale-House in Drury-Lane; the frequenting of this wicked House brought me acquainted with Elizabeth Lyon, and with a Train of Vices, as before I was altogether a Stranger to. Hind is now a lamentable Instance of God's divine Vengeance, he being a wretched Object about the Streets; and I am still far more miserable than him.

It has been said in the History of my Life, that the first Robbery I ever committed was in the House of Mr. Bains, a Piece-Broker in White-Horse Yard; to my Sorrow and Shame I must acknowledge my Guilt of a Felony before that, which was my stealing two silver Spoons from the Rummer Tavern at Charing-Cross, when I was doing a Jobb there for my Master: for which I ask Pardon of God, and the Persons who were wrongfully charg'd and injur'd by that my Crime.

A Narrative of the Robberies, &c.

Unhappy Wretch! I was now commenced Thief, and soon after Housebreaker; growing gradually wicked, 'twas about the latter End of July, 1723, that I was sent by my Master to do a Jobb at the House of Mr. Bains aforesaid, I there stole a Roll of Fustian containing 24 Yards, from amongst many others, and Mr. Bains not missing it, had consequently no Suspicion. I offer'd it to Sale among the young Lads in our Neighbourhood at 12d. per Yard, but meeting with no Purchasers I concealed the Fustian in my Trunk.

On the 1st of August following, I again wrought in Mr. Bains's Shop, and that Night at about 12 of the Clock I came and took up the wooden Bars over the Cellar-window, so enter'd and came up into the House, and took away Goods to the value of fourteen Pounds, besides seven Pounds in money out of the Till, then nail'd down the Bars again and went off. The next Day I came to the House to finish the Shutters for the Shop, when Mr. Bains and his Wife were in great trouble for their Loss, saying to me they suspected a Woman their Lodger had let the Rogues in, for that they were assured the House had not been broken; the poor People little dreaming they were telling their Story to the Thief, I condoling with them, and pretending great Sorrow for their Misfortune. Not long afterwards my Fellow-prentice Thomas acquainted Mr. Wood that he had observed a quantity of Fustian in my Trunk. My Master and I had broke measures, and I begging absent from home and hearing Thomas had tattled, in the night-time I broke through a Neighbour's House and into my Master's and so carried off the Fustian, to prevent the consequences of a Discovery. Mr. Wood rightly concluding I had stolen it from Mr. Bains, sent him word of what had happen'd, who upon overlooking his Goods soon found his Loss, and threaten'd to prosecute me for the Robbery. I thought it was adviseable to meet the danger; and therefore went to Mr. Bains, bullied and menac'd him, and bid him be careful how he sullied my Reputation, lest he might be brought to repent of it. But this was not sufficient to avert the danger. Mr. Bains resolving to proceed upon the Circumstances he was already furnished with; I thought of another Expedient, and acknowledg'd that I had a piece of Fustian which my Mother had bought for me in Spittle-Fields of a Weaver; and she, poor Woman, willing to screen her wicked Son, confirm'd the Story, and was a whole Day together with Mr. Bains in Spittle-Fields to find out the pretended Weaver. In the end, I was forc'd to send back about 19 Yards of the Fustian to Mr. Bains, and then the Storm blew over. I related all these Particulars to Mr. Bains when he came to me in the Castle Room, as well to wipe off the Suspicion from the poor innocent Woman Mr. Bains's Lodger, as for his own Satisfaction.

I abruptly quitted Mr. Wood's Service almost a Year before the expiration of my Apprenticeship, and went to Fulham, and there wrought as a Journey-man to a Master Carpenter, telling the Man that I had served out my Apprenticeship in Smithfield. Elizabeth Lyon cohabiting with me as my Wife, I kept her in a Lodging at Parson's-Green; but Mr. Wood's Brother being an Inhabitant in the Town discover'd me, and my Master with Justice Newton's Warrant brought me to London, and confin'd me in St. Clement's Round-house all Night: the next Day I was carried to Guild-Hall to have gone before the Chamberlain, but he being gone, I agreed with Mr. Wood, and making matters easy got clear of him, and then fell to robbing almost every one that stood in my way. The Robbery at Mr. Charles's House in May-Fair I have confess'd in a particular manner to Mr. Wagstaffe, and to many others.

Jack Sheppard.

The Robberies of Mr. Bains, Mr. Barton, and Mr. Kneebone, together with the Robbery of Mr. Pargiter and two others on the Hampstead Road, along with Joseph Blake, alias Blewskin, I did amply confess before Justice Blackerby, Mr. Bains and Mr. Kneebone being present, and did make all the Reparation that was in my power, by telling them where the Goods were sold, part whereof has been recovered by those means to the Owners.

I declare upon the word of a dying Man, that Will Field was not concerned with Blueskin and my self in the breaking and robbing of Mr. Kneebone's House, altho' he has sworn the same at our respective Tryals; and I have been inform'd that by certain Circumstances which Field swore to, Mr. Kneebone himself is of opinion that he was not concerned in the Fact: But he has done the work for his Master,[1] who in the end no doubt will reward him, as he has done all his other Servants. I wish Field may repent and amend his wicked Life, for a greater Villain there is not breathing. Blueskin and my self, after we had robb'd Mr. Kneebone's House, lodg'd the Goods at my Warehouse, a little Stable at Westminster Horse-ferry, which I had hired for such Purposes. I was so cautious of suffering any one to be acquainted with it, that even Elizabeth Lyon was out of the Secret; but hearing of a Lock or Fence in Bishopsgate to dispose of the Cloth to, Blueskin carried the Pack, and I follow'd to guard him, and met the Chap[2] at an Alehouse; a small Quantity we got off at a very low Price, which was always not ours, but is the constant Fate of all other Robbers; for I declare that when Goods (the intrinsick Value whereof has been 50 £.) have been in my hands, I have never made more than ten Pounds of them clear money; such a Discount and Disadvantage attends always the sale of such unlawful Acquirements. Field lodging with Blueskin's Mother in Rosemary-Lane, we all became acquainted, and being all of a piece made no Secret of Mr. Kneebone's Robbery; we told him the manner of it, the Booty, &c. and withal carried him down to the Warehouse at Westminster, he pretending to buy the Goods. In a Day or two after, to the great Surprize of Blueskin and my self, we found the Warehouse broke open, the Cloth gone, and only a Wrapper or two of no value left; we concluded, as it appeared after, that Field had plaid at Rob-Thief with us, for he produc'd some of Mr. Kneebone's Cloth at my Tryal, of which he became possess'd by no other means than those I have related. I must add this to what relates to Mr. Kneebone's Robbery, that I was near a Fortnight, by Intervals, in cutting the two Oaken Bars that went over the back part of his House in Little Drury-Lane. I heartily ask his Pardon for injuring him my kind Patron and Benefactor in that manner, and desire his Prayers to God for the forgiveness of that as of all my other enormous Crimes.

I have been at times confin'd in all the Round-houses belonging to the respective Parishes within the Liberty of Westminster; Elizabeth Lyon has been a Prisoner in many of them also: I have sometimes procur'd her Liberty, and she at others has done her utmost to obtain mine, and at other times she has again betray'd me into the hands of Justice. When I was formerly in St. Anne's Round-house, she brought me the Spike of an Halbert, with the Help whereof I did break open the same, but was discover'd before I could get off, and was put into the Dungeon of the Place fetter'd and manacled;

---

[1] Jonathan Wild.
[2] Chapman—dealer

A Narrative of the Robberies, &c.

and that was the first Time that I had any Irons put upon me. I in Return rescu'd her from St. Giles's Round-house soon after; but the Manner of my own Escape from St. Giles's Round-House may be worthy of Notice. Having in Confederacy with my Brother Thomas a Sea-faring Person, and Elizabeth Lyon committed several Robberies about Clare Market, and Thomas being in Newgate for them, impeach'd me and Lyon; and the Prosecutors being in close Pursuit of us, I kept up as much as possible; 'till being one Day at the Queens-Head Ale-house in King street, Westminster, an Acquaintance call'd Sykes (alias Hell and Fury), a Chairman, desir'd me to go thence to an Ale-house at the Seven Dials, saying he knew two Chubs that we might make a Penny of at Skettles, we being good Players: I went with him; a third Person he soon procur'd, and said the fourth should not be long wanting, and truly he prov'd to be a Constable of St. Giles's Parish. In short, Sykes charg'd him with me, saying I stood impeach'd of several Robberies. Justice Parry sent me to St. Giles's Round-house for that Night, with Orders to the Constable to bring me before him again the next Morning for farther Examination. I had nothing but an old Razor in my Pocket, and was confin'd in the upper part of the Place, being two Stories from the Ground; with my Razor I cut out the Stretcher of a Chair, and began to make a Breach in the Roof, laying the Feather-bed under it to prevent any Noise by the falling of the Rubbish on the Floor. It being about nine at Night, People were passing and repassing in the Street, and a Tile or Brick happening to fall, struck a Man on the Head, who rais'd the whole Place; the People calling aloud that the Prisoners were breaking out of the Round-house. I found there was no Time then to be lost, therefore made a bold Push thro' the Breach, throwing a whole Load of Bricks, Tiles, &c. upon the People in the Street; and before the Beadle and Assistance came up I had dropt into the Church-yard, and got over the lower End of the Wall, and came amidst the Crowd, who were all staring up, some crying, there's his Head, there he goes behind the Chimney, &c. I was well enough diverted with the Adventure, and then went off about my Business.

The Methods by which I escap'd from New-Prison, and the Condemn'd Hold of Newgate, have been printed in so many Books and Papers, that it would be ridiculous to repeat them; only it must be remember'd that my Escaping from New-Prison, and carrying with me Elizabeth Lyon over the Wall of Bridewell Yard, was not so wonderful as has been reported, because Captain Geary and his Servants cannot but know, that by my opening the great Gate I got Lyon upon the Top of the Wall without the Help of a scaling Ladder, otherwise it must have been impracticable to have procur'd her Redemption. She indeed rewarded me as well for it, in betraying me to Jonathan Wild so soon after. I wish she may reform her Life: a more wicked, deceitful and lascivious Wretch there is not living in England. She has prov'd my Bane. God forgive her: I do; and die in Charity with all the rest of Mankind.

Blueskin has atton'd for his Offences. I am now following, being just on the Brink of Eternity, much unprepar'd to appear before the Face of an angry God. Blueskin had been a much older Offender than my self, having been guilty of numberless Robberies, and had formerly Convicted four of his Accomplices, who were put to Death. He was concern'd along with me in the three Robberies on the Hampstead Road, besides that of Mr. Kneebone, and one other. Tho' he was an able-bodied Man and capable of any Crime, even Murder, he was

Jack Sheppard.

never Master of a Courage or Conduct suitable to our Enterprizes; and I am of Opinion, that neither of us had so soon met our Fate, if he would have suffer'd himself to have been directed by me; he always wanting Resolution, when our Affairs requir'd it most. The last Summer, I hired two Horses for us at an Inn in Piccadilly, and being arm'd with Pistols, &c. we went upon Enfield-Chace, where a Coach pass'd us with two Footmen and four young ladies, who had with them their Gold Watches, Tweezer Cases and other things of Value; I declar'd immediately for attacking them, but Blueskin's Courage dropt him, saying that he would first refresh his Horse and then follow, but he designedly delayed till we had quite lost the Coach and Hopes of the Booty. In short, he was a worthless Companion, a sorry Thief, and nothing but the cutting of Jonathan Wild's Throat could have made him considerable.

I have often lamented the scandalous Practice of Thief-catching, as it is call'd, and the publick Manner of offering Rewards for stoln Goods, in Defiance of two several Acts of Parliament; the Thief-Catcher living sumptuously, and keeping publick Offices of Intelligence: these who forfeit their Lives every Day they breathe, and deserve the Gallows as richly as any of the Thieves, send us as their Representatives to Tyburn once a Month: thus they hang by Proxy, while we do it fairly in Person.

I never corresponded with any of them. I was indeed twice at a Thief-Catcher's Levee, and must confess the Man treated me civilly; he complimented me on my Successes, said he heard that I had both an Hand and Head admirably well turn'd to Business, and that I and my Friends should be always welcome to him: But caring not for his Acquaintance, I never troubled him, nor had we any Dealings together.

As my last Escape from Newgate out of the strong Room call'd the Castle, has made a greater Noise in the World than any other Action of my Life, I shall relate every minute Circumstance thereof as far as I am able to remember: intending thereby to satisfie the Curious and do Justice to the Innocent. After I had been made a publick Spectacle of for many Days together, with my Legs chain'd together, loaded with heavy Irons, and stapled down to the Floor, I thought it was not altogether impracticable to escape, if I could but be furnished with proper Implements; but as every Person that came near me was carefully watch'd, there was no Possibility of any such Assistance; till one Day in the Absence of my Jaylors, being looking about the Floor, I spy'd a small Nail within Reach, and with that, after a little Practice, I found the great Horse Padlock that went from the Chain to the Staple in the Floor might be unlock'd, which I did afterward at pleasure; and was frequently about the Room, and have several times slept on the Barracks, when the Keepers imagin'd I had not been out of my Chair. But being unable to pass up the Chimney, and void of Tools, I remain'd where I was; till being detected in these Practices by the Keepers, who surpriz'd me one Day before I could fix my self to the Staple in the manner as they had left me, I shew'd Mr. Pitt, Mr. Rouse, and Mr. Parry my Art, and before their Faces unlockt the Padlock with the Nail; and though People have made such an Outcry about it, there is scarce a Smith in London but what may easily do the same thing. However this call'd for a farther Security of me; and till now I had remain'd without Hand-Cuffs, and a jolly Pair was provided for me. Mr. Kneebone was present when they were put on: I with Tears begg'd his Intercession to the Keepers

A Narrative of the Robberies, &c.

to preserve me from those dreadful Manacles, telling him, my Heart was broken, and that I should be much more miserable than before. Mr. Kneebone could not refrain from shedding Tears, and did use his good Offices with the Keepers to keep me from them, but all to no purpose; on they went, though at the same time I despis'd them, and well knew that with my Teeth only I could take them off at Pleasure : But this was to lull them into a firm Belief, that they had effectually frustrated all Attempts to escape for the future. I was still far from despairing. The Turnkey and Mr. Kneebone had not been gone down Stairs an Hour, ere I made an Experiment, and got off my Hand-Cuffs, and before they visited me again, I put them on, and industriously rubb'd and fretted the Skin on my Wrists, making them very bloody, as thinking (if such a Thing was possible to be done) to move the Turnkeys to Compassion, but rather to confirm them in their Opinion; but though this had no Effect upon them, it wrought much upon the Spectators, and drew down from them not only much Pity, but Quantities of Silver and Copper : But I wanted still a more useful Metal, a Crow, a Chissel, a File, and a Saw or two, those Weapons being more useful to me than all the Mines of Mexico; but there was no expecting any such Utensils in my Circumstances.

Wednesday the 14th of October the Sessions beginning, I found there was not a moment to be lost; and the Affair of Jonathan Wild's Throat, together with the Business at the Old Baily, having sufficiently engag'd the Attention of the Keepers, I thought then was the Time to push. Thursday the 15th at about two in the Afternoon Austin my old Attendant came to bring my Necessaries, and brought up four Persons, viz. the Keeper of Clerkenwell-Bridewell, the Clerk of Westminster Gate-house, and two others. Austin, as it was his usual Custom, examin'd the Irons and Hand-Cuffs, and found all safe and firm, and then left me; and he may remember that I ask'd him to come again to me the same Evening, but I neither expected or desired his Company; and happy was it for the poor Man that he did not interfere, while I had the large Iron Bar in my Hand, though I once had a Design to have barricaded him, or any others from coming into the Room while I was at work: but then considering that such a Project would be useless, I let fall that Resolution.

As near as can be remember'd, just before three in the Afternoon I went to work, taking off first my Hand-Cuffs; next with main Strength I twisted a small Iron Link of the Chain between my Legs asunder; and the broken Pieces prov'd extream useful to me in my Design; the Fett-Locks I drew up to the Calves of my Leggs, taking off before that my Stockings, and with my Garters made them firm to my Body, to prevent their Shackling. I then proceeded to make a Hole in the Chimney of the Castle about three Foot wide, and six Foot high from the Floor, and with the Help of the broken Links aforesaid wrench'd an Iron Bar out of the Chimney, of about two Feet and an half in length, and an Inch square : a most notable Implement. I immediately enter'd the Red Room directly over the Castle, where some of the Preston Rebels had been kept a long time agone; and as the Keepers say the Door had not been unlock'd for seven Years; but I intended not to be seven Years in opening it, thought they had : I went to work upon the Nut of the Lock, and with little Difficulty got it off, and made the Door fly before me; in this Room I found a large Nail, which prov'd of great Use in my farther Progress. The

Jack Sheppard.

Door of the Entry between the Red Room and the Chapel prov'd an hard Task, it being a laborious Piece of Work; for here I was forc'd to break away the Wall, and dislodge the Bolt which was fasten'd on the other Side. This occasion'd much Noise, and I was very fearful of being heard by the Master-Side Debtors. Being got to the Chapel, I climb'd over the Iron Spikes, and with Ease broke one of them off for my further Purposes, and open'd the Door on the Inside. The Door going out of the Chapel to the Leads, I stripp'd the Nut from off the Lock, as I had done before from that of the Red Room, and then got into the Entry between the Chapel and the Leads; and came to another strong Door, which being fasten'd by a very strong Lock, there I had like to have stopt, and it being full dark, my Spirits began to fail me, as greatly doubting of succeeding; but cheering up, I wrought on with great Diligence, and in less than half an Hour, with the main Help of the Nail from the Red Room, and the Spike from the Chapel, wrench'd the Box off, and so made the Door my Humble Servant.

A little farther in my Passage another stout Door stood in my way; and this was a Difficulty with a Witness; being guarded with more Bolts, Bars, and Locks than any I had hitherto met with: I had by this time great Encouragement, as hoping soon to be rewarded for all this Toil and Labour. The Clock at St. Sepulchre's was now going the eighth Hour, and this prov'd a very useful Hint to me soon after. I went first upon the Box and the Nut, but found it Labour in vain; and then proceeded to attack the Fillet of the Door; this succeeded beyond Expectation, for the Box of the Lock came off with it from the main Post. I found my Work was near finish'd, and that my Fate soon would be determined.

I was got to a Door opening in the lower Leads, which being only bolted on the Inside, I open'd it with ease, and then clambered from the top of it to the higher Leads, and went over the Wall. I saw the Streets were lighted, the Shops being still open, and therefore began to consider what was necessary to be further done, as knowing that the smallest Accident would still spoil the whole Workmanship, and was doubtful on which of the Houses I should alight. I found I must go back for the Blanket which had been my Covering a-nights in the Castle, which I accordingly did, and endeavoured to fasten my Stockings and that together, to lessen my Descent, but wanted Necessaries so to do, and was therefore forc'd to make use of the Blanket alone. I fixt the same with the Chappel Spike into the Wall of Newgate, and dropt from it on the Turner's Leads, a House adjoyning to the Prison; 'twas then about Nine of the Clock, and the Shops not yet shut in. It fortunately happen'd, that the Garret Door on the Leads was open. I stole softly down about two Pair of Stairs, and then heard Company talking in a Room; the Door open. My Irons gave a small Clink, which made a Woman cry, Lord, what Noise is that? A Man reply'd, Perhaps the Dog or Cat; and so it went off. I return'd up to the Garret, and laid my self down, being terribly fatigu'd; and continu'd there for about two Hours, and then crept down once more to the Room where the Company were, and heard a Gentleman taking his Leave, being very importunate to be gone, saying he had disappointed Friends by not going Home sooner. In about three Quarters more the Gentleman took Leave, and went, being lighted down Stairs by the Maid, who, when she return'd shut the Chamber-door; I then resolv'd at all Hazards to follow, and slipt down Stairs, but made a Stumble against a

A Narrative of the Robberies, &c.

Chamber-door. I was instantly in the Entry and out at the Street Door, which I was so unmannerly as not to shut after me. I was once more, contrary to my own Expectation and that of all Mankind, a Freeman.

I pass'd directly by St. Sepulchre's Watch-house, bidding them Good-morrow, it being after Twelve, and down Snow-hill, up Holborn, leaving St. Andrew's Watch on my left, and then again pass'd the Watch-house at Holborn Bars, and made down Gray's-Inn Lane into the Fields, and at two in the Morning came to Tottenham Court, and there got into an old House in the Fields, where Cows had some time been kept, and laid me down to Rest, and slept well for three Hours. My Legs were swell'd and bruis'd intollerably, which gave me great Uneasiness; and having my Fetters still on, I dreaded the Approach of the Day, fearing then I should be discovered. I began to examine my Pockets, and found my self Master of between forty and fifty Shillings. I had no Friend in the World that I could send to, or trust with my Condition. About seven on Friday Morning it began raining, and continued so the whole Day, insomuch that not one Creature was to be seen in the Fields. I would freely have parted with my right Hand for an Hammer, a Chisel, and a Punch. I kept snug in my Retreat till the Evening, when after Dark I ventur'd into Tottenham, and got to a little blind Chandler's Shop, and there furnish'd my self with Cheese and Bread, Small-beer, and other Necessaries, hiding my Irons with a great Coat as much as possible. I ask'd the Woman for an Hammer, but there was none to be had; so I went very quietly back to my Dormitory, and rested pretty well that Night, and continued there all Saturday. At Night I went again to the Chandler's Shop and got Provisions, and slept till about six the next Day, which being Sunday, I began with a Stone to batter the Basils of the Fetters in order to beat them into a large Oval, and then to slip my Heels thorough. In the Afternoon the Master of the Shed, or House, came in, and seeing my Irons, asked me, For God's sake, who are you? I told him, "an unfortunate young man, who had been sent to Bridewell about a Bastard-Child, as not being able to give Security to the Parish, and had made my Escape." The Man reply'd, If that was the Case it was a small Fault indeed, for he had been guilty of the same things himself formerly; and withal said, However, he did not like my Looks, and cared not how soon I was gone.

After he was gone, observing a poor-looking Man like a Joiner, I made up to him and repeated the same Story, assuring him that 20s. should be at his Service, if he could furnish me with a Smith's Hammer, and a Punch. The Man prov'd a Shoe-maker by Trade, but willing to obtain the Reward, immediately borrow'd the Tools of a Black-Smith his Neighbour, and likewise gave me great Assistance, and before five that Evening I had entirely got rid of those troublesome Companions my Fetters, which I gave to the Fellow, besides his Twenty Shillings, if he thought fit to make use of them.

That Night I came to a Cellar at Charing-Cross, and refresh'd very comfortably with roast Veal, &c. where about a dozen People were all discoursing about Sheppard, and nothing else was talk'd on whilst I staid amongst them. I had tyed an Handkerchief about my Head, tore my woollen Cap in many places, as likewise my Coat and Stockings, and look'd exactly like what I designed to represent, a Beggar-Fellow.

The next Day I took shelter at an Ale-house of little or no Trade, in Rupert-Street, near Piccadilly. The Woman and I discours'd much about

Jack Sheppard.

Sheppard. I assur'd her it was impossible for him to escape out of the Kingdom, and that the Keepers would have him again in a few Days. The Woman wish'd that a Curse might fall on those who should betray him. I continued there till the Evening, when I stept towards the Hay-market, and mixt with a Crowd about two Ballad-Singers; the Subject being about Sheppard. And I remember the Company was very merry about the Matter.

On Tuesday I hired a Garret for my Lodging at a poor House in Newport-Market, and sent for a sober young Woman, who for a long Time past had been the real Mistress of my Affections, who came to me, and render'd all the Assistance she was capable of affording. I made her the Messenger to my Mother, who lodg'd in Clare-street. She likewise visited me in a Day or two after, begging on her bended Knees of me to make the best of my Way out of the Kingdom, which I faithfully promis'd; but I cannot say it was in my Intentions heartily so to do.

I was oftentimes in Spittle-fields, Drury-lane, Lewkenors-lane, Parkers-lane, St. Thomas-Street, &c. those having been the chief Scenes of my Rambles and Pleasures.

I had once form'd a Design to have open'd a Shop or two in Monmouth-street for some Necessaries, but let that drop, and came to a Resolution of breaking the House of the two Mr. Rawlins's Brothers and Pawn-broker in Drury-lane, which accordingly I put in Execution, and succeeded; they both hearing me rifling their goods as they lay in Bed together in the next Room. And though there were none others to assist me, I pretended there was, by loudly giving our Directions for shooting the first Person through the Head that presum'd to stir: which effectually quieted them, while I carried off my Booty; with Part whereof on the fatal Saturday following, being the 31st of October, I made an extraordinary Appearance; and from a Carpenter and Butcher was now transform'd into a Perfect Gentleman; and in Company with my Sweetheart aforesaid, and another young Woman her Acquaintance, went into the City, and were very merry together at a publick House not far from the Place of my old Confinement. At four that same Afternoon we all pass'd under Newgate in a Hackney Coach, the Windows drawn up, and in the Evening I sent for my Mother to the Sheers Ale-house in Maypole Alley near Clare-Market, and with her drank three Quarterns of Brandy; and after leaving her I drank in one Place or other about the Neighbourhood all the Evening, till the evil Hour of Twelve, having been seen and known by many of my Acquaintance; all of them cautioning of me, and wondering at my Presumption to appear in that Manner. At length my Senses were quite overcome with the Quantities and Variety of Liquors I had all the Day been drinking of, which pav'd the Way for my Fate to meet me; and when apprehended, I do protest, I was altogether incapable of resisting, and scarce knew what they were doing to me, and had but two Second-hand Pistols scarce worth carrying about me.

A clear and ample Account have I now given of the most material Transactions of my Life, and do hope the same will prove a Warning to all young Men.

There nothing now remains. But I return my hearty Thanks to the Reverend Dr. Bennet, the Reverend Mr. Purney, the Reverend Mr. Wagstaffe, the Reverend Mr. Hawkins, the Reverend Mr. Flood, and the Reverend Mr. Edwards, for their Charitable Visits and Assistances to me; as also my Thanks to those worthy Gentlemen who so generously contributed towards my Support in Prison.

A Narrative of the Robberies, &c.

I hope none will be so cruel as to reflect on my poor distressed Mother, the unhappy Parent of two miserable Wretches, my self and Brother; the last gone to America for his Crimes, and my self going to the Grave for mine; the Weight of which Misfortune is sufficient surely to satisfy the Malice of her Enemies.

I beseech the Infinite Divine Being of Beings to pardon my numberless and enormous Crimes, and to have Mercy on my poor departing Soul.

Middle-Stone-Room in Newgate, Novem. 10. 1724.

John Sheppard.

POSTSCRIPT.

After I had Escap'd from the Castle, concluding that Blueskin would have certainly been decreed for Death, I did fully resolve and purpose to have gone and cut down the Gallows the Night before his Execution.

FINIS.

Jack Sheppard.

AUTHENTIC

MEMOIRS

of the

LIFE

and

Surprising Adventures

OF

JOHN SHEPPARD:

Who was Executed at Tyburn,
November the 16th, 1724.

By way of FAMILIAR LETTERS from a
Gentleman in Town, to his Friend
and Correspondent in the Country.

I've done such Deeds, will make my Story hereafter
Quoted in Competition with all Ill Ones;
The History of my Wickedness shall run
Down through the low Traditions of the Vulgar,
And Boys be taught to tell the Tale of — Sheppard.
        Otway's Venice Preserv'd.

THE SECOND EDITION
Adorn'd with Variety of Copper Cuts.

LONDON, Printed for Joseph Marshall at the
Bible in Newgate-street. 1724.
Price Bound 1s.

THE

DEDICATION.

TO the Vigilant, Trusty, and Indulgent
Guardians of JOHN SHEPPARD, during
his late confinement in NEWGATE-
CASTLE, and the CONDEMN'D-HOLD.

GENTLEMEN,
   Ingratum si dixeris, omnia dixeris; that is, *Ingratitude is worse than the Sin of Witchcraft.* And Nature herself dictates to us, that one good Turn deserves another. As therefore the Heroic Exploits of your late *Guardee,* and

Authentic Memoirs.

the *Hero* of the following History, have been of singular Service to several Honest Tradesmen, and Lyrick as well as Prose Pamphletteers, particularly to the celebrated Author of Ap—by's Journal, and your Humble Servant, who freely owns, he has *crackt* several Bottles of good Old Port, and partook of many a Titt-Bitt *Freecost*, on his Account: I resolv'd to exert my Pen in his Behalf, and oblige the World with the following *Authentic Memoirs*, that they might not be impos'd on by *Romantic Narrations* instead of *Fact*, and to rescue my Benefactor out of the Hands of *Pyrates*.

And as no Man ever came under your Jurisdiction before, of half that Importance and Consequence—to your selves, as he was, nor that ever brought half that *Grist to your Mill* as he did; upon mature Deliberation, I determin'd to lay these few Sheets in the most humble Manner at your Feet, as thinking they cou'dn't fly any where more safely for Shelter and Protection.

I own, indeed, I am in some measure to Blame, and perhaps, may be Censur'd as too presumptuous, in prefixing your *Venerable Names* to a Work of this Nature, without free License and Consent first had and obtain'd: But, as I am an *Anonymous Author*, and expect no *Dedication-Fee*, no Gratuity, the Customary Return for fulsome *Panegyrick*, I take it for granted you'll readily forgive me.

Besides, I dare appeal to your own Consciences, and the grateful Sense you must needs retain of so bountiful, so daily a *Benefactor*, whether you ought not to encourage every Attempt to Record his Fame after Death, whose Life was so near and dear to you, and to secure his *precious Memory* for ever, from being bury'd in Oblivion.

Methinks I hear you very honourably acknowledge the Truth and Justice of this Appeal; but then, to my no small *Mortification*, methinks, a Whisper sounds in my Ears, *We are Pre-engag'd to a more Celebrated Historian;* and I have good Grounds to be Jealous of Mr. Ap—by's Garretteer, as my more happy Rival.

But be it as it may; if so, I'll endeavour to bear my Misfortune like a good Christian, and not dispute his *Prior-Title* to your Favour and Affection: But I hope you'll pardon my Freedom, if I do my self so much Justice, as to assure my *Courteous Readers*, that *My Intelligence* is full as Genuine as *His*, though not usher'd into the World with the Great Mr. R—s's PROBATUM EST. For I received all my *Instructions* from a Gentleman who was intimately acquainted with *Sheppard* in his Infancy, and has had an uninterrupted Correspondence with him during the whole Time of his Confinement, thro' (your most gracious Permission) GRATIS; an Indulgence, as I understand, granted but to *very few;* your *Worships* having made it a Law not to be broke through, but in Cases of extraordinary Emergency, That your *Hay shou'd be made while the Sun shin'd.*

Thus much I thought proper to inform the Publick, in relation to *My Self;* I shall now proceed, whether you shall please to be my worthy *Patrons*, or not, to the Honourable *Thoughts* I had conceiv'd, and still do conceive or your *extraordinary Merits*.

I am very well inform'd, *Gentlemen*, and I firmly believe it, that there has never appear'd that *Conduct* and *OEconomy* in *Newgate*, from its first Erection, as has been visible of late, under your *prudent Administration*.

NEWGATE has, for some considerable Time past, lost its former Character,

Jack Sheppard.

of a *Den of Thieves*, and been crouded with *Gentlemen* and *Ladies* of the strictest Honour and Reputation. Your *Stone Castle*, in which of old resided none but the Giant *Despair*, has, to your no small Advantage, as well as Credit, been the *Assembly-Room* of Persons of Figure and Distinction.

I hope I shall not Shock *your Modesty*, if I mention, with the profoundest Admiration, your Courteous Behaviour and Indulgent Treatment of your *Guardee*, whilst he was under your immediate Inspection.

Never was *Malefactor* so oblig'd before; never was any Inhabitant of your *Gloomy Regions*, 'till now, so pamper'd, so indulg'd, and fed with such choice and delicious morsels.

May the Reformation thus begun in *your House*, from SHEPPARD'S first Arrival in it, be vigorously pursu'd; and may none of its Apartments (as for many Ages they justly have been) be deem'd any more *a* HELL upon EARTH. I am,
Gentlemen,
Your most Obedient,
Most Devoted,
Humble Servant,
G. E.

THE

LIFE

of

JOHN SHEPPARD.

LETTER I.

October 17, 1724.

SIR,

In Answer to your's of . . . Instant, wherein you desire an Account of the Life of Mr. John Sheppard, who hath been so Notorious in the World; I shall give a Relation of what I can find Material in his Life, and in as short and plain a Manner as I can.

He was born in Stepney Parish, and was the son of a Carpenter, who died when he was a Child: He had one Brother and one Sister when his Father died. The Daughter died soon after the Father; and the Elder Brother *Thomas Sheppard* went into a Lady's Family as a Foot-boy, and afterwards was put by the said Lady an Apprentice to a Carpenter, of whom more hereafter. This Younger Brother John was admitted into the Workhouse in Bishopsgate Street, where he continued 'till he was fit to be put out Apprentice, and there received the Common Education. The Trade he chose was a Carpenter and House-Joyner.

His Mother (altho' an Honest, Industrious Woman) was not capable of advancing any Money for him; and therefore apply'd herself to Mr. William Kneebone at the Angel over-against the New Church in the Strand, Woollen-Draper, with whom she then liv'd as a Servant. Mr. Kneebone having considerable Alterations to be made at his Country House at Hamsptead, and being pleas'd with the pretty modest Behaviour of the Boy, agreed with Mr. Owen Wood,

Authentic Memoirs.

who then liv'd in Drury-Lane, that he should take him Apprentice, without Money; and on that Condition, should Repair his House, which Repair was very considerable. To which Mr. Wood agreed; and this John Sheppard was bound Apprentice to him on April 2d., 1717. He had a Mild, Honest, Sober, Indulgent Master, and for four Years of his Time was very Orderly; he was very Ingenious at his Trade, and knew his Business very well, and very early in his Time, in which he far exceeded most of his Years.

As to his being drawn from one Degree of Wickedness to another, take it as he related it to One who visited him in Newgate, and desired to know by what Steps he advanced to that height of Thieving he arrived to, and for which he was Condemned, which was as follows:—a Button-Mould Maker, who liv'd next Door to his Master, leaving off his Trade, and taking a Publick House in Newtoners Lane, drew him, with some other Apprentices, to his House; which being frequented by Loose and Idle Persons, soon corrupted his Manners, and from a Sober Orderly Boy, became Headstrong, Disobedient, and Vicious; staying out of Nights, wronging his Master of his Time, and spending what Money he got with those vile Wretches; and, at this Place it was, he became acquainted with that vile Prostitute Elizabeth Lyon, commonly called Edgworth Bess, (being the Name of the Town she was born in), with whom she contracted such Familiarity as prov'd his Ruin; for being engaged with that vile Strumpet, she soon perswaded him to Steal what he could where he work'd. The first Fact he was detected in, and which he would own, was stealing a Piece of Fustian from Mr. Bains a Piece-Broker in White-Horse-Yard, about the middle of July, 1723, where he was sent to perform a Job. His House-breaking he first began to practise on his Master (Mr. Wood's) House, where, altho' lock'd out at Night, he was sure to be found in Bed the next Morning, by climbing up to a Window which was two pair of Stairs high, and at which he enter'd. His Master and Mistress often caution'd him against keeping that leud Woman Company, but to no Purpose; for he wanting to be more at Liberty, studied all manner of Means to accomplish it, by being Impudent and Abusive to his Master; and under a Pretence of his Master's Way of Jobbing from House to House, was not sufficient to furnish him with a due Experience of his Business, he therefore would step into the World for better Information.

While these Jarrings and Animosities were at Home, Edgworth Bess had stoln a Gold Ring from a Gentleman she had pickt up, and by him committed to St. Giles's Round-House; Sheppard, as soon as he heard of it, went to make her a Visit, and after having talk'd a short Time with the Beadle and his Wife, abused them, and fell on them and having got the Key from them, by that Means set his Mistress at Liberty, notwithstanding all the Opposition they were capable of making. His little Ways of Pilfering were not sufficient to defray the Charges of their Extravagancies, and therefore he resolv'd to try House-breaking.

The first Attempt of breaking open a House, with an Intent to Rob, was the House of Mr. Bains, before mentioned, which he enter'd, August, 1723, the Situation of which he well knew, having work'd in the House on several Jobs; which he effected, by taking the Wooden Bars, and getting in at the Kitchen Window, the Kitchen being under Ground, and went up Stairs to the Shop, from whence he took seven Pounds in Money, and Goods to the Value of fourteen Pounds; he came out at the Street Door, which he lock'd after him, and fastened

Jack Sheppard.

down the Bars again; which made Mr. Bains suspect a Lodger, he having no visible Breach made in his House; which Suspicion remain'd 'till Sheppard was taken for Robbing Mr. Kneebone's House, where, in his Examination, among other Things, he confessed this of Mr. Bains.

The Day after this Robbery, he quitted his Master's Service, and became the companion of the most wicked Thieves, and House-breakers; such as these, Joseph Blake, alias Blewskin, — Doleing, William Field, James Sykes alias Hell and Fury. The Effects of which were as follow;

Sheppard having taken a Lodging at the House of Mr. Charles in May-Fair near Piccadilly, took an Opportunity, on the 23d of October, 1723, to Rob him of seven Pounds ten Shillings in Money, five large Silver Spoons, six Forks ditto, four Tea Spoons, six plain Gold Rings, a Cypher Ring, four Suits of Wearing Apparel, and Linen to a considerable Value.

On the 5th of February following, he, together with his Brother Thomas Sheppard, and Edgworth Bess, broke open the House of Mrs. Mary Cooke, Linnen-Draper in Clare-Street, Clare-Market, and stole to the Value of about sixty Pounds.

On the 14th of the same Month, he, together with his Brother, and Edgworth Bess, broke open the House of Mr. Philips in Drury-Lane, and stole from Mrs. Kendrick, who rents his Shop, some few Goods, but of inconsiderable Value.

Soon after, Thomas Sheppard was Taken, and Committed to Newgate; and in Hopes of procuring Favour, Impeached his Brother John, and Edgworth Bess. Whereupon strict Search was made after them, but to little Purpose, 'till James Sykes, alias Hell and Fury, betrayed his Friend John in the following Manner; Sykes accidentally meeting him, invited him to one Redgates a Victualler near the Seven Dials, to play a Game at Skettles; which was immediately agreed to, and during their Divertion, Sykes privately sent for a Constable, and Charg'd his Friend Sheppard with the two Robberies before mentioned: Whereupon he was carry'd before Justice Parry, who ordered him to St. Giles's Round-House, 'till the next Morning, in order to a further Examination. And for the better Security of his Person, he was lodg'd in a Room two pair of Stairs from the Ground: from whence, notwithstanding that Precaution, he soon gave them the Slip; for, in less than three Hours, by the help of a Razor which he had in his Pocket, and part of an old Chair which he found in the Room, he made a Passage thro' the Ceiling, Untiled the top of the Round-house, and by the Assistance of a Sheet and Blanket, descended into the Church-yard, and by climbing over the Wall compleated his Escape; after which, he mixt himself with the Mob, and the better to Conceal himself, pointed up to the Chimney, asserting he saw Sheppard behind it: Which Notion the Rabble readily came into.

On the 19th of May, Sheppard, with one Benson, a Brother in Iniquity, passing through Leicester-Fields in the Dusk of the Evening, taking the Opportunity of a Quarrel that happen'd between a Gentleman and a Woman of the Town, pick'd the Gentleman's Pocket of his Watch; which he immediately missing, made an Out-cry of Stop Thief, &c. Whereupon Sheppard and Benson endeavoured to slip through the Croud: Benson escaped; but Sheppard taking to his Heels and joining the Out-cry, a Serjeant of the Guards at Leicester-House, seeing no Person run before, suspected him, and seized him. Whereupon

Authentic Memoirs.

he was immediately carry'd to St. Ann's Round-House, in Soho and kept in safe Custody 'till the next Morning. About 9 of the Clock, his old Female Companion Edgworth Bess paid him a Visit, upon which she was detain'd on Suspicion of Confederacy. Both were carry'd before Justice Walters, when Mr. Cook and Mr. Philips appeared against them, and charg'd them with the Felony and Burglary before mentioned.

John Sheppard, in hopes of a more favourable Treatment, made large Promises of discovering several of his Abettors. Whereupon the Justice only committed them to New-Prison, in Expectation of a suitable Performance of his Promise; intending, notwithstanding, in Case of a Disappointment, to commit them to Newgate.

As Edgworth Bess was always look'd upon as the Wife of John Sheppard, they were both secur'd in one Apartment, and that which was reckon'd the strongest, viz. Newgate-Ward. But Sheppard well knowing he had promised more than he could perform, and reasonably supposing the Justice would be incensed at his Disappointment, bent his Thoughts wholly on making his Escape.

As he had the Privilege of having his Friends to visit him, he had several Implements privately conveyed to him, proper for his Purpose, and making good use of his Time, on the 25th of May, which happen'd on Whitson-Monday, very early in the Morning, he had made a considerable Progress towards his Escape, which he compleated, by taking first an Iron Bar out of the Window, and then a Wooden one, though very substantial, by boring it through in several Places. This was only his first Labour; he had then 25 Foot to descend; to accomplish which, he fixed a Blanket and Sheet to the Bars of the Window, and consulting his Mistress's Safety as well as his own, orders her to strip (the best Method he could propose to accomplish their Design;) which Madam readily consented to, and in pursuance to his Directions, was soon landed. Sheppard soon follow'd.

But notwithstanding their Success thus far, they had many Difficulties still to encounter with, for they are now got only from one Prison to another. This puts Sheppard upon Second-Thoughts, and forming a new Contrivance to Escape from thence. This he effected, by fixing Gimblets in the Wall, at proper Distances, which served as a Scaling-Ladder, by which he and his Mistress ascended, and thereby accomplished their Escape.

Though this was a very bold and remarkable Adventure, and what few Villains but himself would ever have attempted; yet they are but Trifles, to the surprising Exploits, which will be the subject of my following Letter.

I am,
Your Friend
And Humble Servant,

G. E.

LETTER II.

Oct. 24, 1724.

SIR,

Having closed my Last with the wonderful Escape of Sheppard from New-Prison, I shall make the Transactions of those few Days of his Release, to the Time of his being Retaken and committed to Newgate, the Subject of

Jack Sheppard.

This. Notwithstanding the apparent Danger of ever appearing in his own Neighbourhood, like one of an undaunted Resolution, the first Night he ventures to pay a Visit to his old Associates Anthony Lamb and Charles Grace, who, laying their Politick Heads together, soon form'd a proper Scheme to Rob Mr. Barton, a Master Taylor, (who lodg'd with Mr. Carter, Uncle, as well as Master, of Anthony Lamb;) which Project they compleated in the following Manner.

On the 16th of June last, Anthony Lamb, early in the Morning, convey'd Sheppard and Grace into the House, well provided with Pistols, &c., for the intended Enterprise. Sheppard directly marches to Mr. Barton's Chamber-Door, and with his usual Dexterity breaks it open. Grace was planted at the Bed-side, with positive Orders to Fire, in case of any Noise or Resistance, during such time as Sheppard should be employ'd in Ransacking the Trunks, Boxes, &c. for Taylors-Cabbage, which, to his agreeable Surprise, consisted of Cash, Bonds, Notes, and other easy Moveables, as amounted to the value of Three hundred Pounds. Among the rest of the Cargo, there happen'd to be a Padasway Suit of Cloathes, the proper Goods and Chattels of a lusty Gentleman, which Sheppard set apart for his own Wear, after a little Alteration.

After Sheppard and Grace had got their Booty safe off the Premises, Lamb leaves the Door open, and steals up quietly to Bed, as seemingly Innocent as his Namesake.

One of the Neighbours happening to Rise somewhat earlier than ordinary, and finding the Door wide open, and no Body stirring, alarms the House. Mr. Barton soon found, to his Cost, that Thieves had stripp'd him; whereupon he, with his Posse, mounted up Stairs to Lamb's Apartment, whom they found fast asleep, or at least in a pretended Dream; but they soon awak'd him, and seiz'd him, on Suspicion, being conscious of his keeping loose and dissolute Company, and directly charged him with the Fact. Lamb had not Courage and Resolution enough to deny the Charge, but cry'd Peccavi, and declar'd his Accomplices, tho' they were too Cunning to let him know where to find them. Upon this Confession, Lamb was immediately committed to Newgate, and was afterwards try'd at the Old-Bailey; but Mr. Barton taking Compassion on his Youth, and listning to the earnest Solicitations of his near Relations, was so favourable in his Prosecution, that he spared his Life, and sate down contented with his bare Transportation.

On the 19th of June, Mr. Kneebone received private Intelligence from Lamb's Father, of a Design upon his House that Night. Whereupon, he order'd his Servants to sit up, and, no doubt, furnished them with proper Provision, to give his intended Visitors a handsome Reception. But something more than ordinary happen'd, that his Guest did not come, which was a sore Disappointment. However, though they were not punctual to their Time, the Visit was paid on the 12th of July following, and Sheppard, Joseph Blake alias Blue-skin, and William Field (as he himself afterwards confess'd) broke into the said Mr. Kneebone's House, about 12 of the Clock at Night; having first saw'd two large Wooden Bars of the Cellar Window, and so made an easy Passage into the lower Apartment.

Having got a safe Admittance there, they soon put back two Bolts, and drew the Staple which fastned the Cellar-Door, through which they proceeded to the Shop, which being lin'd with Shutters, they broke the Hasp,

Jack Sheppard in Newgate

From the *Authentic Memoirs of the Life and Surprising Adventures of John Sheppard*, 1724

Authentic Memoirs.

and convey'd off the Premises about 108 Yards of Cloth and other Effects, to the Value of about Fifty Pounds. Mr. Kneebone, as they did not come at the Time appointed, thought it very ill Manners that they came at all.

On the 19th of July, Sheppard and Blake play'd at Small-Game, stopt a Coach in Hampstead Road, and took from a Lady's Woman Two Shillings and Six Pence, which was all the Profit of that Transaction, as she was alone, and no better provided.

On the 20th, they Robb'd Mr. Pargiter of Three Shillings; for which Fact two Soldiers were Indicted; but as they were Innocent, were honourably Acquitted.

On the 21st, they stopt a Stage-Coach and took Two and twenty Shillings from one of the Passengers.

Mr. Kneebone, being very much out of Humour, at the ill Treatment he had met with, pays honest Jonathan Wild a Visit, and gives him proper Instructions, as well as a proper Fee, to find out his bold Visiters. Accordingly Jonathan sends out his Emissaries, and on the 22d of July, at Night, by his Direction, Edgworth Bess was seized in a Brandy Shop near Temple-Bar, who, in a Fright and Surprise, confest where her Accomplice Sheppard was. Sheppard accordingly was taken the next Morning at Blue-skin's Mother's, (who keeps a Brandy Shop in Rosemary-Lane) by Quilt Arnold, a trusty Embassador of Jonathan's. Sheppard did not, indeed, tamely Resign, for he snapp'd a loaded Pistol, and design'd the Present of the Plumb that was in it for Arnold, for his good Intentions. Arnold thank'd him, as much as if he had accepted it, and secur'd him, without any further Risque.

Sheppard was immediately carry'd to his old Apartment in New-Prison, and carefully watch'd 'till next Morning, at which Time he was convey'd to Justice Blackerby's, and by him committed to Newgate; where he frankly confess'd the several Robberies before mention'd.

On the 13th of August he took his Tryal at the Sessions-House in the Old-Baily; where he made but a very weak Defence, objecting only against the Evidence of Field, as being an old Offender, a frequent Attendant at the Bar, a subtle Seducer of unwary Youths like himself, and an Encourager of all the fatal Practices that procure their Ruin.

This carry'd but little Weight with it; and as the Fact was plainly prov'd against him, the Jury, without any great Hesitation, found him Guilty, and the next Day, in Pursuance of their Verdict, he received Sentence of Death.

On Sunday the 15th, in private Conversation with a Friend, he positively declar'd That Field was no Ways concern'd in the Transaction for which he was to Suffer; and that Blue-skin and he were the only Persons engaged in it.

The Court being out of Town, the Warrant was not sent down for the Execution of the Malefactors Condemned the Session before; in which favourable Interval, James Harman, Lumly Davis, and John Sheppard call'd a Cabinet Council, form'd the Plan of their Escape, and provided themselves with proper Materials to effect it. But having Promises of Favour from Great Persons, they dropt their Enterprise. But alas! they found to their Cost, their building on Great Mens' Promises, was raising Castles in the Air, their Fate was Seal'd, and that 'twas high Time to make some Preparation for their Passage into another World the next Morning.

On the very Day of their Execution, Davis gave Sheppard the Instruments

Jack Sheppard.

by which he accomplish'd his Release; who living in the hourly Expectation of a Warrant for himself, thought it high Time to set his Hand to the Plough, and if possible, give his Keepers the slip. Taking therefore, the Advantage of the Hurry of the Prison, in preparing the others for their long Journey, he began his Operations, and dextrously saw'd off part of the Iron Spike over the Hatch of the Condemn'd-Hold; on Saturday he made some further Progress; on Sunday (being a very Conscientious Gentleman) he rested from his Labours. On Monday Morning, a Friend came to visit him, that knew nothing of the Scheme he had laid, for his Deliverance, and like a good Christian, advis'd him to think of his latter End, for the Time of his Execution would be the next Friday. But Sheppard, who had other Thoughts in his Head, made Answer Yes, so my great Lord and Master says, but, by G—d, I'll do my best Endeavours to make Him a false Prophet, (or us'd Words to that Effect); and he was as good as his Word, for on that same Day, which was the Day the Dead Warrant came down for his Execution on the Friday following, he compleated his Work; and having broken off the Spike, by the Assistance of one Stephen Fowls a Prisoner on the Inside, and his old Confident Edgworth Bess, and another of the same Stamp, on the Outside, he was convey'd with his Heels foremost through the Little Ease, which was but 8 Inches and an half one Way, and 9 the other; and so, like Fortunatus with his Invisible Cap, brush'd through the Croud, and compleated his Escape. As he's an Unlucky and Undaunted young Rogue, 'tis ten to one but too soon you'll hear fresh Advices of him, which, sooner or later, wherever they occur, they shall be faithfully transmitted to you, by

Your Friend,

And Humble Servant,

G. E.

LETTER III.

Novem. 1st, 1724.

Sir,

My last, as well as I remember, closed with the Account of Sheppard's artful Escape out of the Condemn'd-Hold of Newgate; I shall therefore now entertain you with his Conduct since the obtaining of his Fredom. His first Step was to Conceal himself, by taking a Hackney Coach at the corner of the Old-Baily, with a particular Friend, who was planted there, ready to receive him; from whence, the Coachman was directed to drive to Black-Friars Stairs, where Edgworth Bess was appointed to meet him, and there they discharg'd the Coach; from thence they steer'd directly to Westminster Horse-Ferry, and landed safe without the least Suspicion, and Hous'd at the White Heart; after a few hearty Healths and Congratulations for his happy Deliverance, they adjourn'd to a more secure Place in Holbourn, where, by the Assistance of some proper Implements, he discharg'd himself of that disagreeable Clog, his Fetters; and afterwards, tho' he had got his Legs at Liberty, he, and his old Chum Edgworth Bess thought it most adviseable not to make use of them, but to take Coach to another corner of the Town, and, flush'd with their good Success, they resolv'd to fix for that Night at a House in Spittle-Fields, and pay their Devotions to the Shrine of the young God of Love, and drown in softest Pleasures the remembrance of their Dangers past.

Authentic Memoirs.

The next Day (being Tuesday) he sent for a Companion, in whom he could confide, one William Page, a Butcher's Son in Clare Market, who, upon the first Intimation, came to see him. Sheppard, at that Time being special Poor, made bold with his Friend, and told him in plain English, the low Ebb of his Pocket: which was as frankly and generously supplied by Page, as far as his Abilities would permit; and as a further Testimony of the Sincerity of his Friendship and Concern for his Safety, proffer'd to accompany him to some obscure Country Town, where he might live free from the troublesome Apprehensions of a Surprisal; alledging, that no Part of this populous City could be secure enough for him, who was so well known, and so many Blood-hounds in quest of him.

Sheppard, no doubt, was pleas'd with meeting with such sanguine Professions of Friendship, in a Time both of utmost Necessity and Danger, and listned very attentively to any Proposition Page should make to him.

The Scheme, therefore, that Page had laid, was readily complied with, which was, to set out forthwith for Warnden in Northamptonshire; where, he doubted not, but a Relation of his would give them both a Civil Reception, 'till the Storm should be blown over. The Project was soon put in Execution, and Page having provided Sheppard with a Butcher's Frock, they immediately began their Travels. I shall therefore leave them for a while to divert themselves upon the Road as well they can, and make a short Digression, to introduce a Story relating to Sheppard's old Friend Anthony Lamb, who lay (as I mention'd before) under the Sentence of Transportation.

Lamb taking Advantage of Sheppard's Escape, and thinking to induce Mr. Barton to appear in his Behalf, and procure his Release, framed the following menacing Letter, in the Name of his Correspondent Sheppard; which the Reader may depend on to be an exact Transcript of the Original.

Lamb's letter to Mr. Barton, in the fictitious Name of John Sheppard, is as follows:

"Mr. Barton,

"This is to let you know, that with hard shift, I have got my Liberty, ever since last Night, the Gaol not being fast enough for me, nor the Irons which I had on my Legs not being big enough for me, more than the rest of the Prisoners, I play'd at Rob-Thief with the Gaol, which has not been for these many Years; for I have brought my self and my Irons out of the Condemn'd-Hold. I being to Die as next Friday, I thought it my best Way to make off before the Time come, which no Body can Blame me for it: Therefore I beg the Favour of you, to get my Partner off, that is, Anthony Lamb, for fear he should play at Rob-Thief too, as well as I; and should he be taken, Sorrow would come on it on both Sides; and if he don't get out, I am obliged to revenge his Cause, as well as though he was in Presence. Consider, you have been the Author of it, or else he would have been discharged last Sessions. Come, Consider, he is but a young Man, and this is the first Fact, and he has been Punish'd by being so long in Gaol, and I believe you will find the Benefit of it in your Mind, if you help him off from Transportation; and in so doing you will oblige me,

"John Sheppard.

"So no more at Present, but I beg you will send an Answer to A. L——b, and then by some Means or other, I may hear how Stories go."

Jack Sheppard.

Though the Name and Threats of John Sheppard, might prove a Bugbear to some People, Mr. Barton was not so easily to be imposed on. For immediately, on the Receipt of this weak and ill-concerted Letter, (seeing clearly thro' the thin Disguise of it) he went directly to Newgate, and applied himself to Mr. Rouse, for the Satisfaction of knowing whether it was Genuine, or not. Mr. Rouse immediately attended Mr. Barton, and before his Face strictly examined Lamb, in relation to his wise Contrivance; who very strenuously denied having any Hand in the Forgery laid to his Charge. But being Convicted, on full and unquestionable Proof, instead of succeeding in his Attempt, he only made a Rod for his own Breech, was the Cause of being more strictly watch'd and loaded with Fetters, (an Indulgence which before was despensed with) and so continued to be 'till the Hour of his Transportation.

But to return to our Hero and Page, after their Expedition in the Country, and the few Days of their Retirement. A Rural Life, you may easily imagine, could not be over-agreeable to one of Sheppard's Mercurial Disposition: and as Life does not consist in Breathing the Air, but Enjoyment, he began to be tir'd of his Inactivity, and long'd to bear a Part again in the Busy World.

'Tis possible, indeed, a cold Reception might be one Motive, to rouse up this Natural Inclination; for their Souls were alwas aspiring, and scorn'd to lie long under any Obligations. But whether this may be meer Surmise, or real Fact, I cannot positively determine: But as all allow their Accommodation was but mean, supposing 'twas hearty, that was sufficient Inducement to them to seek out for other Pasture; for a Whore and a Titt-Bitt were their favourite enjoyments.

Upon mature Deliberation, they resolv'd upon a Gold Chain, or a Wooden Leg, and at all Adventures to steer Homewards. London is their Scene of Action; and to live in any other Place, is living like Fishes out of Water.

On Tuesday therefore (being the 8th of September,) they arrived safe at their desired Port. In their Passage through Islington, they met with a Milk-Man's Son in Drury-Lane, with whom they had a short Conversation, which was clos'd with a strict Charge from Sheppard, Not to divulge, or mention their Return. Which, on the Word of a Friend, he promised to observe; and so they parted. But a Secret in some Peoples Breasts, is like a Purge in their Bellies, it soon wambles, and will come up. The Milk-Man could hold out no longer, than 'till he got Home, and the News, like Infection, soon spread over the Hundreds of Drury.

A Brandy-Shop in Bishopsgate-Street was their first Landing-place; but a Person accidentally stepping in, who took the Freedom to whisper Sheppard in the Ear, and gave too plain Demonstrations of his being no Stranger, Page and he drank up the Liquor they had call'd for, and soon shifted to another Habitation.

Thus Refresh'd, they determin'd on paying a Visit to some of their old Pot-Companions in Drury-Lane, but not 'till the Dusk of the Evening, lest some more disagreeable Acquaintance should put a stop to their Design.

As the Eyes of a Sharper is always about him, in their Way thro' Fleet-Street, they observed Mr. Martin's a Watch-Maker's Shop to be open, and only a little Boy to watch it; they thought this a Critical Minute to strike.

Page therefore goes boldly into the Shop, and demanded of the Lad, in a very civil Manner, whether one Mr. Taylor did not lodge there? or, if

Authentic Memoirs.

he knew such a Person that dwelt in the Neighbourhood? Having an Answer in the Negative, he took an Hawk's-Eye Survey of the Situation of the Shop, and so departed.

He acquaints his Companion how the Land lay, and with the Weakness of the Fort they intended to lay Siege to. Sheppard immediately resolves upon the Attack, and by a Stratagem that then darted into his Head, doubted not but in a short time to be able to make a Breach.

He enters on the Engagement, and plants Page at a Proper Distance. His first Piece of Artillery, is a Nail-piercer, which he fixes to the Post of the Door; the next, a piece of Packthread, which he fastens to the Knocker and the Nail-piercer, by which he blockaded his Enemy up, and render'd it Impracticable for him to sally out of the Fort.

Having made this formal Preparation, he begins his Attack, demolishes at once a Pain of Glass, seizes three Watches, part of the Enemy's Ammunition, and retreats with the Booty towards Drury-Lane, without the Loss either of a Leg or an Arm.

Flush'd with this Victory, they marched to the Cock and Pye, to wash down the Fatigues of the Battle. They hadn't been there long, before a Barber, an old Acquaintance of theirs, gave them Intimation of the treacherous Discovery the Milk-Man had made of their Return, and represents to them the ill Consequences that might possibly attend it.

Sheppard, nettled to be so treated by a Milk-Shop, resolves immediately to Storm his Cellar, whereupon he takes the Door off the Hinges, and throws it down upon all his Crockery. The Milk-Man gap'd like one Thunder-struck, and thought himself murther'd, seeing so much Milk about his Ears, which, in the Fright, he mistook for Blood.

Sheppard immediately march'd off the Premises, but first told him, this was his first Piece of Revenge; and perhaps, he might take the Pains, some other Time, to make him a further Requital.

The same Night, about ten o-Clock, one Ireton, a Sheriff's Officer, accidentally seeing Sheppard and Page beating the Hoof in Drury-Lane, resolved to Pursue them; which he did, and seiz'd Page; but Sheppard, like an Eel, slipt through his Fingers. The other, he thought a Fish not worth catching, so withdrew his Hook and threw him into the Pond again.

This Surprise, and this happy Deliverance, put them upon a second Rural Expedition. But before they set out, they thought it adviseable to Pawn one of their Watches, out of the three, for a Guinea and a half, to defray their Expenses on the Road.

On Thursday, the 10th of September, early in Morning, they left the Town, and directed their Course to Finchley.

The Keepers having, by some Means, procur'd private Intelligence of their March, made proper provision for a Pursuit of the Enemy: Some on Horseback, and others in a Coach and Four, all well arm'd, set out on this Expedition. Orders were given to disperse themselves in Parties o'er the Common, and in case they met with their Foes, to give no Quarter, if they met with the least Resistance.

They had not long been on the Survey, before two Persons were discovered Trampousing the Common, in Butchers Frocks.

Sheppard cast a Hawk's-Eye at his new Fellow-Travellers, and 'spying

Jack Sheppard.

Langley, one of the Turnkeys, at a Distance, acquaints Page, in their Canting Dialect, that he saw a Stag; upon which they determined to alter their Steerage, and take to a Foot-Path, in hopes to avoid the Enemies Horse. But this Project prov'd abortive: For Langley soon o'ertook Page, who was not quite so Active and Nimble as his Partner, and, Hero-like, dismounts, Sword in Hand, and demands Page to Surrender.

As Resistance would be to little or no Purpose, he submits himself to the Will of his Conqueror, and in a very submissive Manner, begs for Mercy; asks him if he would please to Fisk him; which, according to the Canting Dictionary, is, to Search him from Top to Toe. Which in Point of Prudence and good Conduct, he thought proper to condescend to. Upon strict Examination, he found a Dutchman's Snicker-Snee, and a File upon him, of which he disarm'd him, and then obliged him to attend, like a Prisoner of War, at his Horse's Heels, and assist him in the Pursuit of his Brother Refugee.

Sheppard had taken Sanctuary in an old Stable belonging to a neighbouring Country Farmer: But the Chace prov'd too hot for him; the Hounds got upon the right Scent, and beset the House.

The Farmer's Daughter, or one of his Maids, found the Hare upon the Squat, discover'd him to Austin, another of the Turnkeys, who immediately seiz'd him, and so put an end to their Sport.

Sheppard was as Submissive and Calm as his Brother Page had been before, and readily consented to be Fisk'd and was Fisk'd out of the two remaining Watches that he had before stoln from Mr. Martin, which he had conceal'd under his Arm-pits, and a Broad Knife, fellow to that of Page's.

The Newgate-Birds being now Masters of the Field, without Opposition or Bloodshed, prepare for their return Home, but first dispatch'd a proper Courier to their Lord and Master, with the joyful News of their compleat Conquest.

As Soldiers are all Gentlemen, and as they never beat a Man, but they drink to him, they convey'd their Captives to the first Hedge Ale-house that they came to, and there they were all Hail Fellows well met.

What the Sign might be, I am at a Loss to inform you, but it seems there happened to be this remarkable Inscription upon it, "We have brought our Hogs to a fair Market;" which might very well be construed by the poor Prisoners, as an ill Omen, and too truly Prophetical.

After a short Refreshment, they secured their Chubs in a Coach and Four, and about two in the Afternoon made their Publick Entry through the City.

Sheppard being a Youth of Activity, he attempted, ev'n at the very Door of Newgate, to spring out of his Keeper's Arms and give them a second Chase, but was unsuccessful in that Project.

He was immediately clapp'd into the Condemn'd-Hold, and fastened to the Floor with double Fetters about his Feet. Page was convey'd to Sir Francis Forbes, who committed him to Newgate, for Aiding and Assisting Sheppard in his last Escape.

As Mr. P—t is a Man of great Conduct and Forecast, he thought it was not adviseable to link them together, lest they should set their Politick Noddles to work again, and find out new Measures for a new Trespass.

I shall now, therefore, leave them in their separate Apartments, to Condole themselves for being born under such unlucky Planets, and set on the Stool of Repentance, for not playing their Cards to a better Advantage.

Authentic Memoirs.

If any Thing hereafter should occur that's any ways Entertaining, before they are Truss'd-up, you may depend on a faithful and impartial Account of their Transactions, from

SIR,
            Your Friend
                        And Humble Servant.
                                                        G. E.

LETTER IV.

Nov. 7th, 1724.

SIR,

Any Spirit but Sheppard's would have been depress'd, after such a long Series of Misfortunes; but whilst there's Life there's Hopes, and no Man knows his own Strength, 'till he tries it.

However, Policy goes beyond Strength itself, and therefore he sets his Brains to work once more, and lays the Ground-Plot of a Third Escape.

Some indulgent Friend privately conveys to him a small Watch-maker's File, which, it seems, if us'd artfully, will do Wonders. For the better concealing of which, he puts on an Air of Religion, and a repentant Sorrow for his misspent Life, has frequent Recourse to his Bible, and before his Keepers pretends to have his Thoughts employ'd in Divine Contemplation, that they might have no Jealousy or Suspicion of his Meditations on a Future Elopement.

But this prov'd Hypocrisy to the Life; for the only Use in Reality that he design'd to make of that Holy Book was, a Repository for that darling Implement, his File, where he thought 'twould be most safe; well knowing his Guardians, who had a strict Eye over him, seldom disturb'd their Brains about Matters of a Spiritual Concern.

However, this Project prov'd abortive; for some one more Quick-sighted than the rest, saw thro' his hypocritical Veil, and mistrusted a Snake in the Grass; and on Saturday, the 12th of September, he was stript of his Bible, which being well shook, his File dropt out, and all was discover'd.

Not discourag'd at this ill Success, the Undaunted and Indefatigable Sheppard still entertains Hopes of working his Release; and resolves, like an Egyptian Bondman, to make Brick without Straw.

To Recompense the Loss of so useful an Instrument as his first File, he was supply'd, before the 16th of September, with a fresh Recruit of Tools, viz. two Files, a Chisel, and a Hammer, which he conceal'd in the Rushes of an old Matted Chair; but how he came by them, remains a Secret as yet undiscovered.

But as a Losing Gamester, the longer he plays the deeper he involves himself; so Jack's ill Fortune still pursues him, and his Matted Chair, on the said 16th of September, was plunder'd of all its choice Materials.

Upon this new Discovery, he was examin'd very strictly, by what Means such a stock of Tools was convey'd to him, but absolutely refus'd to confess.

The Keepers, upon a very diligent Survey of the Condemn'd-Hold suspected a Communication between him and his Brother Thomas, through a Hole that led to the Room above the Common Apartment, for those who are consign'd over for Transportation.

This, indeed, was only Surmise; but, for the greater Security of his Person,

Jack Sheppard.

they exalted him almost to the top of the Goal, and confin'd him in the Stone-Castle, which is far distant from any of his Fellow-Prisoners, and chain'd him down with two Iron Staples in the Floor.

Here he remain'd for about a Fortnight together; but as he had Visiters enough of all Sorts and Sizes, the Room seem'd rather a Fair, than a Place of Confinement; and Sheppard kept up his usual Gaiety of Temper, and took a great deal of Pride in returning several smart Repartees, to divert his Company.

One Night, the Keeper coming upon him unexpectedly, found him (to his no small Surprise) taking a serious Walk, for Meditation's sake, about the Room, However, like a Man of Courage and Resolution, he came up to him and sternly ask'd Why he was not upon Duty, and at his Post? Sheppard, in an easy careless Manner, made Answer, 'Twas Troublesome to be always in one Posture, and, that he did it for the Ease of his Legs, and that he had made it his constant Practice every Night during his Confinement; but he hop'd there was no Harm in what he had done, since he never indulg'd himself that Way, with any Design or Prospect of making his Escape.

The Keeper was a Thomas-a-Didymus, a little hard of Belief, and pry'd with all the Eyes he had, to discover if any Progress had been made towards such an Attempt.

No visible Marks at first appear'd; but upon strict Examination, the Keeper took a curious Survey of Sheppard's old Blue Frock, which lay carelessly in the Room, and perceiv'd it was very Black, and, as he thought, Sooty.

Upon this, one of the Under-Keepers was order'd to mount the Chimney, to see if the Iron Bars which lay across it, stood in Statu quo.

Report was soon brought down, that all was safe; however they charg'd him with an Attempt to escape that Way, tho' they suppos'd he found it impracticable. This, Sheppard likewise deny'd very strenuously; but to put it out of his Power for ever, for the future, to take such unlicens'd Airings, they Handcuff'd him, loaded him with new Feet-locks, and took all the Precaution necessary (as they thought) unless they had to deal with the Devil.

The Day following, the Reverend Mr. Purney, Ordinary of Newgate, having been for some Time about Business in the Country, return'd to Town, and soon after paid Sheppard a Visit.

The Substance of the Conversation that pass'd between them, was, you may imagin, of a Spiritual Nature. The good Priest told him, he was sorry to see him so solicitous about the Things of this Life; that his precious Time was wholly taken up in Romantic Attempts to procure his Freedom, and that he employ'd no Thoughts on the dangerous State and Condition of his immortal Soul; begg'd him to consider, that a few Moments Pleasure Here, would never Balance the Torments of an Hereafter, &c.

In short, the Doctor read him a Wall-Lecture, which went in at one Ear, and out at the other; however, Sheppard was very Complaisant, seem'd to listen very attentively to his pious Admonitions, promis'd Amendment, and thankt him very heartily for his ghostly Advice, and hop'd it would tend to his Soul's Improvement. And so the Conferrence ended.

On Thursday the 15th of October, early in the Afternoon, one of the Keepers Assistants, (Will. Austin,) a Fellow of an extraordinary Character, considering his Post, went up to Sheppard, as usual, with his Daily Provisions, and took

Authentic Memoirs.

Capt. Geary, Mr. Gough, and two other Friends along with him, who had a great Inclination to pay their Respects to the Prisoner.

Austin, in the presence of all the Gentlemen, strictly examin'd Sheppard's Hand-cuffs, and his Feet-locks, and was very well satisfy'd, they could not be made more secure. Afterwards he gave Sheppard his Dinner; who entertain'd the Company, during their short stay there, with abundance of facetious Discourse as well as good Manners.

Austin, or some other Assistant, acquainted Sheppard, If what Provision already brought him, was not sufficient, that he would speak in Time; for after they left him, which would be very speedily, they were so busy they should see him no more 'till next Morning. Sheppard returned the Keepers many Thanks for their civil Treatment, and begg'd the Favour, they would be as early as their Business would permit.

Sheppard now began to think with himself, that his good Star began to twinckle, and that next Night would prove the Crisis of his Fortune.

As soon as he was left alone, his Head was as full of Projects as an Alchymist's that Studies the Philosopher's Stone; and Now or Never, Neck or Nothing, is his final Resolution.

When a Man works for Life, 'tis Natural to suppose, he'll put the best Leg foremost; so did Sheppard, and about 12 o'Clock he work'd out his Redemption with Dexterity of Hand, and Magnanimity of Heart.

The next Morning, Mr. Austin, according to his usual Custom, went up to the Castle to pay his humble Respects to his Guardee: But, at his first Entrance, he found the Bird flown, and the Nest most sadly out of Repair, near a Cart-Load of Brick, Stone, and other Rubbish of which it was compos'd, o'erspreading the Room.

The honest Man star'd and gap'd like one that had seen a Ghost, ran down Stairs very hastily, and when arriv'd at the Lodge, could not, for some time, express the Occasion of his sudden Confusion.

However, after a hearty Cogue or two of Right Holland's Gin, he came to himself, and declar'd the Flight of their young Canary Bird.

This News, no doubt, alarm'd the whole House, and not an Augre-Hole was left unsearch'd to find out, if possible, the Place where he was perch'd; since, they took it for granted, his Wings being so closely clipt, he could not fly far.

All the Keys of the superior Apartments were summon'd to be brought up. But they might have spar'd themselves that Trouble, for Sheppard had been before-hand with them; however, he was so Honest, as to leave the Locks, Bolts, and Bars behind him, and only remov'd them a little from their proper Places.

Six strong Doors (one of which had never been molested for Seven Years together) were wrench'd, by which he forc'd his Passage into Newgate Leads, from which, by the help of an old Blanket, that before was employ'd in the Capacity of a Bed, which he fastned to the Wall with an Iron Spike he stole out of the Chapel, (for Sacrilege, nor any thing else, could be any Obstacle to one of his Undaunted Resolution) he descended to the Leads of one Mr. Bird, a Turner, whose House is contiguous to Newgate, and the Door of the Leads being carelessly left open, 'tis presum'd he march'd directly down to the Shop; which, to a Man of his Dexterity, was but a Trifle to encounter with. In short, the Door flew open at his Command, but in his haste he forgot to shut it after him; which, we are informed, he has since acknowledg'd as an Act of ill Manners, and has begg'd Pardon for.

Jack Sheppard.

Many are the Conjectures concerning the Measures Sheppard took to effect this miraculous Escape, but at present 'tis a Secret; and as 'tis allow'd on all Hands, he had no Brother-Companion, no Assistant, (except the Devil,) it must for ever remain so; unless the young Refugee should be out in his Politicks, and stay too long too near Home, and, not Foreclose the Equity of Redemption, by a speedy Transportation of himself out of these his Majesty's Dominions.

As Sheppard must either be as strong as Goliah or Samson amongst the Antients, or be a compleat Master of the more Modern Fawkes's Dexterity of Hand, to accomplish his Release: I shall therefore close this present Letter with a Grub-Street EPIGRAM on this Occasion, which is just come pyping Hot from the Press; and as it has afforded the Author a comfortable Dinner, and the Town some small Diversion, I shall make bold to Transcribe it, and if you don't like it, e'en leave it.

An EPIGRAM on JOHN SHEPPARD's last miraculous Escape.

Samson of Old was a Strong Man, 'tis true,
But Samson was a Boy, bold JACK, to you:
When once Confin'd and Chain'd, he never fled,
But pull'd his Prison-Walls upon his Head;
With Malice in his Heart, his Strength he tries,
And, to destroy his Keepers, with them dies:
But you have shewn Superior Strength and Brains,
Tho' more Confin'd, and Bound in stronger Chains.
You force your Prison Walls, by Dint of Arm,
But then, take Care to do yourself no Harm;
From your Stone Castle mount the lofty Church,*
And leave your watchful Guardians in the Lurch;
From thence with Resolution take your Flight,
And (like a Christian) bid your Fellow-Rogues Good-night.
　　　　　I am,
　　　　　　Your Friend,
　　　　　　　And Humble Servant,

G. E.

* Church is here used, you must know, for the Chapel, by a Poetical License, to chime in with Lurch.

LETTER V.

Novem. 17th, 1724.

SIR,

Liberty and Property are the two Darlings of an English Subject: But Sheppard always made a bad Use of both. What Newgate-Bird but himself, would have projected his Escape from so strong a Cage, and so far gratify'd his unruly Desires after other Mens' Goods, as to have flown away with a Clog at his Tail? However, our Don Quixot did, and walk'd in his Trammels as far as Tottenham Court undiscovered, few Persons travelling that Road at so unseasonable an Hour.

The Weight of his Chains, the Length of the Walk, and the Fatigue he underwent before he set out, must needs incline him to Sleep without Rocking.

Authentic Memoirs.

He ventures to indulge his wearied Faculties, and take a hearty Nap in a more enlarg'd Habitation; the Earth his Bed, and the Heavens his Coverlet.

About three o'Clock he was found in this drousy Posture and singular Dress, by a poor Country Man, who luckily prov'd to be no Conjurer, and a Fellow easily to be impos'd on; who asking who he was, and what he was, and how he came there with such a heavy pair of Boots on, took Sheppard's ready Answer for Matter of Fact, That he had unfortunately got a Maid with Child, and not being able to satisfy the Parish for its Nursling, they had maliciously thrown him into New-Prison, and, contrary to all Justice and Equity, had loaded him with Double Fetters; that he had meditated his Escape from such merciless Tyrants, and had, by G—d's Help, effected his Deliverance.

The poor Man (having more good Humour than Brains, and having follow'd formerly the Trade of Basket-making himself) took Compassion on his Misfortunes, chimb'd with him in his Sentiments concerning his Prosecutors, and instead of endeavouring to Secure him, advis'd him to go farther a Field, that he might be secure.

Sheppard thank'd him heartily for his kind Concern for him, and knowing the Milk-Folks would soon be about, thought he had preach'd very sound Doctrine. So after a civil Salutation, the shorter the better, he takes his Leave, and makes the best of his Way to an old neighbouring Barn, where he conceal'd himself 'till he pull'd off his Boots, and double Japann'd an old pair of Shoes, which he had brought with him, for that Purpose, in his Pocket.

His Legs being now once more set at perfect Liberty, the next Thing he has to think on is, how to make the most on't. He therefore puts on his Considering Cap, examines into the Weakness of his Pocket; and forms imaginary Schemes of a fresh Supply. His first was, to take his Boots under his Arm, go to a proper Translator, and, as they were as stiff and heavy as old Iron, sell them for a Penny a Pound. But Second Thoughts are best, and upon mature Deliberation, he declines that Project.

One might reasonably have imagin'd his Head should have been turn'd another Way; that his Thoughts should have been wholly employ'd on a more distant Flight, and a more safe Retirement: But our Hero, like a perfect Don Quixot, runs at all, and resolves to pursue his Romantic Adventures.

London still he determines to be his Scene of Action; and on the 17th of October, a Gentleman in Leicester-Fields was the first that was let into the Secret, at the small Expence (or rather Loss) of his Silver-hilted Sword.

This mounted our Hero for the present, and a Fit of Filial Piety coming upon him, he bethought himself of his mournful Mother, who knew nothing of her Son's happy Deliverance, and was sitting Disconsolate at Home, all drown'd in Tears, with the dreadful Idea for ever before her Eyes, of her dear Son's Unfortunate, as well as Dishonourable Journey up Holbourn-Hill.

He adjourns, therefore, to an Ale-House, calls for Pen, Ink, and Paper and like a Dutiful Child, addresses his Mother in the following Manner:

A Genuine Copy of John Sheppard's Letter to his Mother.

Oct. 20th, 1724.

My dear Loving Mother,

This, with my Duty to you, hoping these Lines will find you in good Health, as I am at this present Writing; and this is to let you know, that in my

Jack Sheppard.

Attempt, (by the Assistance of God) the Fortune that I had in making my Escape from the Castle of Newgate, save my Life, and I hope that (by the Grace of God) I shall keep my self from any more such Heinous Crimes, and from the Hands of mine Enemies. And, dear Mother, cast your self not down, but be of good Heart, for I hope to be as much Comfort to you, as ever I was Dishonour. I would fain let you know where I am, but dare not, for fear of Miscarriage: So no more at present, but I Rest,
Your Loving, Dutiful,
Misfortunate Son,

JOHN SHEPPARD.

Though this shew'd some Signs of Grace, yet 'twas all Cant and Hypocrisy. For the very next Day, or soon after, he enters on the following Adventure.

Having lain Rough a long while, and being a little in Dishabillee, he longs for some new Rigging; and as Monmouth-Street is a Place of great Temptation in that respect, he cou'dn't withstand the first Opportunity that offer'd.

About Seven a-Clock in the Evening, he surveys a Shop attended only by a young Woman, that was very Industrious in her Vocation, and repairing the several Breaches that Time and long Wearing had made in some of her Second-Hand Commodities, as safe (as she thought in her Castle) as a Thief in a Mill, the Hatch being shut, and fast bolted.

But as Sheppard can handle his Heels better than most Modern Dancing-Masters, the Hatch was no Obstacle to his Intention. He cuts a clean Caper over it, knocks the Woman on the Head, and her Needle out of her Hand, extinguishes her Candle, rummages her Shelves whilst she lies stunn'd upon the Floor, claps five Suits of Silk Cloaths under his Arm, flies over the Hatch again, like an Arrow out of a Bow, and, without the least Noise or Observation, gets into the Street, walks fairly off with his Tackle, and cuts as good a Figure as any Brother Botcher in the whole Neighbourhood.

These Successful Adventures elate with Joy the Heart of our Hero, and having now Money or Money's-Worth at Command, he sits him down in a merry Mood, and entertains himself and his Friends with the two following Ironical Letters, directed to his old Well-wishers, Mr. Ap—by and Mr. A—n.

MR. AP—BY,

This, with my kind Love to you, and pray give my kind Love to Mr. Wagstaff, hoping these Lines will find you in good Health, as I am at present; but I must own you are the Loser, for want of my Dying-Speech: But to make up your Loss, if you think this Sheet worth your while, pray make the best of it. Though they do say that I am taken among the Smugglers, and put into Dover Castle, yet I hope I am among Smugglers still. So no more, but,
Your humble Servant,

JOHN SHEPPARD.

And I desire you would be the Post-man to my last Lodging.
So farewel, now I quit the English Shore.
NEWGATE Farewel.

MR. AUSTIN,

You was pleased to pass your Jokes upon me, and did say, you should not be Angry with me, had I took my Leave of you: But now, pray keep your

Authentic Memoirs.

Jokes to your self, let them Laugh that win: For now it is a equal Chance, you to take me, or I to get away; but I own my self Guilty of that Ill-Manners; but excuse me, for my Departure being private and necessary, spoil'd the Ceremony of bidding Adieu. But I wish you all Well, as I am at present: But pray be not Angry for the Loss of your Irons; had you not gave me them, I had not taking them away, but really I had left them behind me, had Convenience a-serv'd. So pray don't be Angry.

> How Austin and Perry, you did say,
> If ere the SHEPPARD got away,
> That in his room Hanged you'd be
> Upon that Fatal Tyburn Tree.
>
> But that rash Way I pray forsake,
> Though SHEPPARD is so Fortunate:
> I would have you with Patience waite,
> Till that again you do him take.
>
> For you are large and Heavy Men,
> And two the Weight what was of him;
> And if a way to that Tree you take,
> Upon my Word, you'd make it Shake.

So farewel now, my Leave I take, and what's amiss done, you write for my Schoolarship is but small.
This from your Fortunate Prisoner,

JOHN SHEPPARD.

On the 29th of October, he made a new Essay, and was as Successful as before. The Plot was laid against Mr. Rawlins's a Pawn-broker's Shop, in Drury-Lane; and as he was always very Active and Expeditious, wasn't long before he enter'd the Premisses, and travers'd the Shop in quest of proper Booty. In his Travels, he perceiv'd two Journeymen, as he suppos'd a Bed in a Room adjoyning to the Shop; and though the only Actor in this Tragi-Comedy, (like his Brother Scapin) he personates several Parts, and calls to his Comrades Tom and Harry to Shoot the two Dreamers through the Head, if they offer'd to stir out of their Quarters.

The Fellows hearing this tremendous Charge, were as mute at Fishes, pretended to be as fast as two Churches, and suffer'd Jack to take an uninterrupted Survey of their Master's Furniture, which he did with a World of Sedateness and solid Satisfaction.

His Mouth water'd at some of the Materials, and so, without any further Ceremony, he furnish'd himself with a Black Suit of Cloathes, a Silver-hilted Sword, and a light Tye-Wig, as proper Ornaments for his Person, and a few Watches, Diamond-Rings, Snuff-Boxes, and several other pretty little Toys, besides a small Quantity of Ready Cash for the Lining of his Pocket: and thus equipt, he clos'd his Visit with a hearty Curse of the two Bedfellows, for a Brace of stupid, nonsensical Gamesters, to suffer themselves to be Lood, when they had got Pam in their Hands.

A Winning Gamester is most commonly flush'd; and the greater his Success, the bolder his Play. For as Fortune is but a fickle Deity, the best time to

Jack Sheppard.

court her, is, when she is in a good Humour. But there's a Time when the Cards will take another Turn, and the Dame's Frowns are more dangerous, than her Smiles are engaging.

This, Sheppard found to his Cost. For the next Evening he ventures out in his new Rigging, sets sail for the Coast of Clare-Market, to take in Fresh Provisions; but being a little in Liquor, and not minding his Steerage as he ought to do, he runs a-ground upon a Chandlers-Shop; where, being accidentally known, he was seiz'd, upon Suspicion, for a Pyrate, and hoisting up false Colours.

Upon Examination, he was found to be what they suspected, one, who had long infested that Coast, and well prepared with Powder and Ball for new Depredations.

Upon this he was conducted under a proper Convoy to his old Port, Newgate-Castle; where he was receiv'd with uncommon Demonstrations of Joy and Rejoycing on his safe Landing.

So unexpected an Arrival alarms the whole Island: Persons of all Ranks and Degrees flock to the Fort to Visit him, though none are admitted to attend at his Levee, without a Lusty Fee to his proper Officer. In short, not to carry the Allusion any further, Newgate appears more like a Publick Hall than a Prison.

On the 10th of November he was convey'd in a Hackney-Coach to Westminster-Hall; there his Hand-cuffs were taken off, and being brought before the Court of Kings-Bench, the Record of his Conviction for Burglary and Felony at the Sessions in the Old-Bailey, was read; and he making no Objections, Mr. Attorney-General mov'd that his Execution might be speedy, and a Rule of Court made for Friday next. Sheppard address'd himself to the Bench, earnestly beseeching the Judges to intercede with His Majesty for Mercy, and desired a Copy of a Petition he had sent to the King, might be read; which was comply'd with. But being ask'd, how he came to repeat his Crimes, after his Escapes? Pleaded, Youth and Ignorance, and withal, his Necessities; saying, he was afraid of every Child and Dog that look'd at him, as being closely pursu'd; and had no Opportunity to obtain his Bread in an honest Way, and had fully determin'd to have left the Kingdom the Monday after he was retaken in Drury-Lane. He was told, the only Thing to entitle him to His Majesty's Clemency, would be his making an ingenuous Discovery of those who abetted and assisted him in his last Escape; he averr'd, That he had not the least Assistance from any Person, but God Almighty; and that he had already nam'd all his Accomplices in Robberies, who were either in Custody, or beyond Sea, whither he would be glad to be sent himself. He was reprimanded for prophaning the Name of God. Mr. Justice Powis, after taking Notice of the Number and Heinousness of his Crimes, and giving him Admonitions suitable to his sad Circumstances, awarded Sentence of Death against him, and a Rule of Court was order'd for his Execution on Monday next. He told the Court, That if they would let his Handcuffs be put on, he, by his Art, would take them off before their Faces. He was remanded back to Newgate, thro' the most numerous Croud of People that ever was seen in London; and Westminster-Hall has not been so crouded in the Memory of Man. A Constable who attended, had his Leg broke; and many other Persons were hurt and wounded at Westminster-Hall-Gate.

Authentic Memoirs.

On the 16th, he made his last publick Appearance, being the Day appointed for his Execution. His Procession to Tyburn was attended with a numberless Number of Spectators of both Sexes; and being naturally a little Vain-glorious, he begg'd the Favour of being conveyed in an open Vehicle, rather than a close Coach, that he might oblige some loving Ladies, and give them an Opportunity to take a Farewel-Look. His Guardians, as they had made a good Harvest of him, readily comply'd with any Reasonable Request.

But as they did not care to trust him farther than they cou'd see him; and knowing him to be a Man of an invincible Spirit and Resolution, the Under-Sheriff, for the better Security of his Person, gave Orders for his making his Exit in a pair of well-polish'd Hand-cuffs, instead of a White pair of Gloves, to prevent him from being Sly or Unlucky, rightly concluding that a Muffled-Cat could never be a good Mouser.

This Sheppard resented highly, and in a very sanguine Manner oppos'd the Affront, as being the only Means to render abortive his last politick Stratagem, his last Hopes of an Escape.

Upon this Struggle, his Guardians brow-beated him severely, and told him, he acted the part of a Bully, not of a Prisoner. And as the Under-Sheriff never met with his Fellow, was still apprehensive of some Design, and gave fresh Orders for a strict Examination of all his Accoutrements, lest some Weapon of War should lie conceal'd and of a Victim, he should become a Victor.

This was a Cutting-stroke to our Hero, as well as to the Officer that search'd him, and drew both Tears from the one, and Blood from the other. For a sharp Penknife (the whole Dependence of the former) lay loose in his Pocket, and was seiz'd upon him, but seiz'd by the wrong Handle and mortify'd the Fingers of the latter.

These are all the Material Occurrences, 'till he arriv'd at the Triple-Tree, where, contrary to his Expectation, or the Mobs Intention, he hung for about a quarter of an Hour; but was then, in open Violation of the Law, cut down by a Soldier, and deliver'd as 'tis thought, Alive, but 'tis suppos'd very Faint, into the Hands of his Friends, who hugg'd him about with so much preposterous Love, that in all probability, they kill'd him with Kindness.

Give me leave to add one merry Adventure here, tho' introduc'd in a wrong Place, and where, in point of Judgment, a Tear ought rather to be dropt.

Mr. App—by, in Gratitude for the many good Services our Hero had done him, and as sole Executor to the Deceas'd, at his own Expence, hir'd a Mourning Hearse to attend the Gallows, in order to convey the Corps to some decent Place of Interment. But the Mob, misconstruing this good Intention of his Friend, and mistaking it for an Anatomical Preparation of the Society of Surgeons, declar'd Open War against the Charioteer, fir'd their Cannon at him, loaded with Dirt and Stones, and oblig'd him to quit the Field with the Loss of his Standard.

This Day Mr. P—y has oblig'd the World with an Account of his most Learned and Judicious Preparatory Sermon on this Occasion, and the Behaviour of our Unfortunate Hero, before the Finishing Stroke was put to his Execution. But as, he is perfectly silent as to his Dying-Speech, I presume, in reality, he made none. Yet as I have been writing a sort of a Tragedy, and divided it regularly into several Acts or Letters, I cannot be reconcil'd to his quitting the Stage, 'till, Swan-like, he sings his own Requiem. I shall, therefore, in Imita-

Jack Sheppard.

tion of the greatest Poets of the Age, close my Play with an imaginary Speech, and let him take his Leave of the Spectators, like a Man, and like a Hero.

JOHN SHEPPARD'S Suppos'd
SPEECH.

Like Doctor Faustus, I my Pranks have play'd,
(By Contract with his Master long since made)
Like him liv'd Gay, and revell'd in Delight,
Drank all the Day, and Whor'd the livelong Night.
To raise my Name above all Rogues in Story,
I've made Chains, Bolts, and Bars fly all before me:
But, heark, the Dismal Sound! the Clock strikes One:
The Charm is broke, and all my Strength is gone:
The Dragon comes, I hear his Hideous Roar;
Farewel, my Friends, for now Poor JACK's no more.

I am,
Your Friend,
And Humble Servant,

G. E.

POSTSCRIPT.

This Day is Publish'd, by the Executor of Sheppard above-mention'd, a NARRATIVE, much to the Purport of my Four foregoing Epistles; which, he has assur'd the World, is Genuine, and Written by the Deceased himself, during the Time of his Imprisonment. But, as I declare to the World, I take it for a Spurious Copy; and, with Submission, conceive there are no MEMOIRS so Authentick as my own; I think my self oblig'd to give my Reasons for so bold a Suggestion.

The very Frontispiece is an Affront: For he has there represented our Hero tumbling Head foremost out of the Condemn'd-Hold; when 'tis well known, he was Master of more Conduct, and, like a Cat, always pitch'd upon his Legs.

My next Observation is this, That my Rival, Mr. J—s, in his former Account of Sheppard, has oblig'd the World with many of his facetious Jokes, Puns Conundrums, and Quarter-Quibbles; and the Reverend Mr. P—y has this Day Confirm'd his Character in that respect; whereas in the Narrative (last publish'd) there doesn't appear the least Gaiety of Temper, or Flight of Fancy; and, to my poor Judgment, the whole, from Top to Bottom, declares 'tis—ORDINARY.

I must beg Mr. J—s's Pardon, if I think the latter Part of his Relation none of his own, but the Handy-Work of another of Mr. A—by's faithful Garretteers, who is a Wagg by Name, as well as Nature.

Your Friend,

G. E.

LETTER VI.

Nov. 19th, 1724.

SIR,

I had no Thoughts of troubling you any more upon the Subject of John Sheppard, having, in my last attended him to his Dying Hour: But as I unluckily compar'd my Memoirs to an Historical Drama; and presuming the

Authentic Memoirs.

Dedication might pass well enough for the Prologue, I thought an Epilogue absolutely necessary to Compleat the Work. And as most of our Modern Poets have made it a standing Rule, to dismiss their Audience with something Gay and Airy, let the Play be never so Tragical and full of Distress; I have put my Invention on the Wrack, to wind up my Bottom after the same Manner, and entertain you with something Whimsical and Novel.

Sometimes I was thinking to personate Dr. Faustus, and Conjure up the Ghost of our old Friend JOHN, make him take his Rounds thro' all the Apartments of Newgate, put Austin into a second Confusion, and pay a friendly Visit to his Fellow-Traveller Page; then close the Conference, with Mr. P—ny's well-chosen Advice, Not to be Dismayed, &c. insisting, that there was as good Company in the Inf—l Regions, as any in R—s's Dominions; and to keep up the Spirit of Pride predominant in him in his Life-time, make him march off, repeating that Heroical, I wou'd say Diabolical, Line in Milton, Better to rule in H—ll, than serve in H—n.

But as that Thought was Stale, and Tom Brown, of merry-Memory, many Years since, had Publish'd such a number of Apparitions; upon more mature Deliberation, I declin'd it.

My next Project was, to give you a long Narration of Sheppard's coming to Life again, and (as most People thought he dealt with the Devil) assert, his being seen with his Gimlets, Saws, and Chisels, in a Carpenter's Habit, hard at Work upon the Triple-Tree, resolving to carry it off the Premisses, for fear his Friend Page should come to the same Place, and take a Swing that might directly Choak him.

But as this was all Farce, and Supernatural, and consequently, better adapted to an Italian Opera, than an English Tragedy, I could not, as a Critic, comply with that Motion.

At last, however, I came to this final Resolution, that I would Close my Design with a Pastoral Elegy on the Deceas'd, as the most natural Transition I could possibly think of, and ordered my Bookseller accordingly to send me forthwith the Works of Moschus and Bion; in which any Gentleman, that thinks it worth his while, and is a tolerable Master of the Greek Language, may find one very a propos, one that would hit my Case to a Hair, and serve me for a perfect Precedent (as the Lawyers call it) Mutatis Mutandis.

But I found a grand and unexpected Obstacle to this Suggestion: For whilst I was musing o'er the Original, and aiming at an easy Translation, a Friend came in, and inform'd me, that Mr. P—ny had been before me in that Project, and that Mr. Ap—by was very forward with it, and that it would be Publish'd the beginning of the next Week. My Muse being something Modest, and Conscious of the great Reputation of his Pastoral Essays, written in his younger Years, had gain'd with the Learned World, I thought him above my Match, and so resolv'd not to enter the Lists with him. However, as soon as it comes out, as I know you're a Lover of Rhime, and naturally Sympathise with distressed Shepherds, it shall be carefully remitted to you.

As therefore you see my Muse was thus accidentally disappointed, I hope you'll excuse my not sending you the Present I intended. Perhaps, Friendship might have byas'd your Judgment so far as to have thought, an Elegiac Performance of mine equally valuable with his; but I determin'd you shou'dn't

Jack Sheppard.

lie under the Reflection of Partiality, and was very unwilling to Publish any Thing of that Nature, unless 'twas Extra—ORDINARY.

However (as I don't hear of any Poetaster furbishing up a Tomb-Stone for our Hero) I don't see any Reason why my Muse should be so Modest as to be wholly Silent. She may be allow'd sure, to Sing a little, though she cann't Sing like a Nightingale.

As therefore she ventur'd at his Dying-Speech, she shall now pay her last Respects to him after he's Dead, and endeavour to preserve his Memory from Oblivion; as a grateful Acknowledgement, that his Life and Transactions have brought Grist to her Master's Mill, as well as to others.

An EPITAPH,

Design'd for JOHN SHEPPARD's Tomb-Stone (whenever the Carver shall finish it) propos'd to be erected in Tyburn Road; in Imitation of the memorable Monument at Calais.

> Stay, Traveller, stay, and this Inscription Read;
> View well this Funeral Urn, and then proceed.
> Here, the World's Wonder, the Great SHEPPARD lies:
> Cartouch himself did never FRANCE surprise
> With half such bold Exploits, or Robberies.
> He, whom no Goal could hold, no Chains make fast,
> By Death's Superior Bands is tam'd at last;
> Within this Narrow Prison's kept Secure;
> From this Stone-Room he will Escape no more;
> Hard Fate! at Tyburn's Triple-Tree he swung;
> But whilst Alive, was Rescu'd by the Throng:
> On Thousand and Ten Thousand Heads he rid,
> And by his Friends Ill Conduct, not the Hangman, dy'd.

I forgot to Inform you, when Sheppard made his Will, he desir'd his Cash-Keeper and Executor would take particular Care, that one Moiety or Half-part of his Personal Estate, his Funeral Charges being first paid or deducted, might be laid out in a Monument of this Nature, that he might be Recorded, (such was his excessive Vanity) though Recorded for a Villain; but left the Inscription to the superior Judgment and Discretion of his said Executor. I have, therefore, sent a Copy of the above enclos'd to Mr. Ap—by for his Perusal, and free Censure or Approbation.

However, I almost despair of Success; for I am informed since, Mr. Jo—s, as well as my self, is troubled with the Poetical Itch; and as he has, doubtless, superior Interest, as well as Merit, my Performance must of course be rejected.

I wasn't in the least startled at the Intimation; for 'tis an Epidemical Distemper amongst us poor Folks, and as Natural to us, as the Scrub to a Scotchman.

I have but one Secret to disclose to you, and then I shall for ever dismiss the Subject before me.

When I first began my Correspondence with you, I hadn't the least Thought of communicating these MEMOIRS to the Publick; but as you know I have met with Misfortunes, am an unhappy Inhabitant of Alsatia, and a Bookseller offering me some Shiners for my Copy, I cou'dn't withstand the Temptation.

Authentic Memoirs.

I shall make bold to send you a small Parcel by the first Carrier, in **Hopes,** when you are over a Pipe and a Bottle of good October with your merry Country Club, you'll introduce them, and do your utmost Endeavours to promote the Sale of 'em.

This Favour will be gratefully acknowledg'd by the Bookseller, and lay a particular Obligation on,

Your Sincere Friend,
And Faithful Correspondent,

G. E.

P.S. Should any of your Friends or Acquaintance be so Quick-sighted as to discern the Spirit of Indolence that runs thro' my first Epistle, and the little Trips in point of Grammar: Assure them, I had then a Hurray of Affairs upon my Hands, set Pen to Paper late at Night, and frankly own I was half asleep. Desire them likewise to consider, that old Homer himself would Nod a little now and then; and the great Modern Pamphleteer Isaac Bickerstaff, Esq. would often be Dull, but with this Alleviation, That he did it with Design.

FINIS.

Jack Sheppard.

A DIALOGUE BETWEEN JULIUS CÆSAR AND JACK SHEPPARD.

Saturday, December 4th, 1725.*

To the author of *The British Journal*.

SIR,

The following dialogue between an antient and a modern Hero is, we apprehend, designed as an imitation of Lucian or Fontenelle; whether the author has succeeded in that Design or no, we won't pretend to determine. But tho' he has not, we are of the Opinion that the good Sense and Truth which run thro' it, will be a sufficient Apology for making it this Day's Entertainment.

Julius Cæsar and Jack Sheppard.

Cæs. How now, Wretch! What Madness has inspired thee with the Thought of swelling into a Comparison with me?

Shep. Look you, Sir, I have been as excellent in my Way, as you in yours, perhaps more so. And, as we are now in a Place where Glory is our best Portion, I can see no Reason why an Equality in Merit should not be an Equality in Fame.

Cæs. And is it possible? Gods! what do I hear? Are all my Battles compared to Street Robberies? All my Sieges to Burglaries? And must all the Actions of my Life be tarnished by a vile Comparison with a Slave whose highest Character is that of a Gaol-Breaker?

Shep. Softly, good Cæsar! Is it more a Crime to pick a Lock than unhinge a Constitution? Are a pair of Fetters more sacred than the Liberty of the People? And is it more dishonourable to slip through the Hands of a Gaoler, than break through the Laws of one's Country?

Cæs. Now, Friend, I have caught thee. Wast thou not made a Public Spectacle of Infamy for Breach of thy Country's Laws?

Shep. I was; and 'tis there (if any where) I have an Advantage o'er thee: I only infringed the Laws, not overturned them. I did not grow too big a Villain for them to punish me, as you did, and therefore was punished in an extraordinary Manner; but, surely, in fair Reasoning, 'tis the Crime, not the Punishment that is scandalous.

Cæs. That I am ready to grant. But, prithee, what are my Crimes?

Shep. O Lord, Sir, I want Memory to repeat them. Usurping a Tyranny, enslaving your Country, destroying the established Plan of Government, invading Foreigners whose Freedom you had no Right to disturb, and perplexing Citizens, whose Liberties you were obliged to preserve. In a Word, being seditious at home, and troublesome abroad, is the best character you have to boast on.

Cæs. This is a little odd. But, pray Sir, had I no Virtues?

Shep. Very few. Some Accomplishments indeed you had, and so had I, or

---

* The date of the year when this Dialogue appeared was incorrectly given as 1724 when the pasquin was reprinted in *The Bloody Register*, 1764. The error was carried on in the reference to the Dialogue in the memoir of Jack Sheppard in "The Dictionary of National Biography." Mr. J. G. Muddiman, by research in the original files of *The British Journal*, has proved the date to be 4th December, 1725. (1st page.) No. C4 XVII.

A Dialogue.

neither of us had been fit for our Business. Your Purpose was to obtain Power; mine to get Riches. We both took illegal Methods, and therefore some supplemental Qualities were necessary to our Undertaking; you was learned, wise, and valiant; I was fly, cunning, and dextrous.

Cæs. And will you then make no difference between our Enterprises?

Shep. Not until you show me that the one was more warrantable than the other, or less noxious to Mankind; and whichever you prove to be so, I'll allow to be the most laudable.

Cæs. Very well. As yet you have only shewn that our Vices are equal. Now, pray Sir, what are your Virtues?

Shep. Did I ever pretend to any? Sir, you mistake me, I only put in for Fame, to which Virtue is but an indifferent title. Lord, Sir! if either you or I had Virtues, we had been forgotten long since.

Cæs. Hey Day! and so you are content, if I give up my Character for that of Villain, to be thought one too.

Shep. I never aspired to be greater than Cæsar.

Cæs. Presumptuous! And dost thou hope to be equal?

Shep. Why not? My Actions are as wonderful, and somewhat honester.

Cæs. Why dost not thou relate them then? For as yet I have heard nothing but infamous Things of thy performing.

Shep. Cæsar, I hate boasting; but could I write like thee an Account of my Life, it would not be credited, but it would be free from the Censures that may be passed upon thine. Men would find nothing undertaken in it thro' Wantonness or Ambition. I did not ravage as you did in the East for Fame, in the West for Supremacy. All my Actions were enterprized upon a justifiable Score, the Maintenance of Life, and if Glory attended them, she came uninvited and unexpected.

Cæs. I perceive by your Discourse, that you are a Leveller, and not to be conversed with upon such Subjects; but you are pleased to affirm just now, that I had no Virtues, I tie you to that Assertion, and laying aside my Character of Monarch, will join Issue with you upon the Foot of personal Merit.

Shep. Why, now you talk Reason, and I shall hear you with Pleasure.

Cæs. What's your Opinion of my Courage?

Shep. Why! That you had Courage is not to be disputed. But you must allow it to me also; and I think I have shewn it to a greater Degree than you did. I fancy, declaring War, alone and unarmed, against a whole potent Kingdom, is what you would not have ventured upon. Besides Courage is a Quality so many Brutes have in common with us, that 'tis almost a Shame to boast on't. Add that it has such a Dependance on our Constitution, that it is no more a Merit than Birth, Beauty, or any other accidental Ornaments; and a Man is no more to be praised or blamed for having or wanting Courage than for having a fine Hand or a distorted face.

Cæs. What of my Humanity and Moderation?

Shep. Trick and Artifice like my own. Rigour and Cruelty would have undone you. Why! I never purloined any Thing that could be of no Use to me.

Cæs. What say you to my Wisdom and Learning?

Shep. Your Learning I don't understand, but I hope you would not palm it upon me for a Virtue? And, as for your Wisdom, I am asham'd to think

Jack Sheppard.

the World has been imposed on by it. I have contrived a better Plot for stealing a Gold Watch than that by which you stole the Liberties of Rome. Nor was your Scheme for getting the Sword of Power into your Hands, by any Means, equal to mine for procuring one whose only Worth was a Silver Hilt. Oh that I had been Cæsar and you Sheppard! I should have made a glorious Emperor and you but a sorry Thief.

Cæs. Come, good Words and few. I have but one Question to ask. What are your Thoughts of my Resolution? And do you think passing the Rubicon, or swimming from Alexandria to my Fleet, have historical Actions their Equals?

Shep. Hey Day! Did you ever hear of my two Escapes? And do you think the Man who had Resolution enough to attempt them did not surpass you?

Cæs. They were Acts of Despair, not of Resolution.

Shep. I believe you, Sir, you'll find them founded on the same Principle with yours; or if they vary, 'tis for the better. Such of your mad Pranks as you had no Occasion to play, were done for Glory; those which you were forced on, for Life. My Actions were all of the latter Sort, and therefore, as I hinted before, more meritorious than yours; for next to playing the Fool, the greatest Folly is in doing it only with a View to be talk'd of.

Cæs. 'Tis somewhat hard that, tho' I have given up my public Character, you will allow me no personal Merit in my private.

Shep. Sir, I have Reason. You and I have done great Actions in our several Ways, but the Ends for which we did them render them vile. There is no such Thing as personal Merit independent of Society, nor can any Accomplishments deserve that Name, but in Proportion to the Benefit which the Weal-Publick receives from them. Courage, Humanity, Moderation, Wisdom, Learning, and Resolution are fine Qualities, but it is the Use and Application which makes them Virtues, and the only Reason for paying any regard to them, is, that when Men are engaged for the Good of their Kind, such Qualities make them more able to procure it effectually; which Argument is reversed when the Purpose is alter'd.

Cæs. I am almost of your Opinion. You reason well; and I wish for the Peace of Mankind, the Rulers of the Earth had so just a Notion of my Character as you have.

[End of Dialogue* and of p. 1.]

---

* A translation into German of this Dialogue appeared in "Der Neue Pitaval." Leipsig. 1845. Vol. 8, p. 406.

Introductory Note.

JONATHAN WILD.

INTRODUCTORY NOTE by S. M. ELLIS.

It is both remarkable and unfortunate that so few authentic particulars of the early life of Jonathan Wild are available. After he had achieved extreme notoriety and a felon's death, the pamphleteers got busy, for in that age of broadsheets and memoirs, both veritable and invented, there was a large demand for sensational accounts of his career. Grub Street being as obliging as its offspring, Fleet Street and Carmelite Street, was prompt, and, like the cheap press of to-day, provided every possible and impossible detail of a criminal's life and adventures. In the case of Jonathan Wild's professional years, as thief-taker and thief, there was plenty of official record to be had, but of his origin and youth scarcely any genuine details were procured. Even to the present time, no one has succeeded in establishing the date of his actual birthday: all those who have written about him have only been able to say that he was born " about 1682," and these writers have given varying trades as the occupation of his father at Wolverhampton. In " The Dictionary of National Biography " the father is stated to have been a wig-maker, and to make a distinction with but little difference this was changed to a " peruke-maker " by Thomas Seccombe in his account of Jonathan Wild in his " Twelve Bad Men." The authors in question would have arrived at the truth if they had seen the early memoir of Wild, reprinted in this volume from " The Bloody Register " of 1764, wherein it is correctly stated that the father of Jonathan Wild was a carpenter. It is a coincidence that the father of Jonathan's victim, Jack Sheppard, should have been a member of the same trade. No one who has hitherto written about Jonathan Wild seems to have searched for the record of his birth at Wolverhampton. A copy of his baptism certificate has now been procured from St. Peter's Church for this work, and, though the date of birth is missing, it transpires that the father was a joiner or carpenter. The entry records that on the 6th day of May, 1683, was baptised Johnathan, son of John Wildy, " Joynor," of Wolverhampton. It is of interest to note that the surname is quite clearly written as Wildy:

Jonathan Wild.

whether the final letter " y " was an unpardonable flourish of the parish clerk, who could have had no idea that his penmanship would create a biographical problem two centuries and a half later, or whether the surname was indeed Wildy, is a question that it will be very difficult to solve now. Fielding was nearer the truth than he probably realised when he wrote at the outset of his great satire: " Mr. Jonathan Wild, or Wyld, then (for he himself did not always agree in one method of spelling his name)." For it would seem that Jonathan was born Wildy, was Wild during his manhood, and was Wilde in the inscription on his coffin-plate.

Wild's memoirists agree that he was apprenticed to the trade of a buckle-maker, and that while a youth he married a respectable woman, by whom he had a son.[1] Resolving to try his fortune in London, he deserted his family. Having no money and seeing a lady in her travelling chariot, he performed a trick in which he was proficient, namely, dislocating his hip at will. He was invited into the carriage and conveyed as far as Warwick, where surgeons were called in. They could not effect a cure, so the " patient " was taken on to other towns, with the same performance in each place, and so eventually reached London. Here he soon fell in with Mary Milliner, a prostitute, when the two set up a brothel in Lewkenor's Lane, off Drury Lane, at the north-east end, a locality noted for houses of ill-fame since the seventeenth century, when, as Seccombe puts it, the Roundhead soldiers " sneaked into its retirement to practise the vices they more openly denounced." Wild's first blackmailing undertakings in London were those of a *souteneur*, for he preyed upon both the women and the men who used his house. So he passed on to his gigantic system of blackmail, though he was still ostensibly a " bucklemaker," employing and levying toll upon thieves, getting into touch with the robbed and receiving rewards for the restoration of property stolen by his own hand from his own agents—agents sent by him to

---

[1] According to the account of Jonathan Wild in " The Newgate Calendar Improved " (1819), this son, when about nineteen years old, came to London a short time before the execution of his father: " He was a youth of so violent and ungovernable a disposition, that it was judged prudent to confine him while his father was conveyed to the place of execution, lest he should create a tumult, and prove the cause of mischief among the population. Soon after the death of his father, he accepted a sum of money to become a servant in one of our plantations. Besides the woman to whom he was married at Wolverhampton, Jonathan Wild lived with five others under the pretended sanctity of matrimony: the first was Mary Milliner; the second, Judith Nun, by whom he had a daughter; the third, Sarah Grigson, alias Perrin; the fourth, Elizabeth Man, who cohabited with him above five years; the fifth, whose real name is uncertain, married some time after the death of Wild."

Introductory Note.

the execution tree when they became troublesome or dangerous. At the same time he became the most active thief-taker, working in the pay of the Government. He had his offices and clearing-house for the reception of the stolen goods and their return to the owners. No criminal has ever approached the method and wide ramifications of his system and activities, and he far excelled the achievements of the corrupt police in Russia and America of the twentieth century. Thus he would advertise in *The Daily Post*:

"Lost, the 1st October, a black shagreen pocket-book, edged with silver, with some notes of hand. The said book was lost in the Strand, near the Fountain Tavern, about seven or eight o'clock at night. If any person will bring the aforesaid book to Mr. Jonathan Wild, in the Old Bailey, he shall have a guinea reward.—Monday, November 2, 1724."

The "Fountain" tavern was one of the most notorious brothels in the Strand district; and it is obvious that the pocket-book had been stolen by a prostitute in the employment of Wild from some man who was probably of reputation and outward morality; he would thus be compelled to communicate with Wild in order to recover his property, and then pay a handsome reward to secure secrecy concerning his indiscretions.

Second only to his eventual execution, which is duly related in the account that follows from "The Bloody Register," the most dramatic episode of Jonathan Wild's life was the murderous attack made upon him on 14th October, 1724, by Blueskin (Joseph Blake), who succeeded in cutting his throat and very nearly killed him. In the words of Defoe: "Blueskin on a sudden seiz'd Mr. Wild by the Neck, and with a little Clasp Knife he was provided with he cut his Throat in a very dangerous Manner; and had it not been for a Muslin Stock twisted in several Plaits round his Neck, he had in all likelyhood succeeded in his barbarous Design before Ballard the Turnkey, who was at hand, could have time to lay hold of him; the villain triumph'd afterwards in what he had done, Swearing many bloody Oaths, that if he had murder'd him, he should have died with Satisfaction, and that his Intention was to have cut off his Head, and thrown it into the Sessions House Yard among the Rabble, and Curs'd both his Hand and the Knife for not Executing it Effectually."

This incident caused the composition of that song already mentioned,[2] "Newgate's Garland," "being A New Ballad, shewing How Mr. Jonathan Wild's Throat was cut from ear to ear with a Penknife,

---

[2] See *ante*, page 72.

Jonathan Wild.

by Mr. Blake, alias Blueskin, the bold Highwayman, as he stood at his Tryal in the Old Bailey, 1724,[3] To the Tune of 'The Cut-Purse.'" The authorship of this ballad has always been attributed to Swift, though some scholars and bibliophiles, including Mr. T. J. Wise, are now doubtful whether he did indeed write it. But the ballad was included in the last volume of Swift's "Miscellanies," printed for B. Motte at the Middle Temple Gate, Fleet Street, 1727, though of course it was originally sold in the streets as a single broadsheet at the time of the sensation which followed Blueskin's amazing assault. There are seven verses in this not particularly distinguished literary style—

> When to the Old Bailey this Blueskin was led,
> He held up his Hand, his Indictment was read.
> Loud rattled his chains, near him Jonathan stood,
> For full Forty Pounds was the Price of his Blood.
>   Then hopeless of Life
>   He drew his Penknife
>   And made a sad widow of Jonathan's Wife:
> But Forty Pounds paid her, her Grief shall appease,
> And every Man round me may rob if he please.
>
> Some say there are Courtiers of highest Renown,
> Who steal the King's Gold, and leave him but a *Crown;*
> Some say there are Peers and some Parliament Men
> Who meet once a Year to rob Courtiers agen:
>   Let them all take their Swing
>   To pillage the King,
>   And get a Blue Ribbon instead of a String,
> Now Blueskin's sharp Penknife hath set you at ease,
> And every Man round me may rob if he please.
>
> Some by publick Revenues, which pass'd through their Hands,
> Have purchas'd clean Houses, and bought dirty Lands;
> Some to steal from a Charity think it no Sin
> Which at Home (says the Proverb) does always begin.
>   But if ever you be
>   Assign'd a Trustee
> Treat not Orphans like Masters of the Chancery:
> But take the Highway, and most honestly seize,
> For every Man round me may rob if he please.[4]

The intention of the song was political satire of course: but the

---

[3] Blueskin was executed on 11th November, 1724, in the twenty-eighth year of his age. In Gent's *York Journal*, No. 1 (November 16th-23rd, 1724), a paragraph states: "The corpse of Blueskin, lately executed at Tyburn, was interred in a burying-ground belonging to St. Andrew's, Holborn, being attended by a great mob to the grave."

[4] See *ante*, page 42.

Introductory Note.

scansion and rhymes were weak, and Jonathan's " Wife " (who was not made a widow until some months later) was introduced as a rhyme for " Penknife."

It was Swift who bestowed upon the criminal thief-taker the title of Jonathan Wild the Great, and Fielding, eighteen years later, using the designation for his great essay in irony has preserved it in an abiding part of English Literature, a perpetuation which the humble " Joynor " of Wolverhampton, and his wife could hardly have anticipated for their infant son when they brought him to the font of the Collegiate Church of St. Peter in the year 1683. Wild thus engaged the pens of two of the most famous writers of his time; and the whole gang of the garreteers of Grub Street bayed in noisy chorus as soon as his downfall was certain. Every step of his progress to the Triple Tree, and after, formed an alluring subject for their wit. First, there was the invitation to attend his execution—

To all the Thieves, Whores, Pick-pockets, Family Fellows, etc., in Great Brittain and Ireland.

Gentlemen and Ladies, You are hereby desir'd to accompany ye worthy friend ye Pious Mr. J. Wild from his seat at Whittington College to ye Triple Tree, where he's to make his last Exit on ——; and his Corps to be carry'd from thence to be decently interr'd amongst his Ancestors.

Pray bring this Ticket with you.

The said Ticket was embellished with an elegant design of a pillory, stocks, and the Triple Tree itself guarded by Time with his hour-glass and Death with his dart, while below was a sarcophagus.

A bard provided his epitaph, thus—

> Here Jonathan, for want of breath,
> Lies in the folds of icy death;
> The Catcher's catched, we plainly see,
> In that same trap he kept to be
> His bank, which him and Moll supply'd
> With gold enough before he died;
> But if 'tis asked, why he's confin'd
> So close, who has to Death been kind?
> We only can reply but this,
> Being Wild, if loose, he'd do amiss.

Another poet wrote an elegy—

> What mournful muse must aid me in my verse
> To pin on Jonathan's dark sable herse?
> I know in Lethe I must dip my pen,
> To write against the very worst of men;
> For none (I think) can write of him so well
> But what is brought from the confines of Hell.

Jonathan Wild.

Each jailor, strumpet, pirate, bully, thief,
Gamester, old bawd, in tears display your grief;
But ye that can't cry, yet would seem to weep,
Your handkerchiefs in holy water steep;
Then snot and snivel throw about his grave,
And wish Old Nick may soul and body have.
How happy is his unlamenting wife,
Nothing but lucky stars smile on her life;
Some planet has contrived, in a trice,
To make poor Moll a hempen widow twice:
For this good fortune women Molly hate,
And think their husbands deal with death and fate;
But daily live in joyful hopes to be
Widow'd like her at the same triple tree.
Oh! Jonathan, of thee I'll write no more,
No more Parnassus will exhaust its store;
But, Jonathan, art thou sincerely dead?
Yes, yes, I see, and to the Devil fled.

While yet another hymned Tyburn as the blessed spot of Wild's happy dispatch—

Hail! rev'rend Tripos, Triple Tree of State,
Who arbitrates the grand decrees of Fate,
And is the chief defender of the laws,
Three kingdoms joyfully give thee applause.
And universal praises to thee sing,
Since Jonathan upon thy beams did swing.
Tyburn! my muse, by most immortal fame,
In as immortal verse shall soon proclaim;
And that dear halter also consecrate
Which did his exit in thy presence date;
For that and you (I say) together hurl'd
The rogue of rogues into another world.
Yet famous Arnold[5] must not be forgot,
In Newgate annals, who did tie the knot:
That precious knot which made the precious noose,
When Jonathan, for haste, died in his shoes.

Oh! Tyburn, rogues, our laws can never claim
From all their vices, quickly you reclaim;
Men who do once acquaintance scrape with thee
Will seldom (to displease you) vicious be;
Who'd then refuse to smell thy fragrant wood
When it will make a wicked person good?

---

[5] The hangman, Richard Arnet. He died in 1728, and this reference clears up a point Horace Bleackley was in doubt about, for in his "The Hangmen of England," speaking of the execution of Jonathan Wild, he says: "As in the case of Jack Sheppard, we do not know whether Banks or Arnet was the executioner."

Introductory Note.

But yet too many goodness do forsake
Before they will this wholesome trial make.
Thy limbs, which perpendicularly stand,
Are often the supporters of the land;
You safely prop the feeble state of thieves;
A bankrupt, who his creditors deceives,
With oath that's false: all traitors you sustain,
And murderers, to put 'em out of pain;
Wives doubly married for thy succour fly,
All in thy bosom quietly may lie;
And tho' a coiner's money should be brass,
Yet currently it doth at Tyburn pass.

Great Tyburn! thy most ancient lofty trine
With splendor o'er our horizon does shine,
And from the British, to the furthest shore,
Most celebrated rogues thy name adore:
The Church of Rome her orisons do pay
To thee, and for thy future greatness pray;
Some of her prime saints by you were bred
To dye the Romish Calendar with red:[6]
For which posterity unborn will see
In pilgrimage thy sanctified tree.

Some men pretend it is a foul disgrace
That Jonathan, or any of his race,
Should in thy pleasant sweet embraces die,
Who was the very source of villainy:
The very name of most detested Wild
Hath all thy fame and pristine worth defil'd;
For Jonathan, to meet his shroud and urn,
Some country gallows might have serv'd his turn;
Where little, petty scoundrel rogues depart
The world upon a ladder or a cart;
But these reflections thy best friends suppose
Proceed from the antipathy of foes,
Who grudge to live in unity and love
With thee, who of a rogue do well approve?
All the best wits, and other men of sense,
Unanimously join in thy defence,
And say, which we acknowledge to be true,
Men must be *wild* before they come to you:
Who do the poor as well as rich relieve,
And kindly, all alive or dead, receive:
Witness Old Noll and Bradshaw deified
By each blood-thirsty regicide.

---

[6] A reference to the numerous Roman Catholic priests who were hung at Tyburn in earlier times.

Jonathan Wild.

Were all our trees to bear such fruit as you,
Or if thou only hadst but what's thy due,
How blest would most ungrateful England be,
That strives to cheat thee of thy lawful fee.
The cause of justice bravely you'd maintain,
And shew she should not hold her sword in vain;
For men as strong as Sampson you can tame,
Or taller than Goliah bring to shame:
But when such courtiers, who their tailors bite,
Such knavish lawyers who their clients slight;
Stock-jobbers, South Sea Bubbles, tallymen,
Pawnbrokers, bailiffs, who to iron den
Their fellow-creatures hurry, where they die
Between the frightful scenes of poverty,
And that renowned knave, whose hanging looks
Men seeing, without turning o'er the books,
He sells, from trusting him they do refrain,
For fear the cheating pimp should break again;
Where these (I say once more) and you do meet,
Thy glory's absolutely then complete.
But all in time—long look will come at last,
Before the Day of Judgment's here, and past;
Thy fame is then at its meridian height,
On all records till then you will be bright;
For 'twas by you that Wild most justly fell,
And fell into his native Hell.

Seldom has a man been so feared and hated and so mercilessly vituperated after death, and one reason for the obloquy he incurred, at any rate from the tongues of the criminal classes and their relatives, was because he had at his trial provided each member of his jury with a pamphlet entitled " A list of persons discovered, apprehended, and convicted of several roberries on the highway, and also for burglary and housebreaking, and also for returning from transportation: by Jonathan Wild." This document gave the names of 35 highway-robbers, 22 housebreakers, and 10 convicts returned from overseas—67 persons he had brought to the gallows, so he could expect no commiseration when his own turn came to swing there. Criminals hold strongly to the adage that " Dog should not eat dog," and it is remarkable how their point of view against Wild was supported by the hack-rhymesters of the time who voiced the popular execration in terms which made jest of all the horrors of violent death and the tomb. His posthumous reputation grew blacker and blacker, if possible, with the passing years. In a pamphlet, published about 1810, he is thus described—

History of the Life and Times of Jonathan Wild, the Celebrated Thief, and Thief-taker General of Great Britain and Ireland, WHO EXCEEDED ALL MAN-

Introductory Note.

KIND HITHERTO BORN IN VILLAINY, INGRATITUDE, DUPLICITY, AND FRAUD: Giving also an Account of his keeping a Host of Thieves regularly in pay, participating in their Robberies, and then delivering them up to Justice, in order that he might become possessed of the Blood-money; With a curious History of his Office for the Recovery of Stolen Property. London: Printed by and for William Cole, No. 10 Newgate Street. Sixpence.

This work contains an absurd picture in vivid colour of "Blake alias Blueskin cutting the throat of Jonathan Wild, during his Trial at the Old Bailey," wherein Jonathan Wild much resembles His Majesty King George the Third both in the unexpected mildness of his countenance and the costume favoured by the King about 1810.

The romance writers continued the fell tradition. Ainsworth presents Wild as an implacable villain, and his murder of Sir Rowland Trenchard in the Well Hole is an horrific incident. And by 1868, Edward Viles in "Blueskin" makes Jonathan the most devilish creature ever conceived. He murders some one in nearly every chapter; if he needs a horse, he simply shoots an unsuspecting traveller who is riding by, and wherever he goes he wields his fatal bludgeon. In this tale it is certainly true that "the world shall have occasion to remember Jonathan Wild," in the words used by the thief-taker. Fielding in his Satire was content to present Wild as A Great Rogue but not a constant murderer, and thereby came nearer to the truth about this remarkable villain who, as he truly says, achieved a final fate "so few GREAT men can accomplish—hanged by the neck till he was dead."

Dead, Wild's body was probably given to the service of dissection, for the pedigree of successive owners of his skeleton, now preserved in the Museum of the Royal College of Surgeons, in Lincoln's Inn Fields, seems to be authentic. At the time of Wild's execution in 1725 one of the Ordinaries at Newgate Prison was an intimate friend of a surgeon named Brand, who by this acquaintance secured the criminal's body. A medical student under Brand, named Thomas, was much later presented by his master with the skeleton. Dr. Thomas became a well-known practitioner in Windsor, where he died about 1808, at the age of seventy-two. His practice and the skeleton passed to his relative, Dr. Rendall, who in course of time retired and disposed of his practice and the ubiquitous Wild skeleton to Mr. Frederick Fowler, surgeon of Sheet Street, Windsor, who was the owner in 1840.[7] Fowler preserved the grim relic in a glass case, which was open to inspection by all who were interested. Seven years later he addressed

---

[7] *The Weekly Dispatch*, 22nd March, 1840.

Jonathan Wild.

the following letter to Professor (Sir Richard) Owen, then Conservator of the Museum of the Royal College of Surgeons—

To the President and Council of the Royal College of Surgeons, London.
    Gentlemen,
        I beg to offer for your acceptance the skeleton of the celebrated Jonathan Wild which has been in my possession together with my predecessors upwards of 50 years. The peculiar character of the letters and figures on the coffin-plate that accompanies it which were in general use at that period will be an additional proof of the authenticity of the skeleton.
        I have the honour to be, Gentlemen,
            Your most obedient servant,
                    FREDK. FOWLER,
                        Surgeon.

22 Burton Crescent,[8]
    June 18th, 1847.

The coffin-plate bears the inscription: "Mr. Jonathan Wilde, Died May 24, 1725, in ye 42nd year of his age." The height of the skeleton is 5 feet 4.2 inches. The thumb of the left hand and part of the forefinger of the right hand are missing. Three teeth remain in the jaw. Such are the tangible remains of terrible Jonathan Wild the Great.[9]

---

[8] Although giving an address in London, the letter bears the Windsor postmark.

[9] Sir Arthur Keith, the present Conservator of the Museum, to whom I am indebted for some of the above particulars, is quite convinced that the skeleton is certainly that of Jonathan Wild.

Jonathan Wild

From a portrait in "The Newgate Calendar"

The Life.

AN ACCOUNT OF JONATHAN WILD.

Reprinted from "The Bloody Register."

JONATHAN WILD was born at Wolverhampton in Staffordshire, about the year 1682. He was the eldest son of his parents; his father was a carpenter, and had the character of an honest, industrious man. At about fifteen years of age, Jonathan, having made some progress at school in writing and arithmetic, was bound apprentice to a buckle-maker at Birmingham. When his time was expired, he married an honest woman at Wolverhampton, by whom he had one son. But they had not been married two years before Jonathan took it into his head to leave his wife and child, and come up to London. He had been but a few months in town before he ran himself so far in debt, that he was arrested, and thrown into Woodstreet Compter. He says himself (in a pamphlet of which I shall give some account hereafter) that, " by misfortunes in the world, he was subject to the discipline of the Compter, for above the space of four years, during which time it was impossible, but he must in some measure be let into the secrets of the criminals there under confinement; and particularly Mr. Hitchen's management."

Here it was that he contracted a close familiarity with one Mary Milliner, a common street-walker. She had run round the whole circle of vice, knew all the ways of the town, and most of its felonious inhabitants.

The time came when they both obtained their liberty; soon after which it was reported, that they were made one flesh—but without the help of a parson. The first business they went upon together, was that of the buttock and twang, or, in other words, the whores bully. They had not followed this trade long, before they met with some pretty good booties, which enabled them to take a little house in Cockalley, opposite Cripplegate Church.

Jonathan, by his own industry, and his helpmate's assistance, was, by this time, acquainted with all the prigs of any note, within the bills of mortality, and he had cunning enough to dive into all their secrets. He soon knew all their usual haunts, what Lays they went upon, how they proceeded, and in consequence of this knowledge, he had their lives in his power, and from a confidant, became a director.

Formerly, when a thief had got a prize, he could easily find people enough to take it off his hands, at something less than the real value; for the law had provided no punishment for the receiver. But, after the legislature had passed an act, which made it felony to receive stolen goods, knowing them to be stolen, a considerable stop was put to this practice. Those few that continued it were obliged to act very cautiously, and as they ran great hazards, they insisted upon such extravagant profits, that the thieving trade was in danger of coming to nothing.

Jonathan Wild.

But Jonathan contrived a scheme that gave new life to the business; and convening some of his chief prigs, he laid the matter before them.

"You know, my bloods" (quoth he) "that as trade goes at present, you stand but a queer chance, for, when you have made any thing, if you carry it to the fencing culls and flash-pawn-brokers, those unconsionable dealers in contraband goods will hardly tip ye a quarter of what it is worth; and, if ye offer it to a stranger, it's ten to one but ye are babbled. So that there is no such thing as a man living by his labour; for, if he don't like to be half starved, he must run the hazard of being scragged, which, let me tell you, is a damn'd hard case. Now if you will take my advice, I'll engage to pay back the goods to the cull that owns them, and raise you more cole upon that account, than you can expect from the rascally fencers; and at the same time take care that you shall be all bowmen."

This was received with general approbation, and immediately put in practice. No sooner was a robbery committed, but Jonathan was informed what the goods were, when, how, and from whom they were taken. The goods were deposited in some convenient place, but not in his own house; for, at his first setting up the business, he acted very cautiously, tho' afterwards he grew daring. When things were thus prepared, away goes Jonathan, or the bone of his bone, to the persons who had been plundered, and addresses them to this purpose.

"I happened to hear that you have lately been robbed, and a friend of mine, an honest broker, having stopped a parcel of goods upon suspicion, I thought I could do no less than give you notice of it, as not knowing but that some of them might be yours; if it proves so, (as I wish it may) you may have them again, provided that nobody is brought into trouble, and the broker has something in consideration of his care."

People who have been robbed are willing to recover their goods with as little trouble as possible, and therefore it is no wonder, if they easily fell into Jonathan's measures. But if (as it sometimes happened) the person was too inquisitive, "Sir" (says Jonathan,) "I only came to serve you, and if you think otherwise, I must let you know that you are mistaken. I have told you that some goods being offered to pawn by a suspected person, the broker had the honesty to stop them; and therefore, Sir, if you question me about thieves, I have nothing to say to you; but that I can give a good account of myself, my name is Wild, and I live in Cock-alley by Cripplegate, where you may find me any day in the week; and so, Sir, your humble servant." By this affected resentment, he seldom failed of bringing the injured person to treat him upon his own terms, which on such occasions he commonly advanced.

All this while, as Jonathan had his profits out of what was paid to the broker, he took no money of those to whom he restored the goods, by which means he kept up a tolerable reputation, and at the same time there was no law in being that could affect him.

But as he soon became eminent in his profession he altered some of his measures. He no longer applied to those who had lost any thing, but they were obliged to apply to him, if they expected his assistance, and he received them in his office with much formality. At their entrance it was hinted to them, they must deposit a crown as a fee for his advice. This being done, he demanded their names, where they lived, where and how they were robbed, if they suspected any persons, and what kind of persons they were, the particular

The Life.

goods that were lost, and what reward would be given if the goods were returned. These articles being known, were entered in a book he kept for that purpose, and then the persons were assured, that a careful enquiry should be made, and, if they called again in two or three days, he might possibly give them some intelligence.

When they came according to appointment, and desired to know what success he had met with, "Why, indeed," says Jonathan, "I have heard something of your goods, but the person I sent to enquire tells me, that the rogues pretend they can pawn them for more than you offer, and therefore, if ever they make restitution, it must be upon better terms. However, if I can but once come to the speech of the rascals, I don't question but that I shall bring them to reason."

If this did not always prevail with the owners of the goods, to offer an additional reward, it served at least to enhance their obligation to Jonathan by making them imagine he used them very kindly, and took a great deal of pains, if, after their attending two or three times, he helped them to their goods again at their own prices.

Jonathan had always some advantage or other in examining so minutely into the circumstances of a robbery. If, as was often the case, he knew as much of the matter beforehand, as those who came for his assistance could tell him, his enquiries then served to amuse them, and prevent their suspecting his consciousness: But, if he had not already been let into the whole, or any part of the secret, the exact information he received by this means, was such a check upon the thieves, that they seldom dared to conceal any thing from him; and, if they did, or refused to accept of his terms, it was at their peril.

Pocket-books, shop-books, accompts, and other writings, which were formerly looked upon as things of no use but to the owners, and consequently not worth stealing, were now become articles of considerable advantage to the thief, and more to the receiver. Trifling curiosities, toys, and trinkets, would fetch more by being returned to the proprietors, than any body else would give for them.

Jonathan now appeared with a sword by his side, and the first use we find he made of it was in an engagement with the wife of his bosom. She had some time so provoked him to wrath, that he swore by the lord, he would mark her for a bitch, and thereupon drawing his sword, he smote off one of her ears.[1] This occasioned a divorce; but, however, Jonathan, in a grateful consideration of the services she had done him, by bringing him into so large an acquaintance, and assisting him in his business, allowed her a weekly pension as long as she lived.

But, to look a little back, we must here observe that, before Jonathan made any great figure, he was for some time assistant to Charles Hitchin, the City Marshal, in searching infamous houses, and apprehending disorderly persons. After several rambles together for promoting so blessed a work, these hopeful reformers fell to loggerheads about one another's honesty, and so they parted; and each of them separately pursued the business of thief-taking.

In the same year, 1715, Jonathan left his house in Cock-alley, and took lodgings at Mrs. Seagoe's in the Old Bailey, where he went on in his own

---

[1] There does not appear to be any evidence elsewhere concerning this unproved allegation.—S.M.E.

Jonathan Wild.

calling successfully, notwithstanding the Marshal's opposition. The Marshal went to work, and, in the year 1718, published a stupid pamphlet, under the title of, "The regulator: or, a discovery of thieves, thief-takers and locks, in and about the city of London, with the thief-taker's proclamation: also an account of the Flash Words now in vogue among the thieves, &c."

As in this pamphlet, and Jonathan's answer to it, there are several passages relating to his conduct, which are no where else to be met with, we shall make several extracts from each.

The City Marshal's Account of Jonathan Wild, &c.

If these should hold their peace, the stones in the street would cry out of such abominable practices, as are committed and carried on in this city, than an hundred thieves; and in order thereto, I shall take notice here only of one of the aforesaid felonious practices, taking it for granted, that all the rest are of the same management; to wit, a gentlewoman, as she was passing along in the evening, in a coach, on the south side of St. Paul's Church-yard, was there, in an audacious and barbarous manner, robbed to a considerable value, by three of the most notorious rogues; William Matthews, Christopher Matthews, and Obediah Lemon, (who agreed to make himself an evidence) that ever this kingdom was plagued with; which being discovered and sought after, in order to bring them to justice, for so doing, the thief-taker, hearing of the same, and fearing that he might by this means lose three of the most profitable customers, which belonged to his felonious shop, immediately summoned the three aforesaid offenders to a friendly conference, where it was agreed that the only way to save them, at this critical juncture, was, for one of them to make himself an evidence, etc. "Well, then," saith the thief-taker, "in order to blind the justice, and that he may take the information, is to induce him to believe that we are doing something for the good of the public: Therefore you must put into the information a numerous train of offenders, which have been concerned with you, either in robberies or buying or receiving your stolen goods; and at the same time, you must be sure to promise him, the said justice, you will convict them all: and, that there may be a perfect harmony between us, you shall hear me your counsellor, your thief-taker and factor, promise as faithfully, that I will apprehend, take, and bring them to justice for the same. But by the bye, I must give you this caution, to leave out the sixty dozen of Hankerchiefs, that was taken by Mr. Ridley, from a dyer's servant, whom they sent on a sham Errand, for which handkerchiefs, I received thirty guineas from the owner, but gave Oakes, Lemon, and Mr. Johnson, but ten Guineas. That you do not put such and such robberies into the information, because I was employed by the persons that you robbed, to get their goods again, and they not bidding money enough for the same, they were not returned to the right owner. Therefore you know such must be left out, otherwise I shall bring my own neck into the Noose, and put it in the power of every little prig as well as others, to pull the cord at their pleasure, and upon such terms, who the devil would be your factor."

And now let us see what is the consequence of this skittish and felonious information; but deceiving the magistrate, and letting the aforesaid three notorious

City Marshal's Account.

offenders escape the hand of justice, and hanging up a couple of *shim-sham* thieves (Hugh Oakley and Henry Chickley) which he got little or nothing by, in the room thereof. And, likewise, to give the thief-taker an opportunity to rob or extort a sum of money out of all the rest in the information, by making up and compounding the felonies with them, which by a modest computation, cannot amount to less than 100L, or more, &c. Then is it not high time for the citizens of London, and the places adjacent to bestir themselves when the greatest offenders have found a way out, with the assistance of their friend the thief-taker, to escape the hand of justice. This will give them encouragement, and make them desperate, as well as frequent in their robberies, and what the Citizens and others must dearly pay for it, if not timely prevented, by putting a stop to the same. In short, the thief, the gaol, the justice, and the King's evidences, all of them seem to be influenced and managed by him, and at this rate none will be brought to the gallows, but such as he thinks fit, &c. Now if enquiry was to be made, by what means he arrived to this pitch of preferment he is now at, you will find that he hath been a great proficient in all matters and things, that he hath hitherto engaged in.

I. Who, when in a private station, and following the trade of Buckle-making, knew how to plate a crown-piece as well as any that followed that employment.

II. When he became an evidence, did the business skittishly, and as effectually, as any of those he now sets up.

III. When he was a *Twang* (*Bully*) and followed the tail of his wife, Mary Milliner, a common night-walker, no sooner had she picked a pocket, and given him the signal *by a hem*, or otherwise, but he had the impudence and courage enough to attack the *cull*, until the *buttock* had made her escape.

IV. When king of the Gypsies, Jonathan Wild did execute the hidden and dark part of a stroller to all intents and purposes, until, in Holborn by order of the Justice, his skittish and baboonish majesty was set in the stocks for the same.

V. Now King among the Thieves, and Lying-Master General of England, Captain-General of the Army of Plunderers, and Ambassador Extraordinary from the Prince of the Air, hath taken up his residence in an apartment, fitted up on purpose for him in the palace of the Queen of Hell, where attendance is continually given for receiving or buying of stolen goods, as likewise to pay them back again, provided the right owners will give them money enough for the same; but if not, then doth his Excellency fly off, and give you to understand, that the goods he hath heard of are not yours, and that you may be gone about your business; for—he will take a sum of money of the thief, or dispose of the goods some other way. Certainly such a monster in iniquity as this is not to be found in any part of habitable world save only in this kingdom, and this infatuated city, and places adjacent, those places of general corruption.

VI. There being one thing more, which he earnestly denies, and sollicits to be employed in finding out, and setting up evidences against the false coiners, and then you need not doubt but in a little time you will have as many coiners as you have thieves. O London! London! so much found for thy good order; by what means is it now come to pass, that thou art become a receptacle for a den of thieves and robbers, and all sorts of villainous persons and practices?

And here it cannot be taken amiss to examine a little into the trade of

Jonathan Wild.

punishing wickedness and vice, the same being become one of the most mysterious, flourishing and profitabe trades now in the kingdom—and the open, but unwarrantable pernicious practice of the regulator (Jonathan Wild).

And in order thereto, I shall take a view of him in the public streets, which he so much boasteth of, and fain would persuade you, that he doeth so much good to the public, by stopping the whores, and other persons viciously inclined, and forcibly entering the bawdy-houses, and taking them out from thence, and committing them to gaol. And now, I pray, what's the consequence of all this? woeful experience plainly shows, that by the ill-acquaintance and conversation they meet with there, they learn to be thieves, and find the way to the thief takers houses, set up by them on purpose to harbour and train up one breed of thieves under another, and to screen and save them from the gallows, to the end that they might live by the reversion of them. And now it is the general complaint, that people are afraid, when it is dark, to come to their houses, for fear their hats and wigs should be snatched off their heads, or their swords taken from their sides, or that they may be blinded, knocked down, cut or stabbed; nay, the coaches cannot secure them, but they are likewise assaulted, cut, and robbed in the public streets. And how can you suppose it to be otherwise, when there are so many public offices, public and private houses, public inns, and public shops, set up on purpose to harbour thieves and robbers, and carry on the basest designs with them.

Jonathan Wild's Account of himself and the City Marshal.

When two of a profession are at variance, the world is let into many important discoveries; and, whether it be among thief-takers, lawyers, or clergymen, an expectation naturally arises of some Billingsgate treatment. For the satisfaction of the work in this particular, I shall, like a true cock of the game, answer Mr. Hitchen at his weapons.

Says my old old master in iniquity, "one thief-taker brought to justice, is more for the advantage of the city than a hundred thieves." Not to justify the practice of thief-taking, I acquiesce with him in this, if the oldest offenders are to be first prosecuted, and then I'll have the world to judge—Who will deserve an exemplary punishment.

(This looks as if Jonathan was not the original thief-taker, but that he borrowed some hints from the Marshal, and afterwards improved them.)

The information he mentioned, in respect to the setting up an evidence, is entirely groundless, the person accused being perfectly ignorant of it, and there are enough to prove that the evidence voluntarily appeared before my Lord Mayor. And as for not returning the goods for want of a reward sufficient to the value, I shall show what flagrant crimes the City Marshal has been guilty of, of this nature.

(Jonathan does not here deny the charge of not returning the goods, and therefore we may venture to take it for a fact.)

Says this author—"He knows how to plate a crown-piece as well as any that follow that employment." Now, if he could prove this assertion, or any thing like it, is is very rational to suppose, that he would bring the thief-taker to condign punishment, being his implacable enemy.

Account of himself and the City Marshal.

That "setting up of evidence against false coiners is the way to have as many coiners as thieves," is such a piece of nonsense, absurdity, and contradiction that it is not to be paralleled.

And it is a notable piece of inconsistency to say "that taking whores out of Bawdy-houses, makes them thieves." By this way of argument the houses of correction, instead of deterring iniquity increase thefts and robberies, and the reformers of manners are the promoters of wickedness. But, it's no wonder that the Marshal, throughout his treatise, expresses a great deal of uneasiness at the informers, for those persons very much lessen his interest in suppressing houses of lewdness, the keepers whereof have been generally pensioners to him.—I can produce persons who will make it appear that several houses of ill-fame are supported by quarterly contributions to him; besides there being frequently sums of money extorted from libertines for contrivance at their lewdness, and sometimes from persons entirely innocent and unacquainted with the character of these houses. And he has of late been so audacious, as to examine taverns of the best reputation and insist upon yearly compositions from them, tho' the only payment he has met with has been a salute with a crab-tree cudgel and a decent toss in a blanket.

I need not mention his being nearer the pillory than ever a certain person was to the stocks.—And, however a certain diminutive person may resemble a Baboon, it is evident to all that knows the gigantic City Marshal, that he wants nothing but a cloven foot to personate, in all respects, his father Belzebub.

Many other particulars I shall omit, and proceed in matters of fact, by which it will appear, that, instead of a scoundrel author's being entirely free from all the evil practices he has treated of he is guilty of the same crimes he pretends to fix upon others.

After the Marshal's spension in his office, and he was forbid attendance on the Lord Mayor, he, on a time, applied himself to the Buckle-maker near Cripplegate, in the following manner.

"I am very sensible that you are let into the knowledge of the intrigues of the Compter, particularly with relation to the securing of Pocket-books: but your experience is inferior to mine, I can put in a far better method than you are acquainted with, and which may be done with safety; for, tho' I am suspended, I still retain the power of acting as constable; and, notwithstanding I can't be heard before my Lord Mayor, as formerly, I have interest among the Aldermen upon any complaint. But I must first tell you that you'll spoil the trade of Thief-taking, in advancing greater rewards than are necessary; I give but half-a-crown a book, and, when the thieves and pick-pockets see you and I confederate, they will submit to our terms, and likewise contiune their thefts for fear of coming to the gallows by our means.

"You shall take a turn with me as my servant, or assistant, and we will commence our rambles this night."

The night approaching, the Marshal and the Buckle-maker began their walk at Temple-bar called in at several brandy-shops, and ale-houses, between that and Fleet-ditch. Some of the masters of these houses complimented the Marshal with punch, others with brandy, and some presented him with fine ale, offering their service to their worthy protector. The Marshal made them little answer; but gave them to understand, all the service he expected from them was, to give him information of pocket-books, or any goods stolen as "a pay-back; for

Jonathan Wild.

you women of the town" (addressing himself to the females of one shop), "make it a common practice to resign things of this nature to the Bullies, and rogues of your retinues,—but this shall no longer be born with, I'll give you my word, both they and you shall be detected, unless you deliver all the pocket-books you meet with to me. What do you think I bought my place for, but to make the most of it? and you are to understand this is my man (pointing to the Buckle-maker) to assist me. And if you at any time for the future refuse to yield up the watches and books you take, either to me, or to my servant, you may be assured of all being sent to Bridewell, and not one of you shall be permitted to walk the streets. For, notwithstanding I am under a suspension, (the chief reason of which is, for not suppressing the practices of such vermin as you) I have still a power of punishing, and you shall dearly pay for the least disobedience to what I have commanded."

Strutting along the streets a little farther, the Marshal on a sudden siezed two or three dextrous pick-pockets, reprimanding them for not paying their respects to their mighty chief; and withal asking them to what parts of the town they were rambling, and whether they did not see him? To which they answered, that they saw him at a distance (he being big and remarkable enough to be known by them and their brethren) but he caught hold of them so hastily, that they had no time to address him. "We have been strolling" (continued the pick-pockets) "over Moorfields, and from thence to the Blue-boar, in pursuit of you; but, not finding you as usual, we were under some fears you was indisposed." The Marshal replied, he should have given them a meeting there, but had been employed the whole day with his new man. "You are to be very careful, said he, not to oblige any person but myself, or servant, with pocket-books: If you presume to do otherwise you shall swing for it, and we are out in the city every night to observe your motions." These instructions given, the pick-pocket left us, making their master a low congee, and promising obedience. This was the progress of the first night with the buckle-maker, whom he told him that his staff of authority terrified the ignorant to the extent of his wishes.

Another night, walking towards the back part of St. Paul's, said the Marshal to the Buckle-maker, "I'll now show you a Brandy-shop that entertains no company but whores and thieves. This is a house for our purpose, and I am informed, that a woman of the town who frequents it, has lately decently robbed a gentleman of his watch and pocket-book; the advice I received from her companion, with whom I have a good understanding. We'll go into the house, and, if we can find this woman, I will assume a more fierce countenance (though at best I look like an infernal) and, by continued threats, extort a confession, and by that means get possession of the watch and pocket-book; in order to which, do you slily accost her companion,"—(here he described her)—"Call to her, and inform her, that your master is in a damned ill-humour, and swears, if she don't instantly make a discovery where the watch and pocket-book may be found, at the farthest by To-morrow, he will certainly send her to the Compter, and thence to the work-house." The means being thus concerted to gain the valuable goods, both master and man enter the shop in pursuit of the game, and, according to expectation, they found the person wanted; where-upon the Marshal shewing an outraged countenance, becoming the design, and the Buckle-maker being obliged to follow his master's example, the company

Account of himself and the City Marshal.

said, that the master and man looked as sour as two Devils.—"Devils," said the Marshal, "I'll make some of you devils if you don't immediately discover the watch and pocket-book I am employed to procure." "We don't know your meaning, Sir," answered some; "who do you discourse to?" Said others, "We knew nothing of it." The Marshal replied, in a more soft tone, "You are ungrateful to the last degree to deny me this small request, when I was never let into the secret of any thing to be taken from a gentleman, but I communicated it to you, describing the person so exactly, that you could not mistake the man; and there is so little got at this rate, that the devil made trade with you for me." This speech being over, the Marshal gave a nod to his man, who in obedience to his master's motions, and his former commands, called one of the women to the door, and, telling the story above directed, the female answered, "Unconscionable devil! when he got five or ten guineas, not to bestow above five or ten shillings upon us unfortunate wretches! But, however, rather than go to the Compter, I'll try what's to be done." The woman returning to the Marshal asked him what he would give for the delivery of the watch, being 7 or 8l in value, and the pocket-book having in it several notes and Goldsmiths bills. To which the Marshal answered, "a guinea," and told her, it was much better to comply, than to go to Newgate, which she must certainly expect upon her refusal. The woman replied, the watch was in pawn for 40s., and if he did not advance that sum, she should be obliged to strip herself for the redemption; though when her furbelowed scarf was laid aside, she had nothing underneath but furniture for a paper mill. After abundance of words, he allowed her 30s. for the watch and book, which she accepted, and the watch was never returned to the owner.

Not long after this a gentleman in liquor dropping into the Blue Boar, near Moorfields, with a woman of the town, immediately lost his watch. He applied to the Marshal, desiring his assistance; but the Buckle-maker being well acquainted with the walk between Cripple-gate and Moorfields, had the fortune to find the woman. The master immediately siezed on her, on notice given, and, by vehement threatenings, obliged her to a confession. She declared she had stolen the watch, and carried it to a woman who kept a brandy-shop near, desiring her to assist in the sale of it. The mistress of the brandy-shop readily answered, she had it from an honest young woman who frequented her house, whose husband was gone to sea; whereupon she pawned the watch for its value and ordered the sale. This story seeming reasonable, a Watch-maker bought the watch, and gave the money agreed for it which was 50s. Thus the sale of the watch being discovered, the Marshal with his staff and assistants immediately repaired to the Watch-maker's house, and siezed the Watch-maker, in the same manner a person would do the greatest criminals. He carried him to a public-house, telling him, if he did not forthwith send for the watch he should be committed to Newgate.

The Watch-maker not being any ways accustomed to unfair dealings, directly answered, that he bought the watch, and the person he had it of would produce the woman that stole it, if it was stolen, the woman being then present. The Marshal replied, he had no business with the person that stole the watch, but with him in whose possession it was found, and that if he did not instantly send for the watch, and deliver it, without insisting upon any money, but on the contrary, return him thanks for his civility, which deserved five or

Jonathan Wild.

ten pieces, he would without delay send him to Newgate. Upon which, the honest Watch-maker, being much surprized, sent for the watch and surrendered it to him. And since that, he has been well satisfied, that the person who owned the watch made a present to the Marshal of three guineas for his trouble, and the poor watch-maker never had a farthing for his fifty shillings. This story and the following sufficiently demonstrates the honesty of the City Marshal.

Some time ago a biscuit-baker near Wapping, having lost a pocket-book, wherein was, among other papers, an exchequer bill for 100*l*, applied himself to the marshal's man, the buckle-maker, for the recovery thereof; the buckle-maker advised him to advertise it, and stop payment of the bill, which he did, but, having no account of the bill, he came to the buckle-maker several times about it, and at length he told him, there had been with him a tall man, with a long peruke and sword, calling himself the City Marshal, and asked him, if he had lost his pocket-book. The biscuit-maker answered, yes, desiring to know the reason for asking him such questions, and, whether he could give him any intelligence? he replied, no, he could not give him any intelligence of it as yet, but desired to be informed, whether he had employed any person to search after it; the biscuit-maker answered, he had employed one Wild. Upon which the Marshal told him, he was under a mistake, for he should have applied to him, who was the only person in England that could have served him, being well assured it was entirely out of the power of Wild, or any of those fellows, to know where it was—which was very certain, he having it at that time in his own custody,—and desired to know the reward that would be given. The gentleman answered, he would give ten pound. The Marshal answered, that a greater reward should be offered, for that exchequer bills, and those things, were ready money, and could be immediately sold, and that, if he had employed him in the beginning and offered forty or fifty pound he would have served him. The biscuit-maker acquainting Wild with this story, Wild gave it as his opinion, that the pocket-book was in the Marshal's possession, and therefore it would be to no purpose to continue advertising it, he being well assured that the Marshal would not have taken the pains to find out the biscuit-maker, unless he knew how to get at it.

Upon the whole, Wild advised the biscuit-maker rather to advance his bidding, considering what hands the note was in, and for that the Marshal had often told his servant how easily he could dispose of the bank-notes, and exchequer bills, at gaming houses, which he very much frequented. Pursuant to this advice the owner at last went a second time to the Marshal, and bid 40*l* for his pocket-book and bill. " Zounds, sir," said the Marshal, " you are too late!" which was all the satisfaction he gave him. Thus the poor biscuit-maker was tricked out of his exchequer bill. But it happened a small time after, that some of the young fry of pick-pockets, under the tuition of the Marshal, fell out in sharing the money given them for this very pocket-book; whereupon one of them came to the person first employed by the biscuit-maker, and discovered the whole matter, viz. that he had sold the biscuit-maker's pocket-book, with the 100*l* exchequer note in it, and other bills, to the City Marshal, at a tavern in Aldersgate Street, for four or five guineas. The person to whom the boy applied himself, asked him what sort of a person the gentleman was that he took it from, who readily answered, that he was a lusty elderly man, with light hair, which was very apparent to be the same person. But

Account of himself and the City Marshal.

the exchequer bill was never returned to the owner, but returned to another person, though it could never be traced back.

Another instance of the good understanding between the Marshal and the thieves and pick-pockets, take as follows.

Some time since, when a person stood in the pillory near Charing-cross, a gentleman in the croud was deprived of a pocket-book, which had in it bills and lottery tickets, to the value of several hundred pounds; and a handsome reward was at first offered for it in an advertisement, thirty pound at least. The Marshal hearing a suspicion, that a famous pick-pocket, known by his lame hand, had taken the book, he applied to him, and to enforce a confession and delivery, told him, with a great deal of assurance that he must be the person, such a man, with a lame hand, being described by the gentleman to be near him, and who, he was certain, had stolen his book. "In short," says he, "you have the book, and you must bring it to me, and you shall share the reward; but, if you refuse to comply with such advantageous terms, you must never expect to come within the City gates; for, if ye do, Bridewell at least, if not Newgate, shall be your residence." After several meetings, the Marshal's old friend could not deny that he had the pocket-book; but he said to the Marshal, "I did not expect this rigorous treatment from you, after the service I have done you, in concealing you several times; and by that means keeping you out of a gaol. It is not the way to expect further service, when all my former good offices are forgotten." The Marshal, notwithstanding these reasons, still insisted upon what he at first proposed; and, at length, the pick-pocket considering, that he could not repair to the Exchange, or else where to follow his pilfering employment, without the Marshal's consent, and fearing to be a mark of his revenge, he condescended to part with the pocket-book, upon terms reasonable between the buyer and seller. "Whereupon," says the Marshal, "I lost all my money last night at gaming, and except a gold watch in my pocket, which I believe there will be no enquiry after it coming to hand by an intrigue with a famous woman of the town, whom the gentleman will be ashamed to prosecute, for fear of exposing himself. I'll exchange goods for goods with you;" So that the pick-pocket rather than risque the consequences of disobliging his master, concluded a bargain.

The following story shows the Marshal's prodigious courage and forwardness to hang burglars, even his own pupils, for the reward.

One night, not far from St. Paul's, the Marshal, and the buckle-maker his man, met with a detachment of pick-pocket boys, who instantly, at the sight of their master, took to their heels and ran away. The buckle-maker asked the meaning of their surprize? the Marshal answered, "I know their meaning, a pack of rogues! they were to have met me in the Fields this morning with a book, I am informed they have taken from a gentleman, and they are afraid of being secured for their disobedience. There is Jack Jones among them.— We'll catch the whores' birds." Upon which Jack Jones, running behind a coach to make his escape, was taken by the Marshal and his man.

The Marshal carried him to a tavern, and threatned him severely, telling him, he believed they were turned house-breakers, and that they were concerned in a burglary lately committed by four young criminals. This happening to be fact, and the boy fearing the Marshal had been informed of it, he for his own security, confessed, the Marshal promising to save his life on his becoming evidence.

Whereupon the Marshal committed the boy to the Compter till the next morning, when he carried him before a Justice of the peace, who took his Information, and issued a warrant for apprehending his companions. Notice being given where the criminals were to be found, viz., at a house in Beach-lane, the Marshal and his man went privately in the night thither; and listening at the door, they overheard the boys, with several others in a mixed company. They entered the house, where they met ten or eleven persons, who were in a great rage, enquiring what business the Marshal had there, and saluted him with a few *damns*, which occasioned the Marshal to make a prudent retreat, pulling the door after him, and leaving his man to the mercy of the savage company. In a short space the Marshal returned with eight or ten watchmen and a constable. And, at the door, the Marshal, out of his dastardly disposition, tho' his presence was a ceremonious respect, obliged the constable to go in first (but the Marshal and constable were so long in their compliments, that the man thought neither of them would enter); at last the constable entering with his long staff extended before him, the Marshal manfully followed, crying out, "Where are the rebel villains? why don't you secure them?"

The Buckle-maker answered, they were under the table. Upon which the constable pulled out the juvenile offenders, neither of them being above twelve years of age. The two boys now taken were committed to Newgate. But the fact being committed in the county of Surrey, they were afterwards removed to the Marshalsea prison. The Assizes coming on at Kingston, and Jones giving his evidence against his companions, before the Grand Jury, the Bill was found, and the Marshal indorsed his name on the back of it, to have the honour of being an evidence against these monstrous house-breakers. On the trial the nature of the fact was declared; but the parents of the offenders appeared, and satisfied the court that the Marshal was the occasion of the ruin of these boys by taking them into the Fields, and encouraging them in the stealing of pocket-books : and told him on his affirming they were thieves, that he had made them such. The Judge observing the Marshal's views were more to get the reward of forty pounds than to do justice, summed up the charge to the Jury in favour of the boys, who were thereupon acquitted and the Marshal reprimanded. He was so enraged at this, and so angry with himself for not accusing the boys of other crimes, that he immediately returned to London, and left his man to discharge the reckoning at Kingston.

Not much unlike the preceding story, is the following.

A gentleman, who had lost his watch with a woman of the town, applied to a person belonging to the Compter who recommended him to the Buckle-maker for procuring the same; and the gentleman applying accordingly to him, and giving a description of the woman, the Buckle-maker, a few days after, traversing Fleet-street with his master in an evening, happened to meet with the female, (as he apprehended by the description of the gentleman) who had stolen the watch, and coming nearer he was satisfied therein. He told his master that she was the very person described. To which his master answered with an air of pleasure, "I am glad to find we have a prospect of something to-night to defray our expences," and immediately with his man siezed the female, and carried her to a public house, where, upon her examination, she confessed that it was in her

Account of himself and the City Marshal.

power to serve the Marshal in it; telling him, that if he would please to go with her home, or send his man, the watch would be returned, and a suitable reward for the trouble. The man asked his master, whether he might pursue the woman with safety? He replied, yes, for that he knew her: and gave hints of his following at a reasonable distance for his security, which he did with a great deal of precaution, as will appear; for the man proceeding with the female, she informed him, that her husband who had the watch about him, was at a tavern near White-friars, and, if he would condescend to go thither, he might be furnished with it, without giving himself any further trouble, together with the reward he deserved. To which the man consented, and, coming to the tavern, she enquired for the company she had been with but a short time before; and, being informed they were still in the house, she sent in word by the drawer, that the gentlewoman who had been with them that evening, desired the favour to speak with them. The drawer going, and delivering the message, immediately three or four gentlemen came from the room to the woman. She gave them to understand that the Marshal's man had accused her of stealing a watch, telling them she supposed it must have been some other woman who had assumed her name, and desiring their protection; upon this, the whole company sallied out, and attacked the Marshal's man in a very violent manner, to make a rescue of the female, upbraiding him for disgracing a gentlewoman of her reputation.

The Marshal, observing the ill-success of his man, and fearing the discipline of the poker, fire-fork, and fire-brands (which his man was obliged to go through) reserved his fate of this kind to futurity, decently made off, hugging himself that he had escaped the severe treatment he equally deserved with him. The man in the struggle shewed his resentment chiefly against the female; and, after a long contest, wherein he disrobed her so effectually, that she appeared like love without her fig-leaf, she was in that pickle thrust out at the back door, and immediately the watch being called, he and the rest of the men were siezed. In their conveyance to the Compter, the Marshal overtook them, and asked his man the occasion of his long absence. The man answered, he had been at the tavern with the woman, where he thought he saw him. The master replied, that indeed he was there, but seeing the confusion so great he went off to call the watch and constables. This dialogue being over, the Marshal used his interest to get his man off, but to no purpose, he being carried to the Compter with the rest of the company, in order to make an agreement there. In the morning the woman sent to her companions on the Compter, letting them know, that, if they could be released, the watch should be returned without any consideration, which was accordingly done, and a small present to the Marshal's man for smart-money; and upon this, the persons were all discharged, paying the fees. The watch being now ready to be produced to the owner, the Marshal insisted upon the greatest part of the reward, as being the greatest person in authority. The man declared it unreasonable, unless he had partook of the largest share of bastinado. "But however," says the Marshal, " I have now an opportunity of playing my old game. I'll oblige the gentleman to give me ten guineas to save his reputation, which is so nearly concerned with a common prostitute." But the gentleman knew him too well to be thus imposed upon, and would give him no more than what he promised, which was three guineas. The master at first refused, but his man (who had the most right to make a new contract) advising him to act cautiously, he at last agreed to accept the reward at first offered, giving his man only one guinea for his service, and the cure of his wounds.

Jonathan Wild.

One night after this, the Marshal and Buckle-maker being abroad in their walks, not far from the Temple, they discovered a Clergyman pissing against the wall, in an alley to which he had retired for modesty-sake. Immediately a woman of the town, lying in wait for prey, brushed by the Clergyman, he saying aloud, "What does, what does the woman want." The Marshal instantly rushed in upon them, seizing the Clergyman, bidding his man secure the woman. The Clergyman resisted, protesting his innocence (which his language to the woman confirmed) but finding it to no purpose, he desired he might be permitted to go into an Ironmonger's house near; but the Marshal refused, and dragged him to Salisbury-court end, where he raised a mob about him; and two or three gentlemen that knew the parson happened to come by, asked the mob what they were doing with him, telling them he was chaplain to a noble lord. The rough gentry answered, "D——m him, we believe he is chaplain to the devil, for we caught him with a whore." Upon this the gentlemen desired the Marshal to go to a tavern, that they might talk with him without noise and tumult, which he consented to. When they came into the tavern, the Clergyman asked the Marshal by what authority he thus abused him? the Marshal replied, he was a City-officer (pulling out his staff) and would have him to the Compter, unless he gave him very good security for his appearance the next morning, when he would swear he caught him with the whore, and his hands under her petticoats. The parson seeing him so bent upon perjury, which would very much expose him, sent for other persons to vindicate his reputation, who, putting a glittering security into the Marshal's hand (which they found was the only way to deal with such a monster in iniquity) the clergyman was permitted to go off.

The Marshal's next adventure was this: going up Ludgate-hill, he observed a well-dressed woman walking before him, who, he told the Buckle-maker, was a lewd woman, for that he saw her talking with a man. This was no sooner spoke, but he siezed her, and asked her who she was. "You are more like to be a whore" (said the Marshal) "and as such you shall go the Compter." Taking the woman through St. Paul's Church-yard, she desired liberty to send for some friend; but he would not comply with her request. He forecd her into the Nag's-head tavern in Cheap-side, where he presently ordered a hot supper and plenty of wine to be brought in; commanding the female to sit at a distance from his worship, and telling her, he did not permit such vermin to sit in his presence (tho' he intended to make her pay the reckoning). When the supper was brought to the table, he fell to it lustily, and would not allow the woman to eat a bite with him, or come near the fire, tho' it was extreme cold weather. When he had supped, he stared round, and then told her, if he had been an informer, or such a fellow, she would have called for eatables and wine herself, and not have given him the trouble of direction, or else would have slipped a piece into his hand. Adding, "You may do what you please; but tho' we that buy our places seem to go for nothing, I can assure ye it is in my power, if I see a woman in the hands of an informer, to discharge her, and commit them.—You are not so ignorant but you must guess my meaning." She replied, that she had money enough to pay for the supper, and about three half-crowns more. This desirable answer being given, he ordered his attendant to with-draw, while he compounded the matter with her. When the buckle-maker came in again, the gentlewoman was very civilly asked to sit by the fire, and eat the remainder of the supper, and in all respects treated very kindly, only with a pretended

Account of himself and the City Marshal.

reprimand to give him better language whenever he should speak to her for the future.

But, not to tire the reader's patience, we shall omit many other adventures of this sort, which the Marshal and his man had. After the Marshal's suspension, however, it may not be quite amiss to inform the public, that, before his disgrace, he used to have daily meetings with the pick-pocket boys in Moor-fields, and to treat them there plentifully with cakes and ale, offering them sufficient encouragement to continue their thefts. It once happened, that one of the boys, more cunning than his companions, having stolen an Alderman's pocket-book, and, on opening it, finding several bank-bills, he gave the Marshal to understand, that it was worth a great deal beyond the usual price, the notes being of considerable value, and he insisted on five pieces. The Marshal told the boy, that five pieces was enough to break him at once: That if he gave him two guineas he would be sufficiently paid, but assured him, that if he had the good luck to obtain a handsome reward, he'd make it up five pieces. Upon this present encouragement and future expectation, the boy delivered up the pocket-book. And a few days afterwards being informed that a very large reward had been given for the notes, he applied to the Marshal for the remaining three guineas according to promise. But all the satisfaction he had, was, that he should be sent to the house of correction if he continued to demand it; the Marshal telling him, that such rascals as he were ignorant how to dispose of their money.

As a proof of his dealing from the beginning with pick-pocket boys, I need only mention the cause of his being suspended; which was, for his conniving at the intrigues of the pick-pockets; taking the stolen pocket-books, and sending threatening letters to the persons who lost them, under pretence that they had been in company with lewd women, and for extorting money from several persons, and one in particular, who making his complaint to an eminent apothecary in the Poultrey, that knew the villainy of the Marshal, the affair was brought before the Court of Aldermen, where, upon examination the Marshal was found guilty of that and many other notorious crimes, upon which he was suspended.

The following entertaining adventure will exhibit another part of the Marshal's character.

One night the Marshal invited his man, the Buckle-maker, to a house near the end of the Old Bailey, telling him, he would introduce him to a company of He-Whores. The man, not rightly apprehending his meaning, asked him if they were hermaphrodites.—" No, ye fool you " (said the Marshal) " they are sodomites, such as deal with their own sex, instead of females." This being a curiosity the Buckle-maker had not yet met with, he willingly accompanied his master to the house, which they had no sooner entered, but the Marshal was complimented by the company with the title of Madam and Ladyship. The man asking the occasion of these uncommon devoirs, the Marshal said it was a familiar language peculiar to the house. The man was not long there before he was more surprized than at first. The men calling one another " my dear," and hugging, kissing, and tickling each other, as if they were a mixture of wanton males and females, and assuming effeminate voices and airs. Some telling others that they ought to be whipped for not coming to school more frequently. The Marshal was very merry in this assembly, and dallied with the young sparks with a great deal of pleasure, till some persons came into the house that he had little

Jonathan Wild.

expected to meet with in that place; and then finding it out of his power to secure the lads to himself, he started up on a sudden in a prodigious rage, asking the frolicking youths, if they were become so common as to use these obnoxious houses, and telling them he would spoil their diversion; upon this he made his exit with his man. As he was going out of the house, he said, he supposed they would have the impudence to make a ball. The man desiring him to explain what he meant by that, he answered, there was a noted house in Holborn, to which such sort of persons used to repair, and dress themselves up in women's apparel, and dance and romp about, and make such a hellish noise, that a man would swear they were a parcel of cats a catterwouling—"But," says he, "I'll be revenged of these smock-faced young dogs. I'll watch their waters, and secure 'em, and send 'em to the Compter."

Accordingly, the Marshal, knowing their usual hours, and customary walks, placed himself with a constable in Fleet-street, and dispatched his man with another to assist him, to the Old Bailey. At the expected time several of the youngsters were siezed in women's apparel, and carried to the Compter. Next morning they were carried before the Lord Mayor in the same dresses they were taken in. Some were completely rigged in gowns, petticoats, head-cloths, fine laced shoes, furbelowed scarves, and masks; some had riding-boots; some were dressed like milk-maids, others like shepherdesses with green hats, waistcoats, and petticoats; and others had their faces patched and painted, and wore very extensive hoop-petticoats, which had been very lately introduced. His Lordship having examined them, committed them to the Work-house, there to continue at hard labour during pleasure. And, as part of their punishment, ordered them to be publickly conducted through the streets in their female habits. Pursuant to which order the young tribe was carried in pomp to the Work-house, and remained there a considerable time, till at last, one of them threatened the Marshal with the same punishment for former adventures and thereupon he applied to my Lord Mayor, and procured their discharge. This commitment was so mortifying to one of the young gentlemen that he died in a few days after his release.

Thus far have we followed Mr. Wild in the character he gives of his master, which, it must be confessed, he has very notably embellished with all the rhetorical flourishes of his pen; nor does he spare his own, when he acquaints us how deeply he was concerned in all Marshal's iniquitous schemes. Let us now return to Wild's lodgings in the Old Bailey, where we left him in the year 1715.

If his people, as he used to call them, obeyed his orders in letting him into the secrets of their robberies, and committed the goods to his disposal, he assured them they might depend upon his protection; and, indeed, he had so much honour, that to the utmost of his power, he always performed what he promised them. This punctuality so established his credit, that if he sent for any of them, with a promise of a safe conduct, they would go to him directly, though they knew it was in his power to hang them. When they came, if they agreed with his proposals, they parted good friends, but, if they proved obstinate (even though he had an information against them) he would say, "I have given you my word that you should come and go in safety, therefore you shall—but look to yourself, for, when you see me again, you see an enemy."

Nor is it a wonder that he acquired so great an ascendancy over them, when he was not only willing but commonly able to keep his word, whether it was to hang them or save them. If they had followed his instructions, they were sure

Jonathan Wild's House in the Old Bailey

Account of His Methods.

he would not disturb them; and though they were apprehended by others, he seldom failed of procuring their discharge in a little time. He commonly got them to be admitted evidences, as pretending they were capable of making large informations against others, and in this case, if he found they were not sufficiently provided with particulars, he would furnish them with private memorandums of his own. If by such means he could not prevent their coming to a trial, he would contrive some method to keep the principal witnesses against them out of the way, at the time when the prisoners were called to the bar, and then they would be discharged for want of evidence.

But on the other hand, when any of his people presumed to be independent, and took upon them to dispose of what they stole without consulting him, and submitting to his terms, or, by any other act of rebellion, forfeited his favour, they were sure to feel the effects of it. In such a case, no person can be so vigilant as Jonathan to bring the offender to justice, and as he was well acquainted with all their places of resort, there was no such thing as escaping his hands.

Thus by punishing the disobedient he not only got the reward allowed for convicting them but established his authority over the others, and at the same time appeared to have some pretence to the character of being a serviceable man to the public.

If some (who could make free with him) questioned how he could carry on such a trade of restoring stolen goods, without being in confederacy with the thieves? he answered, " I have, indeed, a large acquaintance among such sort of people, and when I hear that such a robbery has been committed at such a time, and that such and such goods have been taken away, I send to enquire after the suspected persons, and order word to be left at the most likely places for them to hear of it, that if they will cause the goods to be carried to such a place, they shall receive such a reward, and no questions shall be asked them. And where is the harm of all this? I neither see the thief, nor receive the goods."

This was his account of the matter, and they could get no other.

We shall now give some particulars of his management: a lady went in her chair to pay a visit in Piccadilly. The chairmen left the chair at the door, and waited for her return at a neighbouring alehouse, and while they were drinking, the chair, with the velvet seat and furniture was carried off. The chairman immediately applied to Wild, and after taking his usual fee of a crown, he told them, he would consider of it, and desired them to call in a day or two. They came accordingly: Wild insisted upon a considerable reward, which they paid him, and then he bid them be sure to attend the prayers at Lincoln's-inn Chapel the next morning. They went thither at the time appointed, were equally surprized and pleased to find their lady's chair under the piazzas of the Chapel, with the seat and furniture in the same condition as when they left it.

On Saturday night, March 31, 1716, Mrs. Knap, a widow gentlewoman, and her son, coming from Sadler's Wells, were attacked in Jockey-fields by five footpads, and she was murdered. A large reward was offered for discovering the villains. Jonathan immediately made it his business to find out the murderers. By the description given of some of them, he knew the whole gang; and, with the assistance of his man Abraham, took three of them, who were tried, and afterwards hanged for the same. But Timothy Dun (one of the gang) was not yet taken, for he had removed his lodgings, and kept himself so close, that not a word was to be heard of him at any of the cafes. But this did not discourage

Jonathan Wild.

Jonathan; he knew that the fellow could not live long in such a private manner, for he must either follow the old business, or starve; and offered to lay a wager of ten guineas that he would have him before the next sessions; some of his acquaintance accepted the offer, and the money was deposited.

Dun, grown weary of his confinement, and willing to know if Wild was still in quest of him, sent his wife to get what intelligence she could. She went to Mrs. Seagoe's where Jonathan lodged, and staid there all the afternoon. When she went away in the evening, Wild sent a man after her to dog her home. She took water at Black-friars, and crossed to the Faulcon. He followed in another boat. She suspecting him, crossed again to White-friars. He was presently after her, and she, perceiving it, took another boat to Lambeth. He followed her, but it being now dark, and he keeping at a convenient distance, she thought she had lost him, and so went directly to her lodgings in Maid-lane, near the Bank-side, in Southwark. But he watched her so narrowly, that he saw where she went in, and, that he might not mistake the house the next day, he marked the door with a piece of chalk, and then returned with the news of his success.

Early in the morning, Wild, his man Abraham, Riddlesden and Horney, and another, went to Dun's lodging, which was up two pair of stairs. He, hearing them at the door, got out of his back window upon the roof of a pantry, the lower part of which was not above seven or eight feet from the ground. Abraham getting into the back yard, and seeing Dun upon the tiles, fired a pistol and wounded him in the shoulder, so that he rolled down into the yard, and then, though there was no fear of his escaping, Riddlesden shot him in the face with small shot.—Thus Jonathan won the ten guineas and Timothy was hanged.

Jonathan got a great deal of reputation, as well as a handsome reward, by the courage and good management, in this affair of Mrs. Knap, and valued himself much upon it.

In the year 1716, Arnold Powel, a notorious house-breaker, was apprehended and committed to Newgate for attempting burglary near Golden Square; Jonathan, understanding that he was pretty flush of the cole, caused it to be intimated to him, that he expected him to come down, or ways and means would be found to have him *topped*. Arnold, not believing it was in Wild's power to hurt him, dared him to his worst. And Wild, resolving to convince him of his mistake, exerted his utmost diligence to find out whom he had robbed. It was not long before he heard that Mr. Eastlick, a glass-grinder, at Fleet-ditch, had his house broke open by Powel. Wild applied to Mr. Eastlick, a prosecution was agreed on, and a bill was found for the burglary. This brought Powel to repentance, and so he struck up a peace with Jonathan, who had his own terms, and thereupon retracted his great zeal, and contrived an expedient for Powel's deliverance.

At the beginning of the sessions, Mr. Eastlick attended with his witnesses. But Wild persuaded them that the first and second day the Court would be taken up with other trials, and therefore they need not loose their time in waiting at the Session-House, but he would give them timely notice when Powel's trial came on. They depended upon this; but, in the meantime, Jonathan so managed the matter that Powel was brought to the bar. The witnesses were called, but none appeared, and Wild, who was then in Court, declared he knew not what was become of them. The prisoner was taken away again and afterwards brought a second time, and so a third, but still no witnesses appeared; at last, the Jury were charged with him, and, for want of evidence, he was acquitted, and the

Account of His Methods.

Court ordered the prosecutor's recognizance to be estreated. But Mr. Eastlick, hearing of this management, the next morning applied to the Court; upon which Wild was severely reprimanded, and Powel was ordered to remain till next Sessions, when he endeavoured to elude a trial by putting himself into a salivation; but, that not availing him, he was tried, and convicted of a burglary, and was hanged at Tyburn, March 20, 1716-17.

Wild had now left his lodgings at Mrs. Seagoe's, and taken a house on the other side of the way, next to the Cooper's arms.

Thus Jonathan, to support his pretences of serving the public, as well as for other purposes, found it necessary now and then to hang up two or three of his people; but this was not sufficient to conceal his other practices. His encouraging felons, and trading in stolen goods, were by this time too well known to be longer suffered with impunity.

Accordingly in the year 1718 (at the instigation and by the procurement of Sir William Thompson, the Recorder) an act was passed " for the farther preventing robberies, felonies, and for the more effectual transportation of felons " : By a clause in which it was made a felony for any persons to take a reward under pretence of restoring stolen goods, except they prosecuted the felons who stole them.

This gave a check to Jonathan's business for a while; but it was not long before he ventured to revive it again, though with more caution than before, and altering his measures, by which he thought to evade the law.

When people had been two or three times with him, in quest of what they had lost, he would tell them, that he had made inquiry after their goods, and received information, that if such a sum of money was sent to such a place, the goods would be delivered to the person who carried it. This being agreed on, a porter was called, the money put into his hands, and directions given him to go and wait at the corner of the street; when he came to the place appointed, or perhaps in his way thither, he was met by somebody who delivered him the goods upon his paying the money.

At other times, the owners of the goods, as they were going home, were overtaken by a stranger, who put the goods into their hands, and at the same time a note, in which was writ the sum of money they were to pay for them.

But in some hazardous cases he commonly put the people themselves upon taking the first step, by advertising what goods they had lost, and offering a reward to any one who would bring them to Jonathan Wild, who was thereby empowered to receive them without asking questions.

In the two former cases he neither saw the thief, nor received your goods, nor took your money; and in the latter, the principal part was your own act, and appeared no otherwise than as a friend, in whose honour you could safely confide; and in serving you this way there was no necessity of supposing him to be a confederate with the felons who had robbed you.

When you had got your goods, and desired to know what he must have for his trouble, he would tell you, with an air of indifference, you might do as you pleased, he demanded nothing, he was glad it had been in his power to serve you; what he had done was from a principle of doing good, and without any views of self-interest; and if you thought proper to make him a present, it would be your own act, the pure effect of your generosity, and he should not take it as a Reward, but merely as a Favour.

Jonathan Wild.

As he had sometimes customers from t'other end of the town, to save them the trouble of coming so far as the Old Bailey, or, perhaps, for some other reason, he took an office in Newtoner's Lane, and placed his man Abraham in it; but, in a quarter of a year, Mr. Wild's business grew so brisk, that he was obliged to send for his man home again to assist him. Abraham had the character of a very faithful and industrious servant to his master, and was entrusted with affairs of the greatest importance, and not undeservedly; as may be seen in the following instance.

Jonathan had been so fatigued in the late hurry of business, that his health was much impaired, and it was thought necessary to take the benefit of the air. Accordingly, leaving Abraham to supply his place, he took lodgings at Dulwich. While he was there, a gentlewoman, in going to the South Sea House, had her pocket picked of bank notes to the value of 700*l*. As soon as she missed them, she went to Jonathan's house, and applied to his man. He desired her to give him the particulars of the notes, and the best description she could of the persons who were near her a little before or after she missed them. This being done, he promised to make a diligent enquiry, and so he did to some purpose, for, in a few days, three pick-pockets were taken with all the notes upon them, and carried down to Jonathan, who thought fit to discharge them upon delivering up all their effects. The notes were returned to the owner, but Jonathan got 400*l* by the bargain.

These three were afterwards transported for other offences. One of them had spoke with a bank note for 1000*l* which he carried with him to Maryland, where he bought his liberty, and then went to New York, and set up for a gentleman.

Jonathan being pretty well recovered, returned to the Old Bailey. Soon after, a mercer at the corner of Lombard-street, sent a porter with a box of rich goods, to the value of 200*l* or more. Three *Prigs*, who were out upon the *kid-lay*, took notice of him, and had a great mind to *speak* with the box; upon which one of them, who was well dressed, goes up to him: "Porter," says he, "can you step a little way and I'll give you sixpence?"—"Yes, Sir."—"Do so much then as go to the tavern at the end of the street, and desire the drawer to give you the roquelair that the gentleman left in the bar—you shall carry my watch for a token. You may set your box down upon this bulk, and I'll take care of it till you come back: but whatever ye do make haste."

The porter pitches his burden, runs to the tavern, and enquires for the roquelair: but nobody there knew any thing of the matter. "May be," says he, "you are afraid to trust me with it; but the gentleman has sent a very good token —here's his gold watch, gold!—Blood—it's nothing but pewter lacquered over." —As soon as he found this, he began to fear he was bit, and hurried back as fast as he could, but came too late, for neither the gentleman nor the box were to be found.—"What must I do?" says he to himself: "what account shall I give to my master? I must never let him know what a senseless dog I have been, to be gulled at this rate; I must invent some excuse, I must forge some lie or other, to bring myself off, or I am an undone man." At last he came to a resolution, rolled himself in the dirt, went home to his master, and told him two fellows had knocked him down, and run away with the box This story was probable and gained credit. The mercer applied to Wild, and told him the same story. "Look ye, Sir," says Wild, "this porter of yours is a lying rascal, and if you'll send for him thither, I'll convince you of it." The porter was sent

Account of His Methods.

for, Abraham took him into a room, betwixt which and the next room was only a thin partition, so that what was said in the one might easily be overheard in the other. "Honest friend," says Abraham, "your master was here just now about a box; we wanted to know some particulars that he could not inform us of, and so before he went, he sent word for you to come hither. Now, if you tell us how you left the box, and what sort of persons took it from you, something may be done."—"Why, two or three fellows came up to me, knocked me down, and ran away with it."—"If they knocked you down, 'tis felony, and therefore I am afraid they won't venture to come in and return the goods."—"Why so?"—"Because they stand a fair chance to be hanged. But, come, you may as well tell the whole truth at once, for, if you don't, we shall find it out some other way. Do you know nothing of a token?"—"A token!"—"Yes; was there no such thing as a watch given you by a gentleman as a token to fetch his roquelair from the tavern?" "Indeed that's the very case. But how the devil come you to know it? I believe in my conscience you are a witch."—"Well, you may go home again now, and we'll try what we can do."

One of these who were concerned in cheating the porter lived at that time in Jonathan's old house in Cock-alley. Wild and Abraham went thither, and listening at the door, heard the man and his wife a scolding.—"Ye bitch," says he, "I'll go to Holland To-morrow." Wild immediately pushed open the door, and said "Will you by G—, but you shan't," and so conducted him to the Compter. Next day the Mercer had his goods again; Wild was satisfied for his trouble, and the prisoner was discharged.

Jonathan's business being now greatly increased, he found it necessary to take a larger house, and accordingly removed to a more convenient habitation, the King's-head in the Old Bailey.

Soon after this, two women came to him with a scheme for breaking a house; but as they were strangers to him, and not having proper credentials, he thought it by no means advisable to fall in with their proposals, and therefore very prudently showed them the way to Newgate.

In Feb., 1718-19, Margaret Dowdell and Alice Wright were indicted for a misdemeanour, in advising and endeavouring to persuade Jonathan Wild, to break and enter the house of John Cook, and steal his goods, Jan. 23, 1718-19.

Jonathan Wild. On the 23rd or 24th of last Month, the prisoners came to my house, and said they wanted to speak with me in private; upon which I looked at them very earnestly, and perceiving one of them to be with child, I did not know but she might want a father for it: However, I took them aside, and desired them to tell me their business. "Why," says Dowdell, "I have lost nothing, but I want to find something.—I believe I can help you to a thousand pounds. Nay, I don't doubt of making it many thousands, if you will be ruled by me."—"O, by all means," said I, "and I shall think myself very much obliged to you for putting me in the way; pray what is to be done"—"Why then," says she, "the business is to break open the house, and take the money. It is the house of John Cook, a Cane-chairmaker, in Worm-wood-street near Bishopsgate; and he has a lodger, an antient maiden gentlewoman, that has got some four thousand pounds in a box under the bed where she lies. Now there is a saw-pit in the shop, and the only way will be for one of the fellows, in the evening, to take an opportunity of hiding himself in this saw-pit, which he may do very easily, and so, in the dead of the night, he may let in his com-

Jonathan Wild.

panions; and then they must take care to secure two sturdy 'prentices, and a boy that lodges in the garret, for they will be apt to be very refractory. But I beg that this may be done, if possible, without committing murder."—" Phoo?" says Alice Wright, " people that go upon such matters must do as well as they can; they must take care of themselves; and act as they shall see best for their own security.—Now when these boys are secured, it is the easiest thing in the world to come at the old gentlewoman's money; for she is gone into the country to fetch more, and her room is underneath where the boys lie. Then opposite to her room, is that where Mr. Cook and his wife lie; but you must take a particular care of him, for he is a dev'lish resolute man, and it might not be much amiss if he were knocked on the head. And, when that is done, you might find money in his drawers, for he never is without. Right under his room lies a gentlewoman and a small child, but I must desire, that neither she nor the child may be hurt "—" and so must I too " (says Dowdell)—" for I would not have them come to any harm for the world." When I had heard all this, I thought it was proper to take care of my chaps.

Mrs. *Cook*. Mr. Wild came and informed me of this design, and described all the rooms in my house so exactly as if he had lived there.—Dowdell had been my lodger five months, and, tho' she was behind-hand in her rent, I was unwilling to turn her out, because I knew she was very poor, and might be hard put to it to get another lodging: but at last she went away of her own accord, without giving me notice, or offering to pay me any thing.

When she and the other prisoner were carried before my Lord Mayor, they both confessed the whole matter. Dowdell called several to her character, who deposed, that she was a captain's widow, had formerly lived in good credit, but was now reduced. Wright called one witness, who said, he knew nothing more of her, than that she had lived in two or three places where he was acquainted, and that she had had a child by a gentleman whom he knew.

The jury found them both guilty of the misdemeanour, and the Court ordered, that they should suffer six months imprisonment.

Jonathan had minuted down in his books a gold watch, a parcel of fine lace, and other things of great value, which Jack Butler had *made* upon the *Lodging Lay* at Newington-Green; and yet he wholly neglected coming to account, and no news was to be heard of him for two or three months. Jonathan swore he would be up with him for his ingratitude; and accordingly spared no pains in hunting after him; but, as Jack had retired from business, it was no easy matter to meet with him. Hearing at last, that he lodged at an ale-house at Bishopsgate-street, he got a warrant, and taking two or three to assist him, went thither betimes in the morning; the door being open, he ran foremost up stairs, with a pistol in his hand, tho' not so softly but Butler heard him; upon which he jumpt out of bed, slipt on his coat, breeches, and shoes, and getting out of the window, (which was but one story high) dropt into the yard, climbed over the wall into the street, run cross the way into a Dyer's shop, and so thro' to a wash-house, where some women were washing. He told them he was pursued by bailiffs, and begged they would let him hide himself, and they directed him to the coal-hole. In the mean time Jonathan had wrenched open the door, and found that Butler had given him the slip, but knew not which way to follow him; however, hastening down stairs, and seeing nothing of him in the street, he concluded he must have taken refuge in some house not far off. At last, seeing the Dyer's door

Account of His Methods.

open, he goes over, and meeting the man of the house told him what had happened, and said he believed the rogue must have run in there, because he saw no other door open. "He can't be here" (says the Dyer,) "for I have not been out of the shop above a minute." "Sir" (says Jonathan) "that must be the very time he slipt in, and therefore I beg you would give me leave to search for him." The Dyer bid him search and welcome.

Jonathan and his assistants went in, and finding the women in the wash-house, enquired of them if they had seen such a fellow? they denied it stiffly, till he satisfied them, that the man was a thief, and then they advised him to look in the coal-hole. Jonathan took a candle and looked round, but to no purpose. Then he went into the cellar, and searched every corner of it, and examined the kitchen, shop, and every other place, but all in vain. He was heartily vexed, and swore he was never so fooled in his life before. He told the Dyer he believed the rogue was got out again. "That's impossible," said the Dyer, "for I have been in the shop ever since, and if he went down stairs, he must be there still, for there is no other way out but at this door and he could not have come this way without my seeing him; and therefore I advise you to look the cellar again, and I'll go with you." Down they all went, and, the Dyer turning up a large tub, Butler immediately made his appearance. "So, Mr. Son of a bitch! have I caught you at last?" says Jonathan; "what have you done with the gold watch, lace, and other moveables that you stole out of your lodgings; ye runagate rascal! you shall certainly swing for it. I'll take care of you, if there is never another rogue in England." But notwithstanding these menaces, Jack knew the secret of calming Jonathan's wrath, and therefore taking him aside, "if you'll step to my room again," says he, "and look behind the bed's-head, you may find something that may make you amends for your trouble." Jonathan went away and was well satisfied with what he found. But, as Butler was apprehended in so public a manner, it was necessary to carry him before a Justice, who committed him to Newgate : and, by good management, instead of being hanged he was only transported.

Jonathan going one day to an inn in Smithfield, observed a large trunk in the yard, and imagining there might be something of considerable value in it, he goes home, and orders Jerry Raun to go and *speak with it*. Raun dresses himself like a porter and brings it off. It belonged to Mr. Jarvis, a Whip-maker in that neighbourhood, who had sent it to the inn, to be carried into the country; but, hearing that somebody had stole it, he applied to Wild, who, after many delays, helped him to most of the goods again for ten guineas. Wild and Raun quarrelled soon afterwards, and Wild found means to have him hanged; but, the day before his execution, he sent for Mr. Jarvis, and discovered the whole affair to him.

Mr. Jarvis was the more inclinable to believe this account, because his own servant informed him, that Wild was at the inn when the trunk was laid down. Wild was threatened with a prosecution for this; but, Mr. Jarvis dying soon after, the design died with him.

'Tis said that Jonathan, resolving to carry on a trade with Holland and Flanders, purchased a sloop, and put the famous Roger Johnson to command her; that he carried over gold watches, rings, snuff-boxes, and other plate, and sometimes perhaps bank notes, which had been *spoke with* by the way of the mail. His chief trading port was Ostend, from whence he travelled up to Bruges, Ghent, Brussels, and other considerable towns, where he disposed of his

Jonathan Wild.

effects, and took in a lading of Hollands, and other goods; returned to England, and usually brought his cargo to land in the night, without giving the least trouble to the officers of the custom-house.

This business was carried on pretty successfully for about two years, when by some mismanagement two pieces of Hollands were lost, and Johnson stopt the value of them out of the mate's Wages. The man was so provoked at this, that he went immediately and gave information of Johnson's running a vast quantity of goods, whereupon the vessel was *Exchequered*, and Johnson was cast in 700*l* damages, which put an end to his trading to Holland.

There had long been great animosity betwixt Johnson and Tom Edwards, who kept the cafe in Long-lane. Johnson was expert at the *passing-lay*, and Edwards at the *waggon-lay*. Edwards was indefatigable in his calling, for he would sometimes follow a waggon for two miles together. He always lay at the same inn where the waggon put up, and when every body else was in bed, he would creep down from his room, and take a box or portmanteau out of a waggon, unbar the inn gates, carry his booty into some private field, and plant it under a hedge, and so return privately to his bed again. One evening as he was coming out of the Black-Lyon alehouse in the Strand, which was then kept by one Butler (the brother of Tom Butler, who received his pardon in order to be an evidence against Wild) he met with Johnson, and seized him, and charging him with felony, carried him to a tavern. Johnson sent for one of Wild's men, who came, with a constable and a warrant against Edwards, and carried him before a Justice, who committed him to the Compter.

It is not certain how the affair ended; but, some time afterwards Edwards, having intelligence of a large quantity of stolen goods, lodged in one of Jonathan's private ware-houses, got a warrant and siezed them. Jonathan was so provoked at this, tho' he did not think it proper to claim the goods as his own, yet he took out an action in the name of Johnson, to whom he said the goods belonged, arrested Edwards, and threw him into the Marshalsea, where he lay one night, but the next day gave Bail for his appearance.

Edwards vowed revenge. He got several informations against Johnson, and only wanted to find where he was. After a long search to no purpose, he accidentally met with him on the Stratford road, siezed him, and, sending for a constable, carried him to an ale-house hard by. Johnson sent a messenger to inform Wild of what had happened. Wild and his man Quilt Arnold went down directly to Johnson. A quarrel arose, and Johnson made his escape.

An information was made against Wild for his management in this affair, of which being informed, he absconded for three weeks, and then, imagining the danger was over, ventured to appear again in public; but he found himself mistaken; for the high constable at Holbourn, hearing he was returned to his own house, went thither with the two Willis's, and apprehended him and his man Quilt Arnold. They were carried before a magistrate and committed to Newgate. From this instant Johnson's cunning and courage forsook him.

The Trial of JONATHAN WILD, *for Felony.*

On Monday, Feb. 15, 1725, JONATHAN WILD was apprehended at his house in the Old Bailey, by Mr. Thomas Jones, high constable of Holbourn division, and carried before Sir John Fryer, Bar. who being indisposed, set up in his bed to examine him. He was charged upon oath with assisting one Johnson, a High-

Account of His Trial.

wayman, to make his escape from a constable at Bow, near Stratford, in the county of Middlesex, and was thereupon committed to Newgate.

The session at the Old Bailey beginning on Wednesday the 24th of the same month, he entered his prayer to be tried that sessions, or bailed or discharged. But on the Friday following, there came down a warrant of detainer, which was produced in Court with several informations upon oath to the following effect.

1. That for many years past he had been a confederate with great numbers of Highwaymen, pick-pockets, house-breakers, shop-lifters, and other thieves.

2. That he had formed a kind of corporation of thieves of which he was the head or director, and that notwithstanding his pretended services, in detecting and prosecuting offenders, he procured such only to be hanged as concealed their booty, or refused to share it with him.

3. That he had divided the town and country into so many districts, and appointed distinct gangs for each, who regularly accounted with him for their robberies. That he had also a particular sett to steal at churches in time of divine services : and likewise other moving detachments to attend at court, on birthdays, balls, etc., and at both houses of parliament, circuits, and country fairs.

4. That the persons employed by him were for the most part felons convict, who had returned from transportation before the time, for which they were transported, was expired, and that he made choice of them to be his agents, because they could not be legal evidences against him, and because he had it in his power to take from them what part of the stolen goods he thought fit, and otherwise use them ill, or hang them if he pleased.

5. That he had from time to time supplied such convicted felons with money and cloaths, and lodged them in his own house, the better to conceal them; particularly for counterfeiting and diminishing broad pieces and guineas.

6. That he had not only been a receiver of stolen goods, as well as writings of all kinds, for near fifteen years past, but had frequently been a confederate, and robbed along with the above mentioned convicted felons.

7. That, in order to carry on these vile practices, to gain some credit with the ignorant multitude, he usually carried a short silver staff, as a badge of authority from the government. Which he used to produce, when he himself was concerned in robbing.

8. That he had under his care and direction, several ware-houses for receiving and concealing stolen goods; and also a ship for carrying off jewels, watches, and other valuable goods, to Holland, where he had a superanuated thief for his factor.

9. That he kept in pay several artists to make alterations, and transform watches, seals, snuff-boxes, rings, and other valuable things, that they might not be known, several of which he used to present to such persons as he thought might be of service to him.

10. That he seldom or never helped the owners to the notes and papers they had lost, unless he found them able exactly to specify and describe them, and then often insisted on more than half the value.

11. And lastly, it appears that he has often sold human blood, by procuring false evidence to swear persons into facts they were not guilty of; sometimes to prevent them from being evidences against himself, and at other times for the sake of the great reward given by the government.

Jonathan Wild.

Besides these informations, an affidavit of Mr. Jones was read in Court, importing, that there were two persons who offered to charge Wild with crimes of a capital nature; namely, John Follard, and Thomas Butler, who had both been convicted, but obtained His Majesty's pardon. These, it was expected, would have been evidences against Jonathan; but he saved the trouble, by committing a felony, while he was a prisoner in Newgate, as we shall soon see.

On the last day of the sessions he moved by his Council that his trial might be deferred till next sessions; and an affidavit made by himself was read in Court, the purport of which was, that the last night he was accidentally informed that the Grand Jury had found a bill against him for felony, since which he had not had time to procure his witnesses, without whom he was not able to make his defence; one of them living near Brentford and another in Somersetshire.

This motion was opposed by the Council for the Crown. They urged, that, as he was in custody, he could not but expect his trial to come on at the ensuing sessions, and therefore ought to have been prepared for it. That, if the single affidavit of a prisoner in such a case might pass, nobody would want excuses, and any trial hereafter might be put off by the same rule. That he had not so much as named his witnesses; and though he says in his affidavit he knows not what he is indicted for, yet he swears that there are material witnesses.

The prisoner then said, that the names of the witnesses were—Hays, at the Packhorse on Turnham Green, and—Wilson, a Clothier in Froom; and that though he did not know particularly what he was indicted for, yet he had heard it was something about one—Stetham, and his Counicl moved that the names might be put into his affidavit, and that he might swear it over again.

The Council for the King returned, that justice would never be denied him, but he stood entitled to no favours; and that they were not sure that the two persons, who had pleaded to their pardons, would be to be found at the next sessions.

Some gentlemen upon the Bench being willing that the prisoner should be allowed time till the following sessions, to prepare for his defence, the court told him, they had no more to say to him. He bowed, and answered, " I thank your Lordship, and am very glad of it."

Follard and Butler were bound each in a bond of 500*l* to appear at the next sessions.

On Saturday, May 15, 1725, Jonathan Wild was indicted for privately stealing in the shop of Catherine Stetham, in the parish of St. Andrews, Holbourn, fifty yards of lace, value forty pound the goods of Catherine Stetham, Jan. 22, 1724-5.

He was a second time indicted, for that whereas fifty yard of lace, value forty pound was privately stolen in the shop of Catherine Stetham, by persons unknown to the Jurors. On the 22d of January 1724-5, he the said Jonathan Wild afterwards, that is to say, on the 10th of March, in the same year, feloniously did receive of the said Catherine, ten guineas on account, and under colour to helping her to the said lace again, and did not then, or at any time since, discover, apprehend, or cause to be apprehended, and prosecute the felon who stole the said lace.

The prisoner, in the morning before his trial came on, dispersed among the Jurymen, and several others who were then walking on the leads before the Court, a considerable number of printed papers, entitled, " a List of the persons discovered,

Account of His Trial.

apprehended and convicted of several robberies on the highway; and also for burglary and housebreaking; and also for returning from transportation, by Jonathan Wild, as followeth, viz. robbing on the highway, 35. House-breaking, 22. Returning from transportation, 10.

Note, several others have been also convicted for the like crimes, but, remembering not the persons names who have been robbed, I omit the criminals names.

Please to observe, that several others have also been convicted for shoplifting, picking of pockets, &c. by the female sex, which are capital crimes, and which are too tedious to be inserted here, not willing of being exposed.

In regard therefore of the number above convicted, some, that have yet escaped justice, are endeavouring to take away the life of the said

JONATHAN WILD."

The Jury having taken their seats, and the prisoner brought to the bar, the council for the King took notice of the prisoner's extraordinary proceeding, in relation to the above-mentioned papers: that such practices were unwarrantable, and not to be suffered in any Court of Justice: this was apparently intended to take off the credit of the King's witnesses, and prepossess and influence the Jury. Though, as he believed them to be men of integrity, he was under no apprehensions that it would have such effect, but that they would give a conscientious verdict according to evidence: and that whatever the prisoner might hope for, from such indirect management, it was far from making his cause appear in a more favourable light. That it was impossible, but that a man who had trained up, and erected a corporation of thieves, a man who had carried on a trade of felony for so many years, and made it his constant known practice to procure goods that had been lost in any part of the town, must have had it in his power to detect those felons he was concerned with. And yet, that there was good reason to believe, that, (to the great scandal of public justice) he had intimidated many from information, and prevented them from making such discoveries, as might have been of public advantage. That if a strict enquiry was to be made, after the motives of his apprehending and convicting those criminals, named in his list, we might find they were private interest, old grudges, or fresh quarrels, and not the least regard to justice and the good of his country.

The prisoner prayed, that the witnesses against him might be examined apart; which the Court granted.

First indictment, for stealing the lace.

Henry Kelly. On Friday, the 22d of January last, I went to visit Mrs. Johnston, who then lived at the prisoner's house. Her husband brought me over from Ireland. I found her at home, and we drank a quarter of gin together. By and by in comes Peg Murphey, with a pair of bracaded shoes and clogs, and makes a present of them to Madam Wild, the prisoner's wife. The prisoner was in company with us at the same time, and when we had drank two or three quarterns more, Murphey and I got up to go away together. He asked us which way we were going? I said, "to my lodging at the Seven Dials." "I suppose," says he, "you go along Holbourn?" We answered, "yes." "Why then," said he, "I'll tell you what.—There's an old blind bitch that keeps a shop within twenty yards of Holbourn Bridge, and sells fine Flanders' lace; and her daughter is as blind as herself: now if you'll take the trouble of calling upon her, you may speak with a box of lace. I'll go along with you and shew you the door."

Court. What do you understand by speaking with a box of lace?

Kelly. To speak with a thing, is to steal it.—So we agreed, and the prisoner, and I, and Murphey, went together, till we came within sight of the shop, and then he pointed, and shewed us which it was, " and " says he, " do you go, and I'll wait here, and bring ye off, if any disturbance should happen." Murphey and I went in, and turned over several parcels of laces, but could not find that which would please us, for it was our business to be mighty nice and difficult. This piece was too broad, and that too narrow, and t'other not fine enough. At last the old woman stept upstairs to fetch another piece, and in the mean time I took a tin box of lace, and gave it to Murphey, who put it under her cloak. The old woman came down again with another box, and shewed us several more pieces; but we could not agree about the price, and so we came away and found the prisoner where we had left him, and told him we had *spoke*. We all went back to the house, where we opened the box, and found eleven pieces in it. He asked us, if we'd have ready money, or stay till an advertisement came out? Stock was pretty low with us at that time, and so we chose ready money, and he gave us three guineas, and four broad pieces. " I can't afford to give any more," says he, " for she's a hard-mouthed old bitch, and I shall never get above ten guineas out of her." I took the three guineas and a crown for my own share, and Murphey had the rest.—I was taken up by means of Butler, and so I made my information.

Margaret Murphey confirmed all the particulars of the foregoing evidences, relating to this robbery.

Catherine Stetham, the elder. On the 22d of January between three and four o'clock in the afternoon, a man and woman came into my shop, on pretence of buying some lace for stocks. I shewed them two or three parcels, but they were so difficult that nothing I had below would please them: and so, leaving my daughter in the shop, I stept up stairs, and brought down another box. Well, that would do, but what was the price? I asked them six shillings a yard. No, they would give me four. I told them I could not take it, and so they went out; and, in about three hours afterwards, I missed a tin-box of lace, which I valued at 50*l*.

Here the prisoner's council (who attended to speak to any point that should arise) begged leave to observe, that according to the evidence given against the prisoner, he could not, in their opinion, which they submitted to the Court, be guilty of this indictment, because the indictment sets forth that HE did privately steal the lace IN the shop; when it is certain that he did not enter the shop. That he might be guilty of a single felony, in being accessary before the fact, or in receiving the goods afterwards, knowing them to have been stolen; but could not, as they apprehended, be guilty of the capital offence, except (as the act directs) it had been inserted in the indictment that he did *assist command or hire*.

The Court, in summing up the evidence, observed to the Jury, that in other cases, as in robberies and burglaries, an accessary before the fact, is a principal. He that stands by, or watches at a distance, being as guilty, and liable to the same punishment, as the very person that enters the house, or steals the money or goods: but as it was not remembered that there had yet been any precedent of

Account of His Trial.

the like construction, being put upon indictments of this nature, it remained a matter of doubt, and therefore in such a case, it was most eligible to incline to the side of mercy.

The second Indictment: For taking money on pretence of restoring the stolen goods, and not prosecuting the felon.

The council for the King having opened the indictment and the evidence against the prisoner, the Court ordered the clerk to read the following clause of an act made in the 4th year of George I on which the indictment was founded.

'. . . And whereas, there are divers persons, who have secret acquaintance with felons, and who make it their business to help persons to their stolen goods, and by that means gain money from them, which is divided between them and the felons, whereby they greatly encourage such offenders: be it enacted, by the authority aforesaid, that wherever any person taketh money or reward, directly or indirectly, under pretence, or upon account of helping any person to any stolen goods or chattles, every such person taking money or reward as aforesaid, (unless such person do apprehend, or cause to be apprehended, such felon, who stole the same, and give evidence against him) shall be guilty of felony, according to the nature of the felony committed in stealing such goods, and in such and the same manner, as if such offender had stolen such goods and chattles, in the manner, and with such circumstances as the same were stolen!'

Catherine Stetham the elder. On the 22d of Jan. last, in the afternoon, a box of lace, which I valued at 50*l*., was stolen out of my shop. I went the same night to the prisoner's house to enquire after it, but not finding him at home, I advertised the lace I had lost, with a reward of 15 guineas, and no questions to be asked; but, hearing no news of it, I went to the prisoner's house again, and then I met with him. He desired me to give him a description of the persons I suspected, which I did as well as I could. Upon this he promised to make enquiry, and bid me call again in two or three days; I did so, and then he said he had heard something of my lace, and expected to hear more in a little time. While we were talking, a man comes in, and said, that by what he had learned, he believed, that one Kelly, who had been tried for putting off gilded shillings, was concerned in stealing the lace. I went away, and came back on the day the prisoner was apprehended,—I think it was on the 15th of February,—I told him, that tho' I had advertised but 15 guineas reward, I would give 20, or 25, rather than not have my lace again. "Don't be in such a hurry, good woman," says he "perhaps I may help you to it for less and if I can I will, the persons that have your lace are gone out of town: I shall set them a quarrelling about it, and then shall get it the cheaper." On the 10th of March he sent me word, that if I would come to him in Newgate, and bring ten guineas in my pocket, he could help me to my lace. I went, he desired me to call a porter, but I telling him I knew not where to find one, he sent out a person who brought a man who appeared to be a ticket-porter. The prisoner gave me a letter, which he said was sent to him, as a direction where to go for the lace; but, as I could not read, I delivered it to the porter; after which, the prisoner bid me give the porter ten guineas, or else, he said, the persons who had the lace, would not deliver it. I gave the porter the money, and he went away, and in a little while returned with a box sealed up, but it was not the same that I had lost. I opened it, and found all my lace, except one piece. "Now, Mr. Wild," says I, "what must

Jonathan Wild.

I give you for your trouble?"—"not a single farthing. I don't do those things for worldly interest, but for the benefit of poor people who have met with misfortunes. As for the piece of lace that is missing, I would not have you be uneasy, for I hope to get it for you ere it be long, nay, and I don't know, but in a little time I may not only help you to your ten guineas again, but to the thief too. And if I can, much good may it do you; and, as you are a widow, and a good christian, I desire nothing of you but your prayers, and for them I shall be thankful. I have a great many enemies, and God knows what may be the consequence of this imprisonment."

Prisoner. I hope the Court will consider the service I have done, in convicting a great number of criminals.—I say that Murphey and Kelly may be called in again, that I may ask them a question or two.—Mrs. Murphey, I desire to know, . . .

Court. You must not propose your question to the witness, but to the Court, and if your question is proper, the Court will require the witness to answer it.

Prisoner. I beg your lordship will ask her who stole the lace?

Court. That's not a proper question; for, as she is upon oath, we cannot require herself to answer any questions to accuse herself.

Prisoner. She swore that on the first indictment.

Court. Whatever she swore upon that trial, we cannot take notice of it upon this, except she was now to swear it over again, which we cannot require her to do.

K. Council. This indictment is laid for taking money of Catherine Stetham, under pretence of helping her to goods that had been stolen by persons *unknown*, and the prisoner would now ask the witness *who stole these goods*?

Prisoner. I would ask her, then, if I stole the lace?

Murphey. No; but he was concerned with those that did steal it, and he received it after it was stolen.

Here the prisoner's council begg'd leave to observe, that as Murphey had sworn the prisoner guilty of a felony, in being concerned with those that stole the goods, they presumed that the act upon which he was now indicted was never intended to affect him, or any other felon, but only such persons as were not felons themselves, but held a correspondence with felons themselves. For as there were old laws in force for the punishment of felons, it would have been wholly unnecessary that a new law should be made to the same purpose; that is, to no purpose at all.—That the very preamble to the clause of the act on which the prisoner stands indicted, intimates, by a plain distinction, that felons are not in that place intended. The words are these, ' whereas there are several persons who have secret acquaintance with felons, and who make it their business to help persons to their stolen goods, and by that means gain money from them which is divided between *them* and the *felons*.'—That by a proviso in the said clause, it could not be supposed, that felons were then intended, without making contradictions and inconsistencies in the act itself. For the words are : ' unless such *person* doth apprehend, or cause to be apprehended, such *felon* who stole the same, and cause such felon to be brought to trial for the same, and give evidence against him.' Suppose now there was but one person concerned in such a case, can it ever be thought that the legislature intended that this very person should apprehend himself, bring himself to a trial, and give evidence against himself? No, certainly.

The Council for the Crown replied to this effect : That it was no absurdity or

Account of His Conviction.

contradiction to say, that the act was intended to affect the felons; for, that a man's being a felon did not any ways hinder him from discovering his accomplices, if he had any. And as to the supposition, that a felon had no accomplices, but committed the felony by himself, it was out of the present question, and no way relating to the prisoner's case; for it was evident, that he had accomplices, and had not discovered them.

The Court observed farther; that Felony was so far from being excepted in the act, that it was principally intended against them; for it particularly mentions those that make it their business to help people to stolen goods. And it was certain, that such persons must be Receivers of stolen goods, and *such are Felons*. That the case of the prisoner came within almost every circumstance of the act, it being evident, that 'He was the person that had secret acquaintance with felons, who made it his business to help people to stolen goods, and by that means gained money from them, which was divided between him and the felons, and thereby greatly encouraged such offenders, and had not apprehended them.' That it was a very surprising plea for a man to say, I am more guilty than you are aware of, and therefore ought to suffer the less: and that it could never be thought that the parliament intended, by this act, to excuse a man merely because he was a felon, and more criminal than another.

The Jury acquitted the prisoner of the first indictment, and found him guilty of the second. *Death.*

What remains, is to take notice of his behaviour under condemnation. and shall begin with the following elegy.

JONATHAN WILD'S *COMPLAINT.*

Confin'd within that dark and dreary cell,
Where terrors reign, and where no comforts dwell;
Where ominous visions wretched souls affright,
Halters and gibbits painting to the sight:
Where some in tears lament, and others swear.
While Purney* sniv'ling spells a godly prayer;
Or while his deputy† with holy qualms,
Devoutly hums o'er one of Sternhold's psalms;
Of life despairing, conscious of desert,
Sad Wild thus vents the anguish of his heart.
Thus of his inauspicious fate complains,
As he with gloomy brow surveys his chains.

Ingrateful country! Zealous for thy good,
How often have I hazarded my blood?
Nor have I arms alone, but arts employ'd,
Swords, Pistols, and damnation have defy'd.
Warm as thy cause, of dangers not afraid,
How great a slaughter has by me been made?
Witness, ye Records of this horrid dome,
Nor let it be forgot in days to come;

---

* The ordinary of Newgate.
† James Wagstaff.

Jonathan Wild.

By me thrice thirty have in halter dy'd,
I siez'd them, and in vain to 'scape they try'd;
'T was I, who evidences did prepare,
And to the purpose taught them what to swear.
  Ye Britons! curs'd with an unthankful mind,
For ever to exalted merit blind,
Is thus your constant Benefactor spurn'd?
Are thus his faithful services return'd?
This dungeon his reward for labours past,
And Tyburn, his full recompence at last?
  More generous *Blueskin!*—O, that thy design
Had ended this unhappy life of mine!
O, that success had crown'd the stroke you gave!
Then had I gone with honour to the grave!
  How will the crowds, that I have sent before,
Triumph to meet me on th' infernal shore!
At me, what looks insulting will they cast,
And swearing cry,—*Old friend you'r come at last!*
  But sure, e'er long, the time will come again,
When watches shall be lost in *Drury-lane;*
Snuff boxes, finely painted, miss their way,
And rings and pocket-books shall go astray:
When Phillis at the Ball or Masquerade
Shall lose a present by some lover made;
Then you, unthinking monsters!—you, that now
Exult at my unpitied overthrow,
Then you'll repent too late:—you then, in vain,
Will wish to have your *Jonathan* again.
  But you, my faithful servants every where,
Whom I have train'd up with a father's care,
Sure you some grateful sentiments will have,
And drop a tear upon your master's grave!
From rags, and saunt'ring bare-legg'd up and down,
With pockets never bless'd with half-a crown,
From selling save-alls, pimping at poor stews,
From raking kennels, and from blacking shoes;
'T was I that rais'd ye.—You by me were made
Successful artists in a thieving trade:
I taught ye to lead comfortable lives,
To keep a train of whores, and starve your wives:
Go on and prosper, bravely play your parts,
Nor leave unpractis'd any of your arts:
Be rogues renown'd, and trample on the laws,
And, like true bloods, revenge your patron's cause.

The Ordinary's account of him is as follows.—After his conviction, he affirmed, that he had fasted upwards of four days, which, together with his lameness and indisposition, had rendered him unable to attend the service of God in the Chapel. He endeavoured to convince people, that at Wolverhampton he knew several persons that would have proved his friends had he thought his case

Account of His Execution.

dangerous, and timely applied to them: but as he carried on the same practice above a dozen years, and was now growing old, he could not be made to believe he should suffer at last, for what he had publickly done unpunished so long. But he was then told by a gentleman, that he had long artfully evaded the law, and escaped justice; which justice had sometime since overtaken one Thompson, who was executed for carrying on such practices but a very short time. That he ought to have taken warning when he was first committed prisoner to the Compter, where he should have observed the misery of vicious people, instead of learning their ways, and endeavouring to understand them and their practices, and afterwards associating with them.—He replied, that his business was doing good in recovering lost goods; that as he had regained things of great value for Dukes, Earls, and Lords, he thought he deserved well.—That he had apprehended the greatest and most pernicious robbers the nation was ever molested with— and had wounds and scars still remaining in his head, body, and legs. He appeared to be very much disordered, and confused in his thoughts, which he said was owing to these wounds, and in particular to two fractures in his scull, which disordered his brain, though covered with silver plates. He never went to chapel during the whole time he continued under sentence of death, saying, he was lame, and unable to support himself on his legs, and much more unable to go up so far. Another reason he added was, that certain enemies of his among the crowd would not only interrupt his prayers by pointing, whispering, &c, but would, he believed, insult him, and if they dared, would raise a tumult;—therefore, as he knew that to pray to God without attention or regard, was worse than wholly to omit prayers, and as he could not attend his duty among so vast a crowd as attended at the chapel, he earnestly desired he might not be carried thither, and accordingly was not.—He kept the other malefactors in order and regularity,—no interruption happening either at prayers, or when the word of God was reading. The day before he died he desired he might receive the sacrament, at which time he enquired the meaning of those words, *cursed is every one that hangeth on a tree.* Also, concerning the disposition of the soul when first separated from the body, and the local situation of the other world, and other questions of such a nature; but he was answered, that they were matters of less moment and importance than other things he might employ his time about; he was advised rather to repent of his sins, to read and study Christ's passion, merits, and atonement, and the infinite justice as well as unlimited mercy of Almighty God. He appeared somewhat attentive to the prayers, especially before he had some expectations of a reprieve, and after he found that all expectations were vain.

The evening before he suffered, he enquired how the noble Greeks and famous Romans, who slew themselves, came to be so glorious in history, if self-murder is a crime?—He was desired to consider, that the wisest and most learned Heathens called self-murder cowardice, in not sustaining the misfortunes which providence laid upon human nature, and that christianity is much more express against suicide.—He confessed that self-murder was impiety, but his confession appeared to be hypocrisy; for, about two o'clock in the morning, he endeavoured to prevent his execution by drinking laudanum; but the largeness of the draught, together with his having fasted before, instead of destroying him immediately, was the cause of his not dying by it.

At the place of execution, Wild having rendered himself delirious by poison,

Jonathan Wild.

began to recover, and united with the other criminals in the public prayers, as well as the tumult and clamour on the occasion would give them leave.

Thus far the Lord Ordinary; to which we shall add a few more particulars.

After taking the liquid laudanum, he grew so drowsy, that he could not hold up his head, nor keep open his eyes at prayers. Two of his fellow prisoners, perceiving his disorder, endeavoured to rouse him: they took him by the arms, and persuaded him to stand up and walk a little, which as he was lame of the gout he could not do without their assistance. This motion awakened him a little, and then his countenance turned very pale, he sweated violently, and grew exceedingly faint and sick; soon after which he vomited till he had thrown up the greatest part of the laudanum.

After this he recovered a little, but still was drowsy, and almost insensible of what he said or did, and in this condition he was put into the cart, and conveyed to Tyburn.

It is not easy to express with what roughness he was treated by the mob, not only as he went to the tree, but even when he was at it; instead of those signs of pity they generally shew when common criminals are going to execution, they reviled and cursed him, and pelted him with stones and dirt continually. By the time that he came to the end of his journey, he was considerably recovered from the disorder the laudanum had thrown him into. The other malefactors being ready to be turned off, and the executioner telling Jonathan he might take any reasonable time to prepare himself, he continued sitting in the cart for a little while, but the mob grew so outrageous at this indulgence, that they called out incessantly to the hangman to do his office, and threatened to knock him on the head if he did not immediately perform it. He found delays were dangerous, and therefore no longer deferred to give the populace the satisfaction they demanded.

Thus ended the life of Jonathan Wild, on Monday, May 24, 1725.

About two o'clock in the morning, after his execution, he was buried in Pancras church yard; but his body did not rest there, for in two or three nights afterwards, the surgeons, as it is believed, thought fit to remove it. A hearse and six was seen waiting about midnight at the end of Fig lane, at which place the empty coffin was found the next morning; but what became of the body is yet a secret.*

---

* See *ante*, page 207.

Horace Bleackley

Photograph by Elliott & Fry

Horace Bleackley.

IN MEMORIAM: HORACE BLEACKLEY.

By S. M. ELLIS.

When Horace Bleackley died, very suddenly, on 30th July, 1931, he had but lately completed the writing of this, his last, book—relating the Life and Trial of Jack Sheppard for the series of Notable British Trials. He did not live, however, to see the work in print; so when Mr. Harry Hodge invited me to do the necessary editing and extensions before publication and add a biographical note, I very gladly consented, for I valued Bleackley both as an author and as a friend. Indeed, craving pardon for a momentary personal digression, I may say that we shared many similar literary interests, and my acquaintance with him commenced with a kindly letter of appreciation and thanks for one of my books he had read and liked. Old-time courtesy was one of his marked characteristics, and this spontaneous letter to a stranger was soon followed by an invitation to lunch with him at his club, which happy meeting was celebrated with a bottle of superlative and mellow hock, the memory whereof lingers to this day. Shortly after, he lunched with me, when he was good enough to praise some Château d'Yquem, which he recalled on several later occasions with affectionate reminiscence.

To Purists and Prohibitionists, whose mental palates may be irritated by these vinic recollections in a memorial notice, I would say that Horace Bleackley's taste in fine wine and food was an essential factor in his choice personality. He loved the good and pleasant things of life, and was at his best as host in his delightful Regency-period house, 19, Cornwall Terrace, overlooking the Regent's Park, where, surrounded by fine Georgian furniture and the mezzotint portraits he revered, he entertained his many friends, most of them notable people with a gift for conversation and wit. Here, at table, and later in his spacious book-lined study, he found the right environment for his urbane and mellow envisagement of life and letters. In his detachment from the rush and noise of the world outside, he seemed like a figure strayed from the eighteenth century, the period whose modes and morals (or lack of such) he ever delighted to recapture and present anew in his

In Memoriam :

books. And yet he was not suggestive, with his gentle and reserved manners, of the typical literary man of the eighteenth century, for he had none of the coarseness of speech and grossness of habits associated with the age of Fielding and Johnson: rather was he approximate to the men of his grandfather's generation, men born at the close of the eighteenth century and who came to maturity during the solid magnificence and elegance of the Regency, in short, such a man as Lockhart—" very fine, precise, dandyish, very shrewd indeed," as the youthful but acute Harrison Ainsworth marked him in 1822. And Lockhart's scholarship and shy hauteur were also evident in Bleackley, for though his bearing was ever calm and courteous there was always, too, something of withdrawment about him, a remoteness from the present company and day. Yet at times he could express his views very forcibly, and would condemn in no measured terms any outrage upon historical and sentimental continuity, such as the destruction of some building or relic associated with the past he loved. In particular, he was jealous of the honour of Literature, and loathed the production of books by what he called " The Scissors and Paste School "—books compiled from the works of earlier students of the subject and containing no fruit from original research and new documentary material. To this present work on Jack Sheppard he attached a note that Jonathan Wild, the notorious thief-taker, might well be made the subject of biographical study, but, he added, the work " would necessitate considerable research, and must not be entrusted to the lazy or incompetent." He himself had a passion for accuracy and first-hand evidence. His own method before composition, as his books will demonstrate, was to make research in forgotten archives and in contemporary newspapers and pamphlets where he would find the sidelights and obscure data he required for the completion of his picture. He would take an infinitude of trouble to verify a date or detail. He liked to reconstruct in his mind the social and archæological and architectural aspects of the scenes he was describing; and so, as in this Jack Sheppard study, he would visualise by means of print and map the old picturesque London of 1724, the high, over-hanging Carolean houses of Wych Street and Drury Lane, and grim Newgate Prison straddling over the City gate, the rumbling coaches and the horses' hooves striking sparks from the rough stone-cobbles, the press of people in their romantic clothes hastening along the Oxford Road to see the death of the criminal by slow strangulation at Tyburn Tree near the Edgware Road. Bleackley had occasion in several of his narratives to present that final scene of pulsating and picturesque horror. He would seize every essential detail and limn it

Horace Bleackley.

with all the literary skill that is the complementary art of a Hogarth or Wiertz in drawing spectacles of sordid terror and death, and he would illumine the sordidness with rich colour. Take his description of the execution of the brothers Perreau for forgery:

"Desperate efforts were made to save the unhappy men. A petition, signed by more than seventy bankers and influential men of business, was presented to the King. Mrs. Robert Perreau, with her three children, flung herself at the feet of the Queen. But good King George III. was a stranger to mercy. On Wednesday, the 17th of January, 1776—a bitter morning, with keen frost in the air and deep snow on the ground—the two poor brothers were led out to die. Shortly after nine o'clock the City Marshals, attended by the full panoply of sheriffdom, started the procession. Next came an open cart, covered with black baise, where sat three of the convicts, and then a hurdle, dragged by four horses, on which rested a pair of wretches condemned for coining. And, last, there followed the sombre mourning-coach—a special privilege—with the unhappy brothers. All around lay a winding sheet of snow, crusted thick on the house-tops, piled in deep billows against the walls. A piercing east wind shot down the Old Bailey, while the prison gleamed in the frosty mist like a monument of hard black ice. Beyond Newgate Street the bell in St. Sepulchre's high steeple rang fiercely over the frozen roofs, as though pealing forth a pæan of exultation upon the procession of death. . . .

"Backwards and forwards around the mourning-coach surged the mob, clamouring with ribald fury for a glimpse of the celebrated forgers. Robert Perreau, sitting with his back to the horses beside one of the Sheriff's officers, pulled down the glass meekly, and gazed out with calm, unruffled features. Standing erect in the cart, George Lee, a handsome boy highwayman gorgeous in a crimson coat and ruffled shirt, doffed his gold-laced hat with a parade of gallantry to a young woman in a hackney-coach. Then, while a hundred eyes and a hundred loathsome jests were turned upon her, the poor girl burst into a flood of tears. In another moment her lover had passed away for ever. Huddled in the same tumbril with the swaggering youth, a couple of Jews, condemned for house-breaking, shook and chattered with dread, their yellow faces livid as death, a strange contrast to their florid, bombastic companion. Shivering with cold, the two tortured coiners were jolted over the snow, bound fast to their hurdle, their limbs turned to ice by the frost. And all the while, the mob—forty thousand strong—shrieked, danced, and hurled snowballs, maddened like fierce animals by the scent of blood. . . .

"Two separate gallows had been prepared, for it was not meet that Hebrew and Christian should hang from the same branch. Having been fee'd by his distinguished clients, Jack Ketch gave a moment's grace while the brothers embraced tenderly. As the cart drew away and their foothold slipped beneath them, their hands were still clasped together. For a full half minute their fingers remained linked as they dangled in the air and then fell apart as they passed into oblivion beside their five dying companions. Four days later, on Sunday, the 21st of January, they were buried together in a vault within St. Martin's Church, Ludgate Hill.

"No mob could have behaved with more indecency than the howling, laughing

In Memoriam:

throng that gazed upon this scene of death, increasing by their wanton rioting the agony of the poor sufferers a thousandfold. . . ."

Or his grim picture of a much later execution, that of the incredible Governor Wall in January, 1802:

"The bareheaded crowd gazes with rapture upon the wooden scaffold. . . . Suddenly there is a second mighty shout of triumph. The rope hangs plump between the two posts, and the tall gaunt form is swaying in empty air. In another moment there are cries of horror, but of horror mingled with applause. The noose has formed an even collar around the giant's neck, while the knot has slipped to the back of the head, which is still upright and unbent. Horrible convulsions seize the huge struggling frame. It is a terrific scene—most glorious spectacle of suffering that a delighted crowd has ever gazed upon—Jack Ketch has bungled. Minutes pass, and still the hanging man battles fiercely for breath. Minutes pass, and not a hand is stretched forth to give him relief. . . ."

We can almost hear the cries and groans from that long vanished macabre Raree-Show, while the odour of the struggling, unwashen mob is wafted down the years. The scene is only one hundred and thirty years ago, and seems impossible. And yet perhaps not so, for to-day with a similar blood lust for a hated man the mob excitement might well be the same if his execution was public; for it is only thirty-eight years ago, in 1895, also outside the Old Bailey, that the crowd rejoiced in similar manner on hearing that Oscar Wilde was convicted, when, in the words of Robert Sherard, "the rabble in Old Bailey, men and women, joined hands and danced an ungainly farandole, where ragged petticoats and yawning boots flung up the London mud in *feu de joie*, and the hideous faces were distorted with savage triumph. I stood and watched this dance of death for a few minutes. . . ."

Human nature does not change despite synthetic civilisation, and the records of crime are ever of historical value. Horace Bleackley was deeply interested in such annals and their archæology, and his interest extended to those persons who may be classed as the adjuncts of criminals, the people who minister to their pleasure and punishment, such as harlots, judges, and hangmen, evidence of which can be found in his books of this category, "Ladies Fair and Frail" and "The Hangmen of England," as well as in the volumes he wrote for the Notable British Trials. He was always in comfortable financial circumstances, so he had no need to seek for popular "best-selling" subjects to write about: he chose to deal with the lesser and unmoral figures of the eighteenth century, but he brought the same zest and historical values to his studies as if he had been engaged with Pitt or Wesley, for he knew that the minstrelsy which commemorated the exploits of Jack Sheppard was as much, or more, a part of the everyday life of

Horace Bleackley.

the Englishmen of those times as the hymnology of Toplady. He put up a very good defence for his choice of subjects in the Preface to his " Some Distinguished Victims of the Scaffold " :

"No apology is needed, save that which the consciousness of inadequate work may call forth, from him who writes a history of great criminals. Without a knowledge of 'The Newgate Calendar' it is impossible to be acquainted with the history of England in the eighteenth century. On the other hand, to him who knows these volumes, and who has verified his information in the pages of the Sessions papers and among the battle of the Pamphleteers, the Georgian era is an open book. No old novel gives a more exact picture of a middle-class household than the trial of Mary Blandy, nor shows the inner life of those on the fringe of society more completely than the story of Robert Perreau. While following the fate of Henry Fauntleroy we enter the newspaper world of our great-grandfathers. And as we look upon those forgotten dramas, the most illustrious bear us company. For a time Wordsworth and Coleridge chat of nothing but the Beauty of Buttermere and rascally John Hadfield. Dr. Johnson thinks wistfully of the charms of sweet Mrs. Rudd. Boswell rides to Tyburn in the same coach as the Rev. Mr. Hackman, or persuades Sir Joshua to witness an execution. Henry Fielding lashes the cowards who strive to condemn a prisoner unheard. To all who desire to understand the eighteenth century 'The Newgate Calendar' is as essential as the 'Letters of Walpole.' By a judicious selection some rare human documents and many an entrancing tale may be found in the crimson pages of the Tyburn Chronicle."

He might have added other illustrious names to those he mentions of The Good Companions who explore with us the shadowy realms of crime. If we raise the dark lanthorn, we may observe Sir Walter Scott making a special detour on his journey north in order to visit Probert's cottage and the winding lane which was the scene of the grim murder of Weare by Thurtell, the criminal with whom George Borrow boasted an acquaintance in Norwich days. And there is every reason to believe that Scott witnessed the execution of William Burke,[1] while most certainly Professor Wilson (" Christopher North ") went to see and report on Burke and Hare in prison, in much the same way as Dickens went over Newgate and saw the terrible poisoner, Wainewright. Dickens and Forster, in 1849, witnessed the execution of the Mannings,[2] while Thackeray attended the hanging of Courvoisier.[3] But the subject of

---

[1] See pages 64, 65, of " Burke and Hare," by W. Roughead, in Notable British Trials, 1921.

[2] Much moved by the horrific spectacle, Dickens wrote the next day to *The Times*, and this letter, and a second one which followed, started the agitation for the abolition of executions in public, a reform duly carried out some years later.

[3] In 1840. His impressions were recorded in " Going to see a Man Hanged," originally published in *Fraser's Magazine*, and now included in Thackeray's " Sketches and Travels in London."

In Memoriam:

the interest which literary men have displayed in crime is extensive, and I must confine myself now to Horace Bleackley. As I have indicated, he was justified in his favourite themes by reason of their social and archæological importance, and he treated them as historical matters worthy of attention and re-presentation by a keen student of manners and morals and by a man, as he was, of exceptional culture and wide reading. His financial ease gave him unusual facilities for pursuing this thorny and unfrequented byway of letters, but he was always far above the habits of a mere dilettante. Both his culture and his money were hereditary, and both had their source in Lancashire.

Horace William Bleackley, born on 19th Janury, 1868, at Myrtle Grove, Prestwich, near Manchester, was the elder son of William Bleackley by his marriage with Janet Kirk Rhodes. His father (born in 1819) was a member of a family who a generation earlier had established a prosperous cotton bleaching business in what was then the pleasant countryside some four miles to the north-west of Manchester. Those were the days when fortunes were rapidly made from cotton in the industrial and industrious North, and William Bleackley had the leisure to pursue many interests outside his business life. He was a man of literary tastes, well acquainted with the classics, and possessing a most remarkable knowledge of the Scriptures, which he would quote with an apt facility, worthy of Cruden himself, on every occasion of domestic, social, and political life.[4] He was an ardent Tory and a connoisseur of fine wine, qualities inherited by his son, Horace.[5] That William Bleackley had very marked literary tastes and post-prandial merits is evident from the fact that, though nineteen years the junior of the redoubtable Manchester bibliophile, James Crossley (whose library numbered some hundred thousand volumes) he was singled out to be the particular crony of the " local Dr. Johnson," as Crossley was styled during the last decades of his picturesque old age. Bleackley was a man after his own heart, for he, too, loved the Scriptures and old wine and was an ardent Conservative. The friends had a further link in their love for bowls, a game, however, to which they were partial more for its Elizabethan associations and pretext for a good dinner

---

[4] Thus, one day, when his friend, James Crossley, observed that relatives were best apart and that he took care not to live near his own people, Bleackley replied, " Unlike the Shunammite woman, you have no wish to dwell among your own people."

[5] During his residence in Lancashire Horace Bleackley was a very active supporter of the Conservative cause, and as the years passed by he became one of the oldest members of the Prestwich Conservative Club. He was an excellent speaker, and was asked to stand more than once for the local constituency, but his health did not permit him to accept the honour.

Horace Bleackley.

after than for the sober excitements it offered in play. Horace Bleackley told me:

"My father and Crossley became intimate in the late sixties, 1869-1879. They were both members of the Cheetham Hill Bowling Club, which met once a week in the summer on the picturesque bowling-green of the Kersal Moor Hotel. They dined at seven, after playing bowls for two or three hours, and sat over their wine—all of the finest vintage—and made speeches till eleven or twelve. The club was 250 years old. I was a member from 1895 until I left Manchester in 1901, the youngest member ever elected.

"Crossley used to dine with my people on his birthday, and after my father's death in 1879, my mother continued the dinner till Crossley's death (in 1883). Of course, all his principal friends were invited. My folks used to say that he generally got through the best part of two bottles of port without turning a hair. Naturally it was good wine, Sandeman's 1851, I fancy."

It was to William Bleackley that James Crossley addressed one of the best of the letters in rhyme he used to send to his particular friends:

> "I know a man—if he were knighted
> How all good folks would be delighted.
> Because on earth there does not live
> A truer staunch Conservative.
> Nor, what to find in vain you'd labour,
> A heartier friend, a kinder neighbour.
> He is not only great in Kersal—
> The deep respect is universal.
> Just see him at a public meeting—
> What orator receives such greeting?
> All Gladstone's false, long-winded proses
> As clear as daylight he exposes;
> Each fallacy he puts his hand on,
> And leaves him not a leg to stand on.
> At Bowling Dinners when presiding
> His eloquence we take a pride in;
> So well the healths and toasts he passes,
> We all fill bumpers in our glasses.
> His Myrtle Grove—full well I know it—
> Beats that of any classic poet;
> And rather there I'd take my Tippy
> Than quaff the streams of Aganippe.
> One only of his fine quotations
> Is worth a score of Whig orations;
> A feast of Scripture texts to dish up,
> I'd put him against Dean or Bishop;
> As a Concordance you may view him:
> Old Cruden's self is nothing to him.
> Such then he is—the opening year
> Shall bear to him the wish sincere—
> Long may he bowl; Long may he live
> With all the blessings life can give.
> "New Year's Day, 1879."

In Memoriam :

Alas! before the year was spent his friend was gone, for William Bleackley died suddenly from apoplexy in September, 1879, at the age of sixty. Crossley was greatly affected, and ever after when Bleackley's name was mentioned his eyes would fill with tears and his voice falter. He wrote his friend's epitaph, "He was loved and honoured when living, and his memory will be long and dearly cherished when dead." Local grammarians took exception to the final "when," and in the controversy that ensued it was decided by the majority that the "local Dr. Johnson" had, for once, nodded.

Horace Bleackley was only eleven at the time of his father's death, and Crossley, until his own death four years later, took the greatest interest in the little son of his valued friend and encouraged the literary tastes he was already cultivating. James Crossley was, of course, the most intimate friend, the *fidus Achates*, of Harrison Ainsworth, the great romance writer; and on the occasion of the last visit Ainsworth paid to his native town of Manchester, in September, 1881, Crossley presented to him young Horace Bleackley, aged thirteen, as a very great admirer of his books. "Which have you read?" asked Ainsworth. "I have read them all," replied the boy—somewhat exaggerating, as he confessed to me in after years, "though not much," for he had entire acquaintance with all of Ainsworth's best work. This meeting took place, very fittingly, in that lovely and ancient haunt of literary peace, the Chetham Library, so intimately associated with both Ainsworth and Crossley through nearly seventy years since the time of their own boyhood, and it was only just in time, for Ainsworth died three months later. So it was, Horace Bleackley had a personal touch with the literary life of the eighteenth century, for Ainsworth, in his own youth, had known well Charles Lamb. The influence of Ainsworth's romances remained with Horace Bleackley until the close of his life, adding illumination and colour to his innate predilection for chronicles of old, adventurous days and the derring-do of picturesque criminals. But at that meeting in 1881, the author of "Jack Sheppard," at the end of life, little dreamed that the boy before him would fifty years hence, at the end, too, of his life, be writing "The Trial of Jack Sheppard." Bleackley was doubly fortunate in his early literary mentors.

Horace Bleackley was educated at Cheltenham College and at Repton, proceeding in due course to University College, Oxford, where he took his M.A. degree and a second class in History. He had already commenced to write, though his first books were novels. He was twenty-four when "A Defender of the Faith" was published in 1892 under the pseudonym of "Tivoli." This "Romance of a Business Man" no

Horace Bleackley.

doubt reflects the surroundings of his youth, and the place called "Estridge" is Prestwich. "Une Culotte, or a New Woman, An Impossible Story of Modern Oxford," by "Tivoli," followed in 1894. "A Short Innings," 1897, was the last work for which he used the *nom-de-plume* of "Tivoli," and in this "Public School Episode" he presented a picture of his old school, Repton, not forgetting the picturesque remains of the priory of the twelfth century incorporated in the later scholastic buildings. While at Oxford Bleackley had resolved to devote his future life to literary work and his artistic tastes: but he had to lay aside his wishes for some years and return to the smoke and business environment of Prestwich. For in the fifteen years which had elapsed since the death of his father, the family interest in the cotton trade had suffered from the absence of a personal head and fallen behind the times. Reconstruction and supervision and direct control were imperative to remedy the effects of a too-long minority. So Horace Bleackley put away, for a time, his pen and the dreams of the books he was to write, and for seven years, 1894-1901, served in what to him was the wilderness of commerce. But he had his reward at the end of his term, when, his business once more in a prosperous condition, he was able to retire from active participation and devote himself to the collecting of his remarkable library, which mainly comprised works concerning the eighteenth century, and the writing of his own books. His life in Lancashire, however, had its interests, and much of this time and his experiences in the work of calico bleaching and dyeing are described in his best novel, "His Job" (1918), a story which reveals his own personal sensitiveness in the delineation of the young protagonist, Ronald, whose home, "Irwell Park," presents in part a picture of the "old" Myrtle Grove.

"In spite of the proximity of a manufacturing town and the contagion of the murky stream that flowed close by, Irwell Park was still a place of some beauty. The square red mansion itself, with its tiers of white-framed windows, standing amidst a girdle of tall trees above which the rooks wheeled and cawed, possessed a certain massive charm enhanced by its environment. In front of the house two twin sheets of water in the shape of an hour-glass, joined by a narrow channel, spanned by a low bridge, bordered the wide lawns of the garden, while beyond, after a short expanse of meadowland, the ground rose abruptly in a long belt of hanging woods that terminated the view. To the right, from the verge of the little park, lay a vista of open fields, with trees and thorn hedges, stretching along the broad plain towards the smoky but invisible city three miles away. To the left nothing could be seen above the cover but a distant glimpse of the old church tower. Irwell Park was a small oasis of forest, lake, and meadow, in the midst of a black country."

There were two "Myrtle Groves." Horace Bleackley had been

In Memoriam:

born in the old house, like his father and grandfather before him. His father built a new house on higher ground, amid the beech-trees, and it was here that Horace Bleackley lived with his mother until her second marriage. After his own marriage, in 1895, with Miss Ruth Gabriel, he moved to a house called " Holmleigh " at Sedgley Park. All through these years he was a keen cricketer—indeed, he was a player until well into middle age—and his interest in the game is marked by two books, " Tales of the Stumps " (1901) and " More Tales of the Stumps " (1902). His comfortable monetary position was much increased in 1898, as co-heir with his brother, by the estate of a cousin, E. O. Bleackley, a very well-known figure in the public and social life of Manchester. Like his younger cousins, he had been born at Myrtle Grove (in 1831), and become a cotton-broker; but he was more interested in his large newspaper business. He was the founder of what became the Hulton Press, and recognising the abilities of the father of the late Sir Edward Hulton, he took him as a partner. E. O. Bleackley acted as trade editor and dramatic critic of *The Manchester Evening News;* he was one of the early Volunteers, and as lieutenant of the 1st Manchesters took part in the famous review in Hyde Park in 1860. He was a keen politician and much in demand as a speaker at meetings, and when he conducted his own case in a trial, heard before Mr. Justice Mellor, two of his sallies caused much merriment in Court and were long after classics on the Manchester Exchange: " The cloth was not damp, but the market was, VERY." And " His Satanic Majesty ought to be trusted—if he paid cash." He married a relative of Lord Brougham, was one of the founders of the Manchester Conservative Club and of the eccentric Nutcrackers Club, and altogether " one of the most popular, as he is one of the best known men in Manchester, where his estimable social qualities have won for him love, honour, troops of friends," as a tribute to him was worded in *Momus* (19th June, 1879), where will also be found a clever caricature portrait by W. G. Baxter, the talented Manchester artist, of E. O. Bleackley.

Horace Bleackley was now fully able to realise his dreams of the literary life; he accordingly left Manchester in 1901 and took a house, " Fox Oak," at Hersham, in Surrey. Here he at once commenced to write the first, and in some respects the best, of what were to be his characteristic books, " Some Distinguished Victims of the Scaffold," which was published in 1905. There was some suggestion of the influence of the style of Carlyle plus Meredith here and there:

" ' Wrong,' cry Farmer George and Doctor Henry, glancing timidly, as with mystical prescience, down the vista of ages to Board School days, and quaking

Horace Bleackley.

at swish of cat and clank of triangles, guilty of as deep anachronism as he who hurled a shell at the tomb of the Mahdi, to the great discomfort of bread-and-milk nerves. For birch twigs and cat—essential forerunners of Standards Six—had much Peninsular and Waterloo work in front of them, and it was just as easy to chain red giants as to hang them. . . . Modern eye can but discern the red giants of a bygone world through a glass darkly. Cruel, crimson, unscrupulous—they were all that: children of murkiness even as we are children of light, and thus let comparison end. One hundred years—as great a barrier as a million miles of ether—has divided our ages, *et nos mutamur*. A thousand pencils—Saxon and Caledonian—have banished with Dunciad scorn the birchen wand that used to betwig merrily the tender fifteen-year-old flesh of ribald lad and saucy maiden."

But he soon shed this mannerism as his own style developed, and there is but little trace of it in his next book, " The Story of a Beautiful Duchess " (Elizabeth Gunning), which appeared in 1907, and later it has vanished entirely. In 1912 he and his family removed to London, to the house I have already mentioned, 19, Cornwall Terrace, and in these appropriate Regency surroundings his remaining years were mainly passed in literary work, adding to his library, and social intercourse with his many friends. He was abroad at times, and one of these sojourns is described in " A Tour in Southern Asia " (1928). He also wrote novels in the intervals between his historical works, though some of the novels can also be classed as historical. Thus " A Hundred Years Ago " (1917) was a tale of the Riots of 1812, while " The Monster " (1920) described the disturbing activities of Henry Hunt at the time he was in Manchester in 1819. In this latter book the author showed he had not forgotten the intricacies of Lancashire dialect. In the phantasy of " Anymoon " (1919) he voiced his antagonism to Socialism with the aim, as Mr. Harold Cox pointed out in his Foreword, of warning how " Socialistic Theories, now so vigorously pushed, would work out in practice." But picturesque, historical biography remained his chief preoccupation and entitles him to remembrance. His " Life of Wilkes " (1917) is generally considered to be his most scholarly and valuable work. In lighter vein may be mentioned " Casanova in England " (1923), which Arthur Symons pronounced to be " vastly amusing, vivid enough, and well written."

Horace Bleackley was very happy in his domestic life with his wife and two sons and daughter. Mrs. Bleackley shared all his literary interests and assisted him at times, as, for example, with her article, " The Beautiful Miss Gunnings," which appeared in *The Connoisseur* two years before her husband's book on Elizabeth Gunning was published. She also shared his love for fine prints, and her List of William Wynne Ryland's Engravings was appended to Bleackley's memoir of that " King's Engraver " who went to the shameful scaffold: his execution

In Memoriam :

in 1783 was the last which took place at Tyburn. " The Hangmen of England " (1929) was the last book Bleackley was engaged upon in England, for he wrote most of this " Jack Sheppard " volume at the Villa Allégria, Cannes. Recurring attacks of asthma compelled him now to be in a sunny climate, and he had purchased another villa with the intention of settling altogether on the Riviera. In 1931 he was staying at the Beau-Rivage Palace, Lausanne, and on 30th July he mentioned that he felt very tired. The words were hardly uttered when the end had come. Thus, mercifully, he died peacefully and suddenly, and was spared all the searing horrors of a prolonged illness and deathbed. A memorial service, conducted by Bishop Bury, was held at Marylebone Church on 7th August, when many of Bleackley's friends were present. The tribute in *The Times* on the same day, written by his fellow-novelist, Mr. W. B. Maxwell, expressed the sentiments of all his friends. He was unreservedly liked and sincerely mourned.

LIST OF WORKS BY HORACE BLEACKLEY.

1. " A Defender of the Faith," The Romance of a Business Man. By Tivoli. Griffith Farran & Co., Newbery House, Charing Cross Road, London, 1892.

2. " Une Culotte, or A New Woman," An Impossible Story of Modern Oxford. By Tivoli. Illustrated by A. W. Cooper. Digby Long, 18, Bouverie Street, London, 1894.

3. " A Short Innings." A Public School Episode. By Tivoli. Digby Long, 1897.

4. " Tales of the Stumps." Illustrated by Lucien Davis, R.I., and " Rip." Ward, Lock, London, 1901.

5. " More Tales of the Stumps." Ward, Lock, 1902.

6. " Some Distinguished Victims of the Scaffold." With twenty-one illustrations. Kegan Paul, Trench, Trubner, London, 1905.

7. " The Story of a Beautiful Duchess." Being an Account of the Life and Times of Elizabeth Gunning, Duchess of Hamilton and Argyll. With six illustrations. Constable & Company, London, 1907. A new edition was published by John Lane, The Bodley Head, 1927.

8. " Ladies Fair and Frail." Sketches of the Demi-Monde during the Eighteenth Century. With sixteen illustrations. John Lane, The Bodley Head, 1909.

9. " A Gentleman of the Road." John Lane, The Bodley Head, 1911. The story of a highwayman who ends at Tyburn.

10. " Life of John Wilkes." With twenty-seven illustrations. John Lane, The Bodley Head, 1917.

11. " A Hundred Years Ago." A Tale of the Riots of 1812. Eveleigh Nash, London, 1917.

12. " His Job." John Lane, The Bodley Head, 1918.

13. " The Lost Diary." Eveleigh Nash, 1919.

Horace Bleackley.

14. "Anymoon." John Lane, the Bodley Head, 1919. With a Foreword by Harold Cox.

15. "The Monster." W. Heinemann, London, 1920.

16. "Casanova in England." Being the Account of the Visit to London in 1763-4. Illustrated. John Lane, The Bodley Head, 1923.

17. "The Trial of Henry Fauntleroy, and Other Famous Trials for Forgery." Illustrated. William Hodge & Company, Edinburgh, 1924.

18. "Night of Peril." John Lane, The Bodley Head, 1926.

19. "A Tour in Southern Asia." With twenty-one illustrations. John Lane, The Bodley Head, 1928.

20. "The Hangmen of England." The Life Story of Jack Ketch through two centuries. Illustrated. Chapman & Hall, London, 1929.

21. "The Trial of Jack Sheppard." Edited by S. M. Ellis, with an Epilogue on Jack Sheppard in Literature and Drama, a Bibliography, a Note on Jonathan Wild, and a Memoir of Horace Bleackley. With twenty-three illustrations. William Hodge & Company, Edinburgh, 1933.

Horace Bleackley was for many years a constant and valued contributor to *Notes and Queries*.

He was the author of plays and a musical comedy which were never produced.

In the Introduction to Volume VII of "The Complete Peerage" it is stated: "Acknowledgments are long overdue to Horace Bleackley, who placed at the service of the Editors his large collection of eighteenth century Memoirs, Tracts, etc., from which much information in footnotes throughout these volumes has been drawn."

The Library of Horace Bleackley was sold at Hodgson's Rooms on 3rd March, 1932.

ADDITIONAL NOTES.

Page 92. The theatrical success of Jack Sheppard had been exceeded, perhaps, sixteen years earlier by Pierce Egan's "Life in London," for, if the suburban theatres are included, there were ten versions running in London during 1822-3. The most popular, as in the case of "Jack Sheppard," was at the Adelphi, where "crowds flocked." There was also a production in Richardson's Booth at Bartholomew Fair.

Page 103. It was presumably the Adelphi Theatre version of the play which was produced again, this time at the Pavilion Theatre, on 2nd April, 1859, as "The Standard Version of the celebrated drama, in five acts and forty scenes, of Jack Sheppard." Jack was now played by a very capable male actor, J. F. Young, with Alfred Rayner as Blueskin, H. Dudley as Jonathan Wild, and George Belmore in the small part of Kneebone.

Page 109. There was an earlier burlesque, produced in the sixties, entitled "Jack Sheppard, Esq." This was written by Sydney French, and Miss Eliza Newton played the part of Jack in America for 500 consecutive performances. She then went on a provincial tour of the piece in England with Captain W. A. Swift's "Comedy Company of London Artistes." When at the Regent Hall, Great Yarmouth, the gallant captain appeared as Owen Wood. C. Hodson Stanley as Kneebone was described as "The Original Chickaleary Cove in ad-Vance of his time." Blueskin was played by Mark Kinghorne, subsequently a well-known actor in London.

Miss Lizzie Wilmore is remembered in Belfast as playing Jack Sheppard there in the seventies.

Page 115. Florian Pascal composed the most melodious song in the score of "Little Jack Sheppard" at the Gaiety Theatre, the romantic ballad, "Silver Star," sung by Miss Wadman as Thames Darrell.

Page 119. When Cecil J. Sharp reproduced the folk-song tune of "Botany Bay" in his "One Hundred English Folk Songs" (1916), he stated : "I do not know of any published versions of this song."

INDEX.

AINSWORTH, William Harrison, 61, 71, 74, 77-90, 91-2, 93-4, 98-9, 105, 106-7, 109, 122, 125-6, 131, 135, 136, 207, 244, 250
Applebee, John, 51-2, 53, 127
Applebee's Original Weekly Journal, 35-6, 127
Arnet, Richard, 48, 52, 204
Arnold, Quilt, 12, 26
Augarde, Amy, 120
Austin, William, 27, 33, 36, 153

BAINS'S house, Robbery at Mr., 4
Ballantine, Serjeant, 97
Barham, R. H., 87-8, 93-4, 99-100
Bedford, Paul, 72, 96, 99, 100-1, 103, 118
"Beggar's Opera, The," 73-4, 78, 111
Beverley, Mrs., 94
Billington, Mrs. John, 103
"Black Bess," by Edward Viles, 91, 134
Blackerby, Mr. Justice, 12
"Black Lion" Tavern, 3, 126
Bleackley, E. O., 252
Bleackley, Horace, 243-55
Bleackley, Mrs., 252, 253
Bleackley, William, 248-50
Blessington, Countess of, 87
"Bloody Register, The," 77, 129, 199, 209
"Blue Dwarf, The," by P. B. St. John, 134-5
Blueskin (Joseph Blake), 5, 9, 10, 12, 25-6, 55, 72, 84, 111, 201-2; as a Stage character, 72, 96, 100, 103, 104, 109, 111, 112, 117-18, 122, 124
"Blueskin," by Edward Viles, 91, 134, 207
Bon Gaultier Ballads, 87, 96, 99, 136
Borrow, George, 60-1, 77, 247
"Botany Bay," song, 117-19, 256
Briggs, Mr., 83-4
Brightwell Brothers, 10
Buckstone, J. B., 108, 113-14
Bufton, Eleanor, 110, 111
Burnett, J. P., 110

"CATHERINE," by Thackeray, 81-4
Charles's house, Robbery at Mr., 5
"Charley Wag, The New Jack Sheppard," 91, 133
Cibber, Colley, 71, 73

Clayton, Eliza, 109
Clerkenwell, The New Prison of, 6-8
Cohen, Isaac, 121, 123
Cook, Kate, 36
Cook's shop, Robbery at Mary, 5, 25, 52
Courvoisier, B. F., 105-8, 114, 125
"Crichton," 96, 106
Crossley, James, 248-50
Cruikshank, George, 77, 84, 85, 90, 92, 100, 131

DAVIDGE, G. B., 92
Defoe, Daniel, 28, 35-6, 51-2, 53, 54, 59-60, 69-70, 126, 128, 136
Dickens, Charles, 66, 79-81, 85, 89, 90, 94, 247
Drake, Lillian, 124-5
Duval, Claude, 64-5, 81, 90, 97, 133

EDGWORTH Bess (Elizabeth Lyon), 3, 4, 6, 8, 20, 36, 49, 56, 65, 68, 78, 90, 91, 111, 114, 124, 133, 135
Egan, Pierce, 122, 256
Ellis, S. M., 55, 58, 136
Emery, S., 103
Enthoven, Mrs. Gabrielle, 110

FARMER, J. S., 71, 118
Farnie, H. B., 109-10, 111, 114-15
Farren, Henry, 102, 104
Farren, Nellie, 104, 115-17, 120
Field, William, 9, 17, 26, 52
Fielding, Henry, 76-7, 84, 92, 136, 203, 207
Figg, Prize-fighter, 50
"Flowers of Hemp," 85-7, 99, 136
Forster, John, 79-81, 88, 90, 106, 126, 247
Fortescue, Lincoln, 91, 132
Fowler, Frederick, 207-8
Frisky, Moll, 37, 59, 71, 76

GAY, John, 66, 73-4, 96
George the First, 36, 41
George the Third, 207, 245
Gilbert, W. S., 133
Giles's Round-house, St., 4, 6, 7
Granville-Barker, H., 119
Grossmith, Weedon, 104, 121-3
Groves, Charles, 112, 122

Jack Sheppard.

HAINES, J. T., 92, 132
Hall, H., 102
"Harlequin Jack Sheppard," 94-5
"Harlequin Sheppard," 71-3, 95, 128
Harper, John, 72, 74, 119
Hatton, Joseph, 91, 121-2
Hayes, Catherine, 81-2, 84
Hayes, Catherine, the singer, 83-4
Hibbert, H. G., 115, 116
Hicks, "Brayvo," 94
Hicks, Seymour, 120
Hill, Mr. and Mrs. C., 102
Hitchin, Charles, 211-24
Hodson, Henrietta (Mrs. Labouchere), 112-13
Hogarth, William, 3, 44, 68, 73, 74, 78, 96, 110
Honner, Mrs. (Maria Macarthy), 101, 102
Honner, R. W., 101-2
Hood, Marion, 115
Housman, A. E., 68
Houssart, Lewis, 43, 46
Howard, Louisa, 102

"IDLE 'Prentice, The," 110-12, 114, 115, 122
Ireton, 19, 23
Irving, Henry, 122

"JACK Ketch, or a Leaf from Tyburn Tree," 102
"Jack Sheppard," by W. H. Ainsworth, 77-90, 106-7, 109, 131, 250
"Jack Sheppard, Esq." (burlesque), 256
"Jack Sheppard" for the Toy Theatre, 132
"Jack Sheppard in Literature and Drama," 64-126
Jack Sheppard plays: Adelphi, 96-101, 108, 113-14, 256; in Ballarat, 104; Bow Palace, 123; at Brighton, 102, 104; at Bristol, 113; Britannia, Hoxton, 109; City of London, 94; Drury Lane, 71-3, 94-5; East London Theatre, 108-9; Elephant and Castle, 124-5; in France (Cancale), 114; Gaiety, 115-20; Garrick (Leman Street), 94; Haymarket, 103, 108; Ireland, 105, 256; Manchester, 113, 123 (Broughton); Marylebone, 113; New York, 102-3; Paris, 104-5, 112; Pavilion, 93, 121-3, 256; Queen's (Tottenham Street), 93; Queen's (Long Acre), 112-13; Richardson's Show, 95-6; Sadler's Wells, 101-2, 103; Sheffield, 102; Standard, 119; Strand, 109-12; Surrey, 92-3, 103, 108, 112, 114; Victoria (Old Vic), 93-4

"Jack Sheppard" Song, 120, 136
"Jack Sheppard, The History of," by Lincoln Fortescue, 89-91, 131-2
Jack Sheppard's "Dying Speech," 67, 192
"Jack Sheppard's Three Fatal Stages" (plates), 130
James, David, 117-19, 120
James, Kate, 120, 136
"Janet Pride," 118
Jefferini (clown), 95
"John Sheppard, A Narrative of all the Robberies, Escapes, &c., of," 59-60, 128, 159-69
"John Sheppard, An Epigram on," 186
"John Sheppard, Authentic Memoirs of . . . ," 60, 128, 170-95
"John Sheppard, The History of the remarkable Life of," 127-8, 137-58
"John Sheppard's Tomb-Stone, An Epitaph Design'd for," 67, 194
"Jolly Nose," 100-1, 102, 124
"Jonathan Wild, or the Storm on the Thames," 108-9
Jones, The Boy, 85
"Julius Cæsar and Jack Sheppard, A Dialogue Between," 76, 127, 129, 130, 196-8

KEELEY, Mary (Mrs. Albert Smith), 103
Keeley, Mrs., 96-9, 103-5, 107, 108, 115
Keith, Sir Arthur, 208
"Ketch, Letter to Jack," 22, 127, 151
Keys, Catherine, 36
Kinghorne, Mark, 256
Kneebone, William, 2, 9, 11, 16, 26, 52, 54, 111, 256

LACY, T. H., 102
Lamb, Anthony, 9
Langley, 19, 23
Lauraine, Nellie, 119
Laurent, Marie, 105, 112
Lecky, W. E., 65
Lee, George, 245
Lee, Jenny, 110
Lee, William, 36, 128, 136
"Les Chevaliers du Brouillard," 104-5, 112
Leslie, Fred, 115, 117, 120
Lewkenor's Lane, 142
"Life in London," 256
"Little Jack Sheppard" (Gaiety Theatre), 115-20
"Little Jack Sheppard" ("The Idle 'Prentice"), 112, 114-15

Index.

Lord Chamberlain, The, 108, 110, 112, 113, 114, 118
Lutz, Meyer, 115, 119
Lyon, Elizabeth (see Edgworth Bess)

"MACCLESFIELD, An Epistle from Jack Sheppard to the Earl of," 42-3, 64, 129
Maggot, Poll, 4, 20, 78, 114
Martin, Sir Theodore, 85-7, 88, 99, 136
Massey, Rose, 112
Mathews, Charles, 133
Mead, Dorothy, 124
Melville, George, 102
Miles, H. D., 90
Mint, The, Southwark, 126
Mitford, Miss, 88-9
Moncrieff, W. T., 93-4
Muddiman, J. G., 196
Myrtle Grove, Prestwich, 248, 249, 251-2

NELSON, Alfred, 104
Neville, Henry, 93, 97, 112
Neville, John, 93
"New Jack Sheppard, A," by Ernest Treeton, 135
Newcastle, Duke of, 39
Newgate Prison, 12-14, 18-21, 25-33, 38-40, 43-7, 246
"Newgate Calendar, The," 77, 129-30
"Newgate's Garland," 72, 119, 201-2
Newton, Eliza, 256
Newton, Kate, 112
Nicholls, Harry, 112
"Nix my dolly, pals, fake away," 98-9, 109, 116

ODELL, E. J., 115, 119
Old Bailey, An Adventure in the, 223-4
"Old London," 112-13
"Old London Bridge in the Days of Jack Sheppard and Jonathan Wild," 119
"Oliver Twist," 66, 79-81, 83, 88, 89, 126
Oxberry, W. H., 95

PAGE, William, 21-3, 37, 69-71, 73, 146, 180-1, 193
Pargiter, John, 10, 55
Parry, Mr. and Mrs. J., 93
Pascal, Florian, 115, 256
"Paul Clifford," 79, 88, 89
Paulton, Harry, 110, 111

Peel, Sir Robert, 85, 100
Perreaus, The, 245
Philipps, Sir Erasmus, 24
Phillips's house, Robbery at Mr., 5-6, 52
Pickersgill, H. W., R.A., 88
Pincott, Miss (Mrs. Alfred Wigan), 102
Pitt, William, 19, 34, 39, 40
Place, Francis, 55, 57
Powys, Sir Littleton, 41-2
Preston, Jessie, 120
"Prison Breaker, The," 74-6, 128-9
Prout, Father, 88, 106
Prowse, Richard, 91, 134
Punch, 80, 85, 89, 136
Purney, Rev. Mr., 24, 39, 46

"QUAKER'S Opera, The," 74-6, 95, 129
Queensberry, Marquis of, 123

RAWLINS'S shop, Robbery at, 37
Reynolds, G. W. M., 86, 135
Richardson's Show, 95-6, 256
Rodwell, G. H. B., 98, 100
Rogers, "Cock-Sparrow," 93
Rogers, Miss, 93
"Rookwood," 79-81, 89, 90, 98, 99
Roughead, W., 247
Russell, Lord John, 85, 107
Russell, Lord William, 105-7, 114

SALA, G. A., 69, 91, 133
Santley, Kate, 110, 111
Saville, E. F., 92-3
Saville, J. F., 96
Scott, Clement, 100, 110, 112-13, 114, 116, 119, 122
Scott, Sir Walter, 247
Seccombe, Thomas, 135, 199
Sharp, Ceceil J., 119, 256
Shepherd, John, 71
Sheppard, Jack: Birth, 1; Robberies, 3-11; Trial, 15-18; Escapes from Newgate, 18-21, 27-33, 156; Conviction, 18, 41; Execution, 51-2; Burial, 54-5; His remains removed to Brookwood, 125
Sheppard, John, of Willesden, 125
Sheppard, Mrs., 1, 36, 37, 69, 125, 126; as a Stage character, 96, 111, 112, 113, 123
Sheppard, Mrs., "Letter to," from Jack Sheppard, 36, 127, 187-8
Sheppard, Thomas, 1, 5, 25, 111
Sheppard, Thomas, senior, 1, 125
Sheridan, Amy, 110, 111
Sikes, Bill, 80

Jack Sheppard.

Sims, G. R., 133
Sitwell, Osbert, 89
Sketch, Jack, 90
Spagnoletti, Peter, 124
Spencer, Walter T., 126, 132
Spurling, Mrs., 20
St. John, Percy B., 134, 135
Stanley, C. Hodson, 256
Stephens, H. P., 115
"Stone Jug, The," 113-14
Summers, Montague, 130, 132, 133, 134
Summers, Thief-catcher, 142
Swift, Jonathan, 72, 73, 202, 203
Sykes, James, 5, 6, 80

TERRISS, Ellaline, 120
Terry, Edward, 110, 111, 117
Thackeray, W. M., 55, 57, 79, 81-5, 88, 247
Thirlwall, Miss, 102
Thornhill, Sir James, 44-5, 57, 69, 91, 134; verses to "On his Picture of Jack Sheppard," 45, 127
Throttle, Obadiah, 132
Thurmond, John, 71
Timbs, John, 89
Toole, J. L., 117, 122
Turpin, Dick, 64-5, 81, 90, 91
Tussaud's, Madame, 20
Tyburn Tree, 50-3, 204-6, 242, 244-5

VENNE, Lottie, 112
Victoria, Queen, 85, 95
Viles, Edward, 91, 134, 207

Vincent, Miss, 94
Vining, Mrs. Henry, 93
Vyvyan, Miss, 104

WADMAN, Tillie, 115, 256
Wagstaff, Rev. Mr., 24, 26, 46, 48, 50, 52, 55, 91
Walker, Thomas, 74, 129
Warde, Willie, 115, 120
Watson, Under-Sheriff, 46-7, 52
"When Rogues Fall Out," 91, 122, 135
Watts, John, 129
Wild, John, 199, 203
Wild, Jonathan, 11-12, 16, 21, 25-6, 40, 65, 76-7, 126, 128, 133, 199-242; Birth, 199; His wife and son, 200, 211; Blueskin's attempt on his life, 201-2; Verses on, 203-4, 239-40; Trial, 232-39; Execution, 207, 241-2; Skeleton, 207-8; as a Stage character, 102, 104, 109, 111, 112, 117, 119, 120, 121, 122, 123
"Wild the Great, The History of Jonathan," by Henry Fielding, 76-7, 207
Wilde, Oscar, 79, 117, 246
Willesden, 125-6, 133
Williams, Arthur, 112
Wilmore, Lizzie, 256
Wise, T. J., 202
Wolverhampton, 199, 203
Wood, Mrs., 3, 80, 106, 124-5
Wood, Owen, 2, 3, 111
Wright, Edward, 96
Wych Street, 3, 5, 126

Milton Keynes UK
Ingram Content Group UK Ltd.
UKHW050643240424
441619UK00012B/579

9 781535 806053